Siege of Troy

D1304625

Siege of Troy

Troy

PAUL ELLEDGE

Charleston, SC
www.PalmettoPublishing.com

SIEGE OF TROY

Copyright © 2021 by Paul Elledge

All rights reserved.

First Edition

Paperback ISBN: 978-1-63837-489-3

Author's Note

The principal setting of this story is re-imagined from a church assembly ground where the author once worked for a summer, but the events of the narrative are wholly fictional. No representations are from life. Nor is the mild satire of institutions and practices meant to disrespect them, or to discredit the value of their formative influence on the author, who honors them still.

~PAUL ELLEDGE

In Memoriam

First Lieutenant Raynor Lee Hebert, USAF
16 January 1938 - 13 May 1964

and

Douglas Joseph Muccio
8 January 1945 - 4 December 1964

"...take my hand, lead me on...."

Entrance

Early June 1959. Twenty miles southwest of Santa Fe. Desert. Midday heat.

"You're Troy," he said, "and you'll bunk with me."

A scrim of sweat glazed his tan; a trace of grin teased his lips.

We faced each other in the crowded lobby of the Jubilee Retreat Complex owned and operated by the Baptist church where several thousand believers enrolled every summer for one paid week of spiritual tune-up. They herded around us, wrestling luggage, flashing annoyance at our immobility; for we held as though stationed by the fix of our eyes on each other, taking our measure, Father might have said, alert for an opening move: curious, cautious, expectant. His hands shoved into his front pockets, his trunk back-tilted, his head pitched jauntily in examination mode. And then his right hand lifted from the Levi pocket to toy and fiddle with a chapstick tube, its metallic paint winking as he rolled the cylinder deftly around his fingers like magicians move quarters across knuckles. He spooled and tickled it around his palm, turned it over the back of his hand and caught it up between the fingers, twirled it, spun it, clinked it against his school ring, tapped tattoos on it with his nails, feigned losing his grip and then grabbed with a snap of the wrist as it fell. And he effected this juggling with what seemed inattention, indifference, as though the gears of his gamboling hands meshed on automatic. He didn't watch the capering fingers; he watched me watching them: watched intently, his gymnast's body poised as if he'd just stuck a perfect landing in the Olympics. Unmistakably, it was a performance, but without self-conscious flash or splash; it was subtle, subdued, silken: unconsciously orchestrated yet shaped and informed by intent, like a choreographed ballet, vaguely hypnotic, faintly seductive. By it, with it, he telegraphed a message: staked a claim and established a hold. I felt it, felt sure of it, but could not have told you what it was.

Then he stopped, pried off the tube cap with thumb and forefinger, and swiped the stick along his lips, greasing them to a glistering finish.

"Lip balm," he said; "for sunburn. This sun out here's wicked mean on lips. Screws up kissing." He paused for two beats, the crinkle of the grin crawling across his waxy lips. "Here," he added, extending the tube: "Take it. It's yours."

"What? Oh," I faltered, "No, I couldn't…." But he reached out and laid the tube onto my palm, folding my fingers around it, warm and moist with himself. "Use it," he purred.

And then, stepping back, at ease: "I'm Monte. Charles Montgomery Trevalyn the Third," laughing lightly at the pretentious grandiosity of it but squinting as if to be sure I'd caught it all. "Swear you'll never ever say the whole of that name to any single living soul on the ever-loving face of this spinning earth, ever! Just don't call me 'Charlie.'"

Swear? I didn't swear. Certainly not here, at Jubilee, within earshot of all these Baptists!

"Okay," I said, snickering; "I swear."

"Good man, Troy! I'm almost twenty. Texas. You're Louisiana?"

"Yes. Eighteen. Rising sophomore."

"You've…well…you've…improved…over your picture."

"What picture? Where'd you see my picture?"

"Your application photo."

"You read my application?"

"No. Is it a secret? Does it hide something I'd better know? Because you'll bunk with me." He played with a curl behind his ear.

"The photo's high school."

"So you'll bunk with me?"

A question now, not the earlier imperative. Something had shifted, re-set the inflection.

"Upper or lower?" I asked.

"Neither!" he hooted, as though triumphal, and paused just long enough for me to start and frown at what, elsewhere, might have been a suspect innuendo. Then, grinning broadly, eyes on mine, he continued, "Not bunks. Beds. Cots. Neighboring cots. Feel better?"

I didn't feel exactly great. Data were crashing in, too numerous, too fast. He hadn't asked my name; he'd used it. He didn't offer a welcoming handshake. He'd touched me. He played games, possibly tricks. I felt slightly dizzy as he rushed on.

"This your bag?" he asked, shouldering it, hitching up his Levis, sucking air. "Let's roll, Trojan!"

We headed out through the throng of guests scrambling to get registered and badged in time for supper. A quick glance around at the Center's interior, stretching far ahead and behind us, left me puzzled by its incoherence and mildly irked by its tastelessness. I'm not a decor nerd but I know tacky when I see it. High against the faux stone walls hung pictures of Jesus in various biblical places and poses — from splashing in the Jordan with John to sailing off for glory against a sunburst — the same sunken face as usual and scrawny frame, showing bones — all painted or printed in reds and greens and golds on hot black velvet. Among them, lower down, dangled wreaths of dried maize, bottom-heavy where the ears bunched up and drooped. Starbursts of maize spattered the walls, interspersed with tomahawks, rifles, and knives, buffalo skins, rugs in dullish hues, beaded shirts, buckskin jackets.

"Navajo," Monte said, over his shoulder, waving at glass display cases along two walls piled with wooly, wide-striped blankets. "Everything you need in there but peyote! And lots you don't!"

I didn't recognize the word but knew it for bait. Showing off again, he practically begged me to ask the question, to belittle my ignorance and arouse more anxiety about what game he played. Even so, his little footnote — "a lot you don't" — opened a door. For he was right. The very last thing I needed any more of was what those glass shelves showcased, extending all the way down the walls to the great arched entrance to the lobby and then along the far side wall facing the slope to the lake: nuzzling up against the blankets were banks of Bibles and hymnals and study guides and Broadman Press books by and about famous Baptist preachers and evangelists and missionaries; and alongside them

devotional tracts and worship aids and prayer leaflets fanned
out inside wide circles of arrowheads and bright strands of beads
and the odd tomahawk or two. Further along came turquoise
trinkets, woven straw baskets, cruciform crocheted bookmarks,
dusty brown moccasins, racks of picture postcards curling at
the edges, and back-lit boxes showing 35mm slides of the assembly grounds. And after that colored rocks and fossils with
little grey, grimy cards giving dates and details; and then some
doilies spread out, and samplers stitched with scripture, a scat-
tering of cheap beaded religious jewelry, silver thunderbirds going dark, braided plastic necklaces and belts and bracelets, a
tray of smudged snake rings. And against the distant rear wall
stood a massive flagstone hearth and chimney reaching to the
roof and supporting a giant chrome-plated Cross flanked by
twin feather-flagged spears, and dispersed around them bows,
arrows, pouches, masks, pipes, a couple of garish head-dresses.
And across the bottom, the gaping black mouth of the fireplace
seemed poised to devour in one gross gulp the whole swarming
sea of rummage laid out before it. No, I needed nothing here.

Outside, Monte lowered my bag onto the white pebbled
path and swept his arm in a wide arc across the vista before us.

"Jubilee," he exclaimed, possessively. "There she lies!"

A thousand acres, the advertising literature said — "That's
one half-acre per Baptist!" Monte said — to the far horizon, of
arid scrub-brushy desert spotted with adobe structures, one or
two levels, some long, like pullman cars, others square and squat,
the farthest back, Monte pointed, Cactus Lodge, our dorm for
the summer, and on the far opposite edge of the campground
Marigold House, for the female staff, "at a distance to keep
them chaste," he added, smirking. The literature had featured

the seven large and gorgeously cultivated flower gardens, each elaborately designed to illustrate a religious theme — Monte pointed seven times — "there and back there and out there and around behind there" — irrigated by a several-acre man-made lake, "Angel Lake," he said, fronting the Central Complex. Off to our left, randomly set out residence halls for the weekly guests who traveled here from all over the Convention to revive their faith, learn new tricks for expanding their numbers, and enjoy what like-minded Christians were forever calling "fellowship," their sanitized word for partying without an assist from alcohol. To the right, the probable site for a lot of that very fellowship, a sprawling dining hall with a vast kitchen where, he said, most of the boys our age worked, and beyond it quarters for the adult staff and barracks for the mostly immigrant grounds crew and sanitation workers. Closest to us and to the Complex stood the immense brick auditorium, or sanctuary, they called it, bigger than a circus tent and as towering, for the nightly services spotlighting celebrated preachers from the denominational ranks.

"They say we don't have to show up every night," Monte added, "but sometimes Sergeant Steph takes staff attendance."

"Who's he?" I blundered anyway, figuring it was another set-up.

"She. Not he. You met her. She picked you up at the depot. Drove you over."

"Oh. Right. Sure. Only she never said who she was. Just pointed us to the jeep and dumped us outside back there."

"She does that. To mess with your head. Make you wonder. She's all right, though."

Was she? Four of us — Travis, Lindsay, and Jordan — had arrived simultaneously by train from Denver through Sante Fe and de-boarded at the Jubilee whistle stop where this Steph person had spotted us as new staff and silently hustled us and our bags into the back of a ratty old mottled jeep, heaved herself under the wheel and flipped on the radio to a country music station blasting at such volume that no questions, no chatter happened during the twenty-mile drive here. Arrived, still without a word, she headed us out toward the Central Complex, spat brown between her teeth, smudged it with a boot toe, re-mounted the jeep and sped off, spitting sand.

"Do it talk?" I asked Monte.

"She'll talk if you cross her," he warned.

Warnings interested me, attracted me: Mother said *Keep away*, I neared; *Don't touch*, I pawed; Teacher said *Don't*, I did.

"She's Dr. Mann's lieutenant, sort of." This would be Dr. Emerson Mann, Jubilee manager, who signed my acceptance letter. Monte always called him, not to his face, The Man. "He's the chief, she's his brave. She runs stuff. She's our boss."

She'd caught my attention back at the station, for her speechless efficiency, her abrupt but effective no-nonsense direction, her quick steps and snappy signals. She was retired military, I soon learned, and looked the part. Late 40s, maybe a tad thick-bodied but not fat, she showed defined biceps that strained against the short, rolled sleeves of her khaki shirt, and her calves, below the khaki cutoffs, were a biker's. I figured she worked out. Her finely-tooled black cowboy boots added height that slimmed her profile. Dark green shades hid her eyes and mirrored you. Her silver-grey crew-cut was probably military issue but not the burr style: it stood up, at attention, butch-waxed. I liked it, liked her for having it. I had one, too. She didn't so much walk as stalk, with a determined step you didn't want to get in the way of. Around her neck she wore a green and white braided lariat with a silver whistle hooked to its end, which she used, Monte said, to train, check, and muster us.

"You always know where SS is," Monte said, "that whistle is so shrill. That whitthle ith tho thrill," he lisped, mocking his own phrase, and giggling.

Monte called her SS. Sometimes, when she riled him, he'd add a third *s* and leak a low hiss, as though letting out her air, for she did, when provoked, puff up. Talking about her behind her back, he'd add an *f* to the end of her name and make his lips flutter and spit fly, and then bring out the balm to grease them over again.

He picked up my bag. "Ready?"

"No," I said; "hang on a sec." It was nagging, and I had to ask. "How come you know so all-fired much about everything out here? Who told you?"

"Oh," he said. "Well, I was here last summer. They, um, invited me back...sort of."

This was weighty news if lightly spoken, and it fixed us both for a moment while I absorbed it. I wasn't sure I liked it. Forget whatever slight advantage, whatever hold, my knowing his full name gave me over him. He had seniority over me. He had experience. He had favor. He knew stuff. He was ahead of me. When had he planned to let me know?

"When did you plan to let me know?"

"I thought you'd figure it out." His omission was *my* fault? "Isn't it obvious?"

"I reckon not or I would've."

"What difference does it make?"

"You should've told me."

"But why do you care?"

Why *did* I care? Suddenly *that* wasn't obvious either.

This sparring put me on edge. He was winning. I wanted out of it.

"Okay," I said; "you're right. I do know now." It was a concession, and it galled. "But maybe," I went on, feeling my way toward making this little spat work for me, "maybe it's a good thing, you knowing all that, being around here last summer?" Conceivably, there was something to be said for hanging out with a Jubilee veteran. "Maybe you could, like, tell me? Show me how...well, you know, to fit in? Adjust?"

He stared for a couple of seconds, making me wait, and then slowly, very slowly nodded, as if reviewing the invitation.

"All right, then," I breathed. "So tell me. Everything."

"I just did," he said, and we laughed.

We'd reached Cactus Lodge now where the door stood open. He set my bag inside the vestibule and motioned me to follow him down the hallway to a lounge with several tatty easy chairs, two sofas upholstered in slick tan vinyl, a couple of fold-up card tables with metal chairs, and a spinet piano and bench in one corner. Several unframed prints of desert scenes were scotch-taped to the walls; pots of cactus sat in the sills, thirsty. We could hear move-in sounds from the hallways beyond and above. Monte shut the double doors, sprawled onto one sofa, patted the cushion next to his.

"Sit," he said. I chose the other end of the sofa, wondering why we'd stopped again before finding our own room. "Now," he said: "Time for you to talk, Mr. Troy. Who are you?"

"Not Mr. Troy," I said. "'Troy' is fine." Monte had nothing to fear from me regarding exposure of his full name. I had always so intensely disliked my own — Timothy Troy Tyler — I wasn't likely to risk revealing it by disclosing his. "Timothy" was way too biblical for me; and "Timmy" was sissy and "Tim Tyler" was tinny and tiny and too mindful of Dickens. I had long ago taken "Troy" for school and everywhere else away from home, while "Timothy" prevailed there. I'd later learn that Monte's one-day early arrival at Jubilee gave him time to wheedle his roommate's name and more out of a woman filling in at the Registration Desk and so had a nickname ready back there in the lobby. I liked nicknames but the parents didn't and forbade them as disrespectful and demeaning. I thought them warm and chummy. When Monte laid his on me I immediately recognized it as one and embraced it cheerfully, even gratefully, notwithstanding some associations that might make it joke-worthy. Trojan: manly; robust. Cool.

"You go first," I mumbled, betraying my fearless nickname straightaway.

He required no encouragement. I suspected preparation.

Monte hailed from Houston, where his father, ex-military and former A-team Baylor fullback, headed a Gulf Oil subsidiary, and his mother lawyered, taught women's tennis at the country club, and chaired a major philanthropic organization. He had no siblings. He mentioned no church affiliation. He would himself return to Baylor in the fall for his junior year, one college year ahead of me. He'd just declared, he said, a triple major in history, French, and political science in case he decided to pursue graduate studies and the professoriate or a government career after finishing one as an Air Force pilot, toward the achievement of which end he already trained on scholarship with an AF-ROTC unit at the University. A competitive swimmer in high school and college, and physically showing it, he also, Monte said, debated, held fraternity office, soloed in glee club, reported sports for the school paper, expected appointment as junior photographer on the yearbook staff...and danced! Danced! "Tap and ballroom," he added; "five years of lessons!" All of this material except the final entry arrived flatly and matter-of-factly, as if rehearsed, but without bravura: a frank, condensed resume of Monte-identity. And yet the delivery was so flat, so colorless and without nuance or modulation — the one exception noted — it felt artificial, incomplete even of essentials. Nevertheless, there was unmistakable challenge in it too: it packaged a dare, if I chose to hear one, to follow with my own recitation of achievements and ambitions, for comparative purposes. I smelled competition brewing, and I disliked, distrusted, the scent.

Not, mind you, that I feared or shunned competition. The totality of my experience to date might fairly be seen as a succession of contests steadily escalating in wattage until culminating, for the moment, in the one that brought me here, to Jubilee, for a climactic bout. For example, there were the elementary school spelling bees, the Valentine and Easter-egg decorating contests, the gymnasium and athletic field rivalries, the Bible drills, the Vacation Bible School scripture memorization tests, the Boy Scout badge trials, the IQ exams, the piano recitals, the try-outs for dramatic roles, the band and orchestra challenges for first chair, the class office elections, the academic achievement prizes and scholarship laurels, the college acceptance letters, the savage popularity wars, the numberless races, and the games: the myriad games in a thousand different guises, each with its own rules and allegiances and risks and hostile threats and ways to screw up; competitions piled on competitions backward and forward to infinity in both directions, with no win final, no loss terminal, for winning fueled the winning yen, and losing quickened the comeback urge.

I had earned my share of wins and was proud of them but ever loathed the stress of the competition, and sometimes sickened over it, however also energized by it. Still, I felt oddly reluctant to open a competition with Monte by parading my own successes for his inspection and possibly his scorn. Something checked my will to trust him with them. He couldn't take them away, no, but could he make me think less of them? Feel ashamed of their modesty? Might he be disappointed by their inconsequence? That thought jarred.

"Which fraternity?" I asked.

"What?" he frowned.

"You said you're an officer in your fraternity. Which frat?"

"Oh, right. KA. Kappa Alpha. We're very big at Baylor. You know, the southern rebel thing and all."

I didn't know. Louisiana College, where I went, didn't allow sororities and fraternities, so it was all, well, Greek to me. Louisiana College, Pineville, LA, was Baptist, you see, totally Christian. My Father could afford to send me there because Baptist pastors' kids got a big tuition break. I didn't mind Monte knowing *where* I attended college but *why* wasn't one of my bragging points. He'd eventually learn my PK — preacher's kid — status, but it was a stigma I'd rather conceal for as long as I could, at least until I'd staked out some other, some respectable, claim on Monte's regard.

"You're Confederates, you mean, you and your frat brothers?" Okay, I was showing off, trying to amuse and charm this guy with a little lame wordplay.

"Well, yeah," he drawled, "we honor the flag...," and then he caught my grin and paused. "Cute," he said. And again, "cute."

Clever, he meant. Not cute. But nothing was gained by correcting his usage. "Which office?" I asked. "What are you, President?"

"Actually, yes," he said, squashing my intent to dis. "I was president of my pledge class. But it's not a real office. You don't belong to the chapter as a pledge. I'll probably be an officer senior year. But KA doesn't have presidents or vice-presidents or secretaries. We have numbers. The President is Number One, and so on. But enough about me. Why don't *you* talk about me for a while?!" It was an old line but he laughed at it. "No, really. Your turn now. Whyn't you tell me about high school. What were you there?"

What *was* I there? He wanted to play out the competitive match, I could tell, and it looked like I'd have to follow through. But the question, What was I there? struck me as curious and provocative, generically. I wasn't quite a Big Deal there, not quite the Trojan. But I wasn't exactly peanuts either: class secretary twice, student body v-p, salutatorian, a Boy's State Supreme Court judge, pianist for the orchestra and second chair sax in the band, assistant student manager and team scorekeeper for basketball games. BUT: lead in the school plays all four years and winner of every speaking and oratorical contest at school and in the district for three of them. Sort of a perpetual also-ran or runner-up generally. But of the stage I was king.

"I did some theater," I said.

"Drama!" he yelped. "I should try that. We could do a play out here! Recite me some lines!"

"It's not that easy." I was taken aback. It's not that easy to stage a play is what I meant, but he thought I declined to recite.

"C'mon," he said, "how about some *Hamlet*? 'To be...?'"

"Or *not*!" I said, a little too loudly. "*No*, even if I knew the lines, I can't just right here up and *perform* them for you without...."

"Whoa! Okay. Easy, Trojan. Maybe something else? You got anything else memorized?"

He sat up, straight and alert, and looked hard right into my face. "Anything? Anything else handy to roll off your tongue?"

"No, of course not. I don't know what you're getting at." But I did almost know.

"C'mon, Troj," now cajoling. "Trust me. I know why you're here."

"Same as you," I said, faintly now. "To work. What're you getting at?"

"All I'm saying is I know why you're here." His own voice dropped to a smoldering conspiratorial whisper: "And we're going to win it!"

2

Every fall, across the South and Midwest, and north up both coasts, hundreds of late teens signed on to the church-sponsored Wilomena Goforth and Silas Blueford Peter Young People's Speaking Competition. The Peters had been famous Baptist missionaries to China for decades until one stormy night a water buffalo herd, terrified by lightening and thunder, stampeded right through the Peters' rickshaw, them in it, killing them both and setting off a denomination-wide grief-fest that eventuated in this memorial contest bearing their names. Local congregations staged early rounds to weed out the rabble; parish (county) and district tournaments followed, and then state finals produced one winner to compete regionally where one was chosen for the national finals here at Jubilee and at another campground on the east coast, always held during the last week of the assemblies' summer operation — "Youth Week," it was named for the hundreds of them who packed in for partying and proselytizing before heading back to school. Most were long ago "saved," of course, in the Baptist tradition, so salvation wasn't at stake for many; the whole understood but unspoken objective of the contest and maybe of Youth Week itself was to ferret out and encourage likely candidates for seminary training and ministerial careers — to collect a passel of heirs apparent for Graham and the rest of them in case, say, of another stampede. The pressure never eased; the expectations of commitment to what was named "full-time Christian service" saturated the evangelical culture, and believers *meant* Full-Time, too, starting yesterday and extending all the way with no letup to the reward of welcoming admission at the Pearly Gates. I knew all about it from long overexposure to it. And I was firmly, fiercely resolved never, ever to follow such a course myself; but back in Madison, my home town, in my father's church, I figured I knew a pretty sure thing when I saw one in this speaking competition, at least through the early rounds, and signed up.

The Madison round turned out to be a pass, for nobody else signed on, the sure thing thing having gotten around, I reckon. So to legitimize my nominal victory there, I had to pick a "religious subject," the instructions said, and compose a speech about it of ten to twelve minutes and memorize it for delivery at the parish match. I found not a scrap of inspiration in my list of predictable topics — prayer, bible study, tithing, witnessing, righteousness, sin (although this last one, like itself, was a serious temptation). So I finally settled on my dog Bruce.

Bruce was the shaggy mixed-breed given us as a pup by a church-member for my tenth birthday, and I'd named him after Batman, outlasting all parental objections and preferences for weird, obscure biblical names (Nebuchadnezzar, Balthazar, Obediah, Jehosaphat: imagine meeting someone and having to say, Hi, I'm Troy and this is my dog Jehosaphat?) that he'd have hated. I wanted "Batman," of course, but the folks weren't having it, so we eventually agreed on the morally neutral "Bruce," ("Wayne" being silently implied by me but never told to the parents). He came without known parentage, but from the black-and-white coat and other appearances and behaviors, we figured border collie and terrier blood combined somewhere along the way. It was my job to feed and water him, groom him, de-flea him, piss and poop him, romp him, scratch behind his ears and stroke his belly. Father trimmed his nails. He slept in my bed, sometimes pillowing my head.

Of course Bruce wasn't himself an obviously religious topic for my speech; but I had taught him to kneel (Father called it "praying"), and I supposed I could spin ten minutes worth of prattle about how "spiritual" Bruce was, how patient and obedient and tolerant, how loving his heart, how forgiving his spirit, how loyal and sweet-tempered and dutiful and so forth like that, and maybe even draw him as a model of Christian comportment. It was every bit true, after all, except possibly that last thing, and I could surely rub it up into something sappy and mushy enough to pass as "religious." Maybe they'd let me bring Bruce along as a sample of himself?

They wouldn't, but I didn't need Bruce at the parish meet in Alexandria where my only competition was Drucilla Patch, a stringy, prune-mouthed, spectacled kid from Tallapaloosa, all zigzagging knees and elbows and pigtails, whose tongue — would you believe it? — kept snagging on the rubber bands of her braces so that her speech snapped and twanged. On then to the district meet in Lake Charles and three girl cheerleaders who collaborated on one speech and were disqualified for it; big Bertha Boone who lost her way three minutes along and fled in tears; and Baxter Thrush from Houma, who thought some Cajun patois thrown in might win him points but didn't. Last on the district program came Drum Drummond, whose name and reputation I recognized: Drum played tight end and captained the Lafayette High squad and deserved all the credit for its annual wipe-out of Madison's team. Drum, I figured, represented my first serious competition; and he *did* give a pretty fair speech even if it was patterned on the old reliable one about Jesus and Satan being opposing quarterbacks in The Game of Life. Drum looked smart in his pads and togs but probably lost points when he fumbled and dropped the football he'd brought as a prop.

My pitch for Bruce as a devout and saintly paragon of religious virtue had improved over the weeks of run-ups to the state finals at Monroe, but as the date for them neared I thought myself into increasing anxiety over the audacity of my idea no matter how original it might be. What if it proved too outlandish, too radical, too secular, too coarse for the alleged refinement of the north Louisiana judiciary? What if they found it profane? The rules allowed for minor tweaking of the original speech as successful candidates advanced but you couldn't change subjects or start over with a new text. I was stuck with Bruce, but maybe I could dress him up a little, sanctify him somehow, consecrate doubtful features I'd highlighted? Render him less playful and more pious in my telling? I set to work on it.

On all accounts, the speech needed upgrading. Because I wasn't yet legit. Except against Drum, I hadn't exactly won, and even that win was arguably suspect. I just hadn't lost. My competitors so far were such winners at losing, really had down pat the art of getting licked, I hadn't yet had a credible shot at proving my superiority. The state finals were certain to present better contestants, more experienced speakers, tougher challenges, and I needed to enrich, add density and color and pizzaz. And drama.

And there was another worrisome thing. I'd signed up for this gig as a sort of lark, a briefly entertaining diversion, without much long-term commitment to serious effort or consideration of the consequences of success, should I achieve any. Yet here I was facing a run-off that just might end with me walking away the Louisiana Goforth Speaker of 19— and lugging around that absurd title (it used to be "Peter Winner" but that slid too easily into "Peter Wiener" and got dropped) for a year of Goforth Speaking with nothing to say and, worse, forever dismissing everybody's expectations of where I was headed now, with all this grooming and practice, for the rest of my natural life, and making up reasons why I wasn't headed there. On the other hand, I couldn't just wimp out at this point: there were parents and friends to please, a reputation of sorts to protect. And there was *me* to please, too. If winning had its complications, losing stung, shamed. I stuck.

Then, three weeks before the state finals, a screaming ambulance, racing down our street, struck Bruce and killed him. Off-leash, Bruce had been following Father on the sidewalk, as he often did, when he spotted an escaped pet rabbit across the road and hell for leather made for it; and although Father called out and ran after, he said, Bruce was too inflamed to heed, all his touted obedience instantly forsworn. A tardy schoolmate saw the accident and, bug-eyed and flushed, reported it to me in class. I ran the eight blocks home, unbelieving and bawling the whole way.

Everybody's lost a dog and knows what that feels like, so I won't even try to describe how Bruce's death pretty much tore me up into little bitty pieces, and I wasn't brave about it. Nobody in Madison ever used leashes except for training but I knew Father felt guilty, worried on my account, although no responsibility could be fairly assigned. Still, for a while I let him think that I might believe he could have saved my dog. And not for a second did I buy his pathetic, lame, even hurtful attempt at consolation: "God needed Bruce more than you did." The way he'd taught me, God, being God, didn't *need* anything. But I sure needed Bruce back. "The Lord giveth, and the Lord taketh away," Father quoted over the backyard grave where we laid Bruce with his filthy green tennis ball and a ragged stuffed badger. Then we cried some more through his prayer that my dog would find good treats in heaven and, I silently added, slow rabbits to chase safely. And that was about it for Bruce.

Only it wasn't. I'm a little ashamed to admit how soon afterward it occurred to me that maybe the Lord also giveth *when* he taketh away, to balance things out. To compensate? Maybe there was purpose and design here, after all, benefit and blessing. What if God figured I should get a little something in payback for what I'd given up and gone through? Because it struck me like a revelation that I *had* gotten it, *already* gotten it back! What you might call a gift, even, had been bestowed: and its name was STORY!

Bruce might become a martyr to my cause, even a figure for the "bruised" Jesus, carrying all the drama and poignance I needed to perfect the address. True, I felt kind of crummy for thinking like this about his passing, but the manner of it was a ready-made tale to move the hearts of men! I went a little breathless at the thought of using it. I could honor my dog Bruce and restore a sort of vitality to him by telling the story of his accident and at the same time add to my speech a compelling narrative with exactly the sort of emotional clout required to complete and climax it. I could keep all the parts about Bruce's loving heart and loyalty and general righteousness and then just let the accident story tell itself, un-elaborated, without my having to punch it up with extra sentiment of the usual sort folks use to swing judgments in their favor. I might even borrow Father's phrase about God needing Bruce: it fit the new strategy, and he would like to be quoted. And if I myself went a little weepy getting through the thing, so much the better for the poignance factor. Remember what I said a while back about sure things? This speech was beginning to shape itself into one.

* * *

The windows in our Cactus Lodge second-story corner room opened down upon the flowered path we'd just walked, and upward back toward the Complex and far beyond it to low purplish hills thick with "pinion…juniper…quaking aspen," Monte said, themselves fading into cloudless azure sky. The spread of Angel Lake fronting the Complex seemed from here a solid plate of blue mirrored glass, a line of swans just then connecting the two small islands — Cherubim and Seraphim — in its midst. Yellow canoes dotted the banks of both.

"Did you crew in high school?" Monte asked. "Row?"

"Um, no. Pirogue, maybe?" But he didn't get it. "Madison Louisiana high school did not crew," I almost scoffed. "I guess you were coxswain?"

It sounded nastier than I meant but there was no taking it back. He gave me a look and moved on. "No, we didn't have crew either, but Baylor does. I just didn't go out for it, or haven't yet. I'm pretty busy. You and I can row here, though. The canoes are free to staff."

"Cool," I said, flashing on the first and only time I'd ever stepped into a canoe, turning it over and hurling myself head-first into the bayou. "You can save me when I flip it."

"My pleasure," he grinned.

Against both walls, starting at the windows, stood the twin beds, two four-drawer dressers with mirrors and unmatched lamps, and nearest the door on the left open closets with straggly hangers across from the bathroom and shower on the right. The only chairs were the beds. The overhead light fixture missed one of two bulbs. Everything looked like Goodwill rejects: temporary, makeshift, uncomfortable, uninviting. Over Monte's bed — he'd already claimed the one on the right, now piled with jumbled clothes — hung that famous print (this copy faded) of Jesus standing in a weedy garden rapping on a rotted door, with the caption, "I stand at the door and knock...." I know it's a sin to say, but I've always thought He looked itchy to use the outhouse. On the opposite wall, above my bed, sagged an also washed-out print of Jesus "calling" three well-muscled, half-naked fishermen.

Monte watched me in his dresser mirror as he fiddled with bottles and cans, sprays and roll-ons, tubes of balm, his Neiman's set of combs and brushes centered in the foregrounded, all in husky greens and blues and dark leathery browns, moving them around like checkers on squares. A while back he'd asked me what I was in high school, and I'd mostly dodged. This looked like a good time to turn the tables.

"So, Monte," I ventured; "what *is* Monte?"

"Well," he didn't pause to plan, "it's short for that name I told you never to pronounce out loud upon pain of death, and also for Montague, which is worse. And it's Spanish for mountain. And it's a card game. Ever play three-card monte? AKA *monte bank*?"

"No. We couldn't play cards at home. Only when we visited The Cousins Corrupt. And then just Old Maid. It's gambling."

"You don't gamble? I'll teach you." He turned around, leaned back against the dresser, crossed his legs, hung his thumbs from his pockets. Posed.

"What's Troy, then, Troy?"

"Me," I said, feebly, still not wanting to go there. Or him to go there.

"Troy," he mused; his brow crinkled, eyes looked up and away, searchingly. "You're named for a city."

"I don't know. Maybe. I don't know that I'm named *for* anything. Nobody ever said."

"Troy in New York or Turkey? God forbid it's the one in Michigan!" He chuckled and I slightly relaxed.

"Wheresoever Helen doth abide!" I smiled back.

"Troy. Illium," Monte said. "I never knew anybody named that before, but it's good. I like it. It's rich. Lots of history, lots of myth in it. A plucky lot, those Trojans. Fierce, cruel, definitely pagan, which isn't to dump on them, of course. Plucky but not conspicuously bright, since they got suckered in the end. Tough, though, durable: so claim the ads on the machines, anyway. You've seen those machines?"

"Smart had nothing to do with it," I snapped back. "They were duped. Unfair practice even in war. Besides, they never heard of gifts bearing Greeks."

Okay, I stole the line from a teacher and had used it before. Monte's brows went up.

"Cute," he said, laughing. "Good! Funny how words get all switched around, though. You know what it meant — Trojan? — during the war? My dad told me. Your Trojan was your Saturday night drinking buddy. If you drank, I mean. You did crazy stuff together, out on the town and all. It was who you didn't care what happened with. Are you that guy? That Trojan?"

"A tough pagan or dumb sucker?"

"Or a carousing buddy? If there's a difference," he grinned slowly, "take your pick. We'll find out soon enough."

There were weighty loads to digest in all of this, and I needed a break.

"I better get unpacked," I said, and made a move toward my case.

"Need help?" he offered, wagging his head no. "Okay, pal, I'll grab a shower and spruce up."

"Wait," I said. "Is this a day of fasting or what? Where do they stash the food?"

"Loaves and fishes comin' up," he slapped me lightly on the shoulder, reaching for a towel, "after my bath." He stepped through the bathroom door, and then stuck his head back out: "Use the balm," he said, and disappeared, whistling.

* * *

Staff breakfasted at 6 a.m. in the rambling dining hall and was supposed to finish in half an hour so to clean up and square away for the onset of Jubilee guests at 8. We had stayed around after supper last night to receive our assignments and get first instructions from Dr. Mann — The Man — and SS, both of whom also laid down some rules about dress and comportment and "mature, responsible execution" of our various jobs. Jubilee furnished squaw dresses for the girls — brightly colored pleated skirts with rickrack and crescent necklines — and recommended white crew-neck short-sleeved T-shirts, tucked in, for us. Each of two men's "kitchen crews" worked alternating shifts of dinner-breakfast-lunch every other day, with the intervening hours off, while the girls laid the tables and cleared them, served the food, refreshed the tea, and generally looked after the diners for all three meals every day. Monte and I landed on the same kitchen crew — the Scrub Squad, I called it — but our workplace wasn't exactly the kitchen: it was, rather, a huge, long room running perpendicular to the kitchen and bakery so that every utensil, every cooking and baking tool and vessel used in those units got shuttled over to ours for cleaning. Dishwashing machines were still primitive and suited mostly for plates and glasses and bowls, not at all for the greasy, crusted king-sized pots and pans, roasters and skillets and casseroles, and the bakery trays and sheets and muffin/cake/pie pans that piled up and up at my station, for that was my job, to scrape and scrub and scour them free of all that hardened gunk so stubbornly stuck. I had stainless steel and wiry, bristly brushes, but those pots were heavy and clunky, and awkward to work with even in my extra-large sinks. And besides them, I was also answerable for the cutlery: we had a machine for it, but before loading you had to be sure every piece, every tine and blade was clear of food scum lest one overlooked bit gum up the works and shut down the appliance. Basically, you had to hand-wash every piece before stacking it in the machine's niches for scalding and steaming. It all looked like hard labor at first, but after a few cracks at it I developed a system and got pretty fast. I even came to like the sheen on the pots and finding my face in it.

Noise levels here in our Sweat Shop, I called it, even with the machines clanging and rattling and banging away, weren't so loud that you couldn't talk with your neighbor, if you had one, but I didn't. Monte scraped and loaded dishes into one of the big washers against the wall behind me; and when I turned to hunt for him that first morning, he was chatting with Travis, who'd ridden from the depot with me and the girls, and was one of three other guys working at the same washer. When Monte saw me looking, he started this little tap dance shuffle, using a big plate as a hat, shimmying it the way vaudevillians do when leaving the stage. I waved and returned to work, the better for knowing where he was.

Not that I wasn't glad to be relieved of his presence and pressure for a bit. After our relaxing, high-spirited dinner the night before with six other staffers — Lance Larson and Dallas Lee, roommates next door to us, among them — I figured that Monte and I would soon enough settle into a comfortable and compatible rooming arrangement as we identified and adapted to each other's quirks and learned to modify our own to achieve and maintain harmony in our close quarters. But not quite yet. Unfinished business remained, at least in my head where, I thought, it probably might best stay if I could sort it all out there. One thing was Monte's intensity. We'd not shared company for twenty-four hours yet, but that was my chief impression of him: controlled but unabated intensity. He seemed always *on*, so to speak, ever animated or coiled to become so, tightly wound, all his springs taut. Exciting, yes, stimulating, for certain, but also tiring. He just never let up: moving, talking, pacing, watching, fondling that blasted tube, bobbing, dancing…and probing, hunting, pursuing! Always reacting and provoking you to. It wasn't nervousness; it wasn't a neurotic twitch; it wasn't a St. Vitus-type agitation. It was Monte practicing and perfecting intensity. He had evidently fallen asleep last night almost upon lights out at 10 —without bedtime prayers, thank God! —but until then he'd maintained a verve, even when posed against his dresser, emitted an air of vivacity, of barely restrained gusto, a zeal always to get on to the next thing also visible in the glimmer of his bright dark eyes. It led one on and wore one out.

And there were "those machines." Of course I'd seen them in public restrooms in highway Stuckey's and in the Men's at Madison's pool room and at our regular Esso filing station, and I vaguely knew what conveniences they sold, but whatever were they doing in Monte's appreciation of Homeric warriors? Had he actually compared me with condoms, in my Trojan identity? And if he had, was it a jokey joke or a serious joke, and in either case what was I going to do about it? Similarly, was the invitation to learn gambling a metaphor for assuming generally base behavior, and likewise "carousing"? Were these locutions merely tossed-off wisecracks or seriously intended proposals, openings? What if they were trial balloons, to test my responses, to draw out secrets or spring traps? Perhaps more important, why was I fixating on them? What about them stirred my interest enough to pick them out for pondering?

They partnered with his prying. He didn't just ask, didn't just open the door for showing and telling: he pried, he thirsted for intelligence, for stories. Mine.

How the devil did he already know the real reason I was here at the assembly? The Peter-Goforth thing? He hadn't alluded to it again, to me, anyway, after his shocking claim to knowing, and evidently hadn't bruited it abroad, for no one else had yet mentioned it either. That we were "going to win it" was too preposterous to take as anything other than a good will wish; but the affected authority of his prediction, together with its conspiratorial hint, seemed to me almost to announce a brewing plot, a strategy of his design and my expected collaboration. Or did that suspicion just express my qualified hope for his continued companionship, my uncertain wish for support as needed from this experienced chum whom, even so, I did not fully trust *not* to set me up to bring me down.

But such worries receded, without vanishing, in the rollicking merriment of the Sweat Shop under Monte's inspired direction. It almost immediately stopped feeling like a workplace and became a playground for screwball antics and infectious horseplay unchecked by Sergeant Steph's oppressive rules. He took over, bouncing around everywhere all the time, lean and limber, with knots and ripples where it counts to have them, packed tight into his Levis and T-shirt, frisky, prancing, clowning, meeting (with handshakes now) and greeting, yakking, spouting one-liners and laughing and making you join. He'd giggle and guffaw, and rake back off his slick forehead a handful of black curls, his sorrel skin shiny, his eyes a-glitter. He'd strut around from one sink to another, showing you how and pitching in, gouging your ribs and slapping your shoulder and slinging gobs of lather at your face and snapping a wet towel at your butt, or zinging you with a chewed-up chicken bone or a soggy corn-cob. Sometimes he'd organize betting games, all of us wagering coins on who'd finish first or last, who'd get caught malingering, who'd have to leave to pee. Oh, it was all silly and inane and juvenile, and if you stopped long enough to think about it you'd feel stupid and embarrassed, and find Monte an over-performing jerk for siring this circus, and then you'd jump right back into it just because it *was* fun and so wildly different from everything else Jubilee offered.

Sometimes, feeling an urge to sing, maybe to show off his Baylor glee-club gift, Monte would climb up onto the long dry-ing-table and, butcher knife for a baton, conduct us, after he'd taught us (these weren't your standard old worn-out church-camp songs, not lame tunes like "I'm Henery the Eighth I Am I Am" or "She'll Be Comin' Round the Mountain" or even "Pack Up Your Troubles" or "I'm Looking Over" or "Irish Eyes" — no, not a one of those!) —he'd teach us and then wave that knife around and we'd raise the roof with "Little Brown Jug" and "Roll Me Over" and "Hava Nagila" and "Blow the Man Down." And then again he'd bang on a skillet or smash a plate to get our attention, and cock his head sassy-like to one side and give us a naughty grin, and sing-drawl, dragging it out:

"You kno-o-o-o-o-w what I like…." and we'd let fly with "Chantilly Lace" and go on to "Good Golly, Miss Molly" and "Hot Diggity Dog" and such like. Such like as "Peggy Sue" and "That'll Be The Day" and "Whole Lotta Shakin' Goin' On," for he thought Buddy Holly was hot stuff because he'd heard him, he said, in Lubbock before anybody else had.

One night right square in the middle of "Peggy Sue," Monte stamped his feet and waved his hands in the football referee's time-out signal, and waited until we stopped singing and moving and had settled into the almost ominous suspension of sound and motion before he swiped his lips and said: "You know, we're just over three months from February 3rd, so maybe we should take a minute to remember Buddy and Ritchie and Big Bopper J.P." Of course we all knew exactly who and what he meant, for that terrible plane crash was probably our generation's first hard encounter with mortality, outside our families, anyway, and it had scarred us, every one. "So if you don't mind," Monte went on, "I'd like to offer a prayer for the peace and heavenly rest of their blessed souls." And he did, in those very words, our heads bowed and our eyes shut amid all those greasy pans and grimy plates, and invited us silently to remember with grateful hearts the many musical gifts of our idols. I believe we did. He allowed about fifteen seconds for it and then said quietly, "All right: now, the next best thing to do," his voice rising, "the next best thing we can do" — his voice louder still — "is to *honor* them all by picking up right where we left off!" I noticed Robyn and Dallas wiping their cheeks, and checked my own. It took us about a minute to recover musical momentum and volume; and our spirits rose with them, and shortly we were bellowing again — honoring, on Monte's instructions.

You'd have reckoned he knew entire scores from all the big shows back then, the way he'd move from *Peter Pan* to *Guys and Dolls* to *The King and I* to *My Fair Lady* and usually end up with *South Pacific*, soloing (we happily let him, his voice was that fine!) on "Getting to Know You" and "Hey There" and "I'm in Love with a Wonderful Guy" and "This Nearly Was

Mine" (which just about wiped me out every time), and bringing us along on "A Bushel and a Peck," "With a Little Bit" and "Get Me to the Church on Time." He wanted "Steam Heat" for our theme song, but we never could get it right, such an oddball tune, so we agreed on "There Is Nothing Like a Dame" instead: he'd do the verses, we'd drum out the rhythms on pots and pound the table and rattle every dish in the joint with our racket, roaring out the chorus, which always brought the girls peeping through the swinging doors to the next door kitchen, thinking we meant them.

Other times: hymns. Monte would start us out on one, reverent and solemn as in church, and then cut us off sharp, with that knife: "Oh, for a thousand tongues to sing, my dear...." Period. Or "On Jordan's stormy banks I stand, and cast...." Period. Or "Mine eyes have seen the glory of the coming...." Period. And we'd all crack up. I oughtn't to mention it, but he also tried to enlist us in this gag where he'd call out a hymn-title and we were supposed to yell "Between the sheets!" right after. It was hysterical at first, like with "Oh, Why Not Tonight" and "Softly and Tenderly," but when he came up with "Jesus, Lover of My Soul" and "Satisfied with Jesus...," well, our yelling kind of died down — you know? — and he quit.

But all of this rowdy commotion paled and dimmed against Monte's appropriation of Judy Garland and Edith Piaf. Judy knocked him out, as he never tired of repeating, as his Edith did us. The way he'd stand up there, still, for once, and deliver "The Man That Got Away," and then, moving again, "San Francisco" and "Mammy" and especially "Sewanee," why, it would raise the tiny hairs on your neck and shiver your spine and maybe even make you want to cry at the wonder and magic of it, he was that good, only you couldn't, not there. He was powerful patient coaching me: he'd borrow from SS the key to the Cactus Lodge lounge where we'd lock the door and rehearse with the piano, me at the keyboard, playing by ear, and Monte demonstrating the dance steps for me to learn by until I finally got the hang of this little vaudeville routine with us taking turns as Judy and Jolson — boaters, canes, white shoes — and belt out "Sewanee" in two-part harmony which was, if I may say so, as good as anything you ever heard on Ted Mack. Whoever was Judy had to don a cruddy old mop-head and stuff napkins under his T, much to the bawdy jeering of the crew, who loved it, as did we, hamming it up right there on the drying-table stage. They were special, those times, for both of us; I think he thought so too. Because once, when Dallas tried to cut in on his own with "Rainbow," he got exactly two notes out — "Some... WHERE...," — before Monte flung his knife hard at the table where it stuck and quivered and hummed. "That," he said, and you could hear the blade in his voice, "That is sacred music."

One night when SS popped by for an unannounced inspection, Lance got so rattled over it that he dropped a whole tray of glasses when unloading a washer, shattering them all. The Sergeant went ballistic, chewed us all out royally in really nasty terms, and threatened collective punishment if we didn't shape up and quit "slouchin'," she said.

"What can she do?" Robyn whispered to me, "Spank us?"

SS stomped around growling for a while, picking at little bitty slip-ups and oversights here and there, nothing consequential but becoming so in her harangue, before stalking off, leaving us sore and disgruntled and dejected. It took Monte about thirty seconds before he vaulted onto the table with a clatter.

"Listen up, you bums! What *is* this, the Bastille or what? And who do you think she is, Madame Defarge or who? You ignorant clowns don't even know what DAY it is! It's July 14th is what it is" (it wasn't, of course)! "And I want to see some respect for it! It's Re-vo-lu-tion time" (to the Howdy Doody tune). "C'mon, you lousy provincial bimbos" (marching and directing now); "everybody up...I want to see everybody out for the French! *Vive*, you morons, *Vive*!"

And he launched right into the chorus of "Milord."

Not that we ever knew, or cared, really, what the words meant. All that mattered was the bewitching melody, the beat, the way Monte strutted up and down, clapping his hands and waving his arms and twirling his apron to whip us up and throwing back his head and rumpling his hair and laughing at how we botched the lyrics, trying to imitate what he sang, but ever at us to keep trying...which we did, ridiculously, howling out that chorus over and over, hanging onto each other till we were clumsily can-canning around that table, hoarse, blundering, hysterical even, looking and sounding for all the world like a pack of Holy Rollers speaking in tongues. Crazy? Nuts? Demented? I guess. Electrifying? Oh, yeah. And nuts or not, such times, Monte in such times, did more than SS ever could've to keep the place up, and our spirits, too.

* * *

A tall, lean guy all the way from small-town Minnesota, Lance Larson shared a room with Dallas Lee next door to Monte and me. Lance was Swede and corn-silk blonde with brows so light they vanished in the sun and a prominent Adam's Apple and pink splotches on both cheeks that often brightened with discomfort, for he was bashful and skittish. Even so, and notwithstanding a high, thin speaking voice unlike a guy's, Lance planned to major in poli sci at Oberlin and enter government service like his hero Adlai Stevenson, whom he affected to imitate in his own stiff formality and stilted speech: he liked to begin sentences with "Furthermore" and "Moreover" and "Nevertheless" and "Therefore" and "The fact of the matter is," no matter the context and despite the non sequiturs; and into the middle of sentences he'd drop "In light of developing circumstances," and "When we take everything into thoughtful account," and "I respectfully venture to suggest...." So conspicuously polite and deferential was Lance that you sometimes wanted to shake him up into a little harmless discourtesy, but he didn't seem to know rude. He liked to wear a formal black bow-tie with his T-shirt — and not one of those pre-tied jobs either: I've watched him knot it, proudly with his eyes shut — and formal black and white suspenders, like you wear for the prom, to keep the Levis up on his skinny hips. Weird wear, and it drew some derisive looks; but pretty soon we got used to it and took it for normal Lance.

His roommate Dallas Lee was actually from Dallas "by way of Virginia," he always said, and if you didn't right away ask, he'd add, "Of the Virginia Lee's"; and if you doubted, he had this Roi-Tan cigar box crammed with Civil War souvenirs and $200, he said, in Confederate paper, and also a big colored chart of The Family Tree, he said; but that's when we left, Monte and I, when he started unrolling it. With a broad face and darting eyes under straight reddish-brown hair cleanly parted on the right, neatly combed over and greased flat, Dallas was large and stout, with thick thighs thumping and burly shoulders swaggering when he walked: kind of a Baylor Bear himself, with the sort of build that at Jubilee usually pegged you for the sanitation crew and its heavy lifting chores, but Dallas asked for a transfer to the kitchen and got it; nobody said why but I figured it was for Monte. They hadn't known each other at Baylor; but I'd spotted Dallas for an operator right off, on the lookout for connections to make and use. You could always smell Dallas's deodorant and after-shave, or both: it wasn't noxious, just loud and distinct. He also sprouted a little growth of brownish-red hair just under his lower lip that might have been the northernmost tip of a goatee, but the chin was clear.

"How come you never asked about Dallas?" I said, back in our room.

"Big D., you mean. What about it?"

"Not it. Him. Him being named for it?" I wanted to see him run with the name, play with it, as he had with "Troy."

"It's obvious. Such a good fit. The 'ass' in 'Dallas' tags him."

"The one in 'Tex-as' too!" I said, forgetting Monte's hometown Houston. "He's double-ass Dallas! Let's christen him 'Double-Ass Dallas'!"

"Hey, that's pretty good, guy!" Monte giggled.

"Well, we can't actually call him that."

"We can't?" he said. "We might. It's pretty apt." He pondered, tinkling his bottles.

"How about the initials?" I offered, after a beat or two. "D. A. Dallas for DoubleAss Dallas. No, wait. DA Dallas. DaDallas. They'll think we mean THE. THE Dallas. Only *we'll* know what we really mean. What we're saying. It'll be our secret. DaDallas. Want to try it?"

"He'll hate it. It sounds like a stutter."

"How about we try it?"

"DaDallas!" Monte laughed. "Pretty fine, Troj. I think I like it. What a team!"

"You mean the double ass, right?" I said, knowing he didn't. "THAT team?"

"DaDallas," Dallas said, after hearing us toss it around a couple of times. "Damn straight!" He laughed. "DaDallas! Da One, Da Only, DaDallas! *TA-DA, TA-DA DALLAS!* " spreading wide his arms in self-presentation. "'Yessiree! Dat be me! By way of Virginia."

Okay. So the joke kind of backfired, in his appropriating revision of it. But we still had our private gag.

Robyn Boyd Byrd was fat. I wish I knew a kinder way to write it but "plump," "chubby," and "portly" don't capture the effect. "Pudgy" gets closer. The bulbous b's in his names closer still. Pouches of blubber bulged from his squat frame, overhung his undefined waist strapped by a pink-and-black belt notched way too tightly against the wan slab of skin exposed by the bunched-up T. Nobody but Robyn wore a belt with Levis; and most everyone but Robyn managed to keep his T tucked. Through his you could see that the wobbly pecs were nearly breasts, outlined against the cotton and jiggling as he walked. Behind big round lenses in tortoise-shell frames, Robyn's pale, puffy eyes squinted and oozed so that he was forever wiping them and polishing the fogged glass with a star-spangled blue handkerchief the size of a table napkin, his initials stitched large on it in orange thread. He was the only person I knew who carried a hanky in his jeans, but as an asthmatic he needed it for coughing and blowing into. He

smeared his pimples with greasy pink salve that caked and crinkled and scabbed over, so he picked at them to relieve the itch.
He told us, one night when Monte randomly proposed a chess
match, that he'd been a master at his Little Rock high school
and was on the chess team at Ouachita College in Arkadelphia,
another Baptist school where chess probably subbed for cards.
Father had tried and failed to teach me chess: I admired the
elegant carving of the pieces but the oddball moves stumped
and flustered me. So I figured Robyn must've been a lot smarter
than all his prattle might have led you to imagine. Monte said
he was insecure and lonely, and the over-talking an effort to
connect and relate, to win allies. I thought him kind of a pest,
always unexpectedly dropping by our room — sticking his head
without knocking through the doorway with a chirpy "Hi-Hey-
Hello-there, fellas" (a greeting borrowed from the goofy kids'
radio show with Big John and Sparkie; nobody said "fellas" any
more either) — and plopping down unanswered on my bed to
snoop and gossip. I have to admit, though, that I felt sort of
sorry for Robyn, stuck as he was with a name so farcical and
damning — more harmful than my own — you had to wonder how sane parents could have so thoughtlessly marked and
doomed a child with it. Some of the kids turned his middle
name "Boyd" into "Boing!" and chanted it as he bounced along
the walkways. But I gave him a break and didn't often mention
it, and tried not to think of him or treat him as a slob. We later
learned that he'd bombed at the Arkansas State Goforth Finals,
which information sort of vexed our acquaintance, but as he
understood, it also opened the door for his advice on my prep,
once word leaked about me.

Ginger-haired and freckle-faced, usually in coveralls rolled up over naked ankles and sneakers, Travis Tuttle lived with parents and two older brothers and a grandmother in Claremore, Oklahoma, where they farmed wheat and soybeans, and tended a peach orchard. He would begin sophomore year come fall at Oklahoma Baptist in Shawnee without an academic major in mind, for the school didn't offer a concentration in art and Travis's chief extracurricular activity at the moment was sketching cartoons for the weekly *Hullaballoo* — "making mutinies," as he put it, "with anarchic art." Failing to nail the right field slot on the baseball team — they wanted him for first base — he quit, having found first base too busy, too taxing: he didn't care, he said, to work that hard. Laid back, easy-going, the embodied antithesis of Monte's intensity, Travis shambled along, poky, often late, never worried or fretful but never lazy either, pulling his weight on the Scrub Squad, just even, slack, his favorite post an easy-chair in the lounge where he slouched, long legs open, his head back and cradled in interlaced fingers, the light frizzle of golden hair glinting along the sun-bronzed arms. Monte ascribed Travis's calm to the pack of Camels he always carried in the oversized coveralls pocket, along with wintergreen Lifesavers, and thought the cigarettes might actually be weed, but the smell was unmistakably tobacco, on the clothes and in the room, and Travis sometimes invited me along to his secret place, so I'd seen the camel on the paper. Travis did light up in their room but only when alone. Of course Robyn had to know, but he and Travis must have made a deal, because smoking was the one and only thing Robyn never talked about. That nobody else did either witnessed Travis's charm — everybody liked him — and maybe we even quietly envied his guile. We weren't altogether comfortable with the trespass but we admired, almost respected it, and didn't want trouble for Travis. Some of us thought he invited discovery by always chewing on an unused matchstick, or sucking on a Lifesaver.

* * *

After our exhilarating blow-out with Edith in the Sweat Shop, all of us, I figured, walked away believing Jubliee might provide and accommodate more opportunities for playful abandon than we'd feared might be permitted. But it fell to Dallas, Ta-Da Dallas, to initiate the next with a proposal to form a club that would meet every week in Cactus lounge to honor and celebrate Piaf's music by learning more about it and her from Monte, and by singing it in more orderly fashion, and with gradually increased understanding of the lyrics, thanks to Monte's translations, for our own entertainment.

"The Sparrow Players, we could call it," Dallas said; "you know, for 'The Little Sparrow,' like Monte said she was? Just a few of us, you see; very exclusive. We'll bid and then elect who else we want. And Monte can have veto power."

That he had it all planned out told me he was up to something else, plotting something more and other, in the evolution of which The Players would be instrumental.

"I don't think he'll go for it," I said.

"Ask him, then. You're his buddy. Only don't say I told you to."

"He won't," I repeated, more stiffly than I felt. "He didn't think of it first."

"Say it was your idea. I don't care. He will then."

"Whyn't you ask?"

"You kidding? After 'Rainbow'? He'd never, if I did."

"What if he vetoes you?"

"He can't. It's my idea. I'm charter. And I get 15% of the dues — a dollar to join and fifty cents a week to belong. As treasurer I'll collect the dues. So if you've got a buck fifty now, I'll go ahead....?"

"Travis will want girls."

"It's a FRATERNITY!"

"Monte won't go for it."

But he did, even when I said Dallas thought it up — except not exactly the way Double-Ass Dallas had mapped it out.

"No frats," Monte said, "and no bids and no charters and no dues. And no Dale." Dale Shivers — "Does she?" I asked, upon first hearing the name and mistaking the gender — was the other staffer who'd been here last summer and now unofficially headed up the second kitchen crew and captained one baseball team. Monte called him, on the sly, Sister Shiv, because he'd converted from the Catholic to the Baptist faith when his folks did but still hung prayer beads from his Levi belt-loop and fingered them whenever Steph raised hell or his team fell behind. "We'll ask Martha and Mary," Monte went on, naming the Moon twins who were backup cheerleaders at Millsaps. "You want Scotty?"

This was bait, for he knew I'd want Scotty before and above everybody else, except maybe himself and Corky Carlisle, who I'll get to shortly.

"I don't mind," I said. "Travis, though. And Lance."

"Fine. And Robyn."

"Why? Why's Robyn got to be...?"

"Why not?"

Why not, indeed? I couldn't say he was fat and pimply. And, on second thought, I remembered to be nice about Robyn, never mind how I thought him at least one-quarter creepy. I had no legit objection.

But Monte was onto me. "Not everybody can be pretty like us! Robyn likes us. He'll work with us. He'll be fine."

"Can he sing?"

"We'll find out."

"Why *not* Dale?" I barely knew Dale but I admired the gutsiness of a former Roman infiltrating this Baptist bastion and figured I might benefit from acquaintance with another Jubilee veteran; but mostly I felt keen to learn why Monte didn't want him for the club.

"Well," he said, stalling; "I don't know, he's…well, he's…. oh, wait: he can't practice with us; he can't rehearse when we do. His crew works when we're off. There's a time conflict."

This was true; but it wasn't the right answer. I let it go for the time being.

"What about Dallas?"

"Ha! Try keeping him out! No, we need him in, keep an eye on him. Ta-Da doesn't want a music club, wouldn't know Piaf from Presley. It's something else he's after."

"A percentage of the dues."

"That, for sure. See if he doesn't veto himself. No dues, no treasury, no treasurer, no percentage…no Dallas, you watch."

"Is that it then?"

"To start. Except for Carolyn."

Babcock. Babs Babcock. She preferred "Babs." I thought it baby-talk, and called her "Carolyn," once. "You wanna be Timmy?" she said. How did she even know?!

"Not Babs," I griped.

"Yes Babs," Monte said. "She'll make you look good. And she knows music."

"I don't care. I don't want Babs in any club...."

"And that's my other condition. You play for me."

"Don't think I know it. Hum some."

"That's not even bad Berle," he snapped.

When I applied to work at Jubilee I'd sort of cheekily hoped to be chosen official camp pianist, and I'd enclosed a list of "Firsts" I'd collected in Madison recitals and "Superior" ratings I'd scored from hotshot northern judges in LSU summer master classes, and didn't neglect to mention all the revival meetings I'd played in small Louisiana towns where Father was guest evangelist. Official Jubilee pianist was a glamorous job, even though you worked every night and twice on Sunday, and without much strain. You were your own boss, mostly, and you'd just spin off a few measures of intro so the congregation recognized the tune and found the key, accompany the singing through four or six verses, and then solo with another hymn while they passed the collection plates, every night. Understand, once you've mastered the basics of hymn-playing, you can pretty much do it comatose. Only, the basics don't satisfy Baptists. For Baptists, you've got to ham it up. Inspired Baptist hymn-playing has to be jazzed up with racy arpeggios and decorative trills and classy octave-runs and big smashing multi-fingered chords all up and down the keyboard that may not, any of them, have much to do with the score as long as they're in the same key with it. You weren't leaving the basics, mind, you were just supplementing them with dress-up ruffly lace. And that's where I figured I had it all over Babs, who was appointed Jubilee pianist after the auditions.

Babs was Nashville Belle Meade and a Belmont junior whose father held high office in the Baptist Convention headquarters and probably influenced her selection as Jubilee pianist, or so I told myself. Short, pudgy, she sported bangs, and wore her straight, fake-blonde hair cut close to her peach-pink cheeks and prim, puckered mouth. Her eyes were small and narrow and pinched, her hands large and fleshy, unpainted nails trim. The thick forearms bespoke years of rigorous piano practice. She carried herself with aplomb and more than a trace of pugnacity: the message read, "Be careful how you mess with me."

It turned out, though, that Babs was every bit as dextrous as I, if not more so, at hymnic pyrotechnics, at embroidering those familiar melodies, for when asked by an auditions judge to "introduce" a hymn — that is, to rattle off a few measures to signal the key and set the tempo and remind everyone of the tune without even finding the score — she banged out thirty seconds of glitzy keyboard commotion way more accomplished than anything I might have managed even with preparation. Asked, she did it again, with another hymn named by the judge, also without opening the book. Mind you, the Baptist hymnal includes over 800 songs! Had Babs memorized them all? Her fancy-dance intro wasn't at all by the routine formula either: it was structurally inventive and sophisticated, its chords intricate, multi-noted, complex, its runs two-handed and over-lapping, its accidentals uniquely daring. I couldn't entirely follow everything she did but it all riveted me as I watched my chances of appointment sinking like a rock.

But Babs had a rule. Or rather a belief, an inflexible conviction. Showmanship she would provide everywhere *except* as accompaniment for congregational singing. For that she returned strictly to the four or five simple notes of the printed score in the hymnal. Anything other or additional was for Babs irreverent, disrespectful, arguably sacrilegious, and borderline blasphemous. Nothing, she held, could be allowed to distract from the words, for they were like holy writ to her — in fact, some *were* scripture — and she would neither participate in nor tolerate any dazzling note-play that in her view distorted or corrupted hymnic texts. This was Babsian law, and she was firmly outspoken about it at the auditions. Her resolution required some whispered counsel among the judges — during which I thought a door might open for me after all — but Babs prevailed, although Dr. Mann reserved the option of changing his mind after determining whether the minimal accompaniment adversely affected congregational singing. Babs would improvise and embellish interludes and preludes and postludes and offertories and introductions but otherwise faithfully adhere to the hymnal notations. This was final.

I could live with it. The decision stung a little but I knew it was the right thing. Babs was better than me. She was virtuosic. I was gaudy. And there was another crucial thing. Babs was a genius at transposition. I was hopeless. I knew I was finished when transposition came up at the auditions. Jubilee attracted a lot of guest vocalists and instrumentalists from across the country who arrived prepared to perform in a practiced key, to which the accompanying piano had to adapt. Several showed up at the tryouts, instruments in hand, and the vocalists always began by naming the preferred key. Babs nailed it every time, effortlessly. I botched every try, and stumbled off burbling about playing by ear if given a minute and a few notes. "I'm afraid that won't be quite reliable," Dr. Mann said, not unkindly. The Babs was in.

* * *

Scotty Hughes did show up, at Monte's invitation.

"You should have let me ask her," I said; "I told you I wanted her."

"I asked if you wanted her."

"And I said I did. You should have let me ask her."

But he asked her and she showed up, and brought sanction with her. A rising sophomore at Ole Miss, Scotty Hughes might, we all thought and said, very well succeed Mary Ann Mobley as the next Miss America, once Miss Mobley finished her reign in six months. Scotty radiated royalty. I don't mean in arrogance or condescension; I mean in consummate beauty. Head to toe, she was a complete knockout. About 5' 5", 115 pounds, shapely slender (what you could make out of her figure through those blousy squaw dresses) and tapered to the bantam waist, the silken auburn hair in a neat page-boy lightly stroking her half-bare shoulders, she moved with an equally silken grace and serenity that made you feel comfortable and satisfied just from looking at her. The pale pink smile was sweet, endearing, the sky-blue eyes warm, the complexion flawless and the face open and wholesome. Her voice was low and velvet-smooth — alto — not Bacall-sultry but heading in that direction — her accent the rich honeyed drawl of deep south aristocracy. Neither perky nor bubbly, Scotty wouldn't have made the cheerleading squad; you'd better imagine her the sedate, majestic Homecoming Queen. She beamed joy and good will. Her mere presence encouraged smiles and converse. She was a little doll-like in her finish, but never brittle. You wanted to touch the skin, stroke it with the back of your finger. I never knew her gloomy.

Her pal was Corky Carlisle. Monte and I had noticed him two tables away in the dining hall on our first night in lively interaction with his mates, jollying them along, not dominating but fully engaged and comfortably delighting in the group.

"Who is he?" I'd asked. But none of us yet knew. "Let's find out," I said to Monte, and then realized I didn't want his help with this one. "I'll find out," I corrected.

I found out by asking a little and watching a lot. And what I determined was this: Corky Carlisle was quintessentially The American Boy, the prototype of ideal Boyness. Start with the name: can you say it without grinning? "Corky" spells cute, sprightly, sunny; it says frisky. It says amiable. "Corky" invites. I learned that he and Scotty had more or less grown up together in Vicksburg, attending the same schools and church there, but when she started at Ole Miss, he'd come over to Tulane, which is where I wanted to enroll but Father couldn't afford the tuition and neither parent would countenance my living in New Orleans, a very Babylon to their way of thinking; so last Christmas back at home Corky and Scotty agreed on a Jubilee summer. Each denied romantic involvement with the other — within the first week, Scotty already had a full dance card — but both professed everlasting and devoted friendship, each with the other. Corky didn't yet date but he became quickly familiar with most everyone, for he and Lynn Crosby were Lobby Boys at the Complex where guest and staff traffic was always heavy. And everybody seemed to like Corky well enough without anybody exactly falling for him.

Meanwhile, I did. About three days into my watching Corky, a sudden turn of his head and a shrugged shoulder revealed the identity of the resemblance that haunted his features and had vaguely perplexed my brain since our first sighting of him. What I caught in that flash was Tony Dow, who'd played Wally on "Beaver," only Corky was older and taller and a tad shyer, in the way he deferred to Scotty. But the hair was the same — dark brown tight curls close-cropped; the torso shapely under the T, tending toward stocky; the forearms beefy, the face a touch puffy, the kind dark eyes set back, the mouth a degree off-center, the one dimple shallow, the lower lip plump, the mouth itself small and rounded, framing slightly rabbity front teeth. The similarity to Dow helped confirm my understanding of Corky as the ultimate incarnation of American boyhood. He was just so thoroughly, categorically *normal,* so free of hang-ups, neuroses, tics, so easy-going, so comfortable, utterly content with who he was and what he did. Not the doltish, worry-free Alfred E. Neuman, no, but a nice, regular guy ever untroubled by anxiety or even mild concern. Steady-on, measured, evened-out, all the time. And he ran with The Queen. Monte was special too, of course, but his attractions were unique, even eccentric, and so always unsettling; and he was never a comforting presence. Corky was blue-ribbon, textbook standard. I craved his favor, coveted his imprimatur. I wanted him for my circle. Had he been the other gender, I'd have courted him, paid him suit.

And on top of everything else, he'd brought his bike! "Nobody said I couldn't," was his sensible, smiling explanation. Dr. Mann and SS were plenty startled when he'd unpacked and reassembled it, and parked it on the wide deck circling the dining hall; but all they did at first was whisper and ask Corky to walk the bike over to the Manager's office tomorrow morning for a little chat. The bike then disappeared for a couple of days until Dr. Mann announced that he was establishing a message delivery service available six days at week 9 to 5 courtesy of Corky Carlisle and his bike. Of course Jubilee had office telephone connections but not in dorm or guests' rooms, and operations were sometimes iffy; so Corky would work off the Registration Desk and distribute written notes free of charge among guests and staff (tips accepted) anywhere on the grounds. He was elated to be relieved of the lobby mops and allowed the liberty of the campus on his bike, as a consequence of which he quickly became something of a Jubilee celebrity for his jolly greetings and winning efficiency. Monte's only comment was surly: "Suffer the little children their toys," he said, and swiped his lips.

I received my first bike at twelve, and was hardly off it until I left for college. It was my second-best pal after Bruce, and I rode it everywhere around Madison, on my paper routes, of course, but also recreationally, for hours, alone, no-hands on smooth surfaces, as fast as I could pedal, back bent, heart pounding, wild crazy with the abandoned passion of it. So I envied Corky's having his bike at hand, and admired his daring, his successful test of Management. It lacked a rider's seat on the back fender, but after we became acquainted, Corky would sometimes prop me on the handlebars for a ride, and later, me astraddle the crossbar, brace me with both his arms.

* * *

To be completely truthful, I *did* feel a *little* pissed when Babs got picked for pianist, but a couple of thoughts helped me past it. For one, it was a fair choice, as I said. Imagine my worry every day that some musician would require a transposition, and my humiliation every time I blew it. Then too, maybe Jubilee management figured I was already spotlighted enough, the Goforth thing and all, and wanted to give somebody else a crack at fame? And in fact I'd rather play for Monte, as he'd said, and the Sparrow Players anyway, once the opportunity came up, even though the "club" turned out not to be much of one, not the way you normally think of clubs, we were so loose and informal about it, which ticked off double-assed Dallas no end. Sometimes, when we'd worked late enough to miss the nightly services and milled aimlessly around the Sweat Shop, Monte would whistle the opening nine notes of "La Marseillaise," ending with a little question mark of a grace note, and if the mood was on us we Players would sing out "Oui, oui, Monsieur," and drift over to the baby grand piano in the dining hall, and meet. All the lights would have been dimmed except the outside floods, which seeped in enough to outline heads and bodies and piano keys. Monte would take the bench beside me and hum a measure or two until I caught which song it was — we had a repertoire of maybe six — and then serenade — yes, I mean serenade — us with those strange, haunting melodies: "C'est L'Amour," "Non, Je Regrettte Rien," "La Vie En Rose," not torch-song style but "softly and tenderly," as the old hymn tells it, quietly caressing the syllables into private meaning for Players unfamiliar with the language. Now and again you might hear Robyn or Carolyn or somebody else humming or la-la-la-ing along in the background, faintly, as though unable to help it, or we might begin to rock gently back and forth to the rhythm, swaying like twilit waves, like the music itself if you could've seen or touched it. But mostly we just huddled around the piano, embraced and comforted by its arcs and curves, pressed against it as against each other, yearning to soak up every shared note into our prickling flesh as he sang.

And as he sang, I became conscious of his face, close upon mine, turning now and then to look upon mine. Ordinarily, Monte's face was, well, ordinary: not distinctively cute or boyish or even especially handsome: commonplace, you might say, or perhaps blank. It was a little long, a little narrow, gracefully tapered to the chin, fair and open, hale, slightly soft, mild, well-shaven with a faint shadow of beard tinting the tan. But ordinary, as in typical, average, unexceptional. *Except* that when Monte was moved to speak or sing or laugh his ordinary face blossomed into mobility and variety — into fluent animated expressiveness that dramatized his discourse, colorfully inhabited his language and informed his whole countenance with radiant visual eloquence, while in its passive mode the plainness of his face highlighted and accented three other properties of it that by themselves and collectively called into question the ordinariness of the thing itself! The plain could not survive the special, nor the average trump elan. What emerged with flux was fixing image.

First, the lustrous dark eyes, flecked with gold and green, rested low and hooded under thick black brows and long lashes. He used these eyes, worked them, widening and narrowing them as the moment and word enjoined, even sometimes shuttering them mid-sentence so to surprise you with an even wider re-opening, arresting in its deep and searching intensity. His dense mane of black shimmering curls, when the light glanced off them just right, tossed about loosely, rampant, tumbling at random onto the high, sun-bronzed forehead and down the slender neck behind. He played with these curls sometimes, fingering one behind an ear, teasing it, teasing you with it, drawing it straight and letting it spring back, watching you watch it. He never used a comb or brush, not that I saw, notwithstanding that ornate monogrammed set from Nieman's on his dresser. His fingers combed the curls, fluffed and mussed them. He was vain of them. I imagined a lightly hairy chest, for his arms, pendant from the pale blue Polo sleeves, were barely fleeced.

The other extraordinary feature, when the face went mobile, was the smile, or the smiles. Monte's full, flush lips could take a dozen different shapes, all comely, some bewitching, all variously charming if you looked for the charm. The perfect teeth behind them dazzled, and most of them shone when he laughed. The fetching thing was, his smiles *developed*: they rarely sprang full-blown, like his eyes popped. They started slowly, the muscles drawing the lips back in a cautious tarry, as though they were undecided, unsure of themselves, faintly a-quiver, as if interrogating the incentive or avid to release. And then they would unfurl, by gentle degrees, and spread, and open, and make light, and beget joy and other music.

I understood right away that hymn-playing and Piaf-playing are widely different endeavors, so I kept the soft-pedal pressed and gave Monte mostly hushed chords as cushions for his dark voice to ride on, his face lifted, his lids half-closed. He never asked us, we never asked, to sing along; we never even asked him to translate. Because you didn't need to get the words to grasp the song; you imagined what it meant by feeling how it moved you: peculiarly, this was, in that right there, at the very heart of a church assembly, the musical moment pulsed with unmistakable secularity and simultaneously dispensed religious warmth too. Monte had named "Rainbow" "sacred music." But these Piaf sessions also in manner and tenor, in spirit and tone, seemed replete with holy mien, their mysterious language enhancing the effect. Swoons threatened among the girls. My own eyes misted.

3

We were heading back to Cactus to refresh after working lunch when Corky wheeled up, slightly winded.

"Sergeant Steph wants you both. In her office. Now."

"What for?" Monte asked.

"Are we in trouble?" I asked.

"I couldn't say," from Corky.

"Or won't?" from Monte. "C'mon, Corky, what's she want?"

"I'm not supposed to say," Corky sidestepped, but you could tell he itched to.

"Is it about the cups?" Monte ventured. Lance had dropped another tray last night. ("Like Adlai E. Stevenson ll," he'd said, "'I believe in the forgiveness of sins and the redemption of ignorance.'")

"It's about the Players," Corky admitted. "SS is pretty mad."

"The Players?" Monte and I said together, and exchanged looks. "What about them...us?" he added. But Corky had spun the bike around and sped off.

"All right," SS barked, standing behind her spotless desk, a framed photo of herself in full military garb, with medals and ribbons featured, facing out. "What're you two *doing* in there with all the lights off?"

"Hi, Steph," Monte bluffed. "Um, where do you mean, and when?"

"You know when and where. In my dining hall. Don't you mess with me here. I want to know what's going on at night in there."

"It's just singing," I said. "We just sing."

"Sing what?" she snorted. "And who's we? Who said you could sing in there?"

"Nobody said we couldn't," from me, borrowing Corky's line about the bike.

"My dining hall's off limits after meals. You know that."

"Um, Sarge," I said; "we're kitchen crew. We work there. You assigned us."

"Don't you sass me, buster. You work there till you finish. Then you leave."

"We have this club," I said; "we like to sing. Together."

"Screw your fairy little club. It's no singing in my dining hall. And besides, you're not authorized to play that piano. It's you playing it, idn it?"

Was this the nub of it? I was out of line at the piano?

"Yes, ma'am," I admitted, with just a tiny swelling of pride. "I'm playing the piano. I know how, you see. What's the problem?"

"The problem, mister smart mouth, the problem is, you're not authorized…to…play…that…piano! And you're going to stop playing it right now!"

"How do I get authorized?" I said, pushing her.

But Monte stepped in. "Okay, Sergeant. Okay, it's fine. We get it. We didn't know. We'll cut it out."

"I'm not cutting anything out," I said. "I DON'T get it! What'd we do wrong?"

"Troy," Monte said, warning.

"Listen up, girls," SS said, coming at us from around the desk, punctuating her scolds with alternating pokes to our chests: "I don't even *want* to know what you do in there in the dark. I want *you* to know that it's stopping. It's over. As in now. You're done."

"Right, Sarge, sure," Monte said. "We understand. We just didn't know. We're sorry. Troy? Okay, Steph? Okay?"

"It's *not* okay, it'll never *be* okay for you and your sissy little singing club to be messing around in my dining room after the lights go out. I find you're back in there at night, you're both on the train home the next day. That's the deal. I mean it. Now get out."

Outside, he turned on me. "What is *wrong* with you?" through gritted teeth. "What were you trying go do in there, get us fired?"

"You shouldn't have apologized. *I'm* not sorry. And I'm not stopping."

"You're stopping, all right. We have to stop."

"But we didn't *know*!"

"Now we do."

"How'd she find out?"

"It wasn't secret."

"I bet it was Caroline," I said. "I bet Babs squealed."

"But why would she? She came. She liked it."

"She's jealous," I said, half believing it. But Monte ignored me.

"I just don't get why Steph is so steamed," he said. "Why should she even care? What's it to her that you're playing 'her' piano?"

"It's not about the piano," I said.

I knew this in my bones. I knew it in my bones because I knew in my bones what it *was* about. And I knew what it was about because I'd seen it before, often before, at church camps before. And not just there but most pervasive and inescapable there. For I'd been to church camp three times before coming to Jubilee and had figured it out.

This was at Dry Water, the church's rinkydink assembly near New Iberia (think Tabasco) where I'd gone for Royal Ambassador Week three summers running. Royal Ambassadors was a sort of sanctified, churchy version of Boy Scouts whose purpose was to train boys in beliefs and traditions and practices and habits, and send them home better Baptists, souped-up witnesses to the faith. It was a week of memorizing and reciting (like the books of the Bible, in order, and verses and psalms), drawing maps of foreign mission fields, writing letters to missionaries, praying out loud, practicing testimonials, passing out tracts and leaflets on the heathen streets of New Iberia. But it wasn't all solemn. "For release," the Directors said, though not what was released, we had a pool, where a mighty lot of horseplay happened, and off to the side of it, near the woods, a wide, cleared circular space for singing along with somebody's ukulele while the campfire died; and frolics in the bunkhouse after lights-out, and food fights and softball and badminton and ping-pong and horseshoes. Good times, happy times, and I romped rowdily through them, proving my PK creds with cocky abandon. But not carelessly; not unwary. Because every activity was monitored, every game proctored, every event policed: a steward of some stripe ever hovered, notebook in hand; a hawk-eyed human steadfastly watched our every move and moment. These presences discharged such suspicion, beamed such distrust, that even if you hadn't broken camp codes in one way or another you felt as though you might have and maybe deserved punishment for it. Mostly innocent, or not seriously guilty, you still quailed under the surveillance, or anyhow knew your heart to skip a beat if you passed a watchdog on the path. Grave misconduct was rare, sharp rebuke seldom, punitive discipline nearly unknown: but threat passed like air among us. And guilt drenched the domain.

That's what I meant by saying Steph's tantrum wasn't about the piano. I recognized a symptom of Dry Water. I don't say it's by conscious design, exactly; I do emphatically declare that church camps thrive on guilt. It's the gas that fuels them, the fire that stokes them. It soaks and abides and suffuses. Guilt keynotes every sermon, tunes every hymn, haunts every conversation, association, and hour. It influences, motivates, inspires, and dooms. It seasons every temptation, checks some of them, prompts others. It is insidious and pervasive. It overcomes every effort to crush it. It racks the souls of youth and age, all victims helpless to quench or purge it. It defines the church camp culture.

What I figured out at Dry Water is that church camps seize every opportunity to cultivate, manipulate, and exploit the in-bred guilt that every participant carries, like a virus, because, of course, it's inherent in the faith itself, founded as it is on the universal need of redemption, which presupposes trespass and its attendant shame. Moreover, salvation comes only by the death of the Savior. The cost of your cleansing is His blood. Your sin occasions His death, which makes you responsible for it. How's that for elevating your guilt quotient?

Sergeant Steph didn't deliberately stage her tantrum to heighten our sensitivity and vulnerability to the corrosive guilt we'd inherited. I doubt that she even recognized it or could have named it. But by long living in its climate, she intuitively sensed the emotional compatibility of the moment with the collective enterprise of the assembly, and with her accusations stirred our reeking reservoirs of guilt. Even I saw that we'd broken a rule. And, though not sorry, I felt the guilt of it.

But after thinking it over for a day or two, Monte came up with a different theory for explaining the Sergeant's hissy over our singing club.

"It wasn't about the piano," he said. "It wasn't even a little about the piano. It was mostly about me. For my instruction and benefit."

"Well," I said, "I told you it wasn't about the piano."

"No," he said, "and I need to straighten out something anyway, so you know, in case it comes up again. It's about last summer, so listen here. Last summer this lovey-dovey couple got caught messing with each other back there in the dining hall after it closed one night, and were expelled and sent home the next day. And SS caught holy hell for not locking up properly. Nearly lost her job, the word was. So they installed those automatic door locks you can't open from the outside after dark, not thinking vandals might already be inside."

"I never knew about them," I said; "we got in there from the Sweat Shop."

"Yes, and also," Monte went on, "they didn't exactly invite me back this summer. Not right at first, anyway. I just about had to beg. Because, the truth is, I'd been a royal pain in everybody's ass all last summer. I mean, I didn't break any laws or anything, and I had a great time, but I was kind of what you'd call a bad boy, a 'disruptive influence,' The Man said, all summer. I didn't actually do any harm or hurt anyone or mess up routines and all like that, but just by being a little 'delinquent' all the time while having fun, well, I ticked off The Man and the Sergeant so bad I had to make a deal with them before they'd let me come back. Not just promise to be a model staffer — I had to swear to that — but also to pitch in, like from the inside, and *help* them, you know, *control* the crews and staff by, you know, sort of keeping an eye out for the rowdies...for punks and those types, and let them know who made trouble for them, or planned to."

"You mean to spy. Snitch."

"Not exactly. Just help to keep order. And if I messed up again, they'd dump me pronto, no questions asked, and I'd be gone. So. When SS found out the club was meeting back there in 'her' dining hall, she remembered last summer and what happened, and went ballistic with us to remind *me* of our deal and what I owed her. She might've been a little pissed at you for playing without permission but the hissy made a point to *me*. It never had much to do with you."

"It sure fell like it did," I said; "she was punching my chest."

"Well, we were't hardly a week into the session then. Steph rolled over us to get out the word on how tough she was, to get everybody in line and keep us there. She yelled at us like we were that couple last summer. You understand what I'm saying here?"

"I dunno. It's kind of roundabout, doncha think?"

"We got the point. She made her point. Word got out. Prob'ly by Corky."

"How come you never said you were bad before? I might wanna hear about that."

"I have to behave now."

"And you actually snitch?" I asked.

"Not yet," he grinned, dabbing balm.

* * *

"We're going legit," Monte announced to the group gathered at his invitation in the Cactus Lounge following lunch three days after the blow-up with Steph. He had forbidden my telling anyone about it but he or Steph must've, for word had gotten round that the Players were finished, though no one said or seemed to know why. You could feel worry in the air, and see it in Robyn's chewing on his lip. What had happened? Were we in trouble? Who had leaked? Guilt was standing by.

"We can't use the dining hall for Piaf any more," Monte went on, "so we're reinventing ourselves. Here's the plan: we'll become a vocal ensemble and perform hymns at the evening services, maybe twice a week. We'll rehearse here, Babs at the piano there. Dallas will manage us: bookings, logistics, advertising, scheduling. Dr. Mann likes the idea and will organize programming and sign off on the hymns. We audition for him and Steph on Sunday. Babs and Troy will pick the hymns and figure out the arrangements — who sings which parts (I'll lead) in what keys and how many verses and with what variations.

Lance and Travis will do sound and lights, Scotty and Corky, dress and make-up. Robyn can work out props and staging, and back up everybody. And all of you will start thinking right now about a new name for the group. Give me written suggestions asap. Any questions?"

D.A.Dallas spoke right up: "How do we get paid?" he asked.

Our salary for working at Jubilee that summer was peanuts, a measly $7.50 per week with room and board, because the real payoff, they said, the true "benefit," was the "privilege" of being there and soaking up all the "spiritual values" of the place and programs. But on Tuesday nights — the night before Transition Wednesdays — they inserted into the service a second passing of the collection plates for guests to contribute to a "love offering," it was named, to signify their appreciation to the staff for Scrub-Squadding and picking up after them all week; and their "love" got split up evenly among ourselves. So we were extra diligent on Tuesdays and dressed for services and pinned on our name tags and scattered ourselves out among the congregants and smiled and nodded...not that such to-do notably swelled the pot, not that I could tell: the take usually came to about $2.50 apiece for us, which averages out to a quarter apiece from them, including the fat cats from Texas, which blew Dallas's stack.

He huffed into our room after the first Tuesday collection, fuming.

"Look at this!" he wailed, extending the $2.50. "Will you just look at this?"

"Love money," Monte said. "You know, Dallas, if I were you I wouldn't advertise how cheap I was. Bad for business."

"It's a bloody swindle," Dallas said. He was forever saying things were bloody. "That's what. $2.50," sneering at it. "This is ridiculous!"

"True," Monte said. "Glad you're owning up to it. And" — reaching out — "if it'll ease your conscience any for over-charging...."

"'Over' my foot," he said, snatching it back and ramming it into his jeans. "It's under, is what, way under. You mean you're actually satisfied with a lousy $2.50?"

"We're ne-e-e-e-ever satisfied," Monte said; "*Are* we ever satisfied, Trojan?"

Tempted, I caved, and profaned the first line of the hymn, singing, "I'm not satisfied with stin-gi-ness," and we both cracked up.

"Actually," Monte said, "it's a good question, the right question from our manager. We should be paid. Other musical guests are. I'll talk to The Man. Anything else? Okay, so break into your little groups and start planning. Meet back here after lunch the day after tomorrow for first rehearsal. Robyn, bring the hymnals."

You have to admire the speed and efficiency and finesse with which Monte handled all of this, and got us past what might have been a killer blow to the group now perhaps more solidly bonded because of it. But even so I felt peeved and grumpy. Why hadn't he let me in on the planning? And what did Robyn know of props and staging? *I* had theater, four years of it, and so did Scotty, it turned out. And what props and staging was he thinking of? We didn't even need hymnals, for such good little Baptist boys and girls were we that we'd long since memorized both verses and tunes merely from overexposure and could warble them asleep. As for sound and lights, make-up and dress, this wasn't exactly Oberammergau! Was Monte just inventing chores to make Scotty and the rest feel welcome? But it was misleading and potentially hurtful. Moreover, it wasn't yet clear to me who would sing and who wouldn't and whether some singers would double as stagehands. Most nettling of all, though, was pairing me with Carolyn aka Babs. It felt like a deliberate affront, publicly delivered to forestall protest. He knew I deplored her hymnic pianism; he knew I didn't much like or trust her. But he also knew she surpassed me in musicianship. I couldn't dispute that.

Back in our room, I spoke up. "I bet Babs already submitted a name."

"For what?" Monte asked, not following.

"A new name for the group," I explained. "She'll want us to be The Carolers."

"Not gonna happen," he said, laughing. "I've already got a new name. The Jubilee Jubilates. It's a praise word. Latin for 'shouts of joy,' with some liberties in the translation. Like it?"

I did. "Whose idea is it?"

"Mine," he said, grinning.

"But they'll call us 'Jubes,'" I said.

"So what do you think of the plan?" he asked.

"How come you didn't let me in on it, before."

"I couldn't be sure I'd get permission. I didn't want to disappoint."

"How do you know you didn't? You could have said something."

"Were *you* disappointed? Now you know the plan, whadaya think of it?"

I welcomed the invitation to comment, late as it was; but did he really want an honest opinion? Did I really want to give him one? Does anybody ever really want an honest opinion when asking for it? Is anyone ever comfortable giving one? Actually, I'd sort of liked to have given him one but I sensed the risk, and dodged.

"I like it that everybody gets to sing," I said.

"Not everybody," Monte said. "Not the Double-Ass. I've heard him try. He can't. We may need more girls, though. What about the Moonies?" He meant the twins, Mary and Martha.

"Why are you asking me *now*?"

"Oh, for God's sake, Troy! Because I want your opinion! C'mon now. You know them. I don't. Should we ask them?"

"Aren't we getting kind of... large? We're practically a choir already."

"Look, everybody and his sister does duets and quartets. Let's be different. Let's surprise them. Let's be fruitful and multiply, and make some noise!"

"Carolyn doesn't like noise. She won't play noise."

"You'll make her play it. That's your job."

"Why not just let me play it? Save a step."

"We need Babs for the...whadaya call?...the transpositions, in case of. And I need you as lead baritone in the ensemble. You can teach Babs how to chord and embellish, so we get your gifts twice."

This was brazen flattery, but it did soothe, without healing.

"Why are you making such a big deal out of all this? Why does it have to be such a circus?"

"Because we're all *clowns*, Troy, or hadn't you noticed yet? We're all just dumb-ass clowns looking for a gig. Only you happened to land one."

* * *

As matters evolved, Babs turned out as ostentatiously competent as I to melodramatize the hymns; she just preferred not to do it as congregational accompaniment. And in any case the songs The Man approved for our use were all the "invitation" hymn type: downtempo, pianissimo, syrupy, designed to draw respondents into the aisles and to the "altar" down front (Baptists didn't believe in "altars"; "communion tables" replaced them in the jargon) in public acknowledgment of a hard decision for Jesus finally made, usually to the confessional chords of "Just As I Am," the perennial favorite rendered so by the Reverend Billy's everlasting addiction to it. Babs's chords were dense and complex, packed with harmonic combinations and variations and inventive, unexpected tonalities I'd never have imagined much less achieved, her right hand sparkling arpeggios supported by bass-registry sonorities under her strong fingers. Encouraged by Monte, she showed-off flashes of virtuosity at rehearsal but settled down to apt complementary reserve as backup for us, with solo piano intervals between where she could strut again. The auditorium light crew admitted Travis and Lance to the booth on their solemn oaths never to touch the switches; but Travis said he'd rather sing. Lance claimed timidity in excusing himself from the ensemble; but the resulting slot for a substitute had to become two, for the Moonies never split. Robyn said he was drafting a map for getting us all in orderly fashion onto the stage and off again, and for lining us up just so, only he'd need musical assistance in positioning voices each to each for maximum effect, and for dividing us into smaller units of 4-3 or 3-3-1 (with Monte by himself as lead) or 2-3-2? We could always count on Robyn to snarl the simple.

The day following Monte's announcement of the plan, Scotty Hughes cornered me after lunch: "Walk me back to Marigold?" she asked.

She wanted to talk about her assignment, with Corky, to consider "dress and make-up," Monte had said, for ensemble appearances. "Not the make-up part," she giggled; "the girls can work that out. I mean, for the guys. You always dress well. What should the boys wear? Don't say T-shirts."

"I dunno," I fumbled, still flabbergasted that we were even talking. We never had. "Maybe suits?"

"Did you bring some?"

"Just one."

"What about blazers and slacks? With club ties?"

I wasn't dead sure what club ties were but it seemed shaming to ask a girl. "Sure," I said. "Bow ties are pretty smart." I happened to favor bows, and tied a knock-out knot.

She gave me a look. "Would everybody have one? And know how to tie it? I've never seen Corky wear one, except at the Prom."

"You could be right. Maybe best stick with regular...club?... ties. With red in them."

"Will everybody have navy blazers? And gray slacks?"

"If not, they can borrow them. And black dress shoes. Shined. No weejuns."

"Oh, I think polished weejuns would be okay."

"With socks," I said. "No naked ankles poking out. Black or gray socks. Do we all have to dress alike?"

"Uniform is best. Neater. The ties can be different colors."

"With red," I insisted; "with some red. White shirts or blue? I think blue. No patterns or checks, right?"

"Then solid blue it is," she agreed.

"What will the girls wear? Don't say squaw dresses."

Scotty laughed. "No, we'll do long-sleeve sweaters and straight skirts. Different colors. It's cool enough at night for sweaters. Stockings and low heels."

"We'd better say belts. The slacks better be belted. No suspenders."

She laughed again, way back in her throat. "No, no braces. Not even on Lance. Pocket handkerchief?"

"No. Too sloppy. And Robyn would be forever using his."

"Is that it, then? That was easy. I'll write it up."

"What a team!" I ventured, shakily.

But Marigold was not yet near. We were quiet for a minute.

"I'm thinking about starting a Jubilee newsletter," she said. "You know, for staff? What would you think about that?"

"Do we need one? Do we actually make news?"

"We might if journalists were around to report it. Would you care to work with me on a paper? Maybe as my executive editor?"

"What, ME?! Oh, I don't know anything about writing!" This was a flat-out lie. I played at writing all the time, even then. I got A's in writing. I would major in English. I'd written a winning speech. Why am I lying?! "Actually," I faltered, "maybe I do know a little. About writing, I mean. What would I do?"

"You see?" she said: "That's a news story right there, why you lied." She paused. Was I supposed to whip up the story of my lying for her first issue? "We'll figure out what you do as we go," she continued. "You speak well, so you must read a lot. You'll recognize good writing, and maybe know how to make it better. You'll help me with editing…and other stuff around the office."

"What office? There's a newspaper office?"

"Steph said she has a vacant little cubbyhole in Central we can use, and a couple of beat-up typewriters and a mimeograph machine and an old telephone in there she can reconnect. She's fine with the idea of a staff newspaper, so long as she gets to review copy."

"You told her you were asking me to help?"

"No, not yet. I didn't know whether you would. Is there a problem?"

"Possibly. She's not a fan."

"She will be. Besides, she likes Monte."

"Is Monte involved?"

"Should we ask him?"

"Could we decide later? See what our needs are first? What will we write about? I mean, what kind of stories?"

This could prove interesting: working closely with Scotty might be the dream job I hadn't yet dreamed. Was that why I'd lied about writing? Had the idea come down the pike *too* fast, preempting desire for it? The opportunity felt almost scarily ideal, so perfectly designed it inescapably had to be flawed! Where was the catch?

"Would it be just the two of us?" I asked.

"Oh, no!" she said.

(Wait. What's wrong with "no"? Just plain "no" would have sufficed. The "oh" made "the two of us" unthinkable.)

"We should ask Lance," she said, "who could write editorials à la Adlai…."

(When she did ask Lance, he had a Stevenson line at hand, which she reported to me later: "Adlai E. Stevenson II said, 'Newspaper editors separate the wheat from the chaff, and then print the chaff.'")

"Yes, but what would he editorialize *about*," I asked. "I mean, what's news around here? The only 'new' items are the different groups coming in on Wednesdays and they all look pretty much the same. No 'new' there. So where *is* the news for a paper?"

Clearly, I was arguing against my own interests here, if Scotty was one of them, but I felt something faintly artificial or inauthentic, or at least half-baked, about the whole idea of starting a newspaper, and I needed to probe it, lightly.

"I edited my high school paper senior year," she offered, "and I felt the same thing when we started. Everything looked as routine and repetitious as Jubilee does; but we *always* had news, or what we called news. I'm just saying that if we have the medium in place, we'll find the copy to fill it."

"You got a name for it yet?" I asked.

"*Hughes' News,* I thought about," Scotty Hughes said.

"Oh," I said; "I like *that!* Would you want, say, regular columns? What about?"

"Haven't decided. I'd like to bring Travis along, as a regular cartoonist. That's what he already does at Oklahoma Baptist. And Robyn for a gossip column? M&M are already photographing for the yearbook and could double-up…as they already do!

And Corky could freelance since he and that bike are always everywhere and he knows what's happening. My friend Hollis can report sports, if those baseball teams ever get going."

"Hollis is a girl, right?"

"And Dallas can sell personal ads!"

We laughed. But my doubts, my uneasiness, were growing.

"Why," I asked — and I heard some petulance in my voice — "why does the Sergeant have to approve copy? I don't care for censorship."

"Well, without it we don't publish. That's my understanding of what she said."

"Then we'd better find another job for Robyn. Besides, he'd swamp us with rumor and tattle. Who'd care?"

"Maybe let him interview one staff boy and girl for each issue? Get interesting background; also feature interviews with adult staff, Steph and Dr. Mann? Personality profiles?"

"How do we choose without playing favorites? Or creating favorites?"

"We could do food reviews. Corky cooks, knows a lot about food."

"But would reviews change the menus? I doubt it. Just stir up ill will in the kitchen."

"Wait! There's Babs. She's got oodles of time. Let's invite Babs aboard."

"Babs doesn't know or care about anything but music. And who's going to read about music...except Babs?"

"Should we ask Dr. Mann for a brief devotional?"

"He'd probably do it, but aren't we overloaded with that sort of thing already? There's no news there."

"Troy," Scotty said, exasperation edging her alto; "do you want to help or not? You're not helping yet."

"I'm sorry. Really. I guess I just don't see the point of it. Or what news we'd report that anybody cared to read. What purpose or need it serves."

"What if we run it by Monte?" she said. "Monte might have some ideas. You want to talk it up to him?"

"You know what?" I said, gentling down my tone; "I don't think I do. Feel free to yourself, if you want to. I'm just not keen. And I don't think I'm your guy for a job with the paper. It's a great idea and all but I don't think I'm enough interested, not really. So I'll excuse myself, if you don't mind."

"Well," Scotty said right back, "I kind of *do* mind. I think you're perfect for the job, if you'd give it half a chance. I think we'd work very well together, don't you?"

This felt like a sudden hard left turn. "I don't know. As you said, I've not been much help here."

"Because there's this other thing I wanted to bring up," she said. She turned her head toward me with a sweet, quirky little grin. "I've been wondering why you never asked me out."

"What?" I may have gasped. "Oh, well, you know, Corky...."

"Corky and I don't date. That's our deal. We're best friends. Maybe you didn't want to ask me?"

"No, no," flustered; "it's not that, no. I wanted.... I'm sorry. I mean, I just didn't think...."

"Don't think, Troy, Ask."

"Oh, well, okay. Would you...um...could we, sometime, you know...like, go out?"

"How about Sunday," she said, "after the auditions? Maybe eat together?" She paused. "And Troy," she added, "use my name. Scotty." She turned sharply into the Marigold door.

What just happened? I'd had an actual conversation with The Actual Queen. And sort of a quarrel. And we had a date for Sunday. But how? And what did I do now? Except float back to Cactus in a blur, not without stumbling?

* * *

Back at Cactus, a barefooted bathrobe was knocking at our door, the occupant's head down, apparently listening. I didn't recognize it.

Dale Shivers turned. "Troy?" he said. "I'm Dale." The voice was soft, gentle. "I live down there at the end. We haven't met, but I kind of need a favor, and Monte's not answering."

"I don't know where he is," I said, "but what can we do for you?"

"I'm really sorry," he said, sounding like he was, "but our shower drain's clogged, and the room's flooded, and I'm working tonight and need to bathe. Do you think I could maybe borrow your shower?"

"Of course you can," I said, opening the door. "Should I look for a mop?"

"No, no, my roommate's reporting it. Somebody'll take care of it." He looked at me kindly, his eyes damp. "Thank you," he said quietly. "I'm glad to meet you." He extended his hand.

"Me, too," I said, taking it. "I've heard a little about you. From Monte." I reached into the closet for a fresh bar of Lifebuoy. "You need a towel?"

Dale nodded. "Thank you," he repeated. "You're being awfully nice," he smiled, and stepped into the bathroom, then turned back. "I nearly always sing," he said; "I may need to."

"Fine," I said. "We favor singing here. Go for it."

Whether all of this would be fine with Monte, I suddenly felt uncertain. Where was he, and how soon back? I remained clueless why he didn't want Dale for the Jubilates. Would he also mind this courtesy?

"You left the shower running," he said, closing the door. Then he stopped, lifted his head a notch, sensing: "Is somebody in there? What's going on here?"

"It's okay. Give me a sec to explain." He frowned hard, almost scowled; his eyes narrowed. "It's Dale," I added; "from down the hall. You know."

"That jerk Dale Shivers is in our shower?! What the *hell* is happening here?"

"Easy, Monte. Everything's fine, all right? Just listen."

"Better make it good, buster! It ain't lookin' so fine from here!"

"Dale's bathroom is flooded. His crew's on tonight and he needed a shower. He asked to use ours. There's nothing wrong with letting him. He won't be long."

"You're in no position to know whether there's anything wrong with letting Dale Shivers use our bathroom."

"I know there's a lot wrong with *not* letting him use it. He had a little problem. We could help. There's no harm. I'll clean up when he's done. So cool it, okay?"

And just then the voice — the pure, clear, honeyed, tenor-sax voice — lifted from the shower and prickled my scalp: "'Only you…

…can make this world feel right,
Only you can make the darkness bright;
Only you and you alone
Can thrill me like you do,
And fill my heart with love for only you.'"

"Jesus!" Monte said, wagging his head.

I later learned, from Dale himself, that the family had moved from Catholic New Orleans to Baptist Memphis when the father, an experienced, crack insurance salesman with trophies to prove it, was recruited by the corporate headquarters in Memphis of the famously successful Promised Land Life Insurance Company and offered a vice-presidency at an executive salary several steps higher than the one he had, on the condition that he recant his Catholicism and embrace Baptist doctrine so to mesh, religiously and politically, with all the other highfalutin managers at the firm. PLLIC, Dale said, had made a lot of its vast fortune by insuring Baptist preachers and missionaries and teachers and other church officials worldwide, not because these laborers in the vineyard earned good salaries but because there were so many of them, and because, with their righteous and abstemious life-styles, they tended to live into their late eighties and nineties, a lot of them still working and paying premiums that long. The founding patriarch of PLLIC believed his company blessed with prosperity partly *because* every employee from the CEO down to the pubescent mail-boy had to be a baptized (i.e., immersed; dunked) believing Baptist and belong to a mainline Baptist local congregation and tithe his/her income and attend services regularly, no exceptions. All of these provisions were contractually spelled out, Dale explained, and his daddy wasn't officially hired until he'd signed off on them all: the Company claimed that it could not afford or tolerate outliers, or its multitudes of clients would instantly defect in bitter disillusionment. The elder Shivers, having already sired six spawn, figured he'd done his Catholic duty in that regard, and in any case entertained hunches about fiscal hanky-panky in the New Orleans diocese, and awaited somewhat anxiously signals of direction from the still new Pope John XXIII; and moved by the PLLIC offer to remember the increasing pecuniary pressures of his issue, he found himself able to consider shifting allegiances in ecclesiastical alliance, with assurances that his evening martini wasn't jeopardized. PLLIC regulations did not include families, so Mother and the sibling six could pick their own theological sanctuaries. Mother followed Papa; Dale had called himself "Christian" on the Jubilee application form, and made up a Baptist church name for an affiliation, meanwhile quite liking, as he put it, weighing and balancing the claims of contending denominations. He was still weighing, he said, even after a previous summer at Jubilee.

Dale was taller than most of us at around 6'1" or 2", thin, not skinny, with a longish face, arrowed chin, and a modest mouth, short light brown hair combed up into a shy pompadour, and soft, warm brown eyes. His ears stood out a little, giving him an alert, not goofy, air. In the bathrobe, his bare feet looked long too, his hands of notable breadth. Faint ripples under both eyes marked where bags would develop. The frame was trim, looked fit, but the motion of it didn't show athletic: it was gently, subtly supple, with the artful flow of dance, but naturally, without effort or intent. He was mad for the hapless St. Louis Cardinals, and sported the team's red and white cap with the interlaced initials, and a short-sleeved jersey bearing Musial's number 6.

I caught up with Robyn the afternoon following the shower loan. "What might you know about Dale Shivers?" I asked him.

"He's good people," Robyn said. "Memphis. Rising junior at Southwestern. Rooms with Lynn Crosby. Heads up the second kitchen crew. Why?"

"Just wondering. We met last night. He was here last summer, right?"

"I've heard that. Why?"

"No real reason. What's the deal between him and Monte?"

"What deal?" Robyn reached for his handkerchief and slowly unhitched the temples of his glasses.

"That's what I'm asking. I think there's a history. Maybe from last summer?"

"I don't know about that. Was anybody else here now here then? We could ask."

"No, I don't want to start anything. I was just wondering."

"What about? What made you wonder?" He rubbed his hanky around his lenses and squinted at me.

I'd figured that if anyone knew the story here, supposing there was one, Robyn would. But now that I'd laid the scent, it might be hard to extinguish. He rose to it.

"You know," he said, "there's a copy of last summer's Jubilee yearbook at the Registration Desk. We could check it out. For, like, clues?"

"Jubilee does yearbooks? Like school annuals?"

"Exactly like. Called the *Thunderbird*. You knew that. It's what the Moonie twins are already taking pictures for."

"And there's a copy of last summer's?"

The 1958 *Thunderbird* turned out a revelation in at least one respect. Dale Shivers was everywhere in its pages, and Monte Trevalyn wasn't. Monte appeared only in the staff section — in one one-and-a-half by two-and-a-half inch senior-year school photo in the alphabetical sequence — and again crowded into a group shot of a kitchen crew. Dale had his individual picture, of course, and one as chief of the other kitchen squad, and then stood out as player-coach of the baseball team in its photo; twice as an actor in a play; thrice as a vocal musician (chorus, quartet, soloist in a choir-robe behind the auditorium pulpit); once in a candid shot saluting from horseback; once laughing with Dr. Mann; once with a very pretty girl's head on his shoulder; and, climactically, in a full- page coat-and-tie pose, as handsome Mr. Staffer 1958.

"They might as well have crowned and sceptered him," Robyn said.

"Turn back to page 57," I said. Page 57, in its lower right-hand corner, showed Dale and Sergeant Steph standing against a bench with Angel Lake spread out behind them, both grinning broadly, and Steph holding Dale's extended left arm high — his hand a fist — the way boxing refs raise the winning fighter's.

"What's that about?" I mused aloud. And to myself; *if there's anywhere a clue, it's in this shot.* But it didn't speak.

"I want Dale for the ensemble," I said matter-of-factly to Monte as he rearranged his toiletries for the umpteenth time.

"You want *what*?" he snarled. "What did you say?"

"You heard. We should get Dale for the Jubilates."

"Sister Shiv?! No, I told you. He can't rehearse. The times don't work."

"We change the times so they do. I've figured it out. Look, we can use that gorgeous voice. He'd like to join. I've invited him."

"God *damn* it, Troy!" He smashed the dresser top, rattling bottles and cans. "You had *no fucking right* to do that! It's *my* group, damn it! I invented it. I named it. I *own* it. You can't just invite anybody to join without...." He sputtered to a halt, his face flushed, neck veins prominent.

"He's not anybody. He's Dale of the Golden Tenor Throat. You heard him. You know we don't have a voice that rich and ripe. Not even yours. We have to bring him in.

"I cannot *believe* you actually asked him to join without asking me could you. What has *happened* to you?"

"What has happened to me has happened to you. We both heard his voice and knew it for great. Only you won't admit it. You're behaving very badly here, Monte, unreasonably. What's the deal with you and Dale, anyway? Why don't you like him? It's becoming kind of obvious why you don't want him in the group."

"Just shut the fuck up. You don't know shit about any of it."

"Well, why don't you tell me shit about all of it? It's something to do with last summer, idn' it?

"How the hell do you know that? Who told you that?"

"Nobody. Why don't you?"

"I don't talk about it. It's none of your business anyway. So don't try to change the subject to that. The Sister Shiv's not right for the group."

"Don't call him that; it's stupid and wrong. Dale is the rightest one of us all. And why you don't want him is very much part of the subject here. I don't think you want me to guess any more about that."

"Well, you got *that* right. But I don't talk about it. It's nothing, really." At least he had stopped shouting. "Who mentioned last summer?"

"I told you: nobody. But I've looked at last year's *Thunderbird.*"

"There's nothing in there about…." He stopped abruptly.

"There's a lot about Dale," I said quietly.

He moved to the bed, sat, reached for his balm, swiped. His hand shook. I sat too, and waited.

After a while he nodded. "Yeah," he aid; "there sure as hell is. A *lot.*"

More silence. He shifted. "You don't have a cigarette, do you?" he asked.

"Let me check my pockets," I said, stepping to the closet. I found two of Travis's Camels, and book matches in a drawer. His hand still trembled as he lit up.

"I don't think," he began after a couple of drags, "I don't think I entirely know why Dale irks me so much. He just does. I don't like being around him. It upsets me to be around him. He doesn't have to do anything. He just *is*…upsetting. And so is your talking him up. But…yeah. Something did happen last summer, something big, and after it I didn't much like Dale anymore, not that I'd actually *liked* him before it did. And I didn't like finding him back out here this summer."

"But he must have done something to tick you off?"

"It's kind of hard to say, really. It's not completely clear. Which is partly why I don't talk about it."

"Maybe it might help to?"

"I dunno," he said, and paused again, tugged at a curl, his hand steadier now but still quivering. "I dunno, but I'm thinking I might like to tell you, I don't know why, maybe to help you understand? But, really, Troy, you can't repeat any of it, ever. I have to know I can trust you with the story. And I'm pretty sure, if I do tell you, I may not want to talk about it ever again even with you. It all has to stay between us, forever. In silence between us. Understood?"

"Understood," I said, a little scared by his somber mood; 'intensely' somber.

He spit on the butt, tossed it toward the trash, took a deep breath; he leaned forward, elbows on his knees, hands clasped under his chin, the knuckle of a forefinger tapping lightly against it. It occurred to me that this didn't look like an act at all.

"We weren't friends," he said, "but Steph asked Dale and me to drive with her to Santa Fe to pick up supplies, to help her load and unload them. We hitched a small trailer to the jeep — a different jeep — to carry them and headed back when a bunch of chicken coops packed with the birds bounced off an open truck-bed right ahead of us. We crashed into them, Steph lost control, and we flipped over a couple of times into a ditch. Dale and I were thrown clear but my head hit a rock and I passed out. So what happened next is fuzzy. I'm not sure of any of it."

He paused for a few seconds. "You understand what I'm saying? I'm not dead sure."

"Yes, okay. Go on."

"Well, Steph was pinned in, couldn't move. And something sparked the gasoline — it had sprayed everywhere — and the jeep took fire. Dale squeezed in and somehow got Steph loose and dragged her out onto the grass before the firetrucks and ambulance drove up, I don't know who called them or how. The jeep burned and all the supplies, but except for some bruises and scratches we were all okay. Now, understand, I didn't actually *see* anything after we smashed the crates and spun out off the road; I was out cold for the fire. But Steph is almost sure she remembers Dale dragging her out, like he says he did. That's how she told it, too. Back here, everybody rejoiced and prayed thanksgiving for the 'miraculous deliverances,' and things went on pretty much as before once Steph replaced her jeep with this other ratty old used one. But...but I never much liked Dale after that, I can't say why."

We let it settle for a bit. "That's a really scary story, Monte," I said, "a terrible accident. It was a very lucky escape for you guys. I don't wonder you don't want to talk about it. Thank you for sharing it with me. But where were you during the fire?"

"I don't know. I don't remember. It's a blank."

"And you dislike Dale...because of that? I don't quite get it."

"Me neither. I told you. I can't figure out the why either."

"And you've tried?"

"Of course I've *tried!* I *can't!*"

"Maybe it's best you don't. Obviously it's a hard thing to remember, and to tell. Thanks again for telling me. I'll respect the confidence. But…" I said after a pause, "but we still have Dale. We have to sort out Dale. You and Dale."

"I don't know what that means. There's no me and Dale."

"You have to want him for the Jubilates."

"But I don't. I can't."

"Monte, you have no musical reason not to include him."

"It's personal. I don't like him. He's not a good fit."

"I'm not in love with Robyn Byrd either, but he's a good fit in the group. Dale's a better one, musically. Forgive me, Monte, but you're being petty and unreasonable, and you need to stop. We're wasting time here."

"Tell you what, then: set up an audition for him with Babs. If Babs approves, I'll reconsider."

"She already has. She's already writing harmonies especially for him."

"What? Babs has heard him sing?"

"And wants him. But you have to invite him. He wants you to ask him. You're not the only one uneasy about this affair. Dale wants you to welcome him in."

"I can't, Troy. It would upset me!"

"Have you any idea how infantile that sounds? How wimpy?"

"It's how I feel. I can't do it."

"Then I'll quit the group. I might even quit the speech contest and go home. You know I'm not real keen on that thing anyway. You don't change your mind about Dale, I'm gone. You need to grow up here, mister: you're being a brat. Okay, you had a serious accident a year ago that you somehow blame Dale for and can't even say why, and you're nursing a grudge with zip basis in reality. It's mean and pigheaded and ornery and absurd. Straighten yourself out here, fella, and welcome the man."

"You'd actually quit? The contest?"

"In a heartbeat."

On the way to work later that afternoon, we met Dale coming back to Cactus.

"Hey, Monte," he said. "Thanks for the bath."

"Dale," he said. "The Jubilates rehearse tomorrow at 3 in the Cactus lounge. Be there."

"Yes sir," Dale said, with a snappy salute, and walked on, grinning.

4

Babs showed up at rehearsal with several large sheets scored for musical notation on which she'd scrawled additions and variations she deemed vocal improvements on the hymnal versions of the approved songs. Happily, we learned that the Moonies studied voice at a conservatory near Milsaps and not only read music but were experienced performers, even in opera. Scotty and Corky sang in the senior choir at Vicksburg First Baptist, and Travis played principal trombone in high school band. Robyn said he "took piano" for three years before quitting but thought he remembered enough to make do; and he turned out to have a pleasing tenor voice, just not enough breath to sustain it for long, his being so…oval…and all. We gathered around for Babs's instructions.

"People," she said, "Welcome Dale Shivers! He's Troy's and Monte's find, and I'm glad to have him. Dale's from a different tradition, so he won't be as familiar with our hymns as you are. Cut him some slack while he catches up. Feel free,

Dale, to take a hymnal home. He'll match with Mary and Robyn and maybe sometimes solo. Take a bow, Dale." A light pattering of applause.

"I think I'm caught up on hymns," Dale said; "remember, I was here last year."

"Sorry," she said; "I forgot. All the better. #934, 'Softly and Tenderly,' key of A-flat. Everybody in four-part harmony on verse 1. Monte and Martha on the soprano line; Scotty and Travis, the alto; Robyn and Mary and Dale, tenors; Troy and Corky, bass. On verse 2, Monte sings melody to Scotty's alto. Monte solos verse 3 while we hum behind him in four-part. Everybody sings verse 4, harmonizing. We all sing the chorus, in harmony, after every verse. I'll do a brief piano interlude after verse 3; and after verse 4 and the chorus, we'll all hum a chorus reprise in full harmony, fading out toward the end. All clear? Let's try it." And she began a strong, heavy-chorded intro to the hymn.

This one was a snap: we all, even Dale, knew the tune and some of the words, and needed the hymnal for minimal help with the harmonics, which got just a tad tricky for the altos on "weary, come home." Finishing a satisfactory, not brilliant, run-through, Babs let fly with a big, fortissimo crashing TA-DA chord. "Not too shabby," she said, and reached for her prepared scores, passing copies to Monte and Martha.

"This," she explained, "is a descant for the chorus after the final verse. Monte and Martha will sing it in unison over the rest of you, who'll continue the chorus in four-part harmony. Then we'll hum the chorus through again, in parts, Martha and Monte singing the descant words. Got it?"

"That," Robyn said in the quiet after we ended, "that was *amazing.*" It was. Jaded as we normally were about stuff so familiar, so worn, we were frankly surprised, even a little moved, by how affecting we sounded.

"Good," Babs said, sucking in a deep breath. "Good. Now let's try the descant again, minus the piano, with Monte and Martha a little stronger. And pick up the tempo. We don't want draggy. Oh, and Robyn, how about a little less face. No drama. All eyes on me."

Monte soared, and carried Martha with him, gloriously.

"That nailed it," Babs beamed. "Make it just like that for the auditions."

I'd expected to be impressed by Monte, and was, but I also had to hand it to Carolyn, who seemed downright professional, if a little as though she'd been trained by Steph.

"Next," she said, "is #675, 'Wherever He Leads,' key F-major. Lots of easy repetition in this one. Everybody in harmony on verses 1 and 4; Monte solos the melody on 2 and 3 while we back-up hum. We finish with the chorus twice, the second time extra slow, very hushed. Ready?"

But just into the second line of verse 1, Babs started and frowned, and then on the repetition of the same musical line in the chorus, she stopped and banged the keyboard hard.

"No, no, no!" she yelped. "Somebody's off. Everyone, restart the second line, verse 1, 'I gave my life....' Here's the chord." We got as far as "to" in "I gave my life to ransom thee" when Babs broke in again. Everybody tried not to look at Dale.

"Troy and Corky," she said, "listen: here's the descending chromatic line," sounding the keys: "F, E-flat, D-flat, C. Together now, both of you. 1-2-3-4." We sang them, perfectly.

"Okay," Babs said, "now separately." Separately, also perfectly.
"All right, now the tenors: A, C, B-flat, G-sharp, A. Go." Robyn
and Mary and Dale in perfect in unison. "Okay, now all of you,
all four, together, starting at 'gave.'"

At "to," we strayed, or I did. "It's me," I said. "I'm screwing
it up. I think it's the tenors' G-sharp that's throwing me off. I
can't find my D-flat."

"Let's try it again, you and Robyn."

Again, I couldn't find my note. "I'm sorry," to everyone. "I
don't know why...I can't understand it."

"Try it with Dale. You okay with that, Dale?" He nodded.
I failed again.

"Try holding a hand over one ear," Dale suggested. We did.
No good.

We kept trying, alternately with Robyn and Mary and
Dale. It was a signal turning point in the score, an unusual and
arresting harmonic juncture, and it had to work. I could sing
well enough the preceding F, E-flat, D sequence, but the D-flat
eluded me. I could hear it from Corky, I heard it in my head, but
I could not voice it; I simply could not pair it with the tenors'
G-sharp. We tried it with the identical sequence in the chorus's
"I'll follow my Christ who loves me so," and every time I messed
up "who." I was utterly mortified. Babs fumed. Monte glared.
Scotty looked away. Corky blushed. Robyn rolled his eyes. Dale
stared, nonplussed, thumbed his prayer beads. I sweated with
embarrassment.

"Look," Babs said at last, taking charge, "for now, Troy, just
don't sing that note. Mouth it but don't sing it. Let the others
take it, Corky louder, and you come back in on the C in 'ransom.' Let's try that."

We did, and Babs thought it passed. But the spell had broken. All of us had gone sour and sullen over one lousy note. My note.

"Auditions in the auditorium tomorrow at 2," she barked, gathering her sheets. "Bring your hymnals." And we broke up, bummed.

I lingered, though, taking the piano bench vacated by Babs, going back over the problematic notes, softly sounding and singing them, at perfect pitch. I could also sing the tenor sequence flawlessly. And the bass-tenor mating I could also manage as long as no voice sang the G-sharp: the human G-sharp unaccountably threw me off. It was maddening and disheartening. But being back at the keyboard was consoling, coming back to it alone, without snoops or crooners or swooners hanging on, no Monte, even, just me and some comfort-notes. I drifted on my own harmonies...until a light rustle behind roused me.

"Troy?" It was Corky The All American Boy.

"Hey," I said. "What's up?"

"I just wanted to be sure you're okay," he said. He must've biked over to the Complex snack bar, for he held out an iced Coke and a pack of Oreos. "Thought you might like these after that workout."

"Ah, Corky," I almost teared up. "That's so sweet, and kind and thoughtful. Thanks a lot. Let's have a cookie," unwrapping the cellophane.

"You okay, Troy?"

I swallowed hard, took a sip.

"Sure," I coughed; "I'll be fine. It was just so embarrassing. And weird. I don't know what happened. It messed up Dale's first time."

"Shit happened," he said; "it does. It's just shit. Dale's used to Jubilee shit. Had a whole summer of it! Don't let it get to you."

"It already has. Got to me, I mean. I've ruined us. Really. I don't know how we go on, after that. I think I have to quit."

"Whoa there, Troy! Hold on, my man! Nobody wants you to quit. Of course we'll go on. We're terrific, and we're just starting. Babs found a great way to get past this. Remember how we sounded before? We were fantastic. She said so."

"But it's not right, not to sing. It's cheating, what Babs said. I'll be faking. It doesn't feel right. I should drop out."

"All right, then: drop out for one note, that's all. One frigging note. Do it for the good of the group. Where's the harm? You're actually *helping* the group. The group *needs* you. Monte and Scotty and I and the rest are counting on you, to help us. Today was just a little part shit. It's over and it's cleaned up and it's all fixed. Have another cookie."

"You really don't think it's cheating?"

"It's obeying. You got an order. Listen: something broke; it got patched. It's done. Nobody cares. Why would you?"

"Corky...you're...."

"I'm good," he smiled, laying a hand on my shoulder. "C'mon, let's ride the bike."

"You're being really sweet. Thank you."

The next day's auditions ensued with unexpected success. No one mentioned, exactly, my rehearsal glitch, and no one verbally noticed my silence on the cursed note except maybe Corky, standing close and kind of leaning into me. Steph actually went a little teary over "Softly and Tenderly" and even congratulated Monte on organizing the Jubilee Jubilates. The Man briefly addressed us, cautioned us to represent the Assembly faithfully and respectably, prayed over us, and put us down for a premiere showing on Tuesday night, the very night of the "love offering."

"This is great!" Ta-Da Dallas squawked when he heard; "we'll make a bloody killing! And the Jubes should get a cut of the take. How about 40%?"

"I told you," I said to Monte.

"Or maybe 45%," Dallas refigured. "We're more than half the draw."

"Your math's cockeyed," I said.

Babs detained us after the bosses left. "Attention, Jubilates," she said, drawing more large pages from her folder. "I've sketched out another descant here, for the chorus of 'Wherever He Leads.' Maybe it'll help smooth over the rough patch around G-sharp D-flat. Mary and Martha will sing it, soprano and alto, and we'll oooh a four-part harmony back-up on the chorus." She rolled out an arpeggio of introduction and led us through verse 1 to the chorus, where the Moonies just about lifted off in the descant, operatic gifts patent.

"Wow-wie!" Babs whooped. "*That* was *fabulous!*" She actually pumped her fist, likely as thrilled by her own composition as by their rendering. "Once more now, though, girls, and maybe not quite so much volume. Let's don't scare them."

She called a dress rehearsal for 5 p.m. Tuesday: "Right here, before the herds gather. Dress as instructed. No hymnals or pages. Memories only. If necessary, ask Troy to rehearse you in Cactus. If you're down to work that night, speak to Steph; she'll excuse you. Dallas, be sure we're in the program leaflet, everybody's name spelled right and their parts named. Robyn, you've copied the line-up directions? And Dallas, arrange for reserved seats, first row. Monte? Dale? Anything else?" Monte signed a thumbs-up. Dale saluted. We milled.

And then Scotty was there, in my face.

"Want to head down to the lake?" she smiled, her head at a distinctly coy angle.

"Let's hit the snack bar first," I said, pointing that way; "I'm a little dry."

Shorts forbidden the girls, Scotty wore the standard squaw dress with the scooped neckline showing a fair portion of bare shoulder and upper chest before flowing out into pleats from the narrow waist. It was bright yellow with brown rickrack more or less matching the auburn hair she'd swept back into a brush ponytail trussed at her neck by a blue band. A choker of tiny blue beads graced her throat, and an identical bracelet her dainty wrist. Except for the barest hint of rouge and lip gloss, she showed no makeup. Her very white feet tucked into blue flats.

"You look nice," I said.

"So do you," she replied. "The madras is cool."

The madras shirt was one of two I'd saved A&P pay to buy at Simon Brothers in Baton Rouge for $5.50 each, and I liked to show off both of them. I hadn't yet seen any other madras at Jubilee.

"Thanks," I said; "tartan is fun."

We strolled on over to the Complex and found the snack bar crowded with guests and staff. Normally, only girls serviced the bar unless demand required Lynn Crosby, the remaining lobby boy, to step up. He was back there now, and his head was one of several that turned toward us as we sidled up and made space for ourselves.

"Hey, Lynn, could we get two cokes on ice in cups with straws?" I asked him, reaching for my wallet.

His eyes clicked back and forth between us for a second.

"Is there a problem?" I asked. "Just two cokes, please."

He ladled some ice. "No, no, no problem. Coming up."

"Hey-hey, Scotty," from a tall, sturdy girl I didn't know. "Long time! Who's this?"

"This is Troy Tyler. First kitchen crew. Troy, this is Hollis Mosley, also from Vicksburg. She works Oklahoma Hall."

Out came quite a large paw. "Pleasedtameetcha," Hollis said, biting into a Baby Ruth.

"Hollis plays first string girl's basketball for Mississippi State," Scotty explained.

"Say," from me in frisky mode, "I've always wondered why they call them strings: what's stringy about them?"

In jeans with a zipper fly and a loose, plaid, timber-man's untucked shirt and a black baseball cap, Hollis loomed. Big, broad, strapping, a little coarse-grained against Scotty's refinement, she checked me out, head to toe, not the least bit daunted by my wise-ass question.

"It's from archery," she said, chewing slowly. "Your first string in archery is your bowstring, your main string. If it snaps, you've got a second or third string in your quiver to replace it — like second-string subs in basketball. Anything else?"

"Really?" I asked, subdued and surprised. "Is that actually true, Hollis?" I looked at Scotty, who was grinning. "I never knew that. Did you know that, Scotty? That's really pretty interesting, Hollis. Thanks for telling us. So second string is actually a string!"

"Not in basketball," Hollis said. "And it's second-rate on the court."

"Hollis is first team," Scotty said, "and team captain."

"I'm the Power Forward on my squad," Hollis said, wadding up the wrapper and dusting her hands. "I'm big. I have some muscle. So that's my position, Power Forward. I play a lot of defense, back to the basket. I snag rebounds. I take jump shots. I dribble us out of jams. I'm not too bad out there."

"I made second team one year," I admitted, "second-rate out there, I guess. I'd like to see you play sometime. Congratulations! It's good to meet you, Hollis."

"Same here," she said. "See you around. Bye, Scotty." And she drifted off, vacating space immediately filled with Monte.

"Well...," he exclaimed, "Hello, people!" his eyes darting back and forth between us before narrowing. "Fancy meeting you two here! Um, what's going on? *Is* something going on?"

"We're getting cokes," I said.

"We're walking to the lake," Scotty said.

Monte paused, looked away, looked back, pulled out his balm, twindled it. "Okay," he said; "I'll come along. There's something I want to...."

"Monte," I interrupted, "no. We're, ah, we're like together."

"It's a date," Scotty said. "You've heard of dates?" reaching for the cokes Lynn held out.

"A date? A date. I see. Oh. Well. Then. Fine. I'll just...," he shrugged.

"Come with me up Baldy on Wednesday?" I asked him.

"Whither thou goest," he said, staring.

I settled with Lynn, tipping liberally, and lightly touched Scotty's elbow, guiding her toward the wide double-doors, the pleats of her skirt brushing my knees.

"What was that?" she asked, "what Monte said?"

"You know," I replied. "Book of Ruth. In the Bible?"

"Oh, right. But what did he mean?"

"Beats me," I lied.

White pebbled paths threaded the grassy slope down to the lake, weaving the gardens into a resplendent multicolored mantel itself then formatted into discreet patterns of religious import: an open Bible, for instance, with red petals signifying Jesus's words; a Cross (sans the Body, of course) of entirely white blossoms against an entirely blue background; a huge floral map of both hemispheres with tiny blooming cacti where the Baptists staked missions; an ichthyic (fish) in brilliant gold bordered by royal blue blooms. SS would have named the flowers; I can only report the colors and invite your imagination to fill in with every other tint you've ever loved. These gardens were a triumphant constellation of choreographed color anchored at the bottom by the slate blue lake far surpassing the brochure photos that made them famous. Scotty and I paused to breathe it in.

Teak garden benches perched here and there. "Shall we?" I said, pointing to one about half-way down.

"That was pretty cool," I began, "what Hollis said about archery, didn't you think?"

"Yes, but your question was kind of snide."

"Do I need to apologize? I will, but what would I say? And you were kind of nasty yourself with Monte, about dates."

"He was being a jerk."

Was he? This struck me as a novel concept. I postponed consideration.

"So," I said; "let's talk. Not about the paper."

Now, it isn't like I'm exactly "experienced" in relations with women, although I did "go steady" with Allison Lockhart from freshman year all through high school; and while we never went "all the way," as people doubtfully said back then, we came as close as it's possible to get to it without finishing the job or the joy, depending on how you look at it (as if it's possible to look at any of it except in one joyful way). In a moment of reckless conceit and condescension shortly after graduation I broke up with Allison as a shade puerile for the college man, and then with truly titanic arrogance, just last spring at Prom time, I actually volunteered to escort her if she couldn't get a date for it! *That's* how stupidly little I understood women. But I did know you got them to talk by asking about themselves.

I learned that Scotty didn't believe in beauty pageants and would never be a contestant. I learned that she twirled a baton but had quit the Ole Miss squad even after making it as a freshman, because training for halftime shows took too long. I learned that she read novels but spelled poorly, and intended to major in English anyway. She'd pledged Tri-Delt. She belonged to the Baptist Student Union but skipped meetings. She liked football and played softball. She liked to fish. She'd dated but never gone steady, as her parents forbade it. Her father owned cotton gins and deaconed at First Baptist. Her mother sewed and knitted but couldn't get Scotty interested. She loved music, singing, but didn't play. Her older brother was third year at Emory Law School. She'd taken Home Economics and cooked well. Her favorite food was spicy hot chili. Her least favorite food was snails. She'd performed in high school plays.

"What? Wait!" I said. "You did high school plays?!"

"Oh yes," she said; "every year."

"You're not kidding? What plays?"

Okay, you're not going to believe this next part, except that every high school in the country in those days staged Thornton Wilder's "Our Town" at least every five years. Madison did, starring me, and as it turned out, Vicksburg did, staring Scotty as Emily, the beautiful hometown girl who loves, marries, gives birth, dies, and gets to visit her own funeral and wax wise on life. Winning the lead in tryouts, I was still let down because George, not me, got to kiss Emily on stage.

"'Our Town'," she said, "to sold out houses all four nights."

Somewhere from the cellar of my memories I dredged up a couple of lines from my role referencing Emily and spoke them softly there on the bench.

She turned to stare, then pushed herself away for a clearer view. "How do you know…? You know this play? Wait! You're the….?"

"Stage Manager." In case you're one of the half-dozen who've never seen this old chestnut, the Stage Manager, the lead, delivers a running commentary on the action all the way along, occasionally stepping into the action and then out again.

Scotty whooped. "No, really? You played Stage Manager? Unbelievable! I mean, unbelievable that we…"

"Also four nights," I said. "And we took it around town and then to three other high schools in the parish."

"Phenomenal!" she cried. "Don't you still just love that play?"

"Except I can't see it without crying."

"Me, too," she said, her lip barely trembling.

"And didn't you just love that role? All that knowing, all that power? Sort of like God?"

"Only I never got to kiss Emily."

"Would you care to kiss her now?"

* * *

Dr. Mann dismissed Da-Dallas's petition asking that Jubilates' share of the "love offering" include pay for performing at services, but our reception was so warm that nobody but Dallas much minded. I was relieved, for Dallas's whole mercenary shtick bothered me. It feels odd to write here that I have a favorite Jesus-story but I do like the one where He bounces the merchants and traders from the temple, because (1) He shows some temper; (2) He shows some machismo; and (3) He purges the place of commercial stain. Oh, I understand well enough that the institutional church requires money to survive; I always understood that my family's livelihood depended entirely upon the weekly collection of "tithes and offerings" from the congregation, and Lord knows how I exploited that practice when playing piano for Father's revival meetings in small-town Louisiana churches where I repeatedly got more in (yes) "love money" for splashy playing than he did for lofty preaching, I being such a flamboyant little prodigy, and all. Of course, I always had to tithe my take, but losing 10% of it didn't allay my vague sense of shame for charging the church, so to speak, for supplying spiritual provision — for accepting hard cash in return for religious inspiration and enrichment. It didn't compute. These people were finding satisfaction in some dimension of themselves on a whole different plane from where I delivered whatever produced it. They paid for an uplifting experience it cost me nothing to provide and which originated in a sphere of being not just indifferent but arguably hostile to the country where their souls sojourned. The equation sat askew. Something of the same disconnect obtained in my discomfort during church financial campaigns, when elaborately and expensively designed brochures begged parishioners to fund next year's budget, and all manner of time and resources were dedicated to increasing annual pledges. And just generally, mindfulness of money seemed implicit in every program, every operation of the church: the whole enterprise soaked in grasping materialistic consciousness indigenously at cross-purposes with its proclaimed sacred mission. If it wasn't explicit in Sunday School lessons and pulpit messages, you would feel its presence pushing just behind them awaiting an opening, a summons into articulation. Somebody's hand was forever fluttering about my pocket, poised to pick it.

As long as I'm into discomfort territory here I might as well mention another item or two nagging at me. The kiss among the flowers happened, all right, but barely: a brief, glancing, ethereal brush of lips against lips before we both broke into giggles at the suddenness of it, the flukey, impossible coincidence of it, and, on my part at least, the hopeless dissatisfaction of it! For certain, it wasn't the George-and-Emily kiss of my fantasies. And the whole business of the date itself had come to pass far too fast, and right on top of the newspaper squabble, most of both at Scotty's initiative. All of that was disorienting, and, well, felt unnatural, as though she'd stolen my lead, so to say, and was Stage Managing *me*. And the squabble had stalemated, inconclusively, and opened up again with the date arrangement.

The conversation had been mostly one-sided, perhaps a result of my questions. But surely she might've asked a few herself. And then she'd accused me of insulting Hollis. And she'd called Monte a jerk. The demerits were piling up. But it was largely the speed of the flowering that unnerved and rattled me: we'd raced from the ask to the kiss without passing through all those delicious cautions and clumsy fumblings, all those doubtful hesitations and wracking uncertainties and aching apprehensions called "getting to know" each other. Yes, we had only twelve weeks, eight now, but we had already, precipitately, arrived at an endpoint, a climactic moment (if you discount the final one, as our environment pretty well dictated that we do) with nothing to look forward to. Haste — impetuous haste — had forfeited days of luscious angst! And then on top of that, what, *what,* to think of Monte's displeasure, if that's what it was. What was it?

* * *

"How was it?" he asked. He lay stretched out on his bed, head pillowed against the wall, twiddling with his balm. "Your date. You used the balm?"

"Fine," I said; "it was okay. What'd you do?"

"What did *you* do? What'd yawl do?"

"I told you. We walked to the lake. We talked."

"What'd you find out?"

"Why're you grilling me? What is it you want?"

"I want to know what's going on. What's going on?"

"Nothing's going on. We talked. I learned a lot."

"What'd she teach you?"

"I meant, I learned a lot about her, her life."

"She taught you about life? Already? Wasting no time!"

We sparred like that for a while longer, getting nowhere, he making his point: *I'm pissed*; me making mine: *I don't care.* Except that I did. I just didn't know how to work it.

He uncapped his balm, smeared his lips: "I think Robyn knows something."

"Robyn knows nothing," from me.

"I think he thinks he does, or is trying to find out."

"Are we playing 'I've Got a Secret' here?"

"Well," he said, looking hard at me; "you do."

"What?" I started.

"You do. You've got a secret." He let it sink in. And then leapt off the bed, laughing. "The Goforth Secret, you dope!" he slapped me on the shoulder. "The speech competition! What'd you think I meant?" And after another pause and look he began pacing the room.

"Lindsay says Robyn's been asking around about you." Lindsay is one of the two girls — Jordan the other — who shared SS's jeep with Travis and me that first day from the depot. They both worked the Registration Desk at the Complex. "Lindsay says Jordan heard The Man talking to Steph about Youth Week, and your name came up. Something about kitchen crew schedules, but she didn't quite catch the connection."

"What's that have to do with Robyn?"

"Robyn and Jordan hang out sometimes. Maybe she'll tell him too. And maybe he's been pumping her. What do you know about Youth Week?"

Monte and I had not talked about the Goforth Speech Finals since his mysterious announcement days ago that I'd "win it," as though by unspoken understanding we knew not to discuss the competition between ourselves or among others

without mutual consent. This suited me so amiably that I sometimes almost forgot the impending showdown amid the stir of
other, more agreeable affairs. The truth is, I didn't want to think
of it lest anxiety poison everything. I didn't want news of it to
bring attention my way. For I often felt a little ashamed of my
success, always embarrassed by an asinine title, and troubled by
an imminent obligation likely to set me apart as different just
when I'd found belonging such bliss. It might be pleasing to win
the contest without exciting attendant expectations, but I saw
no road opening for that to happen; it might be satisfying to
participate indifferently, without anyone assuming my performance *meant* anything — signified *anything* about me and my
intentions or implied anything about my future. Where was it
written, I wondered, that everything always has to mean something else other than itself? But I already knew that to most
minds it usually does. And I knew exactly what to expect from
any win. But I also knew I couldn't deliberately lose. What I
knew about Youth Week was its coincidence with the national
contest finals, so Dr. Mann's naming the one triggered alarm
about the other, especially as my own name had been attached
by management.

"I believe it might be the last week," I said. "It might be the
Goforth Finals week."

"That's what I was thinking," Monte said. "I remember
from last summer. Can you find out for sure?"

"I'll look. I must have the date somewhere."

This was textbook dissembling. I did not want to go there
yet, for I knew that any confirmation of a forthcoming date
would launch Monte upon another Big Deal operation certain

to engage me and to foreground my scheduled address. I bleakly dreaded any such furor.

"Does Robyn know anything about Youth Week?" Monte went on.

"He might know it's when the Finals happen. You remember he lost at the Little Rock state finals."

"So why should he care a fig about the national finals here?"

"You don't know that he does. Why not ask Jordan if he's said anything. And why he's poking around. Ask her to say again what she overheard, about me."

This was both counter-intuitive and self-contradictory. I prompted prying open when I had better be shutting down.

"I think I will," he said. "Robyn's up to something. We need to find out what."

"Do we? Monte, listen: I don't know what you'll find out, if anything, but if it's to do with the speech thing, I really wish you'd drop it. I'd rather not fool with that right now. Let's let it lie. I'm not ready to think about it, okay?"

"Depends," he said. "If they're talking about it, we have to. To control it."

"I don't even know what that means, but I wish you wouldn't. And by the way" — I just remembered that I'd intended to ask — "how did *you* find out about the speech thing. I never told you."

"Steph told me," he said. "Before you came. I thought you'd figured it out."

* * *

A large outcropping of rugged rock lay just inside the eastern border of Jubilee, the bare, flat top of which — Old Baldy

— offered a wide, encompassing view of the Assembly campus at that distance radiantly bejeweled by the gardens and lake. Monte said that an oil-rich Texan and late convert to the Baptist faith after a nearly fatal Beechcraft crash donated tens of thousands for the construction of an artificial waterfall at the top southern edge of Baldy with a natural rock bathing pool at its base, but Jubilee staffers had found the site irresistible for hanky-panky after hours, so it had to be ruled off limits for night use. I thought it a beautiful piece of work, tall and noble, especially in sunlight with rainbows dancing amid its mists. The surprising feature of it was the noise it made: some engineering trick or mechanical device gave its tumble a thunderous roar up close audible as a steady, low hum all the way back to the Jubilee gardens. Two faint paths edged by occasional benches led in opposite directions from the base to the summit of Baldy, each requiring moderate stamina and an hour to scale. And two roughly matching, designated Prayer Gardens were laid out just off both trails about half way along, featuring trellises and small arbors hung with looping flowered vines. It wasn't exactly a demanding climb, but steep, narrow corners and tricky rifts and fissures might challenge novices. Dating staff couples, I'd heard, routinely found privacy along the paths. In fact, I'd planned on inviting Scotty for a hike up when Monte turned ugly about my date, and I with palliating intent switched my bid to him for Wednesday. He, after all, had almost said he wanted to chat.

I turned into one of the Prayer Gardens for a breather.

"Did you talk to Jordan yet?" I asked him.

"She wasn't much help. She *had* told Robyn what she'd heard The Man tell Steph, and he'd asked her to repeat it exactly word for word but she couldn't remember it all that well. And he wanted to know what she knew about Youth Week, which was nothing. Oh, and he asked if she knew or could find out where you're from."

"Why would he want to know that? And why wouldn't he just ask me?"

"That's what she said, to him. I don't think he said. Anyhow, no, not much help. But at least we know he's actually digging around into you."

"It's got to be something about the speech."

"And you still don't want to talk about it?"

"I don't. There's nothing to talk about."

"Well, there is. Obviously. We just don't know what it is yet."

He shifted on the bench, reached for his balm. Used it.

"Want some?" he asked, offering.

"No thanks."

He pocketed the tube, reached for a curl behind his ear.

"Troj," he said softly, like imploring; "Troj, there's something I need to tell you, talk over with you. Okay?"

"As long as it's not about the speech," but my heart thumped.

"It's not. Troj," entreating; "I've lied to you."

I figured this was probable, beyond the lie about returning to Jubilee this summer, and because of that one, but I thought it best to let him own it.

"Or at least I didn't tell you the whole truth. When I told you about myself, that first day, when we met."

My heart thumped a little harder. He sucked a deep breath, let it out. I dimly sensed that this might be staged. "Go on," I managed.

"I told you I won an Air Force ROTC scholarship to Baylor, and that part's true. I told you I wanted to fly, intended to pilot Air Force planes, maybe as a career. That part is also true. What I didn't add is that…well…I'll probably enlist as a chaplain."

"A what? A chaplain?"

"Yes. A minister. Clergyperson."

"I know what a chaplain is. I'm just…well…surprised." Dumbfounded was more like it.

"I think I may have a calling, like a vocation."

Was he kidding? He did like to kid around. But this seemed seriously sincere, alarmingly so. His face had gone a little pale.

"You really mean this, Monte? I don't understand."

"I'm not certain. But I think so. I think I might like it."

"But it seems so…unlikely? I mean, you don't seem…." I had nowhere to go with that sentence and so lapsed into silence, and repetition: "I don't understand it at all."

I should probably explain here that true Baptists believe with a sort of plain-faced literality — an earnest gravity — that God "calls" certain chosen mortals into divine service as "Christian ministers of the Gospel," in the church's phrase for it. A narrative of this experience is a favorite homiletic trope of ordained preachers: my own Father never tired of recounting his own "call," heard or felt as a late teen while praying for discernment at a tree stump in a field near his rural Arkansas home. These visitations of divine will usually follow the pattern of God's "call" to Old Testament prophets and patriarchs — think Moses, Abraham, Samuel, Jonah — and are always resisted, fiercely resisted, with feeble and unworthy excuses eventually vanquished by wise persuasions or wilted will. A frequent joke of waggish parsons holds that Mother's craving for a clerical son is often mistaken by said son for God's call to ministry. But Baptists are usually firm in believing, and encouraging youth to believe, that an ultimately irrefutable Deity anoints the heart and mind of the chosen one with a conviction of "call," and then blesses its acceptance. Such did Monte almost claim to have heard or felt.

"I can't quite understand it either," he said, "not entirely. But I can't not sense it. I can't not imagine it. The chaplaincy feels like a fit. Almost comfortable. Right now, though, I'd mostly like a cigarette. You got one?"

The non sequitur was so unexpected, so outlandish, we both cracked up; the tension eased. He knew I didn't smoke; only that once, over Dale, had I seen him hold a cigarette. But I'd have inhaled one too, had Travis been there with the Camels.

I stood, pocketed my hands, looked down at him. He seemed shrunken, drawn.

"I don't know what to say, Monte. I never thought…I'm just so, well, sort of shocked." I wanted to say, straight out, "disappointed," but knew I couldn't. "I don't know if I can handle this right now. It's so different…."

"I just wanted you to know. Almost nobody does. But I wanted you to. Are you pissed off?"

"No, oh no. Not at all. I'm just going to need some time, you know? To get used to it. Look, thank you for telling me. Yes, thanks. For trusting me with it. I see it wasn't easy. How about giving me a little time to, you know, process? What if I meet you back at Cactus, before dinner? Okay if I cut through and take the other path down? Don't be sad. You look sad. I'll see you later."

"Troy," he said, with a limp, wimpy little wave.

I headed down to the lake and skipped rocks across its surface for some while. That I could skip them six times told me I was mad. Pissed.

By packaging his intended profession as an Air Force chaplaincy, Monte had endowed it with a glamor, a mystique wholly absent from the bland, drab designations of "preacher," "parson," and even "minister." By styling it a military office, he'd invested it with status and stature, with cachet and prestige. He'd ribboned it. Conferred honor upon it. But for me this ornamental uplift amounted to nothing more than cloying sugar-coat, a shabby veneer draping a reality I knew all too well. And I *knew* the idea, the plan, was all wrong.

First, you didn't ever just accept a call. You resisted it, you fought it, you struggled mightily against it. You didn't even recognize it *as* a call or admit its authenticity. You tried to ignore or escape it. You made up excuses to reject it. You agonized over it day and night. You said no to it in every conceivable way for as long as you could, and then at last gave way to the inevitability of acceptance while nearly always doubtful whether the call might have reached a wrong number. But to all appearances, Monte had rashly embraced it.

Second, ministry would ruin him. It would suppress and contain his intensity. It would paralyze his imagination and emasculate his creativity. It would depress his charisma. It would strap his energy. It would repress his vibrancy. It would dull his wit and shade his sparkle. It would crush his spirit, warp and disfigure his whole identity.

Third, he would fail at it, probably die of it.

The fourth, I vaguely sensed, had to do with me: the idea, the plan, was somehow all wrong, too, because of me. I couldn't find me in it. It disappointed me, yes; it hurt me, for certain. Because I couldn't see how I could go there with him. I couldn't go *back* there, even with him, in his company. That's as far I got with Number 4, for I began unaccountably to weep hot tears.

What stopped them was the stunning novelty of the notion I'd just imagined. Whereof the whim that Monte and I would ever go anywhere together, post-Jubilee — that there was even life, for us, afterward? I'd never imagined it. We'd never spoken of it. How did I even get into the picture? He hadn't invited me, hadn't even hinted I had a place in it. I hardly realized there *was* a picture. And whatever made me reject a possibility never presumed to exist, an occasion or opportunity never entertained? And why was I crying again?

Muddled and tired, I drew some shaky breaths and headed back to Cactus, stopping by Travis's room on the way. I'd walked away from Monte with really rotten timing: he'd done a brave thing, telling me, and I'd let him down by disrespecting it, selfishly. I didn't understand it and I didn't like it but I could've let him try to explain it, and comforted him while he did. Deserting him like that was a dirty trick.

He stood at our windows, looking out, his back to the door. "Hey," I said, "you all right?"

"Yes I am," he said evenly, not turning around.

I walked over, stood beside him, and reached into my shirt pocket.

"Here," I said, palming two Camels and book matches: "let's smoke."

5

"Hi-hey-hello there, fellas!" Robyn said, poking his round face through our doorway. "Can you talk?" waddling in.

"Last time I checked," I said. "Hey! I still can."

Robyn knew he'd been gypped in the looks department and tried to compensate with flowering, skin-clinging, silky shirts when off duty, tucked into the tight waistband but always slipping loose. He also favored white chinos too snug for someone half his weight, too tightly belted. Everybody else breathed a lot easier than Robyn, who never seemed quite able to catch his.

"It smells like smoke in here," he said, sniffing.

"Maybe your brakes?" I cracked.

He ignored this and eased himself onto Monte's bed as though afraid Monte might still be in it. Out came the big blue hanky with the orange monogram. "Monte's not here?" he asked, going after the thick, round lenses with vigor. Of all the Jubilee guys I knew, only Robyn carried a handkerchief; but then he was also the only one who polished his glasses every five minutes, as though his eyes tried to help him breathe, and steamed them up.

It was a slow, grey morning, more October than July, with low clouds and drizzle and fog which at that altitude drifted past our windows like fine gauze, hugged the adobe walls, clung, cooling, to your skin: perfect for lying around. At least that's how it began. We'd worked the breakfast shift and returned to a quiet dorm with twenty-four hours of freedom ahead and nothing planned. So even though Robyn wasn't my nearest and dearest, I didn't much mind his dropping by. Besides, a visit might furnish information Monte wanted.

"What's he doing," Robyn asked.

"Being Monte," I offered, "which is a pretty good act."

"Where? When's he coming back?"

"On the handiest stage and whenever the applause stops."

I was enjoying this. Actually, Monte'd only stepped over to the Complex for mail and Burma Shave but on queer impulse I resisted saying so. Maybe it was Robyn's rapped-out little questions, his sharp little what's and where's when none of it was his business, like a prying reporter hunting a scoop.

"How come he's not here? You're always together."

"Is this on the record?" I ventured, an idea forming. "Official?"

"What? Whadaya mean 'official'"?

"No," I said, "I'd better not. I can't go public with it."

"What 'public'? What're you talking about? Where is he?"

"I don't think I'd better say anything yet. No, I better hadn't. You'll tell."

"No I won't either. Honest, Troy. I wouldn't. What's going on?"

"You sure? I can trust you?"

"Sure I'm sure," his eyes really popping out. "Honest, I won't tell. What?"

"We-l-l-l-l," I loitered; "I guess maybe I do need to tell somebody, get it off my chest. You sure you want to hear, though? You can leave if you'd rather not."

"I'm not leaving," he said, but how he perched on the bed, bird-like, hinted he might, only I figured he wouldn't, not now. "What the hell is it?" his voice raised.

"Okay, if you're sure. And you promise. I was only trying to cover for him, it's so awful. And you're going to find out anyway; you'll all learn soon enough. I might as well tell you and you can help me handle it, if there's any way to handle it. I just don't know. Something terrible's happened, Robyn, something really bad."

A little jar shook him, like he'd been bumped from behind, so he almost plopped onto the floor. "Not to Monte," he said, "not Monte...."

"Something we'll all be ashamed of for a long time. I don't know if Jubilee'll ever get over it, it's...well...such a scandal. I can't hardly believe it's true myself, but it is. You sure you want to hear this?"

"I'll hear it," he said, choking on it, gulping.

"All right then. The fact is...what happened is...Monte's been arrested. Steph and the Santa Fe sheriff came to get him right after breakfast, handcuffed him right where you're sitting, took him to jail. No bail, Steph said. No, wait, let me finish: No bail, she said, it was too horrible, what he did. I'm real sorry to tell you this, Robyn, I know you like him and all, but Monte... well, Monte is a peeping-Tom."

"Shit," he said. "I don't believe it. It can't be true. You're kidding, right? Where is he, really?"

"He's in jail. He confessed to it, sitting right there, said he can't help it. And when they asked whether what the girls said was true, how they saw him last night right outside Marigold windows stark bare naked looking in, and, you know" (I made the jerking gesture), "well, he didn't deny a thing, only started crying and apologizing and asking them please not to tell and give him another chance and not arrest him. But they did, took him right off. Didn't even let him tell me goodbye."

Robyn's pouty lips hung open, his glasses so steamed I couldn't make out his eyes, just moony hoops staring; and he was wheezing, the asthma acting up.

"Naaaaaaw," he said; "Monte's not…Monte couldn't, he wouldn't…."

"But he did. You think I'd make up something that disgusting about my roommate? I was here. I saw it, heard it. Not an hour ago, when they hauled him off."

"He actually admitted it? You heard him confess?"

"I'm afraid so."

"And he's in jail? It's just not possible."

"In Sante Fe by now."

He removed the glasses with one hand and reached for the handkerchief with the other. For a second I thought he intended to blot his eyes, but he blinked away the tears — there really were tears welling up — and wiped the lens in slow circles.

"Oh my God," he said, a coarse croak. "My God, Monte did that. I'd never, never in a zillion years have imagined…. Troy," he looked at me, like begging, his face yellow-gray and sagging;

"Troy, what are we going to do? We have to do something. We have to help him."

All right. Okay. I know. I shouldn't have. I just didn't think it'd be so easy, that's all. It being so easy — Robyn being so easy — sapped some of the fun out of it. It got weird when Robyn didn't get it. Anybody else would've figured it out. If he hadn't been so gullible…. It's just that once I got going I couldn't stop. The thing just took off, on its own. Maybe you can tell why. But really I *didn't* think what Monte did was anybody's affair but ours. Certainly not Robyn's. Nevertheless, I had to own up.

"Robyn," I said. "Hey. Look at me; listen to me. It's a joke. I *am* kidding. There's nothing wrong. It's just a story. Okay? Monte's fine. He'll be right back. Okay?"

That little bump goosed him from behind again and he stared unblinking for a few seconds, looking numb.

"You're crazy, Troy. You know, you're really fucking crazy."

"I know," I said. "You're probably right. It was a crazy thing to say."

"I'd call it about the meanest thing anybody ever pulled… anybody ever tried to pull on me. You're completely nuts."

"Maybe. Sometimes."

"But I knew it wasn't true. Monte couldn't do that. You've got a sick mind, Troy, you know that? Making up all that about him. Sick and perverse."

I knew he wanted an apology, waited for it; and because he did, I held back.

He thought it over while we were quiet, then slipped on his glasses, stashed the hanky. And when he looked back up at me, this crooked, piggy little smile crawling across his lips, something about it out of kilter, off balance, unsure of itself.

"It *was* kind of funny, though," he giggled. "Funny weird. But you really are a kook, Troy. They oughta lock *you* up." He took a long breath. "So when's he coming back?"

"Look, you asked *me* when you banged in here whether *I* could talk. You want me or Monte?"

"Oh, well, both of you, actually. Together. I wanted to mention something."

What he wanted, it turned out, while ignorant of our curiosity, was to tell us pretty much everything we'd wondered about his nosing around.

"Jordan says you're from Madison, Louisiana, right?"

"Yes, but why didn't you just ask me? And why'd you want to know?"

"Wait. Wait. My mother's older sister lives there, in Madison. My Aunt Agnes. Her husband's mayor."

"What? Mayor Hoytt?"

"The same. Bo Hoytt. And Aunt Agnes attends your father's church. Maybe you know them?"

I didn't; but this was getting interesting. Unless Robyn was making up a story to repay mine. "No, but go on."

"So Mom and Aunt Agnes were talking long distance a while ago and Mom said something about me being out here at Jubilee for the summer, and Aunt Agnes remembered reading a notice in their church bulletin about her pastor's son winning a state speaking prize and getting to compete nationally, she couldn't remember where. But Mom figured where because I'd lost the Arkansas state competition and didn't get the free trip out here for the final round. So Mom called me to ask if I'd met any guys from Madison, Louisiana who might be national finals Goforth speakers, and I had to ask around for Louisiana kids.

And then Jordan said Dr. Mann mentioned you and something about Youth Week, which is, I knew from state finals, when the run-off happens; and I finally worked it out when Jordan put you in Madison." He took another deep breath. "It *is* you, idn' it?"

It was almost dazzling, this little history, rolled out with such detail and fluency and polish. Rehearsed? A bit of a stretch, maybe. Heavy on coincidence, for sure. Fudged and fuzzy around the edges. A few holes. But not necessarily for those reasons implausible. And in its conclusion, incontestably right. Perhaps Robyn was entitled to the smug on his face.

"Bravo," I said, muting it. "So long as you're not making it up."

"It *is* you, idn' it?"

"It is. But you can't say anything. Not even to Jordan. I don't want it to spread around."

"Okay. Monte knows, though? I wanted both of you to know. Because I've been through it. I thought I might could help you get ready. And because...because I thought...I think I might know who your competition is."

"How could you possibly know that?"

"Because he beat me."

"Who did?"

"An Indian."

"Most of my best friends aren't Indians," Monte said from the doorway, one fist gripping the brown sack and cocked on his hip, his right arm angling up and propped against the jamb. A jaunty pose.

"Hey, Monte," Robyn said, grinning, and struggling to his feet. "Come on in!"

"Just might do that. It's our teepee, I believe. What kind of pow-wow is this anyway? War? Hunting? Planting? How about fertility rites? Always a good day for fertility! Wait, I know: it's in-i-ti-a-tion day" (to the Howdy Doody tune). "High time these boys learned what 'Brave' means!" And he thumped the dresser top in tom-tom rhythm.

"Robyn was saying he got beat by an Indian."

"War, then," Monte said gravely. "Let's have a look at this paleface's scalp," poking around Robyn's head.

"Monte," Robyn squeaked, pulling away and flopping back onto the bed. "This is serious."

"War usually is," Monte said. "Better break out the paints, Troj."

Still frisky — stubbornly unserious — he began whooping and shuffling about in this madcap imitation war-dance like a six year-old. I thought it hilarious but figured Robyn had had enough for one morning — not to mention my own readiness to resume business — and stuck out a foot so Monte sprawled.

"Oh," he said with a look, arranging himself into a cross-legged position there on the floor. "You mean serious serious. Why didn't you say so?"

"He's an Indian," Robyn continued. "Native American. Full-blooded Kiowa. Black Wolf."

"That's Jewish," Monte said.

"Stop it," from me.

"Black Wolf Warren," Robyn said. "Wolf Warren, the papers call him."

"Wait," Monte said. "Wolf Warren?" scrambling up, suddenly alert and engaged. "You mean from Oklahoma?"

"That's his tribal home. But he's at University of Arkansas, Fayetteville."

"I know where he goes to school," Monte sounded slightly annoyed. "Everybody does. But he's native Oklahoma."

This looked like Robyn's moment coming on, and he was trying to take his time getting there, deliberately fiddling to get his glasses just so and wiping his mouth with the hanky. But his fingers trembled; and you could see that he twitched inside like his skin wriggled with fleas...or he needed real bad to pee. I half-expected to see hickies popping out among his pimples any second, or a gusher down his pants.

"For your information," he began at last....

"Wolf Warren," Monte cut him off, "Wolf Warren is the Razorbacks' starting quarterback this fall. He's a sophomore and only nineteen. Skipped two grades somewhere. Every school in the country tried to recruit him when he graduated, and every school in the country is scared to death of him now. With good reason too: he's the absolute best out there. About 6'2", 195, rock-hard but as fast and agile and beautiful as God ever made. Their freshman squad played Baylor last year — skunked us — and I never saw anything like the way he moved. Like the way he danced out of the pocket and, oh man, floated, *floated*, on air back there, and then connect on a pass from fifty yards, no loft either. And he's clever, thinking all the time, you can just see it. Nobody can touch him for passing, or beat him running and dodging and faking and thinking."

"Or speaking," Robyn said, bouncing on the bed.

"And he's coming here," from the rapturous Monte.

"He's making it up," I said. "There's no black wolf or any other color coming here, so you can just calm down and forget about burnt offerings. Robyn's pissed because I joked around with him before and he's onto payback now with this crap about wolves. And you fell for it."

"The hell I am," Robyn squawked. "I was *there*. He beat *me*. And it was the best damn speech I ever heard by anybody my entire life. Shit, man, I'm *glad* he won, so he gets a crack at *you*, you friggin' phony! And he'll lay one fuckin' whippin' on you too, you just watch!"

"I can see why you lost," I said, "dropping your g's."

But his words hung there, crackling like static.

"Don't ever talk like that in this room," Monte said, quiet and even. "Not ever. Now. Before I kick your sorry ass out of here, is he or isn't he coming? You lie, and I'll break your face."

"I'm not lying." But he was right on the edge of crying, catching his breath in quick, wet gulps. "I'm not sure but I think he's coming. Honest. So help me, I think he is. But I said it only to warn Troy…to help him…prepare…."

"Some help," Monte said. "More like a trap. Now get out."

"I'm sorry, "Monte. I only meant…."

"*OUT!*"

He walked off, a scruffy, drenched duck, like maybe he had leaked, after all, his white pants sticking.

Monte took my shoulders in both hands, turned me to himself: "Troj," he said, the big smile beaming, "Looks like we've got a little problem."

6

Noon Wednesdays at Jubilee was scrambled eggs. I don't mean for lunch. I mean traffic jams, gridlocks, congestion, with the prior week's guests heading out — revived, revved-up, prepped for another year — and the next batch heading in, and most of the staff granted "furloughs," Monte called them, to enjoy outings organized and chaperoned — oh, so conscientiously chaperoned! — by Steph with her whistle and other adult coun- sellors, more or less patterned on "youth socials" offered after Sunday night services at our home churches: bowling, minia- ture golf, ping-pong tourneys, swimming pool parties — always with safe refreshments. These were entertainments for "blowing off steam," someone always said, though nobody ever explained what produced the steam. Monte was nevertheless right: these occasions only briefly and lightly relaxed Jubilee constraints that waited in place to be clamped back down again: whether any pleasure in our "leaves" and their liberties was enhanced or reduced by undimmed awareness of their brevity is uncertain. If

Wednesday afternoon at Jubilee wasn't Sunday, we remembered that Thursday would be.

Still, we looked forward to Wednesdays, and not just for the outings. Also to the sideshow provided by Da-Dallas who, after Monte vetoed the Sparrow singing club with its bids and elections and dues, formed his own Dallas Lee Porter Service, Inc., and conned nine or ten guys into buying shares that authorized them to work the guest dorms on Wednesday mornings like bell-boys. They hauled down over-stuffed luggage and helped pack trunks and gassed up the cars and gophered sack lunches and snacks and ice and Kleenex and maps and maybe some junky last-minute souvenir for Aunt Gladys back home and hung right in there for tips, which Dallas collected and paid them from, according to how many shares they owned. Mind you, Ta-Da didn't scoot around like them from pillar to post: through the week Dallas would spot who drove the Pontiacs and Buicks and Cadillacs, point his investors to them, and then just hang around among the guests spouting off about Virginia and the Lees. Not the smoothest operation on the planet — that would be Corky, zipping hither and yonder on his bike delivering messages, also for tips — but they raked in the cash: you had to hand it to DA for knowing what folks would pay for, even Baptists. We got a kick out of it, Monte and me, watching Dallas make a fool of himself.

(I should admit, though, my ambivalence: I might have bought in, if TA-DA hadn't been running it, and if Monte hadn't said no, like a threat. After all, it did mint money, and Scrub-Squadding, where you also looked foolish, didn't. So if you're going to be a fool anyway, why not earn money at it? I didn't push it though, after what Monte said.

"No," he said.

"Dallas says he cleared $16 the first week."

"It's pimping," Monte said.

"And Travis $9"

"But don't you see what that makes Travis and the rest of them?"

"Richer," I said.

"Whores," he said.

So we had to settle for the measly love offering.)

Actually, I liked the outings quite a lot, never mind their inevitable ending and inescapable oversight. They eclipsed by a long chalk the "youth socials" of home churches because always including new sites and sights and sounds and stories and even stimuli, you might say, to thought and imagination. And they also — the main thing — gave Monte opportunity and room and inspiration to feature some new and surprising and beguiling aspect of himself. For instance, on the rodeo afternoon, he swept into our room with cowboy boots, hats, Levi jackets, all neat fits...

"Where'd you get this stuff?" I asked, excited to have it.

"Don't look a gift horse," he said; "all true Trojans know better than that!"

...and spurs, and a couple of looped ropes, and bright bandanas for our necks, and nothing would do but that he help me dress:

"No, no," he said of my jeans, "not those. A tighter pair, *tight*, man...lower on the hips...lower...no belt...scarf inside the collar, like this, rumpled...two buttons open...cock the hat...here, the old rakish angle...boots okay? Can you walk in heels? Not so fast, though…pokey…yes, perfect! Some kinda dude!"

…like I was his manikin and he the window-dresser at Simon's in Baton Rouge. And later on at the show he talked just about non-stop, explaining the "artistry," he said, the "subtlety," he said, of calf-wrestling and -tying…

"…flip the loop with the wrist…it's all in the wrist, not the arm, which everybody thinks…and then jerking, so the horse'll know…not jumping, that'd screw it up, but falling on him, and never losing count of the seconds, ticking them off in their heads all the time…."

"…and bronc-busting and brahma-riding…working their heels, sitting high and loose, slack, otherwise they'd split right in two…and no king's horses and no king's men to put'em together again…," laughing and punching me in the ribs.

And later at the Santa Fe restaurant, Monte led me through the seven-course à la carte menu…,"

"…look out, 'cause all those peppers and spices and herbs aren't just hot; I mean, they're mostly aphrodisiacs too…."

…and footed the bill, since Jubilee paid for just three courses. And then at Greer Garson's ranch, where by her very own invitation we picnicked along the Pecos River, he confided stories of her film career and marriages, and hinted why she'd hidden out…

"…in that fortress back there, fenced and guarded, Pinkertons prowling. 'Cause after *Miniver* and *Chips,* she'd got too famous, everybody after her, no privacy, so she couldn't, you know, do what she wanted with whoever she wanted. So it's not just a hideaway, more like a seraglio…."

And touring the film set of *Cowboy*, you'd have thought him the equal hotshot of Glenn Ford and Brian Donlevy, the way he introduced himself and squatted comfortably among the smoking, card-dealing extras — rough-hewn exotics who might as well've dropped in from outer space, for all I knew, and for how tongue-tied I got meeting them.

"...no different from you and me, though," he said, "same parts, same glands, same juices...."

And he sparkled like that, effervesced like that, at Carlsbad and the Santa Fe museums too.

Yes, I know. We were, Monte and I, outrageous, preposterous, way over every imaginable top. He was, in fact, far, far less than my fantasies made him. I knew that, and I didn't care. It didn't matter, not essentially, for now, for these minutes, if he pretended or exaggerated or fabricated or conjured: such forms, such modes, don't signify when you're caught by magic, swept away by an incarnate magic compelling faith in illusions. So I didn't care, except about his wacky plans for seminary, and those I could shelve, at least on Wednesdays. Otherwise, I pretty much let him take over, run the show, run *me,* like Scotty had tried to. It was as though Monte had earned me, won me, although I hadn't much resisted, and the Jubilee competition wasn't stiff, except maybe from Corky, except probably from Corky. Monte had the old ring in my nose — clamped back in there pretty tightly after the blow-up over Dale — and never had to tug, until later. And when it finally dawned on me that I might be running up against the First Commandment here, well, I didn't care about that either. Because I couldn't help it, how I felt. But I didn't try to help it, either.

As Gaylord Bryce brought up the First Commandment there, I'd better introduce him. Gaylord Bryce has lived behind-the-scenes (but ever observing them) in my head since I was ten, not as an imaginary playmate but as a presence of that general species, only solemn and somber. Gaylord Bryce is a spectral shadow, a sheer, smoky spirit, only not even as visible as they might look, if you could spot one. Gaylord Bryce is an apparitional, phantasmal entity, a disciplinary, monitory agent who turns up whenever doubtful thoughts or intentions or temptations invite me to stray into forbidden territory, whenever and wherever mischief beckons or folly woos. I never see him; he never speaks; but when he is there, he is categorically, unmistakably there, here. He merely arrives as a silent alarm against imminent error. Gaylord Bryce is my blinking yellow caution light. Here's his story:

Already at ten, I'd gained something of a reputation for keyboard showmanship at revivals Father preached around central and south Louisiana but I'd never gone as far south as Marquette, Cajun country, where Catholics dominated. We'd left Madison in the Plymouth after Sunday dinner and driven the two-lane through acres of sun-baked cotton and then into dense corn flanking the highway and finally into the fields of sugar-cane spears so high and tight you couldn't see light between them: like so many needles of church steeples jammed together, those shoots stabbed at the sky, blotting out sky and distance, closing in, until deep into swamps south of Baton Rouge you couldn't see horizon or sky except right overhead and along the road, or feel any light at all. The highway slid, snake-like, through this tunnel of frowning black-green oaks and cypresses and spiky palmettos that pressed from both sides, drooped from above, trapped the heat, muffled the engine. Like dusty, moth-chewed old drapes, Spanish moss hung the branches, hiding something fearful and unspeakable. Thick, greenish-black vines coiled the cypress stumps whose gnarled and contorted roots grabbed at the mud, like monsters' claws, slick with sweat. And everywhere, clogging your nose and slowing your blood, the sour, green odor of scum-choked swamp-water. Cajun haunts: knit and split by a zigzagging, criss-crossing tangle of bayous with frogs and lizards and gators and snakes and other slimy, scaly, skulking critters poised to snatch or bite or sting or stain you: still as death, sluggish, olive-lit like skies turn before a tornado, the whole brackish, stinking bog camouflaging and concealing those alien, silent half-breeds squatting in stilted shacks or tottering lean-tos, scratching out subsistence however they could from earth and water. Those not voodoos were Catholic, Father said, the two sharing ritual traits. But a couple of intrepid Baptists had braved what was said to be the incivility of the tribes, and what was known to be the enmity of the priests, and established a mission in Marquette several years before.

About 5, we pulled off the dirt lane running alongside the church into the yard where a small crowd already gathered among the tables and chairs prepared for "dinner on the ground," as it was always called. Three large metal vats with tea, water, and lemonade sat in ice under a spreading oak.

By 8, a larger crowd — large and charitable enough to chip in $7.49 for my playing — seemed ready for the finish, whether brought there by Father's sermon or the heat and mosquitos, I can't say. Anyway, keying up "Just As I Am" as the invitation hymn, I noticed a woman moving along the lane outside, kind of edging down the far margin of it as though avoiding or hiding something: she wasn't exactly tip-toeing in her boots but she did sort of creep, as to escape notice? She wore denim overalls over a white, long-sleeved blouse, and a red John Deere baseball cap with her short brown ponytail pulled through the little window in back and tied with a red ribbon. A big golden hoop dangled from her earlobe on the near side and winked in beams from the exterior floods. A little black pouch of a purse swung from her fingers. The only one up on the dais, the only one facing that way, I alone could watch her through the floor-to-ceiling clear-glass windows lining the walls. And I alone saw her stagger and fall, though everyone of course heard the two shots.

And everyone scattered. I got hustled off, while Father went for a deputy, to spend the night at the preacher's place, where I remember listening from my bed to the dogs, near, then far, then circling nearer again, and to the noise of men shouting commands or curses or both in an unknown tongue, and it came over me what poor Eliza must have felt, scrambling for that freezing river. In the early gray light came a blood-roiling scream, the kind scared and wounded rabbits make, the kind that pops goosebumps on your arms because you're pretty damn sure you know what caused it, and the fainter, broken, quivering one that followed it and made the hard thudding beat against your pillow.

Father and the local preacher were still away by breakfast, but his wife — a plump, granny-type whose crinkled face looked like it had known happier days than this one — she told me that Gaylord Bryce had "done murder" from his front stoop at the end of the lane where he lived alone, and had "answered for it."

"Answered how?" I asked. "Who made him?"

"Never you mind, son," she said; "just eat your grits."

"Did they lynch him?"

"It's all right," she said. "It's all done over now."

"But they cut him up first, didn't they?"

"Just eat, son. You want some red-eye on it?"

"Was it a posse? I bet it was."

"Yes, a posse."

"From the church, wadn' it?"

"Nobody can…nobody will prove that," she said.

"Why not?"

But she clammed up, just carried on about my playing. Father wouldn't say either, on the way home, except to echo her, as though they'd agreed on the script: "It's better not to think about, Troy. Try to put it out of your mind. Pretend nothing happened." And maybe I might've, I don't know, after I'd spent the $7.49, if I hadn't stumbled on the full truth in a Madison *Messenger* clipping Mother had tucked into her Bible, I guess because Father was mentioned in it and quoted as a witness at the inquest.

Gaylord Bryce had killed a man, Max LaRousse, not the girl I saw in the lane. I mean, he'd shot the *person* I'd watched walking past the church, but she wasn't a girl. She was Max. Word got around that Gaylord Bryce had hollered and swore and screeched that *he'd* thought her female, too, one Emmilene Hebert (pronounced "A-bear") who, the paper said, owned a "house of business" on the shady side of Marquette's tracks and had financed Bryce's renovation of the abandoned downtown pool hall and then watched his mismanagement bankrupt it, and had lately brought a very public suit against his home and land to recoup her losses, so that the feuding, said the paper, had gone mean and threatened to get nasty. Bad blood between

Max LaRousse and Gaylord Bryce dated back to high school rivalries for girls and thereafter routinely erupted over just about anything, locals claimed — politics, race, religion, sports — and last Friday in a fistfight around a domino table in the town square when both accused the other of cheating, and Max pulled a knife. The clipping went on and on about these squabbles and strife but I lost interest beyond the basics. What caught me instead was Gaylord Bryce's *mistake*! What seized and held and focussed my concern was his blunder, his miscalculation. Oh, sure, he might've been drunk, as the paper said he often was, and the dusk might've dimmed his vision; but, still, he misread; he mistook; he misinterpreted. I couldn't get over the plain, bald, stupid *error* of it. And what really knocked me out, what hounded and haunted my dreams for months afterward, was that both of us, Gaylord Bryce and I, and we two only, had made the *same* mistake: at effectively the same instant, we had both misidentified a live person, and he was dead of it, with a rope around his neck and a pitchfork in his gut, hanging out there like ragged moss in that foul and rotting swamp. Gaylord Bryce was dead for thinking a man was a girl.

* * *

"You like it here," Monte said quietly, to himself as much as to me.

I liked it the way I liked most things, except maybe him and Corky: sort of, with reservations.

"It's okay," I said. "Hadn't we better get back to the others?"

The others, a little dimmed by distance, splashed about in the shallows and scampered along both banks a quarter mile or so upstream from where we knelt on a slab of rock sloping down into the Pecos. Deep here, it slipped, glassy, between the tall cliffs, reflecting them, slowed to serenity. A light breeze, nippier by the minute, moved down the canyon, raised goosebumps on my neck.

"What, to Robyn?" he said. "Why?"

"That dope."

"What does that even mean, 'dope'? And what do you actually mean by calling him that?"

This seemed downright peculiar to me. Here we were on Wednesday afternoon away from Jubilee in horsing-around terrain if ever I saw any with no wardens in sight; and here he was — quiet, pensive, asking classroom questions about "meaning," for heaven's sake!

"Well he is," I said, "a textbook case."

"He's fat and foul-mouthed and meddlesome and jealous. Does that add up to 'dope'?"

"You left out whore."

"Whore, then...on Wednesdays around Da-Dallas. I repeat, does that add up...?"

"And whadaya mean 'jealous'?"

Okay, so I knew. I just wanted him to spell it out.

"Of me. Of you. Of me and you. Of Wolf Warren. Probably of everybody else. All of which is why he'll make a crackerjack preacher."

"Wait. What? *What?!* Robyn wants to be a....?" I couldn't even spit it out.

"It isn't a matter of want. It's a calling. He's felt the call, just like me."

Don't do that! I wanted to scream. *Don't ever say that! Don't ever say that about you and him! It's not true!*

What I said was: "I don't believe it. And I don't care."

"I thought you knew. He'll apply to the New Orleans seminary."

I took a second to breathe, shook my head, gathered my wits: "Let's see if I've got this straight: you just said Robyn's already guilty of at least four of the seven deadly sins, and that's going to make him a crackerjack…?"

"Robyn knows all those faults about himself, all his little flaws and tics; he admits them, doesn't try to cover up. He's honest and above-board about who he is, and he knows his best chance for learning how to handle them, how to turn to advantage his little foibles and frailties, maybe even getting shed of them, is seminary. Don't you know that cut-throats become surgeons, pyromaniacs firemen, and bullies policemen?"

"And dopes preachers? I think I've got it straight now."

"Low blow," he said, shaking his head.

I happened to know that theory about murderers and the rest from a magazine article; and I also pretty much knew his logic was askew, his smart-alecky parallels crooked. But I didn't know how to say how.

"You've got nothing straight, and you needn't get bitchy. Why can't you like him? What's your problem?"

"You said it was Wolf," I countered, grabbing the opening to quit a topic — or topics — that annoyed, puzzled, and oddly ruffled me. "Look," I went on; "Is this Warren person really as good as you said? As Robyn said?"

We hadn't — because he hadn't let me — talked about our "problem" since he'd named it one. "Put it out of your Trojan mind for a while," he'd said, like Father did of Gaylord Bryce. "Just forget all wolves, no matter what their colors! We'll work it all out in good time." Which advice I'd followed with zip success.

"At quarterback he's the greatest," Monte said. "And Robyn must be right about his speaking."

"Why 'must be'? Robyn's only trying to make himself look good by building up Wolf. He can't be that sensational. Wouldn't take much to whip Robyn."

"Hold on, Troj. I've done a little research for you. Robyn's got clippings, pictures and all, from the Baptist state paper, carries them in his wallet…"

"He would."

"…and showed me. Arkansas Baptists are wild for Wolf, already comparing him to Dr. Graham and Criswell and Abernathy and the rest of them. But you know what, Troj? I think you can take him. I think you can beat Black Wolf Warren. If."

He stopped there and stared at me, his face blank but for the eyes, full of cold black fire. I made him wait, uncertain myself of the conditional and wary of his possible exploitative use of it. What choice had I really, though, but to ask?

"If what?"

"If you really want to, of course."

He maintained the hard stare for a bit, looking straight through my eyes, hunting around behind them for something or other, although I couldn't have told you myself, for sure, at that point, what was there, except a lot of dizzying, confounding perplexity.

"I've been thinking," Monte finally said. "How'd you feel about me coaching you some?"

"I'd need to consider it," I said, stalling. "I mean, what do you know about....?"

"And Corky, too; he's pretty cool with the ad lib."

"There's no ad lib. It's all fixed. Memorized."

"And also Lance. You know how he talks, all formal and proper. And Robyn."

"Robyn! Are you nuts? You heard what he said, back in the room. He'd never...."

"He will if I ask. He'll do it for me."

Well, what might you have done? To win or not to win: a question I didn't know how to answer. Losing wouldn't pose a problem, I figured, if that's what I wanted to happen. This Warren character didn't sound like another Drum, taking pratfalls and preaching tired old sermons everybody'd heard before, not if he was forever thinking like Monte said. He needn't be Cicero to crush Robyn. And yet Monte appeared to want this hero of his to get licked — which I wouldn't have minded, except that it probably meant my winning, depending on the strength of the other competition which we had no present means of calculating. Whipping Wolfe was one thing; winning was a whole mess of others, the way I figured it. And beside all the fawning drool I'd have to splash through if I did win, and all the bonehead assumptions, imagine what'd happen if I didn't: think how squelched I'd feel, how mortified, how disappointed family and church and friends would feel, especially if Monte and the others out here helped me prepare, as he'd offered. And why *did* he offer? Why'd he even care whether I won since he must've guessed I wasn't that keen to try. I'd *told* him I wasn't! Lance and Corky would be all right, and maybe Scotty too, if really I did have to rehearse for them. But Robyn? True, Robyn might know if and where Wolf was soft, but then he might just as well trick me, lie about Wolfe and tactics, to engineer my loss. He had reason enough to connive at my defeat, and Monte knew it. So why bring Robyn in? Why take the chance? Unless...unless Monte *didn't* want me to win, wanted instead to save his hero (from *me?*) and planned to use Robyn for that? After all, they'd colluded over those confounded clippings, even after he'd kicked Robyn out of our room. And Monte seemed mighty all-fired eager to explain and forgive Robyn's rotten conduct and warrant the cure for it. Moreover, if you think about it, there's a fishy little twist in what Monte said — "He'll do it for me" — that Gaylord Bryce and I didn't like the smell of, not one bit.

"I don't know," I said. "Let me think about it. We better get back to the others now."

"No," he said; "let them play." He bent toward the water and trailed his fingers against the current. "No, because you do like it here, away from them. With me. That's why you think we oughta go back," glancing over his shoulder and frowning. "Right, Trojan?"

I felt funny, kind of queasy in the stomach and wobbly in the head: a little cross, a little thrown: muddled and nervous. "Maybe," I murmured. "It's just that they might be wondering, you know, what we're doing."

"Let them. Aren't you wondering the same thing?"

Yes, I'd practically leapt at the offer to take this short hike. But he'd seemed so reserved along the way, pre-occupied, and once here, so serious and reflective, so focussed on Robyn and Wolf and the contest, but also holding back, holding in something you couldn't quite put your finger on but messing with your head anyway, developing an air of suspense thick with tension, like right before the curtain rises or between the lightning and thunder when you know Something is about to happen but not what or how close to you or how you'll take it — all this Monte and his magic (was it black?) had conjured up, and it all came together in an eerie apprehension of when...*when*?

"Yeah," I said, "what are we?"

"Ah, yes," he breathed, after a pause, "that really *is* the question, isn't it? Philosophers' meat and potatoes from Socrates on — you know about him? That one, and why we are."

"Doing," I said, belatedly. "I meant what're we doing, off down here?"

"I know what you meant but you didn't ask that. There's a difference. Unless you think what we are and what we do are the same. Are you what you do?"

"More likely, I am what I think. You know, Descartes and all." This kind of show-off, smart-ass remark got me into trouble all the time. (Where is Gaylord Bryce?) I know I'm wading in way over my head and yet I rashly press on anyway. We'd never talked like this before, Monte and I, heading toward serious serious, as he'd once said, and if it was half-scary, it was also half-invigorating, this exposure of a new side of him and a new (was it new?) angle of interest in me. So I didn't quite want to retreat or divert: I might as well dare to make that Something happen and get it over with. "Or maybe," I plunged on, "maybe I am what I *don't* do?"

"And you don't do what you think?"

"Of course not. Neither do you. Nobody decent does."

"You're sure," he said, in neutral.

"Well, it's pretty risky, idn' it, to go around doing every-thing you think about doing, paying no never mind to other folks, other people's rights; I mean, it's pretty selfish, idn' it, and egotistical and, well, like, insensitive. You're talking anarchy — chaos — if everybody did whatever he thought and just as he liked. That's crazy. That gets you jailed." I was talking very fast, thinking: *No, not invigorating. Not even interesting. Let's finish this and get out of here. Nothing here is working right. What am I doing? Why am I letting him do this to me?* "I mean, that's what laws are *for*, to keep folks from doing what they think." *After all, Gaylord Bryce was dead for doing what he thought, and we in trouble for singing Piaf, and Robyn a dope and Dallas a pimp.* "And besides all that, if you 'always and exactly' do what you think, you leave yourself wide open, don't you, like at bay? And not just to the law, either: you can get hurt, paid back by every-body you've run over doing what you thought. You can get hurt, and you deserve to get hurt, if you hurt them." I almost panted.

"It's risky, all right," he said, brass in the voice. "That's the fun of it." But he wasn't laughing.

He rolled onto his back, propped his elbows at the water's edge, stretched his legs alongside mine, faced me: flaring nos-trils, daring eyes.

"It's risky," he repeated, tugging at a curl, "unless other peo-ple think like you do. And if I'm talking anarchy, you're talk-ing lying and dishonesty and hypocrisy. And you're confessing, Troj; like it or not, you're actually confessing. To dishonesty, first, and to selfishness and to fear. And by golly, if you were't so afraid, if you weren't so almighty terrified, you — not me — *would* be a revolutionary, wouldn't you? You might as well confess it. I know anyway."

"You don't know squat, and *I* don't know what you're talking about. All I said was, nobody does what they think. For very good reasons. And you don't either."

"But I *do*. Not 'always and exactly,' maybe; it depends on the person and the situation — but I mostly do. Like right now, for instance...."

"And I'm not confessing...to anything. Whod'you think you are, that I should confess...?"

"Like right now, for instance."

But I wasn't taking any more bait. "Listen," I said, sitting up, "I truly don't know what you're getting at. Fishing for. You asked me whether I am what I think, and I tried, I mean I really tried to give you a straight answer, the best I could to such a dumb question. And you *accused* me, you accused *me*...."

"You answered me," he said, softening a little; "and your answer, I guess you expect me to believe, is what you are. But I wonder, I can't help wondering after being so much around you for so long, living with you, I can't help wondering if you're telling the truth — even if you believe you are. Because, don't you see, you're assuming that what people think is what they *want* to do but *don't* do, or won't do. You're equating thoughts with desires, and making every act a denial of them, a betrayal of them. And you're leaving no room at all for pleasure, for *fun*! Do you really believe everyone's that unhappy? Are *you*, God forbid! Do you actually believe that everybody's that frustrated, that neurotic and sick?"

"I think you're trying to make us all liars and hypocrites."

He sighed: "No, Troj, I'm not trying to make you anything you aren't already or don't want to become. If you're a phony or whatever, you're a phony or whatever without any help from me.

Are you? When's the last time you didn't do what you thought about doing?"

I could see Father standing waist-deep downstream in the river, his hand reaching toward the bank.

"All right," I said. "Okay. Sometimes, maybe. Maybe sometimes I do what I think. Sometimes not. Like you, okay?"

"Not like me. Not yet anyway. What about the other part, the secret part: the part of you that thinks and wants but doesn't get. Sound interesting?"

"Could be," I said, faking a nonchalance I could not feel. *For Father had moved nearer the bank, his open palm and spread fingers pawing for it.*

"I meant, what do you think about."

"I know what you meant but you didn't ask that. There's a difference with you. Like me, you're not doing what you're thinking, which proves my point."

"Touché," he said, grinning. "But let's push it, just to see. All right, then, what do you think about?"

"About how the others must be wondering what we're doing." *Father had stopped but the others swarmed around the spot he reached for on the bank.*

"The others," Monte sneered, whether put off by them or me, I didn't know. He turned away, again sighing, then brightening: "Yeah, and very likely what we are and why we're doing it. I hope so, because they never would understand. But you..." and those hot bright eyes drilled me again, "I think you can. If you want to, and try. C'mon, slide over here and have a look."

C'mon, they'd all by their surging toward me seemed to say. Come on, come on!

He shifted to the side of the rock where backwash lay in a deep, still pool. "Right there," he said, pointing at the two dim faces staring back at us, "is what we are. And that's also what we're doing."

"Doesn't say much about what we're thinking, though. Isn't that what you were…?"

"Yes, but wait. What we are and doing. Just there."

"Two kooks eyeballing themselves in the Pecos, you mean."

"Not kooks necessarily," he said. "Faces, just faces. Now watch." And with one finger he traced in large capitals across the reflections M, O, N, until he'd spelled the name. The faces rippled, ruffled, disintegrated on the water, then floated together again.

"Now you, " he said.

"Monte, I really don't see the point…."

"Now you."

And now you, Mother had said as I stood trembling, the last, the showstopper, the one all those others had been waiting for, the reason they'd gathered. Father beamed at me, water from previous baptisms still splashing against his chest. Mother nudged me toward his hand. The eyes of the others, the eye of the sun, burned into my back as I stepped, shrinking, into the water.

I carved the letters, a mirrored finger reaching up to mine. Again the faces wrinkled, vanished, drew together.

I'd watched Father perform the rite hundreds of times but never without fear: that he, forgetful, might bungle his lines, mangle the convert's name; that he, slight, might drop one of those heavyweight river-boatmen and spoil propriety with unseemly splashing and sputtering; that he, careless, might hold them under too long and raise not a newborn being but a dead one; that he, my Father, who couldn't swim, would, someday, lose his footing, slide away on the current, strangle among the razor-bladed sedges of the riverbed. No such fear blighted Mother's bathing me, cleaning and caressing at once, giggling gaily with me, squeezing sponge-water over my head, down my ribs. And yet she pushed me at him; they all, I knew, shoved me toward the top half of him bobbing out there in the deep water.

"So not boneheads necessarily," Monte continued, "because '*bonehead*' is just another name. So even if we behave like boneheads, that needn't make us one. Or if you behaved like a Trojan, or thought like a Trojan, that wouldn't automatically make you Trojan. The same's true of 'Christian' and 'Baptist' and 'Catholic' and 'Communist' and 'Democrat' and even 'whore' and 'pimp.' The point is, they're all just labels — other kinds of faces — convenient, even essential. But you saw what happened when you tried to give it to yourself. You dissolved."

The two reflections — my thin frame, his out-reaching hand — closed on the surface, almost touched. I shivered, and the water carried it to him.

"Essential I mean negatively," Monte said. "They have to be wiped out, forgotten, just like the faces, our faces, have to be erased if we're ever going to be, and know we are, anything except what they show us to be and say we are. Mainly, they're distractions."

"In obedience to the command of our Lord and Savior...." His left hand reached for the sun behind my back, his right — cupping the handkerchief like a mask — lay on the water against my chin, threatening to crush my face, erase it.

"What we are, then, isn't our names or faces or just what we do: what we are, fundamentally, is down under there, in that deep dark water. And what we're doing, out here right now and at Jubilee all summer, you and me, is trying to learn what *is* down there, way down, deeper than we've ever gone before. Because we have to learn that before we'll ever know what we can and should become. If we don't know what's way down there, we can't plan our future…know how to prepare for it, make it happen."

"…*and upon your profession of faith and pledge of allegiance to Him….*"

"And what we're going to find out is what you think… about…and why you are what you don't do, if it's true you don't. It's down there, that secret, somewhere. And we have to go after it. Because what we'll become, you and me, depends, positively and negatively, on what we are right now."

"…*I therefore bury the old life that was, and baptize thee, my son Timothy Troy Tyler, into the new life to be, in the name of the Father….*"

The sun burst, and spears of light pricked my eyes as he tilted me backward, and I heard the other voices murmuring from the bank.

"…*and of the Son….*"

He flattened the handkerchief across my face, the fishy stench of it gagging me: blotted me out.

"…*and of the Holy Spirit.*"

My knees went limp as he dragged me under, and his left arm slipped off my back and he grabbled with his right, his nails scraping my cheek as I slithered free of it; and I wrapped my knees in my arms and sank, sank down and away, off and away with sweet glee, with aching bliss sank over the ledge and abroad on the current: sank to the bottom and settled there, his white mask flattening on the flood while his thrashing arms sliced wide swaths, hooked and writhed and arched, spun broad circles, seeking, far above me. For an instant I was safe there, the mud a soft lap, the water cradling, rocking me. And then I watched his feet moving toward the ledge, inching along it, fingers groping. And I sprung, shot from the water and churned toward the bank and into Mother's arms, surprise at survival mixing with rage, anger erupting in sobs, for he shouted, somewhere behind me:

"This is our beloved son...."

Blasphemy! my mind howled at him. Sacrilege! How dare you?!

"...in whom we are well-pleased."

"No-o-o-o-o-o!" A protracted roaring bellow. And a drop spattered the faces, smashed them.

"Are you crying?" Monte said, and reached toward me.

"Don't," I said, and looked at the hand on my arm. "It's nothing."

"Hey, did I say something?"

But Steph's shrill summoning whistle pierced our quiet.

7

Sunday: 5 a.m. DMT: Monte leaning out our door, shouting: "Mush, you huskies! Mush, I say!"

Sunday: 6:30 a.m. CDT: Father leaning in our door, singing: "Good morning, Breakfast Clubbers, morning to ya!"

Charming, right? Some choice, right? Sergeant Preston yelling or Don McNeill chirping. I could've used more sack-time.

But that's how they kicked off Sundays, the principal day of the week in Madison as at Jubilee; and except for our Scrub-Squadding duties, the days unfolded similarly in both sites, like mirror images of each other: Sunday School, Morning Worship, a big dinner, an afternoon break for "meditation" (or, if you were pouty, for clearing your head of the a.m.), Training Union, Evening Worship, followed by some manner of young people's "social," which I've already mentioned but now need to lay out so you'll fully understand its intended function and effect beyond just "letting off steam." They could be, these socials, about as social as a wake, because whoever managed them ("wardens," I said) never let you forget it was still Sunday; but they could also, if we the subjects of them broke out and got crazy and took them over and made them our own — they could also become jolly if kind of juvenile fun. In Madison, for example, we'd sometimes head out for bowling at the Lucky Strike — Percy, Eugene, Billyclyde, the whole pack of us — and just as sure as you guttered your ball, Miss Geraldine Null, our Sunday School teacher, would pipe up:

"Is that where your mind is, Troy? The ball goes where your mind is. Get your mind out of the gutter and you'll do better."

With her so well-informed about it, I figured Miss Null's mind must've been there too, because a lot of the time she was right about where mine was. Or out at Link's Links and Putting Pasture (Link was an ex-con and mulatto; and since nobody knew who fathered him, that's all he ever was, just Link, living in a shack behind the property and running the place for Mr. Spraddle, Father's head deacon who also owned two gins and the John Deere store and so could afford to set Link up after jail) — if we went putting, we had to pretend the balls were these various sins we'd done last week, actually name and re-name them, like Envy and Lying and Sassing and Pride at every hole; and when you sank one, that meant you'd buried that particular sin for the time being. And if you couldn't think of another one at the next hole — could *you* have come up with eighteen? — Miss Null always had one handy, usually Lust. She knew a mighty lot about sins, for a warden. But maybe that's how she learned, being one. Or why she nailed the job in the first place. Yes, it was all puerile inanity. But what else were we to do?

The Jubilee post-service Sunday hour was the same, of course, only more so, with about one Null, male or female, for every five or six kids and no bowling alleys or putting greens, so you had to get along without props. We'd pick up Butterfingers and jellybeans and sodas at the snack bar and group around the fireplace — its orca-mouth still yawning at you — for games. Yeah, games, at our age, all of them just plain stupid and hokey. You'd spare me trouble if you could imagine some but I doubt you can — much less ever played such bonehead games, so I'll have to describe one. Here goes:

(slap your thighs)　　　　(clap)　　　(snap)　(clap)

Everyone: "Who stole the cookies from the 　 cookie jar?

　　　　　(slap)　　　　　(clap)　　　(snap)　(clap)

#1: "Number 4 stole the cookies from the 　 cookie jar."

　　　　　(slap)

#4: "Who sir, me sir?"

　　　　　(clap)

#1: "Yes sir, you sir."

　　　　　(snap)

#4: "No sir, not I, sir."

　　　　　(clap)

#1: "Who sir, then sir?"

(slap)   (clap)   (snap) (clap)

#4: "Number 3 stole the cookies from the   cookie jar."

(slap)

#3: "Who sir, me sir?"

But if #3 didn't remember in time who she was — which number she was — before the next clap, and accuse another number of the theft, she'd go to the end of the line and we'd all move up. And the rounds went on and on like that, faster and faster, and louder and louder until we yelled and laughed and fell all over each other in giddy hysteria.

See what I mean? Pretty dim, huh? You could, if you were clever, vary the chant in other contexts and improve upon it, as Monte did one night walking back to the dorm after: "Who got to Martha in the wet flower-bed?" he asked.

"I don't know," I said, "who?"

And he had to start slapping and clapping before I got it.

Understand, now: all of these games were very physical exercises, and kept us mobile while still mostly stationary. I mean, we weren't exactly training for track and field but we never stopped moving either, not for long. Together with all that slapping and snapping, we were forever standing and sitting, bending and kneeling, crossing and uncrossing our legs, facing left and right and back again, smacking hands against our neighbors', linking and unlinking arms with them — always,

always to a hard heavy rhythm from stamping feet or clapping hands or maybe a marching song or a Null banging a tom-tom lifted from a display case: a steady knocking throb, like a metronome whose ticks tocked louder with every beat. It wrought your blood — you know? — hammered at your glands, kind of like horsing around in the Sweat Shop did. You could get hyped, never mind how dumb you felt. Sometimes the dumb got lost in the hype.

These recreational intervals, though, were ingeniously shrewd, foxy even, as warm-up sessions for the main event. What followed was the pitch, the hard sell, when you were worked-up and hot, whipped down and sweaty, and just wanted…well, it's hard — and risky, tricky — to say just what we wanted but it couldn't have been what we got. That's when they especially didn't let you forget it was still Sunday. The Nulls would divide us into small groups of four of five each, herd some toward the lake, head others to the prayer-gardens, and if all the dark, private spots were taken, they'd make for a dim corner of the lobby or a dorm, and then start in on you.

But that particular Sunday, the one after the Pecos River excursion, feeling a mite low, I drifted away from our group to be by myself for a while: maybe it was the sermon — it was the one about Ishmael and his exile to the desert for being a bastard (not that the preacher used the word); or maybe I missed our Sunday afternoon horseback-riding adventures (escapes from the recommended "meditation" rigor) — with Eugene and Percy and C. J. and Billyclyde, missed racing along the turnrows and hunkering down behind stumps on Plaquemine Bayou and shooting the heads off sunning turtles with our .22's, missed how we'd sometimes carry on later, toward dark. Or maybe I was a little homesick, missed being there, at home on Sunday night, with my people, if golf got rained out or the Nulls ran out of games and hidey-holes: how the family would lounge around the TV with cold chicken sandwiches on white bread with mayo, and popcorn and sweet milk…while Sunday petered out:

Father: munching on what popcorn he didn't dribble across the rug, checking out Arlene Francis and that diamond-heart necklace she always wore, maybe studying how to buy Mother a fake one like it; chuckling and wagging his head and going pink-faced over smarty-pants wisecracks from Bennett Cerf and John Daly. He wasn't so hot on Dorothy Kilgallen: "She bullies them," he said; "she's hard, not gracious like Arlene," as though he and Arlene were pals. Cerf bullied them too, I thought, in a sleazy-greasy way for a man, and pouted when he lost. But Father never noticed that, perhaps because they favored each other in the head, both of theirs slick and shiny, and because Cerf sat next to Arlene. Father had been bald since twenty-five, but he'd turned it into an asset, made clever jokes about it before you could, sometimes predicted a similarly bare pate for me, and got laughs for that too, if none from me. Stretched on his recliner, feet up, he lay reposed, motor off, cooling down, glad like me to have done with the toughest day of the week, not showing it if disappointed or grumpy because none of his exhortations and alarms from the pulpit had paid off.

Mother: puttering with dishes and padding out to the kitchen and back, and force-feeding us: that was Mother's "line," force-feeding food (like Father did religion): "C'mon," she'd urge, "eat! It'll stick to your ribs. You want to grow up to be pretty like me, you eat what I set out." *She* ate hummingbird portions, but they stuck to her ribs, all right, and just where it counted too. Never quite quiet, never still, not really watching to see who the Mystery Guest was, she chattered about what somebody wore or said or did, or where they went for vacation and why couldn't we, or what sort of feathers she needed to order for the hats she fashioned for neighbor ladies. She fussed about with pillows and throws and magazines and books, dusted her ceramic bell collection and Father's antique bottles, my shells and brother Mark's rocks, her needles tick-clicking as she knit baggy, crazy-quilt sweaters and socks for her "boys," not meaning G.I.'s.

My brother is Matthew Mark, unluckier even than I in the biblical-names sweepstakes, as he got two. At age five, he took "Mark" and never afterward answered to "Matthew," never, anywhere (I liked the look and sound of "Mark Tyler" on his baseball roster): oiling his glove or squeezing on a hard rubber ball or sketching football plays with x's and o's and long dotted lines or razoring balsam for model airplanes or playing with broken-down old clocks or radios or car-parts he'd found over in Frenchie's junkyard, and talking mostly baseball standings and "stats," which he knew, for I'd now and then check the sports section, to be sure.

Now that I've recollected, though, I'm not sure homesickness drew me away from my Jubilee cohort that Sunday night. We know what familiarity breeds; and while I can't go that far, I'd rather have this silence than that noise, this privacy than that company: what I liked about the home parlor on Sunday night was the letting-down and loosening-up and cooling-off and breathing-spell ambience I could almost sense in us all when I'd snuggle back into the pillows of my rocker and let thinking rest.

Monte's voice rang out from the shower as I returned from my ramble: "'Ba-a-a-a-by face, you've got the cu-dest li-ddle ba-a-a-a-by face...,'" and then not from the bath at all but standing right there in front of me, inches away, rummaging through the clothes rack, his tanned shoulders sleek and beaded as though with bath oil. "'No one could ever take your place...'; oh, hi, didn't know you were home."

"Sorry," I said; "I should have hollered."

"Hollered what?" he laughed. back-stepping out of the closet in a thigh-length terrycloth; "Male call?"

"Male call" was what guys were supposed to yell upon entering Marigold Hall, the girl's dorm.

"I might've shrieked!" And he shrieked, and laughed, and started singing again.

The same song Father sang, driving me and grandpa to the hospital where Mother was, with Me-Ma, her mother, and a surprise, too, Father said, "the finest surprise of your little life."

"Better than Peg?" I asked, my biggest surprise so far. Once, when Mother's folks visited us in Madison, grandpa had bought Peg for me, not for Christmas or birthday like the rocker and the pogo-stick but, he said, hugging me, "just for love." If it sounds like a weird name to you, you don't understand how partial I was to that Mobile Oil horse, spinning atop the pole and pawing the air, and the story grandpa told about him and the springs and the stars.

"Better than Peg," Father said, through a big grin. "Better than a whole barn full of rocking horses, or real ones either!"

I looked at grandpa to verify, and he nodded his big, heavy head, slowly, three times, in this way he had, almost like he was dozing off, and smiled his wide, kind smile, and moved his fingers around in my hair, strong and soft. "Much better, son. You'll see."

"But at the hospital?" I said.

I'd never seen my sprightly Mother so still, lying there white under the white sheets in the white room in light so white and hard you could feel it pulling at you, like a magnet, draining the color out of you and making you pale so you'd fit in.

"How's my girl?" grandpa said.

"I'm just dandy, thanks," Me-Ma said, the gold in her teeth flashing and blue-silver stars winking her eyes and her five chins jiggling like jello. "Nice of you to ask. You *might've* asked after Prissy." Her face was all soft, moving folds from about a hundred years of smiling, like a pillow you want to put yours against, and feel it give.

"Still doing okay?" Father asked Prissy his wife.

"Mmmmmm," just a sigh, with a tiny piece of voice hanging onto it. "Much easier than Troy," her lips quivering. "Hey, Troy," and her long white arm reached for me.

"Hey," I said. "Is it catching?"

Grandpa's big laugh boomed, cracked the light, and Me-Ma's chins bounced and rolled, and Father burped a chuckle, and a bright tinkle of giggle, like one of her glass bells, tickled her lips.

"Not that I ever heard tell of," grandpa said, "and not if you're the man I think you are, from your grandpa's stock. No, son, you can't catch it."

"Are you coming home now?" I asked, slipping into the crook of her arm.

"Pretty soon," she said, and crooked me to the bedside. "I'm better now you're here."

"Now *he's* here," Father corrected. "And twelve days early. Hard to believe, after Troy. Nothing slow about this one."

"Which one?" I asked. "He who? Where's my surprise?"

"You haven't told him," she sighed, and closed her eyes.

"Tell me what?"

"You want to?" he said.

"No, you," and she reached back her arm and covered my hand with hers and trailed her fingers across it, raising goosebumps.

"Tell you what," Father said, after glancing at grandpa, who nodded, and Me-Ma, whose chins jumped: "I heard tell the hospital has this little baby boy, brand spanking new, that they just might give to us, to take home and keep, to be your little brother. They *might*, mind you, let us have him, *if* we all agree we *want* him, and that includes you, you most of all. So you have to think it over and decide if you want him. And if you want him for your brother, you have to ask them if you can, ask them nice and polite and proper, like you know how to, if we can take him home for keeps."

"A baby?" I said. "A baby boy brother?" The grin spread and joy bloomed and tingles raced around under my skin and star-tips prickled it like July 4th sparklers had ignited behind it until I couldn't stand it, standing still, any longer, and bounded, skipped around the room, bounced off the three of them, dizzy with the wonder of it, and clapping, and singing, "A baby! A baby brother! To take home!"

"But you have to ask them first," Father said.

So I asked Dr. Sawyer, could we, could we please have the new baby to take home, to be mine? And he frowned and pulled his chin and hemmed and said well maybe if I promised not to pick him up or feed him hard candy or cry when he did and to do my chores and help Mother out, well, then, maybe… and I promised, crossed my heart if we could have him to be my brother, please; and please, could I see him now, my own little brother?

And it was, I knew it was going to be, a happy-ever-after story. Except when, a few days later, Mother came home. When they took Mark in with them, to share their room, and closed the door. When they shushed my knocking, shushed me, said I'd wake up the baby, said go back to sleep. But I couldn't, for wondering. So I mounted Peg and rode him there in the dark, rode him hard and rough, rode him off that pole, galloped him out and over and away, across and beyond, harder and faster, thrashing his haunch with my belt, gripping, hugging his flanks with hips and thighs, my hot cheek against his surging neck until his foreleg detached from the rocker and lurched me off as it cracked, fractured, and split. Sprawled and gasping, I heard his faintly ticking limp and knew I'd fatally lamed my Peg.

* * *

I'd seen plenty of nude men before Monte — "Naked as a jay-bird," Mother would've said — turned into me, fresh from the shower and half-erect, there at the closet in our room. Of course I'd seen them in the locker rooms for gym class from fifth grade on; I'd seen them skinny-dipping with Billclyde and me and others in Plaquemine Bayou and at the big pond on Eugene's farm; skittering in and out of showers and up and down the halls of my college dorm; even around the house where brother Mark paraded his maturing form shirtless in shorts and bare feet; and in fine art books from the library where my favorite was the Michelangelo "David" with the amazing eyes and very cool slingshot. And I liked looking at them, mostly because they were mostly beautiful: proportional, contoured, lithe, shapely, tailored, elegant. Younger, I liked looking at other pictures of them — Jack Beanstalk and Prince Charming and Pinocchio and Aladdin, and then Tom Sawyer and Penrod as I imagined them from the stories; and in the illustrated Bible grandpa had given me of Adam and boy Samuel and hunk Samson and stud Joseph and young Moses and the same David over a laid-out Goliath. I suppose I've always found the human male form divine (to mangle Blake's line), although I know not to say so out loud: the beauty of it also charmed me because I don't have it, not in the way I mean here: not in body, which is why, skinny-dipping, I kept my T-shirt on when messing with the guys. I *envied* them their naked bodies, which tells you how effectual the Nulls' goofy golfball burying routine was. So when C. J. loaned me the comic book with the barbell ad inside the back cover, I determined to buff myself up for $29.95.

As my thirteenth summer had been lousy for revivals, for spending-money I'd been reduced to hustling Christmas card orders on long August afternoons. Embarrassing, that was, traipsing around Madison with Father's beat-up typewriter case packed with sample boxes, and jawing about Christmas in 95-degree heat. But once potential customers got past my sales pitch ("My stars!" they'd gush; "dear me!" they'd flutter: "Christmas cards already?"), these bony old no-lip spinsters with darting sparrow-eyes and buns screwing down their grey hair so tight they must've scraped skin, they'd invite me in for sweet milk and oatmeal cookies and, before ordering a box or two, always work in a little lecture on how short Mother's skirts were and how Father preached too much about the budget. Widowers were even likelier targets: their rooms stank of old and stale and pharmacy, and made you feel moldy yourself, and they'd go soggy at the word "Christmas" and then order five boxes. I felt sorry for them, to tell the truth, for I figured they didn't know a hundred people but I couldn't refuse an order without letting on I knew how lonely they were. The church deacons didn't exactly tickle my ribs either, especially not Mr. Spraddle, forever harrumphing in that rushed, blustery way busy businessmen let you see how busy they are; but they bought too, one token box, maybe figuring to secure their heavenly mansion by helping out the preacher's kid.

I already had my paper route, a 90-minute grind from 5 every morning and 4 in the afternoon delivering the *Times-Picayune* (on this side of the tracks) and the Madison *Messenger* to poor white trash (on the other) ("You call them 'brothers in Christ,'" Father said) along the Bayou. This was another embarrassment, and a dubious deal too. For at least once a week I'd have to ride against roaming, yelping dog-packs and mean, snot-nosed kids who got their jollies chunking gravel at moving objects: I'd hang my khakis in the bike chain, take spills right out of The Three Stooges with the rascals howling and the dogs yapping, and then listen to Mother fuss about patching the pants. I could bear it, though: I wasn't laying out cash for a chain-guard and she didn't offer to. What I truly hated about the job was begging payment from those deadbeats twice a month and never getting more than half they owed, and making up the difference from my Christmas card profits.

So I took up selling Bibles ("One cash dollar down and fifty cents every month for ten months, no carrying charge")

to Negroes ("You call them 'colored brethren,'" Father said),
Shadrach and Jambalaya and their neighbors who lived behind
the gins and who you could depend on to dig up that fifty cents
every month and right on time, too. This wasn't embarrassing
so much as uncomfortable and oddly worrisome: the thing was,
a lot of them didn't read; but, really, they didn't need to, in this
matter. I'd flip through the pages to find the "deluxe illustra-
tive artwork" (my instructions said) — "Samson Grinding at
the Mill," "Jacob Wrestling the Angel of the Lord," "The Good
Samaritan," "The Prodigal Son" — my best selling points, I
thought, and *they'd* start telling *me* the story behind them better than I could've. They especially liked the flowered blank
pages reserved for family histories — births, baptisms, marriages, deaths, etc. — and said grandchildren would fill them
in. They didn't much care for the maps — "Honey," said one,
"I ain't studyin' goin' there" — or the section called "Questions
and Answers" — "Sonny, I done had all my questions answered
a long while gone" — so since they knew the stories, I didn't
feel quite right about hard-selling the product. Once I said so to
Jambalaya, who sometimes helped out Mother in the kitchen;
but she replied, "Chile, you can't never have too many Bibles
in the house," reaching out a little black change-purse from between her breasts. I might have differed on that point but didn't
push it.

So I saved the quarters and dimes, the bills and the I.O.U's,
stashed them in a sock under my pillow; and how I could bear
not spending a cent of the growing collection was by watching
my brother Mark's body thicken and swell in all the right places;
and by nurturing my special, happy secret, knowing what would

surely come to pass, because the ad, now buried in a bottom drawer, promised to renovate my body for $29.95.

Monte, clad only in jockey shorts, stretched down the center of our room, doing push-ups.

"But when'll it start to show?" I asked Father. He'd seemed almost pleased when the set arrived, after making sure I'd tithed my profits, and didn't ask where or how I'd got it, though Mark did.

"They're super," he said. "Where'd you get them?"

The truth is, I was faintly embarrassed about having to get them, and didn't want Mark meddling. "None of your business," I said.

"How come you got them?"

"Don't be dopey," I scoffed. "You know what they're for."

"Yeah," he said; "I know. Do you?"

I flushed. "I know you're prying into noneoyourbusiness. So cut it out. I saved and bought them. They're mine."

"Can I use them when you're not?"

"So when'll I see something?" I asked Father.

"It's not so hard," Monte said, pushing hard, "once you get the rhythm. You know, it's a completely natural motion." He grinned. "Right, Troj?"

"Patience," Father said. " You need to learn a little patience, Troy. Patience and practice and persistence. Just like with your piano. Always keep at the three P's, to get anywhere in life. You can't expect miracles overnight."

Mark stood next to him, watching me.

"The trick," Monte said, "is to spread your hands away from your body (pant), and keep your legs and feet tight together, (pant), and catch yourself on the way down so you (pant) spring back up and don't have to push, and don't (pant) break your rhythm and lose momentum." He flattened, sucking air.

"*Not counting on overnight miracles,*" I sneered. "*I'm working, every day; I'm doing exactly what the book says, in front of the mirror and all, and nothing is changing. When will it?*"

Monte rolled onto his back, hooked his hands behind his head. "You might be a little sore the first couple of days, in your wrists and along your arms and in your shoulder joints, but that wears off...."

"*He's got blisters,*" Mark said; "*show Dad the blisters.*"

"*Well, then, you see?*" Father said. "*It's showing already. Those blisters will turn into callouses in no time. And those little aches and pains shooting around under your skin are just blisters, too, only invisible. Why,*" he squeezed Mark's biceps, "*muscles aren't anything but callouses trying to get out.*"

"*But when will they?*" I whined. "*The ad said by now. And I told C.J. already.*"

I expected a "What ad?" but he moved on. "*In due course, son. If you just keep at it. Remember the three P's! You have to work and wait. And have faith.*"

"It's a must-do," Monte said, rattling around his bottles and cans on the dresser top, "if you want to feel your best. Be your best." He paused to spread balm on his lips. "Brings blood to the surface, sends it zipping around so your whole body gets all fiery and tingly, you know? I promise, it can get pretty exciting. Besides, you don't work on your build, you can't expect to attract anybody, to get their hooks into you and set them there. The girls, well, the girls start developing sooner than we do, and sort of naturally, without needing to work out or anything. They just...ripen. But exercise is the only way we have for catching up to them, to even things out and make them notice what they see, and like it. Otherwise, they think we're little boys."

Was he actually talking to me, instructing me? Or just prattling on to pass the time and fill the space? Was he even conscious of me, aware I was there?

"A lot of guys," he continued, pulling up his jeans, "a lot of guys, I've noticed, think they can make it with a pretty face — take you, for instance: ain't nothin' wrong with sweet blonde hair and blue bedroom eyes and James Dean lips and lashes to make Scotty drool and — you never had pimples, did you? — and smooth tight skin. That's a head start, 'cause they notice above the shoulders first. But the second and third looks get their palms itching, when they check out shoulders and biceps and the rest of you. You've got to think about that and prepare for it. Look, Troy," — he turned to face me squarely, hands on hips: "It's none of my business or anything, but, well, what the hell, you've got good bones, a good frame, better than good, really, what, 5' 9," 125? — it just needs some solid muscle hung on it. It just needs some beef. Anybody ever tell you your body had lots of potential?"

"You have told me that and told me that," I said to Father, *"to wait and be patient and practice and it would all come right, and it doesn't and it's not true. The book said fifteen days and it's been twenty already and it's not true. I do what the book says and nothing changes, and with these blisters I can't even practice piano anymore. It's a lie, I know from my body in the mirror. And if you know so much about it and are so faithful and all, why aren't you strong like Mr. Tanner and never got anywhere in life? Whyn't you just take your stupid p's and cram them where the sun don't shine, dammit, for all the hell I care!"*

"Can I have the weights, then?" Mark asked.

"No," I said to Monte; "nobody ever told me that."

He had worked himself up. After we tucked in, cut the lights, and were quiet for a time, I heard him, turned to watch him, humping his mattress. And as he finished with a whimper, I touched myself.

* * *

"Can't he-a-a-ar you," Robyn called from the murky well at the rear of the auditorium.

Monte had assumed management of my participation in the Goforth speaking competition upon learning of it, without asking me, but only after Robyn's revelation of the Wolfe factor had he begun taking steps, presumably on my behalf. He'd called this early meeting, and secured Steph's permission to use the auditorium after the service dismissed for our "orientation and preliminary practice session to reconnoiter the premises," Lance called it, as though we weren't thoroughly habituated by presence *in* them four or five nights every week. Monte had rounded up members of our regular gang to investigate the site with the contest in mind, for word about the finals had circulated, thank you, Robyn, and the staff had grown curious, and interest and chatter of exactly the sort I dreaded had spread. A lot of the Jubilee student employees now seemed to know who I was and what was up, which was embarrassing even while the attention felt complimentary. Ta-Da of course was present, to collect any loose change lying about, and Lance, perhaps to edit my speech for elevation à la Adlai, and Corky, probably to leaven everything with his reliable good will, and Scotty because Corky was and to cast into pretty mode whatever happened and maybe to take notes for the newspaper that hadn't yet materialized, and Travis with tobacco and Lifesavers in case of need. Babs wasn't there, as no music was yet planned, although M&M (Martha and Mary) turned up, mistakenly thinking the Jubilates were rehearsing, and brought along Dale, who imagined he'd forgotten the date for the next practice session. Relations between Dale and Monte had coasted along routinely through rehearsals and performances, once Dale joined, if with a noticeably stiff formality and distance-keeping on Monte's part while Dale warmed up to the rest of us and we to him. Babs hadn't yet brought him forward as soloist, aware as were we all of Monte's presumptive ownership of the slot; and Dale appeared cooperatively content where he was. I believe all of us felt, though, and Robyn privately said, that our performances lacked the luster Dale would surely bestow upon them as soloist. He strode boldly down the center aisle with Mary hanging on one arm and Martha on the other, the three of them giggling and flirting, until Monte stepped into it holding out his open palm like a traffic cop. "Hold up there," he said; "why're you here?"

"It's not rehearsal?" Dale asked, looking around.

"It isn't," Monte firmly said, mild annoyance shading his voice. "We're working on a project."

"Need help?" Dale asked cheerfully. "We can."

"I doubt it," Monte said; "it's private."

"Secret?" Dale asked. "That's my favorite kind."

"It's not secret any more," I said.

"It's supposed to be private," Monte said, "and we prefer to keep it that way, if you don't mind. I'm afraid I must ask you, Dale, to leave."

"We do need to keep our *plans* confidential, Dale," I said; "but there's no reason you can't be trusted with them, once we make them. These good folks are helping me prepare for a contest."

"Oh," Dale said, "it's about the big speech, then. I heard about that from the girls." And after a second, "Oops!" He clamped a hand across his mouth.

"Shit!" Monte said.

"Actually," I said, "you might *could* help," an idea forming.

"I could try," Dale said, probably eager to redeem himself for the slip. "But Jesuit High didn't teach speech. And anyway, Catholic priests are pulpit pussies compared to your Baptist bible-beaters. I don't know anything about that."

"I'm not preaching," I said.

"Thanks for the offer, Dale," Monte said, and you could almost hear his grinding teeth, "but I don't think there's a place for you on this team. We need to get to work now. So if you don't mind...." He pointed toward the rear door.

"Now just a second," I said, standing up and waving the group toward me. "Gather 'round and listen up, people. You too, Dale. Monte? Put it on hold. Permanent hold, please. I have something to say." I paused, letting the moment collect consequence. I felt consequential.

"All right," I said. "Here's the thing: I'm betting that Dale Shivers is the only person in the room — on this team — who's ever actually witnessed a Goforth Finals Speaking event. Monte skipped last summer's runoff. He told me. But you, Dale, you were there, weren't you. You were right there — *here!* — in this very auditorium, and saw it all happen, didn't you. You watched, you heard contestants vie for the Goforth national title; and you heard and watched one of them win it, didn't you. You know how the whole complete operation, start to finish, unfolded and ran and ended. Don't you."

He nodded. "I guess I do," he said quietly, "if I can remember."

I turned to Monte: "How's *that* for a resource?"

He stepped up very close to me, his lips to my ear: "You don't sound like somebody ready to quit," he said.

"What'd he say?" somebody asked.

Robyn sang out again from the rear: "I can't HEAR you!"

"NOBODY'S TALKING TO YOU!" Monte yelled back, but took it as a signal to get started. "Okay," he said; "Okay, Dale. As long as you're already here. Everybody but Troy, scatter around out there so we can test for audio. Troy, get in position behind the pulpit and just recite the alphabet or something so we can get a read on your voice."

Aye, aye, sir. Ever the Captain.

"Still can't hear," from the back. "WOLF PROJECTS!"

"So PROJECT!" Monte said.

Projected alphabet letters followed while Monte sent Travis to find the hall light switches; then came "okay" signals from the pews, and Monte called everybody back to the platform, directed us to settle on the floor. "Here begins Operation Wolf-Wreck," he said; "here's how Troy wins!

"First, Lance: get a copy of the text from Troy and upgrade it to eloquence. No offense, Troy, but Lance knows formal. If you've already got it, Lance won't tinker. What we want is pithy. I want it dense and tight. Not long: max twelve minutes. And pay special attention to tempo, Lance, rhythm. It's got to have a beat."

"Hang on here," I interrupted, my blood rising. "You haven't even seen my speech yet, or heard it either. How do you know it's not already...pithy...and what else you said? It's already won three times. Maybe I don't want to change it, or have it changed. I'm pretty sure I don't want you or Lance messing with it."

From Lance: "Adlai E. Stevenson II said you can tell the size of a man by the size of what makes him mad."

"What's the speech about?" Scotty asked.

This checked my temper and impetuosity. I couldn't exactly say, "My dog Bruce," and I couldn't explain, to the group, how the speech made him a shining example of Christian virtue, not without getting laughed off the stage.

"I can't say before the finals. It's supposed to be confidential," I improvised.

Robyn waddled up from the back: "Nobody ever told *me* that," he said. "Besides, everybody's heard it three times. It's not a secret."

"I'd rather make it a surprise," I said. "And I don't want anybody fooling with it. I've got it memorized."

"What if you say it to Lance in private," Monte said. "Just let him hear it, and see if he wants to...well, suggest any...im-provements? You don't have to accept them. Just see if more formality feels right to you? Are you okay with that, Lance?"

"All things considered," said Lance, "I don't know. If I go to the inconvenience of hearing Troy deliver it and making notes for changes and improvements and refinements, and he doesn't approve…? When we take everything into account…."

"Lance," Monte said, "just do it. You okay with that, Troy?"

"I'll have to think about it," I said.

"You've got two days. Stand by, Lance. Somebody has to hear it before you go on, Troy. I probably better. But I'll do it in private too, if that's what you want."

"I may *not* want you to hear it first."

"Robyn," Monte turned toward him. "You make a list of Wolf's weak points. Anywhere he's shaky, vulnerable."

"That's nowhere," Robyn said.

"Then write down everything you can remember, every detail about what he said and how he said it, especially how: delivery's the key. Write it all down, and we'll figure where to nail him."

"I'm not sure," Robyn said, "about all this help we're giving Troy. I don't know whether it's fair, whether we should."

I'd actually wondered the same thing but was happy to let Robyn carry the challenge to the Cap'n.

"Nobody's said we can't. And besides, this is war. Everything's fair. And it's not as though we're doing anything Troy wouldn't do for himself if he could and had the time."

This may have been true.

"What about *me?*" DaDallas griped.

"What *about* you?" Monte countered.

"Well," Dallas went on, "for one thing, I've got this recording of General Lee's farewell to the Confederate Army at Appomattox, read by Reverend Edmund Jennings Lee the

Fourth — he's in the family — and he was a missionary to Asia somewhere, only Episcopal, for about twenty-five years, so he knows all about preaching, and it's so beautiful, how he reads, Troy might pick up some tips...."

"It's not preaching," I said; "it's speaking."

"...and you could borrow it for fifty cents a day or as long as you need...."

"I don't believe this," Monte groaned. Scotty and Corky were laughing.

"...until after the contest, anyway."

"Dallas," I said, "shut up!"

"Okay," he said, "a quarter a day."

"*Dallas!*" Monte said.

"I could help Troy dress," Scotty volunteered, "like for the ensemble. Does Robyn remember what Wolf wore?"

"I know what to wear," I said, "but Scotty can help me dress anytime she likes."

Everybody laughed, relaxing the tension a little. Scotty blushed.

"Ladies," Monte said to M&M: "Work your cameras. Get shots of everything: rehearsals, award announcements, the follow-up celebration. The yearbook should have heavy coverage. And the newspaper too. Scotty? And your other job, M&M, is to find out from SS the format for The Night Of — whether there's a regular service and whether the ensemble can perform. And get back to me."

"How can I help," Corky asked; "anything I can do?"

"Yes sir, there sure is," Monte smiled. "It's a big, important job, Corky, and you're exactly the right man for it. YOU are Troy's escort for the afternoon before The Night Of! I'll fix it with Steph so you'll spend the whole afternoon before he speaks that night distracting Troy from thinking about it. Are you listening, Troy? Your job, Corky, is to relax him, loosen him up, keep his mind on anything *but* the speech. I don't care how you do it — maybe involve the bike? — just keep him focussed somewhere else, or many places else, but not on the competition. Get him back to Cactus by 6 so he can shower and dress. Think you're up to it?"

"Wow," Corky breathed. "Just us two? All afternoon?"

"Is that yes or no?" Monte asked.

"Do I get a vote?" I asked.

"*I* can't do it, Troy," Monte said. "There's other stuff I've got to take care of in the afternoon. Let Corky do this."

"Sure I will," Corky said. "Of course!"

"Anything for me?" Dale asked.

"I'll think of something," Monte said.

You had to give him credit; you had to admire the efficient competence of his management — of us — even if he ticked you off by his smart-ass manner and his attempt to kick Dale out and to hijack my speech. But at least I now knew, almost for certain, that he wanted me to win this thing. Whether *I* did remained uncertain, but his commitment meant something, as did the interest of the others. But Monte's keenness also felt a little like competition. It was as though *he* had something to win too, by engineering my victory: as though ownership, possession, of something was at stake. What might *reward* this effort for *him* escaped me. And made me uneasy.

"So," I asked back in our room, "what's your assignment for Dale?"

"I said I'd think of something. But why don't you do it? You're the one who called him a 'resource.'"

"Well, he is. Obviously. Or should be. He was here."

"You said that. Several times."

"Don't you want to take advantage of it? Of what he remembers?"

"I think you should do it. You know what you need to know better than I do."

"You think?!"

"But you should grill him. Like you grilled him back there. Take him aside and press him hard, get every scrap of every detail out of him about that runoff: what they wore, how long they talked and what about, how they delivered, how they screwed up, who won and how, what kind of staging and props, how many judges and which sex, where the winner came from: we might even look him up. Make Dale remember stuff he doesn't know he knows. Get him talking about it for as long as he will. Take notes. Then tell me. Let's see just how good a 'resource' he is."

✳ ✳ ✳

The Sweat Shop was pretty much exclusively male terrain, so when Scotty swished through the swinging doors the next morning after breakfast, work almost stopped with surprise. She paused, spotted me, and walked right over — passing Corky without a look — purpose in every step. Corky got suddenly busier.

"Hey, Troy," she said. "I need a conversation. I'll wait for you on the porch. Meet me out there as soon as you're done here, okay?"

"Sure thing," I said, "but what's going on?"

"I'll tell you then." She turned and went, giving Corky the slightest of nods as she passed. His eyes followed her.

We hadn't chatted since the garden kiss and the newspaper wrangle, just exchanged heys and waves, and I knew I'd been neglectful, probably disrespectful, and felt a little embarrassed by what had happened then and what hadn't. And I hadn't yet given her a firm answer on the newspaper offer. I knew she was moving ahead with a plan, and had lined up Travis for cartoons and Lance for editorials, but nothing more about where it stood. She must have expected follow-up on both matters. She sat on the porch steps with her arms around her knees, her chin resting on them.

"Look, Scotty," I said, "I'm sorry I haven't come around since, well, you know...."

"This isn't about that." She stood up and faced me. "I'm not worried about that. A little curious, though.... It's not about the newspaper either, but my offer stands. It's something else. It's about Monte's plan."

"Which plan? What?"

"I think he called it 'Operation Kill the Wolf' or something like that. You know."

"'Wolf-Wreck.' Yes, what of it?"

"Let's walk," she said, and took a few steps in silence, broody. Then turned to me, interlaced her fingers in the prayer configuration, and clasped them under her chin, as if about to plead. "It's Corky," she said. But she said the name in a way nobody ever said Corky's name. There was no grin in it. The tone was serious serious. She went silent again and moved slowly on. I felt a chill.

"What about him? We just left him. He seemed fine. What?"

"I have to tell you something about Corky, Troy. It's something important you should know. But it has to be completely confidential. You cannot say a word about it, not to anyone."

"Seems like a mighty lot of secrecy going around these days, have you noticed?"

"This has to be top secret. No kidding."

"What?" I asked; "is something wrong?"

"No. Nothing at all is 'wrong.' Don't think that."

"So what? What's happened? What're you saying?"

"Troy," she looked me directly in the eyes and said quietly, "Troy: Corky's queer."

I almost laughed. She had to be joking. But she wasn't laughing. "No, he's not," I said flatly. "You're kidding. Why would you kid about something like that? He's not."

"He is. It's why we don't date. He's known forever, and he doesn't care. I mean, he doesn't mind it. His folks know, and they don't mind either. He just has to be very careful out here."

"I don't believe you. You're putting me on. So stop. He's not...what you said. Corky couldn't be that."

"It's not up for debate, Troy. He can be and he is. And he wants you to know it."

"*What?* Why would he want me to know something like that?"

"He likes you."

"Well, of course I like him too...I mean, wait. Wait. What do you mean?"

"I mean he likes you; thinks you're cool. But he's afraid to tell you...about himself. He's afraid you'll be mad, hate him.

It's happened. So he asked me to tell you. He's trusting you with a secret nobody here knows. But he thought you might. And that's okay with him. And then Monte put you two together for the afternoon before The Night Of and I figured I'd better tell you, before then."

"But I'm not...you know."

"Nobody's saying that. Corky just likes you; he wants to know you better. Run with you, only you're always with Monte. He'd like to be friends."

"He's everybody's friend. He *is* my friend. I just never thought...."

"Which is why he wants you to know."

"But he's just so...you know...*normal.*"

"Of course Corky *is* normal. He just happens to like guys the way some guys like girls. It's nothing bad or wrong. For him it's the most natural thing in the world. And he's not ashamed of it. You shouldn't be either."

"I don't know," I said; "I really don't know what to say or think. You're sure this isn't a trick? I can't hardly believe Corky is like that."

"Name it, Troy. Call it 'queer.' Call it 'homosexual.' Corky does. I do. The name isn't going to bite you. 'Infect' you. It's a step, naming it."

"I don't know. Does Monte know?"

"Not that we know of. And we don't know if we trust Monte to know. You cannot tell him. Corky wants you not to tell anyone, at least not until Jubilee is over, and so do I. We're trusting you to keep it completely confidential, unless you want to talk about it with Corky. He'll do that. But it would ruin him, you know, if word leaked out; and he's actually having a very good time here. He just thinks he'd have a better one if you knew. And I agree. But you must promise me — promise us — to keep it a secret. As a favor to me?"

"When did Corky decide? *How* did he decide?"

"It's not a decision, Troy. It's a recognition. He recognized it when he couldn't *not* recognize it"

"I think I'd better go now, Scotty. I actually need to go now. I'll tell you good night now. Thanks, I guess, for telling me. Tell Corky hey."

"Mum, Troy!" she said, forefinger at her lips.

* * *

Gobsmacked is the British term for what I was, first by Monte's masterfully designed strategy for my winning the speech competition. But it was almost as disturbing as it was impressive for the intensity — remember what I wrote about that? — of its focus on, well, me. I think the focus had vaguely unsettled me from the start, but I'd set aside the unease in the pleasure of the notice. But the force and the concentration of the notice were so enchanting, his hanging out with me so pleasing, that it frightened me, even as at the Pecos he teased and puzzled and even hurt me a little. It all appeared to me, when I thought about it, like he either wanted and expected something from me not yet named, or, if he was that solicitous and friendly just to be that friendly and solicitous, I knew I'd eventually have to pay Dallas prices for all the fun I took in it, most likely by losing every scrap of it through some stupid blunder. Because by now Monte was known to be and have everything for all of us — the Leader, the chief, #1, Ace — a certainty to win the Mr. Staffer Award at summer's end. We returned mostly star-eyed wonder, which might've been a pretty good bargain both ways. But what bugged me was this: Monte didn't stand to gain a thing by running with me, and he might lose points by doing it. And yet he'd turned down, turned away, at least a dozen staffers of various stripes, male and female, who forever threw themselves at him, practically strewing palm branches in his path, and singled me out for his...what?...favors? discipline? direction and instruction? I don't mind admitting again that I was caught, but also confused, comfortable and fretful, thrilled and edgy, and all for knowing that calamity was imminent. It always is, when you feel as good as I did nearly all the time.

Just as concerning was how I sized up the others and the way they might get to Monte — use him, or try to. Quite a lot of younger versions of Miss Null, male and female, were hoofing it around Jubilee, ever about their Father's business as they unoriginally put it, and once it dawned on me that Monte might, could have been, about the same business, at the river, say, I couldn't dismiss the possibility, especially in light of all this hullabaloo around my speech. I disliked it, got impatient with it, but couldn't shake it. He'd dug around inside my head, all right, tried to drag some manner of confession out of me, and nearly agreed to confess something himself so that we could get shut of what our names and looks meant. And by the ritual of the water he'd sealed us in some rare union, by unspoken consent, let's say — joined our presents and futures, maybe, possibly our pasts too in how he talked of depths, as though he'd sounded them. The whole Pecos affair, I knew, was as secular as Tuesday, but it also conveyed the goose-pimply feeling of some variety of consecration there on that rock, his hand in benedictory blessing on my shoulder, in a new kind of "laying on of hands." But he might have been softening me up for something less compelling, absent goosebumps, some maneuver vaguely familiar and threatening. Because when the Nulls started their quiz number about my "calling," as they called it, I recoiled against the reprise of other days, other queries, knowing that if I conceded space for pressure, then space for development of whatever Monte and I had going would surely shrink. But not at the Pecos, not during this fuss over my speech, not in conversations I'll report later, could I determine, for certain, why precisely he did and said things, what moved him to say and do them, where he was headed with them and how we together were supposed to get there.

* * *

It was four days after Monte had given me two to work with Lance on my speech, and I hadn't made a move in his direction or he in mine. I didn't intend to either, but I needed to cut bait with Monte on the issue. We had worked supper and skipped services and were on our way back to the auditorium for another meeting of the group he'd called for tonight.

"About Lance," I said. "I won't work with him. My speech doesn't need Lance. But maybe I should tell you something about it."

"That would be helpful."

"Well, it's not exactly what you'd expect."

"Maybe that's good, maybe not. What's it about?"

"Okay. It's actually about my dog Bruce who got killed."

He stopped. "What? You're giving a Goforth competition speech about a dead pet dog?"

"Sort of, yeah. I make Bruce a paradigm of Christian virtue."

"Was he baptized?" But Monte was grinning. At least his question reflected the spirit of the thing.

"Don't know. But I could bring that in."

"You're kidding, though, right? What's it really about?"

"No, it really is about Bruce and how good and loving and loyal and obedient and decent he was, and how God must have needed him more than I did and so took him to a better home."

"And you won three times with *that?*"

We both laughed, though I felt mildly miffed. "It's better than that. I work in some Bible verses and some good deeds he did for needy people and how he visited kids sick with polio in their iron lungs to cheer them up and let them pet him, and once he jumped into a pool after a baby fell in, you know, to 'save' her, if you get my drift...."

"He rescued a drowning infant?!"

"Well, no, but he did jump in.... And I tell how he died and what we said at his burial."

"It gets sad? Dramatic and sad?"

"I guess, kind of."

"Wait a second. Let me think."

He stopped again and dug around for his balm, toyed with it.

"You know what, I...think...you...just might have some potential here. How'd he die?"

"You think it just might? Hey, guy, it won three times!"

"How'd he die?"

I explained.

"He was...obediently...following your father, and then *disobeyed* him, and got hit. Right?"

"Not right. He didn't disobey. I'm not saying that."

"But you just did say it. And that's the way it needs to be to work in the speech. You understand, don't you, what we can do with that? How we can use it?"

"I'm not doing it. I'm not saying Bruce disobeyed and paid for it."

"But it's perfect for the speech."

"Not my speech. It's not true. And it's, well, disloyal. I won't."

"All right. Let's postpone that part. Tell me more about the rest of it."

And when I finished, he, giggling, skipped into a little jig of joy: "Oh, brother, Troy, this is great. This is just *great!* It's drama; it's sappy; it's sweet and poignant and...familiar — everybody's lost a pet — and gut-wrenching to boot. It's even kind of saintly! What an idea! This is sure-fire winning material. Maybe a little short on funny, but we can fix that. Wow! But listen: let's not say anything to the others. Not a word. This has to be a knock-out, home-run *surprise* for everybody, okay?"

"You really think it'll be all right, then? It's just feels so... different, like peculiar."

"That's its brilliance. Nobody — none of the judges — will ever have heard a sermon about a dog."

"It's not a sermon, Monte. I wish you'd try to remember that."

"If *you* remember to rethink the 'disobedience' part."

"Not doing that," I persisted.

We entered from the rear, where Robyn had already positioned himself on the back pew, evidently anticipating a rehearsal of the speech. "C'mon to the front," Monte said. The others were gathered there, awaiting the Cap'n and his minion.

"Slight change of plans," Monte announced. "I'm scrubbing the rehearsal. We won't need one. Troy wants to keep his speech private until The Night Of, and we should respect that. But I've read it and it's terrific, only a little shy on funny, so you all could be thinking of jokes to perk it up. Tonight we'll go over what we did and add a few flourishes."

"Moreover, I don't get to assist?" Lance asked. "I thought you wanted me to...."

"Troy's speech doesn't need formal. Formal wouldn't work. Adlai wouldn't work. But hang on, Lance; I've got another assignment for you."

"I don't think my speech needs anything, Monte," I said. "I mean to speak it, deliver it, just as I already did, the three times I won with it. If it was good enough then, it's good enough now, without any tinkering."

"That doesn't follow," he said; "this is national."

"What we need here," Ta-Da offered, standing and hunching his shoulders, "what we need here is a trainer from the Desomthenes School of Speech and Drama in Dallas. I've seen their billboards all over...."

"Dear God," Monte groaned. "It's Demosthenes, Dallas, and we don't."

"Whoever. They've got billboards all over Dallas, and ads in the paper. I could call them. I'll even pay for that. We can get a dollar apiece from the whole staff — you know how everybody wants Troy to win — and that'd cover expenses for a Desomthenes teacher to come over for a day and show Troy what to do. And I'd only take 10% for setting it up. It can't miss. I can call right now. How about it?"

"How about shoving it?" Monte said.

"No, really," Dallas said. "I can."

"When Cicero finished speaking," Lance said, "folks said how well he spoke; when Demosthenes finished, they said, 'Let's march.' That's what Adlai E. Stevenson II wrote."

"But it's so sure to work!" Dallas said. "You're throwing away the chance...."

"Dallas!" Monte snapped: *"Screw* your Desomthenes!" That subdued temper for a minute while Robyn waddled up from his rear perch: *"What's* Dallas screwing?" he said, his voice trailing off as he realized what he asked halfway through it.

"Lance," Monte said, picking up the thread, "what if you and Travis team up with M&M for a little art project? Travis, you're an artist, right? So M&M will get photos of Troy and yawl and Lance will chose which to use and make multiple copies of. And Travis and Lance will design badges with a slogan for staff to wear to whip up enthusiasm for Troy between now and The Night Of and turn out a crowd in support. I'll get Steph to help with supplies for the badges: we'll want bright colors and Troy's photo and the slogan. How about 'Go for(th) Troy!'? Whadaya think, people?"

"It'll become 'gopher,'" I said.

"Nevertheless, it's stupid," Lance said. "Childish."

"It's cool," Robyn said. "I like it."

M&M were nodding and grinning.

"Let's vote," Corky said. "All in favor of badges...?"

"Everybody's hand went up except Lance's and mine.

From Lance: "Adlai E. Stevenson II said, 'A free society is one where it's safe to be unpopular.'"

"That's it, then," Monte said. "Lance, please help make the badges. Could ya'll get me a design within three days? I'll need to approve it."

Operation Wolf-Wreck had now swollen way beyond all reasonable and tolerable proportions, and I felt crabby about it, but I saw no way publicly to restrain and contain it. I'd have to take it up in private with Monte later.

"Next," he said, "is Robyn's...doubtful...list." Monte had showed me the three-page, play-by-play account of Wolf's Arkansas state win, which was sweet enough to induce a diabetic coma but also, if you drained off the sugar, pretty near as full and clear and even smart a description as you could want. Except for its uselessness. To Robyn's adoring eyes, Wolf had no weaknesses, no soft spots we could target for exploitation. On the one hand, it looked like Robyn really meant to help us after all; at least it might have looked like that unless I'm the looker. For on the other hand, maybe Robyn didn't want to expose any Wolfian deficiencies that might enable me. Or maybe he decided to back us to curry favor with Monte so, if I won, he'd take partial credit for it and make Monte beholden. Hard to tell, with Robyn. But now that Monte had openly judged the list "doubtful," he'd pulled the plug on Robyn's ploys.

"Overplayed your hand, sweetheart," I muttered, as if I knew squat about cards.

"There's nothing here," Corky said; "Wolf looks solid as a tank."

"That's for sure," Travis chimed.

"I tried," Robyn said, "but I told you before."

"Well," Monte said, discarding the pages; "let's move on. Troy's talked with Dale and reported to me. We've got info, some info, on last year's finals; time will tell whether it's useful. If you think of anything else, Dale, tell Troy. All right, people! Jubilates rehearse on Saturday afternoon."

"I can't," Dale said. "I've got a ball game."

"Reschedule it," Monte said.

"I'll take care of it," I said.

"Anything else?" Monte asked.

"Yes," Robyn said; "there is something else. Troy's going to need a microphone. I really couldn't hear him back there last time. He won't be heard without a mike."

"Is that right?" Monte asked, searching our faces. "Ya'll couldn't hear?"

"He was a little faint," Scotty said, and M&M nodded.

"Worse than faint," Robyn said; "he was IN-AUD-IBLE! Not like that!"

"Truly?" Monte asked, frowning. "Why didn't somebody say? This could be serious." He paused, studying, looking around. And his face brightened. "Wait...wait a second," his lips spreading and unfurling in that slow smile. "Maybe Robyn's got something."

Robyn had nothing but flesh as far as I could tell, but Monte was suddenly squirming with excitement.

"What? What've I got?" Robyn wheezed.

"Hang on, troops," Monte said, specks of black fire dancing in his eyes, "and say what you think of this: Look, Troy, they expect you to use the pulpit, don't they, the lectern there," he pointed up to it; "but you won't. They expect all the lights to be up, right? They won't be. Just one spot, on you. They expect you to preach, right…?

"No," I said, "I've told you and told you…."

"Right, right, sorry. They'll expect preaching, which means shouting and snorting and Bible-thumping, right? You won't do any of that. Now listen," and his voice dropped to a low purl, like the sound cats make when you rub them, and his eyes flashed: "You're going to pray that speech, Troj: you're going to *pray* it, whisper it to them, soft and…like….alluring. You're going to take that mike off the mount and stroll with it, amble around the stage with it, play with it, toss and catch it, toy with it…."

"Monte," I said, "it's not lip balm."

Everyone laughed, Monte too, but on he rolled; "No, but you can g-r-e-a-s-e your voice with it! Croon that speech, Troy, right into the mike on your lips. I want you to b-r-e-a-t-h-e it, Troj, dream it, sigh it, *knead* them with the oiliest lines you can float off that sweet tongue of yours. You need to milk every syllable for all the juice that's in it. And stroke the mike, fondle it, hell, man, make love to it, so we can hear your pipes humming. You're going to ravish those yahoos, my man, make jelly of them, melt them down to runny slush. And that's what we're going to have when you're done, one big lake of whimpering, moaning drool. To drown Wolf in. Can you do it?"

I could. I liked it. Of course it was outrageous, even scandalous, maybe *too* extravagant for a winning strategy. But it opened the door to *performance*! No longer mere recitation, my speech became high drama: I had a role to act. I had spectacle in my sights!

"You, Robyn," Monte said, "plan to be here, in the front row, as prompter, with a copy of the text — Troy? Travis, you'll cut the house lights backstage — you know where — the minute Troy gets the mike off the mount. Dallas, Dale, Corky, Martha, Mary, Scotty: you six space yourselves out through the crowd: dress up, suits and heels, no name-tags, no badges. Wait exactly three seconds after Troy finishes — count 'em off, one-a-thousand, two-a-thousand — three seconds after the spot goes off, and then start the applause if it hasn't, clapping and whooping and whistling and stamping like crazy. I want bedlam. And keep it going as long as you can. The judges will notice. Think you can manage that? Without pay, Dallas? No slip-ups here, I mean it; no screwing around! All right, then. Everybody out now, except Troy. Scram! I need to review the speech. But it has to be a total surprise for everybody else. Ya'll can't know anything about it. So scat now! You're up, Troj: let's hear you make love to that mike."

Afterwards, from his dark bed, a whisper: "You were good, Troj. Really good. Ol' Wolf's done drown-ded dead."

"Killed with love," I said.

* * *

The next night I met Dale as his crew finished clearing after supper.

"How about we skip the service," I asked, "and have another go at last summer's run-off? Maybe you've remembered more?"

Our earlier chat hadn't produced much. Monte was right about the usefulness — or …lessness — of what it did. Dale had tried, all right; he'd proved well enough that he was there, had witnessed the event; but details were scarce.

"I don't think I have," he said. "I'm sorry."

"Do you recall anybody using a mike?" I asked.

"I'm pretty sure they didn't," he said, after a pause. "I remember, because some of them where kind of hard to hear. And because several guests on my pew made a commotion of moving closer after the first one or two."

"That's good, Dale. That's the kind of thing we need to know. Let's keep pushing. Did you notice how they dressed? The speakers, I mean."

"Oh, everybody dressed up. Suits and all. I'm sure."

"Nobody looked different? Nothing stood out?"

"Not that I recall."

"Anybody have props? At one of my semi-finals a guy brought a football."

"I don't remember any. Wait. One girl sang at the end. She ended her speech with a soft little song. I don't know what it was."

"Did somebody play for her? The piano?"

"Don't think so."

"Did she win?"

"No, a guy won. I'm sure of that. But I don't know anything about him or where he was from."

"Did the audience applaud?"

He thought a second or two. "Maybe after it was all over. Dr. Mann may have asked everybody to applaud everybody?"

"Don't make anything up, Dale. Just what you remember."

"Okay. Sergeant Steph was there, I remember. She was sort of in charge, organizing stuff. Kept things moving along."

"That's good to know. What about judges?"

"There were several. They went out at the end, and reported back."

"Men *and* women?"

"I think there were women too."

"Spotlights? Any special lighting?"

"I don't think so."

"Anything else? This is very good, Dale. If you think of anything else, don't hold back. We really appreciate your help. I'll tell Monte."

"I'll keep trying to remember."

"Speaking of whom: Monte told me what happened last summer. That terrible accident and the fire. You were very brave."

He looked at me, and looked away. "Not really," he said quietly. "The Sergeant was trapped. Somebody had to help her."

"And you did. Where was Monte?"

"Monte wasn't there."

"You mean he was out cold. From hitting the rock."

"No, not for long."

"So where was he?"

"Can we just say he wasn't there? I don't remember him being there. But I was kind of busy. He came back."

"From where?"

"I don't know. He never said."

We both went very quiet. Dale fingered his beads.

"Monte was there, and then he wasn't, and then he was," I said, almost whispering.

"That's what I remember. I might be wrong. It was kind of crazy there for a while. What did Monte say about it?"

"He said he didn't remember anything after the crash."

"That could be true."

"But you doubt it is."

"I'm not sure anymore. I try not to think about it anymore. I don't think we should talk about it anymore."

"But don't you want to know? Where he was?"

"Why do you?"

I thought for a second. "Well, maybe I don't," I said.

Did it matter? How could it not? But what difference would it make if it did? In what connection might my knowing matter?

* * *

"Dissembling," I believe, is the word for my part of the conversation with Scotty about Corky. Please blame the shock for my defensiveness. Let me clarify:

Of course I know what queers are. I'm not sure what they do, but I know to dive for cover when the word comes up, and it hadn't come up within my hearing at Jubilee except that once from Scotty. Mind you, I don't think I've had anything to hide in this regard, other than a general curiosity and a few random, scattered thoughts from time to time like everybody else has, and a little harmless adolescent experimentation I'm about to describe, and maybe that dirty postcard of naked men messing with each other that I once accidentally left on the back seat of the Plymouth, and, oh yes, I almost forgot, I liked checking out how my chum Butch Moreland's skinny jeans profiled his prodigious, prominent, and permanently stiff cut prick tracking down the inside of his brief-less left thigh. It's also odd, and interesting, that I remember the first time I heard the word "queer," at Lester's Barber Shop where a couple of rough boys were trashing Mr. Cameron, our school principal and husband of my third-grade teacher, for offering to play with two basketball stars, and I don't mean on the court. He'd been investigated and fired, and these boys were sneering and laughing about it and gave me a funny look when I asked, "What'd he do?" It was the same shop, by the way, where Father walked in one day and caught me reading "Playboy," and snatched it away and ripped the pages out and let Mr. Lester have what for: one of my more memorable humiliations. I think the high school locker crowd used the word contemptuously and indiscriminately against anybody and anything for any reason or none at all without knowing any more particulars than I knew about the queer species and how it got on. But then along came Fletcher Sterling, a Hallmark artist who lived in Madison and commuted three days a week to the headquarters in Baton Rouge and shopped every Friday night at 8 in the A&P market where I clerked part-time and always waited in line at my check-stand where he bought two cartons of Viceroys and seven cans of cat food with every order. He always wore sports jackets and brightly colored ties, a lit cigarette dangling on his lips, his thinning hair neatly parted and combed, and he liked to ask me how school went and what piano score I was practicing and how play try-outs were going. Sterling — he told me to call him Sterling — once took me to dinner in downtown Baton Rouge and afterward to a traveling production of "My Fair Lady," my first and only Broadway show to date, which plumb knocked me over. And later on he asked could he pick me up at 9 after work and bring me home to inspect his record collection; and while I did he called out from the kitchen that I should spend the night there sometime. The notion startled, even scared, me a little — Why would I want to do that? And why did Sterling hide in the kitchen to invite me?—so I hit the door and walked all the way home on my own and told Father about it the next day. He said: "I don't know why people like that don't just get married...." But Mr. Cameron *was* married.

Overnights with boy friends were the equivalents of girls' slumber parties back then, and both were popular around Madison for a time. My parents allowed me separately to invite Gary and Louis and Grady and other town boys for sleepovers where we joked and giggled and talked dirty but never fooled around sexually, which did, I admit it, mildly disappoint my curiosity: I kind of wanted to know if what was happening to me in those situations was also happening to them.

But then we had our Sunday afternoons that more or less recompensed the disappointment. Sunday afternoons at the Bayou with Eugene and Billyclyde and Purvis and them, after our horseback riding for an hour or so, were more specific and vivid. We'd actually warm-up for the Bayou during the morning church service. Once done with standing up for prayers and hymns in the service sequence, we'd settle back into the pew, hunch our hips out, spread our legs so the crotch material loosened up, get erect, and flex our dicks so you could see them stir and poke up and rise and fall, and sometimes we'd place hymnals gently on them and try to flex the books off. If we did, we'd get so red-faced from suppressed giggles that Father once had to scold us from the pulpit. At the Bayou, we'd skinny-dip and splash and romp and water-wrestle until tired, and pull on our jockeys and lie around joking until somebody started fiddling with himself and we'd all pull down our shorts again and compare sizes and jerk off and notice how burned we'd got, and then untie the horses and trot home, like nothing unusual had happened. It hadn't. We never touched each other *there,* except maybe in a graze when wrestling, but we all so to speak peered, eyes aslant.

I won't say I didn't enjoy these sessions; but I enjoyed them less for the indifferent, routine, even slightly boring sex than for the act and the fact of transgression. This was big-time sin. And not because anybody ever *said* it was. Nobody *ever* said "masturbation" except us guys to each other, and we usually used a slang phrase for it instead. It was almost literally unspeakable. I believe that's how we knew it was wrong, for the silence wrapping and stifling it. It was the great unspoken offense, short of The Big One for which it substituted, of course, but momentously grave on its own. Father didn't even say "self-abuse;" I'd picked up the idiom from a book, *For Boys Only,* he'd bought to fill in the gaps he'd left when "explaining" sex to me. The very idea of "self-pleasure" — a deliciously apt term, I thought — was utterly taboo. What precisely excited *me* about these afternoons was performing a universally acknowledged but utterly benign wickedness, the easy and rapturous indulgence in harmless evil: the complete joy of being sinlessly bad.

This was all junior high fun and games. It pretty much stopped with sophomore year when some guys found girls and others of us went private for sex, which probably *is* unnatural. I didn't know (of) any queers in my class or in my school. Anyway, when I wrote above that I "fell" for Corky, I didn't mean what I'd have to mean if I said it now, after Scotty spoke the word. But I'm not so shocked that I'm not interested. I want to talk to Corky. Or rather, I want Corky to talk to me.

And what I particularly want him to talk about is why, as he intimated to Scotty, he thought I might suspect he was queer. What about me would make me believe that about him? Did he

also suspect me? Was he projecting? I don't know if there's a cer-
tified stereotype against which to measure oneself — a checklist
of symptoms? — but *For Boys Only* identified "effeminate boys"
as sufficiently distinct from the standard to attract ridicule and
derision, and suspicion of "abnormal predilections," it said. What
they were, it didn't. Now, I've been called "sissy" often enough
in my time, for throwing baseballs like girls do and for skipping
rope with them and hop-scotching my way across those chalked
sidewalk patterns, and even for playing piano and liking po-
etry, and once for lip-synching "Hernando's Hideaway" in drag
with castanets, no less, for drama class, which landed me the
lead in "Charley's Aunt," another drag role. And I never earned
higher than a C+ in gym class or lettered in any sport although
I made second-team basketball junior year and ran track senior
and was a whiz at paddle ball. But I don't understand how any
of these "predilections" insinuate aught about my sex life and
sexual preferences, for I also "went steady" for two-and-a-half
years in high school with a sweetheart of a girl as randy as I am
24/7. And Corky knows I like Scotty. But then Scotty noticed
I'm "always with Monte." Is Monte some manner of cue here?
Shall I ask Corky about that? What if he asks *me* about that?

8

When accepting our applications for employment, Jubilee management strongly recommended that staff continue through the summer the practice long traditional among good Baptist families of reading together designated scripture passages every day along with a brief commentary on them; these materials were published and distributed quarterly by the Convention in a small booklet including on the page for each day the names of missionaries whose birthday it was so we could mention them in prayers supposed to follow the readings. At home we routinely observed this little rite upon finishing breakfast every morning of the livelong year, parents alternating reading day by day the scripture verses, the meditation, and praying aloud. Neither Mark nor I was keen on any of it but protests were futile: the parents were rock-solid locked into it. Monte and I had talked early about the recommendation and, seeing it was unenforceable, agreed to pass unless one of us wanted it for a change, but always omitting the praying part. Occasionally he'd suggest we do it, him reading, and I'd go along, the familiarity of it vaguely comforting.

He was sitting on his bed in Jockeys and a T, his sleeping uniform (and mine), a Bible on his lap, when I got home late after a flatware dishwasher jammed and I had to hand-wash a mountain of scummy cutlery and dry it too. Corky offered to help but I politely declined, not yet ready to talk, as I knew we had to, but for sure not there in the Sweat Shop.

Without preliminaries, Monte asked, "How do you figure Judas?"

"Judas? What's to figure? He sold out, that's all. Why?"

"'Why' is exactly the question, why he did it."

"I meant, why're you asking?"

"Because I'm interested in why he did it. 'He sold out' is the God's truth, all right, but how did he get there? Sit down, let's sort it out."

"It's not that hard, Monte. Thirty pieces of silver. Does that sound about right?"

"Don't be a smart-ass. I'm serious. I mean, the whole story is bogus. It doesn't add up, how they tell it."

"You honestly think we're going to find holes in it after two thousand years? Nothing's going to change. What's the point?"

"The point is why he did it. Think about it with me: thirty pieces isn't that much dough. It's a bargain bribe. Second, Jesus isn't hard to spot: He's been hanging around town and country for a while, kicking up a fuss too, making lots of racket, so just about anybody'll know Him and His people and His hangouts. The high priests don't *need* to have him pointed out: they *know* their guy. So, they don't round up Judas; he looks *them* up, which must mean he's not hard up for cash, wasn't much interested in the money. All he cared about was the dirty deed: the betrayal itself. Otherwise, he'd have advertised his availability on the sly and waited for the priests, and bagged a better payoff than thirty pieces. Also, remember that after trucking along for all that time, he suddenly for no reason we know of turns sour and decides to sell out. Something must've happened. Something turned him off the whole pack. Something happened that Matthew and the rest want to keep secret."

"Or don't know or don't think matters. "*He's* not the hero, not who the story's about."

"Maybe not, but how can you say unless you know why he fingered Him, what made him do it."

"I dunno but I'll bet you think you do. What's all this about, anyway?"

"I'm only saying the whole story starts to fall apart if you don't know why he did it."

"No," I said, "it or something like it would've happened anyway, with or without Judas. Jesus had to die. You know that. I don't see how the why matters. Or how the story falls apart. It would've all turned out just the same."

"Exactly!" he exclaimed. "The authorities would have caught Him and killed Him. The hero's heroics would have come off just as they did. So the question is: Why is Judas there at all?"

I didn't know, didn't answer. Couldn't say why Judas was there, couldn't figure where Monte was headed with this zany set-up. Was he trying to divert me — move my mind off Wolf and the contest? This seemed a passing strange way to do it, and in any event the contest wasn't where my mind currently strayed. Whether intended as diversion, the fiction was starting to resemble a strategy, for Monte's hypotheses, his scenarios, stirred with disquieting effect. I could feel how his reasoning was wacky but not pinpoint where. I knew his suppositions were creeping up on heresy if not already arrived there. They didn't themselves trouble me so much, though, as *his saying* them, maybe even buying them. Because it was one thing for a pre-seminary student to play worldly connoisseur at rodeos and film sites and fancy restaurants but something else again to horse around with Holy Writ within earshot of any Nulls who might happen by our door. And who was I, anyway, to accuse him of hypocrisy or heresy or worse — to come charging in like some inspired cavalry to rescue sacred scripture from his blasphemous trifling with it? Hadn't I better be surprised and gratified and encouraged by his dredging up from the deeps behind his own face this challenge to the old orthodox take on the story, a doubt potentially sealing the pact half-made back at the river? What if he was, then by word, now by act, teaching me to do what you thought, to be certain I understood it wasn't a one-off deal, as with the speech? But I couldn't feel pleased. Because all of it was spooky, carried a whiff of mischief and risk that alerted Gaylord Bryce, who hung around its edges in my head. Gaylord Bryce and I figured something doubtful was cooking with this Judas spiel, and it looked mighty like the makings of a trap, secular or religious or threaded with strands of both. We knew it, and still I said:

"I don't know, but you've obviously got a theory, so why'nt you just spit it out? Why *is* Judas there?"

"We have to go back to the start. Suppose you're walking along one day minding your own business when this gang of guys comes up and their leader — tall, lean fella, long hair, in white — he says, 'Hey, buddy, follow me,' and that's all. What'd you do?"

"Dumb question. I dunno. *You* don't know either." He'd taken the long way round but now I had some inkling (or thought I had) where he was going.

"I mean before you decided, what would you do?"

"All right, if we have to do this. I guess I'd try to find out what he wanted."

"Yes. But all he does is look at you — dark eyes, maybe — reads you, and says 'Follow me.' You can't pry anything else out of him. In other words, he's asking you to trust him. What'd you do now?"

"Say forget it."

"No, 'cause you've not given yourself a chance yet, or him either. All he's asked for is a little faith in him. And you can't say no without some reason, which you haven't got. Try to imagine the whole scene. What would you do?"

"Really, Monte, what has this to do with Judas? Or anything?"

"We're getting to that. What would you do?"

"Geeze. But this is nuts! Well, I guess I'd look them all over and try to guess what they want."

"And what do they look like?"

"Bums."

"No, now. Be serious. What?"

"Hoboes."

"*Troy!* This is serious."

"Oh, is it? Classy hoboes then."

"Nice enough, you mean. Husky, rural types, right? Poor, though."

"Most bums are."

"But happy, would you say? Content?"

"If you say so."

"You're not scared of them, though. They don't look like beggars or robbers or lepers."

"If you say not."

"And you don't think they mean you harm?"

"I don't know, 'cause…."

"And have you anything better to do? Than joining up, following…?"

"Oh, well, if I scratched around *real* hard, I might find…."

"*Troy!* C'mon!"

"I can't say, because…."

"Because you don't know what they want from you. What he wants. Right. What would you guess he wants?"

"Are we about done? This is tiresome."

"Hang on. What would you guess he wants?"

"Maybe they need a mascot."

"You mean it as a joke but you could be right. Think of it this way: you've said they're nice, prob'ly harmless, friendly enough. So even though their mission is secret, everything you see says it might be interesting, possibly important. So what does the rest of it matter? Wouldn't you think it might be kind of a lark to wander around the country with this bunch of nice friendly guys? How half the fun might be in *not* knowing what to expect?"

"I don't think so, and I don't…."

"So, if you've got no hard negative evidence, if it's likely to turn out fun, if you're willing to trust him for a little while, you've no reason for not following him, like the others, right?"

I had to concede that it was pretty well done. But by forcing it so far and so hard, he didn't leave me much choice.

"Maybe, but I'd still say forget it. And if it's all the same to you, why'nt you forget it too, okay? I need some sleep."

"It's not all the same to me and I won't. Because you're *right!* Of course you'd say forget it *now.* But *why?*"

"What?"

"Of *course.* Because you've now *counted* them. You've counted out *twelve men.* You'd be number thirteen and odd person out. And you know what that could mean."

"I don't know, or care, what any of this means, so please dummy up and let's get to bed."

Sure, it was a lie. I mean, I didn't know, no, but I mighty well *cared* all of a sudden. When Gaylord Bryce gets as jumpy as he was just then, you lie if you think it will shut down whatever's making him, not that it did.

"Right. You wouldn't go. Let's review: Judas was the last one to get called; you wouldn't go but he did; what he must have thought about, eyeballing those twelve nice-looking dudes; how *everything* sailed along smooth as silk over all that time until something happened, something happened inside their little club that nobody'll talk or write about; remember how he ID'd Jesus to the soldiers and what happened next: he joins, he's happy, he's not, he leaves, he talks. Now try to imagine the... whadaya call? the *dynamics* in there. Did somebody get fooled? Was somebody disappointed? Hurt? Did somebody get mad? Did somebody cross a line? What went down in there? What secret came out?"

The dusky shadow of an idea — profane, prohibited, but for all that teasing, titillating — lurked around the margins of my muddled mind where Gaylord Bryce skittishly patrolled. It showed crazy, ludicrous, and also tantalizing. And if Monte thought it too, possible?

"You mean he...," I faltered. "You mean Judas was...?"

"Imagine it, Troy!"

"No, I don't think that...." I trailed off, confounded.

"What, Troy? What if...? Go for it!"

He waited, his eyes very wide.

"What if," Monte said, slowly nodding his head, "what if... Judas was a girl? What if Judas was Judy?"

He smirked, and winked, and switched off the lamp.

9

Corky wheeled up after lunch detail the next day in snug white shorts, a pale blue polo, and white Keds showing off well-tanned legs. "Got a minute?" he asked, dismounting and stepping alongside.

"Sure," I said. "You look good. What's up?"

"I talked to Steph this morning. She had news." He was lightly flushed, and his eyes danced above the bright smile. Clearly, he itched to spill. "They've heard about your competitors in the finals."

"Why're you talking to Steph about the finals?"

"No call to be cross, Troy. I didn't go see her about that. It just came up."

"Oh, sorry. What did?"

"Well, the Convention has told them who else your competition is, besides Wolf. Or not exactly who but how many. There're four others, so six of you in all. The Convention said reserve four rooms for five for three nights and meals. You're all from west of the Mississippi."

The denomination operated a twin of Jubilee in North Carolina, older and larger and more popular than ours, so Goforth champions from eastern states competed in nationals there. Not all Southern Baptist states were ever represented, and some regional winners always dropped out before finals, which accounts for limited numbers at the national run-offs the same week at both venues. My research back before I entered in Madison said six was about average for Jubilee finals.

"So who are the others?" I asked.

"Steph says she doesn't know. They're supposed to show up the day before and leave the day after the day after The Night Of."

"Can't she find out about them? Somebody has to know."

"Maybe you should put Robyn on it," Corky said, "or his mom."

We laughed. But it was mildly vexing. The identities of these finalists couldn't be secret. Mine certainly wasn't.

"I'll see what Monte can dig up," I said decisively.

"But why would you?" Corky surprised me by asking.

"Well, to prepare, I guess. To know the competition."

"But you're already prepared. You've given this speech how many times now? Monte says it's terrific. And he's choreographed the whole show down to the last stroke of the mike. What's left to prepare?"

"Well, it just might help me to know…how…to know what…you know."

"No, I don't see it. What could you possibly learn, from knowing who they are, that would make you change your plans? And why anyway would you want to let your competition redefine them, revise *you* in their own terms? You'd only get data to worry you, raise your anxiety level, distract you from the task at hand, which is what you're already prepared to perform and all of us are prepared to help you bring off a win with. Why would you want to mess with that?"

Wait. Who *was* this? Who was *this?* Where did that advice come from? Startling, yes, but I saw right away how smart it was, how right.

"Wow, Corky," I said, "where'd you get all that? It's really good. I like it."

"I've been thinking. It's my assignment to 'distract' you. You don't need distractions by competitors or their plans. And we're not thinking about changes in yours."

"You're prob'ly right," I said, "only I *would* like to know who…."

"Nope. Not. Here's better distraction: Steph's arranging the day off for you, that day. No duties. Dr. Mann thought of it. Said it was only fair, as your competition wouldn't be working."

"Really? That's great! But what'll I do?"

"I've got that covered. You've forgotten I'm your guardian angel for that afternoon, in charge of your care and feeding. I'm also getting the day off."

He paused, letting me take this in.

"That's why I saw Steph this morning," he continued after a beat or two. "I've been wondering if you've ever seen Bandelier?"

"What's Bandelier?"

"It's a national park, honoring an ancient Indian civilization. I think we should go there, together, spend the day visiting sites there — pueblos and caves and ruins and such. It's just up the road a piece, and it's said to be historically significant and fascinating and a popular tourist stop. We could look around and grab a meal and make it back in plenty of time for you to rest and change and get to the auditorium. How about it?"

He reddened a little and smiled spaciously.

"But how'd we get there? The bike?!"

"Ah, that's the other thing. Steph says that Mr. Mann owns a second car besides the big Buick, that their son uses when he flies in from Miami for visits; and as it's otherwise just sitting there could use some exercise. Steph thinks Dr. Mann might let us borrow it for some 'distraction' time to help you unwind and relax away from Jubilee. Wouldn't that be cool?"

It would. No doubt of it: an ideal plan for spending those fraught hours before the speech. Why did I waver?

"It sounds good, Corky. It does. But let me think it over."

"What's to think? I'll need to get back to Steph about the car. We could go right now and see her. Tell me why you're iffy?"

"To be honest," I said, "I don't know. I just feel kind of funny about it. I don't know...."

"Are you being honest?" he frowned.

"I think so. I'm just not sure about the trip."

"You don't know, or you won't say why not?"

"I'm not sure about that either." My heart was beating very fast.

"I'm your friend, Troy; I'm trying to help. Can't you help me help you?"

"That's just it, Corky. I'm not certain what you're trying to help me with. How you want to help me."

"I don't know that we know that yet. But spending some time together might help us find out, don't you think?"

"Maybe."

"Maybe? *Maybe?* Troy, are you frightened of me? Do I scare you?"

I felt myself wilt. "Oh, Corky," my voice trembly, tears in my throat. "I've talked to Scotty...." I stopped.

"I know," he said, tender now. "She told me."

"And it's true, what she said?"

Big smile. "Of course it's true."

"And you're sure?"

He actually laughed. "Oh my goodness gracious yes, Troy, I'm dead sure; have been for years. Do you mind?"

What if I *did* mind? Could everything go back to how I thought it used to be? Could he change back? It didn't sound like he wanted to.

"Do you mind?" he repeated.

"No, you don't scare me. I'm just not sure what to think."

"I don't want you to mind."

"I don't think I mind. I'm trying not to mind. It's just that I don't know anything...."

"Tell you what, Troy: let's try one thing at a time here. Let's firm up the car with Steph. Agree on the trip. Work up toward talking about.... Well, what shall we call it, since you don't like the word Scotty used? Let's invent another one. How about... 'Qwork'? It can be The Qwork. The whole subject can be The Qwork. That all right with you? Say it."

I said it, and laughed.

"Attaboy," he said, also laughing. "And the trip?"

"Okay. Let's plan on Bandilier by car."

"Done."

"Only: we have to put the speech first. We can't screw me up for giving the speech. We can't" — I felt the giggles rising — "we can't 'distract' me so much I lose my lines!"

"I mightn't be that good," he said, and we both cracked up. Later I wondered whether he'd said "might" or "mightn't."

And also why Gaylord Bryce hadn't made his presence felt.

In Steph's office we found Monte inspecting the raw materials for the badges she'd somewhere found. He seemed mildly ticked to be interrupted.

"What's going on with you two?" he said, barely looking up.

"We wanted to see Sergeant Steph about the car."

"Right," she said, smiling, and standing up behind her desk. "You want it, then?"

"Yes, ma'am," Corky said, "we'd love to use it for the day, if it's still available."

"May I ask what for? Dr. Mann will want to know."

"Of course," Corky said looking at me. "We were thinking about driving over to Bandelier or maybe up to Taos for the day, if that's okay."

"Super ideas," she said, still smiling. "I'll just step into Mr. Mann's office and ask him. Wait here."

"What?" Monte said. "What's all this?"

"For 'distraction,'" Corky said lightly. "You remember."

"I remember what I said. Who's idea is this?"

"Both of ours. We figured getting out of Dodge might be good, and we've never been to either place."

"I have," he paused. "Yeah, that'll prob'ly work. I'd go back to Taos. Just keep an eye on the clock. Troy's good with it?"

"I'm right here, Monte," I said. "You can ask me. Yes, I'm good with it."

"Listen, Troy," Monte said, "do you carry a picture of Bruce?"

I caught his eye, flicked mine toward Corky, twitched my head "no." But Corky saw it.

"Who's Bruce?" he asked.

"Not here," Monte said, as Steph returned with Dr. Mann.

The Man was rarely seen around Jubilee by staff, and by guests only when he showed up to deliver announcements and pronounce the blessing before their meals. Tall, stately, with curly grey hair and blue eyes behind gold rimless glasses, and a kind, open face, he strode right over, hand out, to shake Corky's and mine, getting our names right too.

"It's only a '55 Ford Fairlane," he said, "but it runs reliably if not pushed too hard, and you'll be gentle with it, of course. And where will you take it?"

"Taos or Bandielier," Monte said. "I suggested Taos."

"Either would offer a fine day of interesting entertainment. I'll ask you to sign the car in and out with the Sergeant, noting times. Show her your driver's license. She'll type a note on Jubilee stationery granting permission to use the vehicle, which I'll sign, and copy out information from the licenses. And I'll have Dallas wash and fuel the car and leave it here at the building. You know to keep under the speed limit. We need Troy back in good shape for the contest. Enjoy your day!" Smiling warmly, he nodded to us and to the Sergeant, and withdrew.

"How about *that*?" Corky beamed.

We handed over our licenses and chatted amiably with the Sergeant while she copied out information, promising the signed note would be in the car on The Day Of. She asked me, as everybody now did, how the speech was coming along. I muttered assurances. Monte trailed us out.

"How come she's being so nice?" I asked.

"She likes your work," Monte said. "She says we're her two best. She's thinking of making us Shift Heads."

"What? Shift Heads?"

"In charge of the two crews. To keep order, to speed things along."

"But we'd be on different teams. And you know it would become 'Shit-heads.'"

"Who's Bruce," Corky said.

"I'll take it," Monte said to me. "I'll tell you, Corky, but you can't say a thing about it…without ruining Troy's speech. This has to stay an absolute secret among ourselves. If it leaks, Troy's toast. Swear to me you won't breathe a word to anyone, not even Scotty. I'll personally cut out your tongue if you do, and I'll know if you do."

"Okay, sure. I can keep a secret." He looked hard at me.

"No," Monte said; "I believe you'll try, but I want an oath. Swear it."

"All right. I swear I won't tell. So what is it?"

Monte, enjoying the drama, glanced at me. I nodded assent.

"Okay," he said. "Now listen and lock up your lips. Bruce is Troy's dog. And Troy mentions Bruce a couple of times in his speech. Actually, more than a couple. But for optimum impact, Bruce has to be a complete surprise. Nobody can know beforehand, or it's all up in smoke, right, Troy? Understand, Corky? Success depends on Bruce being a surprise."

"All right. Fine. I can do that. No leaks from me. You're really preaching about a dog, Troy?"

"No, dammit, I'm not preaching. I wish people would get that straight. It's a *speech*! Okay?"

"Geeze," Corky said. "Okay. Speech."

"I mention Bruce. That's all."

"So, Troy," Monte stepped in, "do you carry a photo of Bruce?"

"No," I said, faintly sorry I didn't. "I don't have one here."

"I was thinking," Monte continued, "we could add a picture of Bruce to the badge but not identify him. Put you and him together on the badge, with the slogan, but never explain why the dog is there. Maybe stir up some curiosity about what the badge means. Maybe increase interest and attendance that night. Jack up the appetite?"

I thought it clever, wondered if I could turn up a photo, get the folks to send one.

"Hold on," Corky said, digging out his wallet again. He extracted a card, handed it to Monte. "That's my dog, Dixie."

"So?" Monte said.

"Nobody here," I said, getting it; "nobody here knows what Bruce looks like. Isn't that where you're going with this, Corky?"

"And nobody here but Scotty knows Dixie," Corky said. "And, trust me, Scotty sure can keep a secret!" Again he looked hard at me.

"Hold on," I said; "isn't Hollis also from Vicksburg?"

"Yes, and goes to our church. But I don't think she's ever been to my house. I'll ask Scotty."

"Dixie doesn't attend church?" I joked. "Unlike Bruce?"

"That's not disqualifying," Monte said.

He studied for a few seconds. "So you might lend us Dixie's picture here for M&M to copy for the badge? I could get Travis to design a badge with Troy and Dixie and the slogan, and let folks try to figure it out? You'll have to convince Scotty to go along without telling her why, and make her swear not to give it away about Dixie, certainly not to Hollis. You okay with this, Troy?"

I was charmed that Corky had thought of it. It had class and wit. I wondered whether Bruce would mind being Dixie for a while, and figured he wouldn't if it helped me win this stupid thing. I still questioned the badge notion but couldn't deny Monte's point about publicity. A badge with a boy and a dog, even if somebody else's dog, would get folks talking and smiling.

"Let's see the picture," I said. Corky stepped over with it, leaned into me to look again.

Dixie was a nearly white golden retriever adult holding a Westminster pose, her long coat combed and draping perfectly, her tail a flag. Her shapely head faced the camera, her mouth barely showing a trace of teeth and tongue, like she was herself about to smile.

"Good Lord," I said, "what a beauty!"

"She is, isn't she," Corky agreed.

"So Dixie can be Bruce," I smirked at Monte, who winked and nodded slowly. "And Bruce Dixie."

"I think we ought to try it," Monte said. "We don't lose unless somebody leaks."

"Won't be me," Corky said. "And I'll talk to Scotty. She'll go along."

"But it's cheating," I said. "It really is deceitful."

"We'll never say it's your dog," Monte said. "We'll never claim Dixie is Bruce. If people assume, we can't help that. They'll make the connection from the badge."

"But we make the badge," I said, without conviction. I did feel sort of preciously puritanical in expressing reservations but the very secrecy Monte demanded witnessed a moral ambiguity, at the least, in the plot.

"Look," he said, "we just put something out there, without any comment at all. And then when you say 'My dog Bruce' on The Night Of, Dixie's face pops up in everybody's mind and stays there till you finish. And you DO want them to *see* Bruce, don't you? We're helping them, that's all."

"Actually, I don't describe him in the speech. I probably should."

"Not *now*!" Monte said. "You shouldn't *now*!"

"And you don't think we're misleading?"

"Troy, we're illustrating your text! Illustrations mislead all the time, and nobody thinks a thing about it. We're illuminating with illustrations, that's all, opening a whole new dimension on a speech you wrote. What's your problem with that?"

Gaylord Bryce made a quick pass through my mind, and dissolved.

10

A popular Jubilee tradition was the "Christmas in July" celebration scheduled, I reckon, to break up the monotony for staff and to provide a mid-point social lift, the centerpiece of which was a prodigious feast laid out on Tuesday night after guests had dined and retired to pack, and we briefly had the dining hall to ourselves. The garden crew felled and anchored a mighty fir at the center of the dining hall, and Steph with help from other adult staff hung it with colored lights and baubles and tinsel, and strung streamers around walls and windows, and sprayed the panes with snowflakes, and rolled out butcher paper for tablecloths and left on each table a 24-pack of crayons for adorning the paper with seasonal art, and also dressed the tables with crepe and holly and wreaths and tall red candles and even wee votives and white cloth napkins, and set around the hall's perimeter blooming potted plants from the gardens in place of the usual poinsettias. Under Monte's officious direction, our regular group, including Dale and Robyn and Dallas, settled at a single table and shared what you might call Christmas conviviality as though we were and ever had been best friends for life. Steph strolled by with book matches and, once we'd lit our candles, dimmed the overhead lights to a chorus of "oohs" and "ahaas" around the room — Babs's signal to bang out a spirited intro to "Jingle Bells," which we all, some harmonizing, belted out at top volume. Dr. Mann then pronounced a blessing over the bounty and invited us to self-serve from the groaning board.

It groaned with crocks of Caesar salad, and heaps of roast turkey and hen and sliced ham, and cornbread dressing, and mashed potatoes and gravy, and squash and green bean casseroles, and corn pudding, and white beans with onions and red beans with pork, and cabbage with ham hocks, and asparagus and broccoli, and greens with chipped turnips, and English peas and black-eyed peas, and deviled eggs, and apple sauce, and fruit-salad jello, and spiced peaches and dill pickles and celery stalks and green and black olives, and dinner rolls and biscuits and butter pats, and tea and lemonade and sodas, with optional second and third servings as long as food lasted; and on every table clustering the shakers stood containers of catsup, mustard, vinegar, sugar, honey, and hot pepper sauce. Released from her self-imposed musical restraints by our eating, Babs showed off spectacularly with variations on carols during the meal, nibbling from a plate Corky kindly filled for her. We devoured wantonly, of course, incautiously forgetting that a final course, often triumphantly, always followed dinner and supper at Jubilee, so we too groaned when Babs sounded a trumpet-like tattoo and the swinging kitchen doors burst open and a parade of carts bearing huge bowls of fresh strawberries and of heavy whipped cream in peaks and trays of spongy shortcake moved among us, the drivers our bakers unloading as they came. Monte had spoken of this extravaganza and particularly of the dessert, mentioning that the berries, if smaller than California's, beat them for sweet succulence. He was surely right, and they just kept on coming, crowned with cream, until in our unleashed, abandoned delight we followed Corky's lead and flicked dabs and spoons of it at each others' faces. Other tables took the cue, but before bedlam broke out, Steph and the Nulls, having largely abandoned their surveillance till now, resumed it at Steph's whistle, and we fell back into line. Still, the whole affair gave us all a jolly high old time, everyone laughing and joking and carrying-on, with tensions relaxed, high spirits ascendant. Dr. Mann and Steph passed around to everybody little white, red-ribboned packages containing small medals inscribed "Jubilee 1959," fit for wearing on bracelets or necklaces or maybe as a pin on your baseball cap. Steph whistled again, and Babs played the opening chords of "Away in a Manger," which we sang one verse of a-cappella, and after that Dr. Mann uttered a quiet "Amen."

M&M had buzzed around the hall during dinner, popping flash bulbs for pictures, and now Monte had withdrawn with them to check proofs of me for badges, or so Travis explained when I caught up with him, though not why I didn't get to help choose. I tracked Travis because I wanted to smoke. A sugar-high, maybe, I needed to climb down from?

"Can we go back to your room?" I asked him, "or is Robyn home?"

"I think he's with the twins," Travis said, "sniffing out Monte's business."

We laughed. "Why were they so busy with the cameras tonight?" I asked him.

"For the yearbook, I guess," Travis said; "but maybe also for *Hughes' News,* if Scotty can get it together."

"How's that going? Things coming along?"

"Not really, no. I've given Scotty about a dozen cartoons, and Robyn's written an article about how Jubilee started, and Lance is supposed to be editorializing on the need for improving relations between staff and guests, whatever that means... like we're running a dating service or something; but I haven't heard anything about an actual issue or seen a production schedule. Maybe Scotty's waiting for you to come aboard? She still wants you."

"Is Monte aboard?"

"He's hanging out around the edges. Like he wants to be an advisor or something. I don't think he has an assignment yet."

"Could I get a Camel, please. I need one."

"Here you go. Is something wrong?"

"Not sure. I'm a little tense. You have time?"

"Yeah, but I want to sketch out some scenes from the dinner before I lose them. You can stay, though."

"No, no, I don't want to bother. Just smoke one with me."

We opened the windows and lit up and went quiet for a minute.

"You okay with the badges, Troy?"

"I guess I'll have to see one first. Have you designed it yet?"

"No. I've got an idea or two, but I've still not seen any photos. I meant, are you fine with the badge *idea?*"

"Are you not? It's okay with me if you're not. But I'd like to know what *you* think of it, as an idea?"

He took a deep drag, exhaled. "It's kind of hokey, doncha think? Corny?"

"Maybe," I said; "but with a classy, dignified design...?"

"Not sure how to make that slogan classy. It's kind of not."

"Monte loves it."

"Monte loves everything he thinks of. And nothing he doesn't. You know that."

"I do," I agreed, a little edgy.

"Here's what I'm getting at, though," Travis said: "is the badge really fair? To the other contestants?"

"Well," I said, "to be honest, I've thought about that too. I even brought it up to Monte, and he shot it down. But I don't know that it *isn't* fair. It's not going to influence anyone with any decision clout. If the judges see any random badges around, they won't, they can't, be swayed by them, not even if, as Monte thinks, they might swell the crowd a little. And how do we know the others won't bring their own cheering sections? I just don't know of any rules we're actually breaking with our plans."

"You think they're innocent?"

"No, that's the thing. What we're planning doesn't *feel* innocent. It doesn't feel exactly guilty either, though. So why do I?"

"Doesn't it feel wrong to you?"

"Well, it doesn't feel right."

"It may be cheating. It looks a little like cheating."

"I can't see that it hurts anybody. Who does it hurt?"

"It could hurt everybody."

"No, I don't see that. That's not a risk."

Travis didn't pick up. "So what should I do?" I asked him.

"I can't help you with that, Troy. Wish I could. You'll have to sort that one out for yourself," he said, crushing his butt against the sill, and spitting on it. "Toss yours in the toilet on the way out," he said, holding out a Lifesaver roll. "I better get on my sketches now. I'll work up a classy design."

Groggy and sluggish from the meal but remembering to take an allergy pill — I'd once "reacted" to strawberries — I returned to our room relieved to find Monte still out, for I wanted time alone to sort through recent issues and remarks, and reach decisions about them, including the "fairness" of the badges and other Montesque contrivances, and the Qwork surprise, and the Corky trip, and who my finals competitors were, and maybe even the Judas tale, which for the moment appeared to me either the worst shaggy-dog story ever told with the best punch line or the scary exposure of a seriously diseased mind intent on corruption; and of course on what Dale told me and didn't tell me. So I flung onto my bed, propped my pillowed head against the wall, and drifted...drifted into somnolent remembrance:

Shadrach, balancing six crates of strawberries, kicked at our back screen door. I unhooked it and returned to my jigsaw at the kitchen table.

"Mass Sweeney say dese heah de ripes' ah de crop. Yawls gets de bes'."

And Mother, fluttering: "Oh my goodness, we couldn't possibly use...six, we couldn't. Here, Shad, you keep one. No, you take it now. And you make sure to give Mr. Sweeney my thanks and the Reverend's. Now you go on and take it," nudging the box against his belly when we both knew he'd already stuffed his pants with the best berries from all six crates. You could see the bulby shapes there, poking out and damp.

"We could too've used six," I said, surly.

"No call for greed," she said. "Don't you imagine Shad's boys like them as much as you?" One of Shad's boys was Overnight, about my age and an occasional playmate. "It's only right we share. Mr. Sweeney gives to us, we give to the less fortunate."

"But Shad stole ours. And you helped him."

"Of course I didn't. Stop saying that."

But part of her reasoning scored. I didn't figure she meant to let the cat out, but her remark confirmed a suspicion I'd always pondered: that we were welfare too, pretty near: that congregational gifts (I never thought they quite made it as tithes) — from batches of turnip greens to the battered old TV — were crumbs for church mice; that we were "fortunate" only because one rung higher than Shad and Overnight, thanks to our color and Father's job, on the ladder of charity cases.

"So," I said, "Mrs. Tyler, like God, helps those who help themselves. Who help themselves to our berries."

"That's not what the scripture means, Timmy. You're twisting it."

"It's not scripture," I said.

"Of course it's scripture. I forget where right now, but it's in the Bible. And don't you be saying it's not."

"But it's not. It's Greek. It's just a proverb."

"Maybe it is in Proverbs. It sounds like it might be there."

"It isn't," I insisted. "It's not biblical. Listen to it and you'll hear how it can't be biblical. It says that God helps those who steal, who help themselves to other people's stuff. What else can it mean?"

"Well, it doesn't mean that, and you know it. You're being blasphemous, Timmy. So cut it out."

"I'm only saying Shad stole our berries. He cheated us. You helped him cheat us. You helped him steal Mr. Sweeney's present to us."

Perched there on the low stool, her breasts resting on the counter's edge, she leaned into the sink stemming berries, rinsing and slicing each into neat quarters. The yellow print sleeveless clung like skin to hers, its hemline hiked above her knees, showing crossed thighs. Fixed on her task — tongue-tip arrowed between her lips — she could have been a child cutting out paper dolls, even at 33 might've passed for a sister or schoolmate. But when I said she helped Shad cheat, the blue eyes widened, smoked over, her body started and flexed. Mother recurred.

"You know he'd helped himself, stuffed his pockets full. So why'd you give him a whole more box, what was left of it?"

The nylons sang as she uncrossed her thighs and slid from the stool, her wrist snapping like Mark's as she shut off the faucet so hard the pipes rattled below. And before she wriggled her skirt back down, I saw how her stocking seams were crooked, warping the fine curve of her calves. A bra shoulder strap sagged across her left arm. Sometimes, before Sunday services, she'd step from their bedroom into ours, spin on her toes, and ask: "How do I look? Are my seams straight?" as though beauty and style and acceptance depended on straight stocking seams. Hers didn't, no, but I understood why she thought they might: everybody remembers how scarce and pricey nylons were during the war, which meant she'd gone without them. Also, she was almost miserly about the few she had, and sealed up even the tiniest run with clear nail polish. Then, too, every item in what she called her "limited wardrobe" had to be fare-thee-well perfect. Because apart from her four nice outfits — two for fall and winter, two for spring and summer, alternated Sunday to Sunday year round — apart from *them, the only changes in her appearance Sunday to Sunday were the hats and the nail polish. Hats she made, re-made, made over again a third and fourth time from whatever lay handy. She was so creative and gifted at it Father pushed her to sell some, but she allowed as how she wasn't in the hawking business. (Well, she wasn't.) Some were flimsy strips of veil sprinkled with rainbow sequins; others sprouted petals snipped from wrapping paper, glued, and fastened to scraps of chicken wire. The best ones sported pheasant, duck, dove, and quail feathers sent over by wives of hunters in the church, prob'ly, I figured, with the notion of getting them back on a hat. The nail polish came compliments of Geraldine Null, local Avon lady and gutter expert, whom you've met. Every quarter, Avon turned out a new color, and once Miss Null had peddled it around town, she gave Mother whatever was left of the sample. Saturday nights she'd scrape off flakes of old polish, dabbing on the remover (clearing nearby nasal passages in no time!), and in three dainty strokes paint each nail in Paris Pink or Moonglow or Tulip Pastel or Sunset Cerise, ritzy names like that. "Now don't touch," she'd laugh, spreading her fingers and dancing away from my mock swipes at her body: "Don't touch me till I'm dry," as if touching would be okay then.*

"Your seams are crooked and your strap fell down," I said.

"I did no such thing," she said, jerking at the strap. "And you need to back off, young man, and watch your mouth! What was that you said about God?"

"Young man." I hated that. It could mean anybody.

She stepped close in bare feet, spread fingers — minus the wedding rings laid on the sill — bracing her hips. If I raised my eyes I knew they'd study her rising falling breasts.

"I didn't mean nothing," I said. "I meant he stole our berries, and you helped him do it."

"Anything," she corrected. "And you don't know he stole any-thing. I won't have you accusing him, Timothy. You know better. I've taught you about judging. We don't judge. You know the verse."

"But you helped him cheat. You did. And you're judging me right now!"

"Stop messing with the puzzle." She leaned down and stirred the pieces.

"Hey! " I said. "Cut that out! You're ruining...."

"Don't sass me, boy! And stand up! Look at me!" She took a breath. "Look, Timmy," she said. "I'm just trying to help you under-stand what's fair and what's not. You're being very unfair to Shad by accusing him of cheating when you don't know he did. That's why judging is wrong. The accusation is false. Now, what was that you said about God, about God and me?"

"Nothing. I didn't say anything else. I just asked why you gave him more when he'd already helped himself."

"Yes you did too. And don't you take to lying on top of inso-lence. You said something about God." She clasped my shoulders with both hands. "Don't make me shake it out of you."

I could feel the tremble in her hands, almost feel the heat in her face and words, but I could not understand a growing anger so much bigger than anything I'd done, so out of balance with it. Besides, if she really hadn't heard what I said, why was she mad over it? And if she had heard, why should I make things worse by repeating it?

"I didn't mean to upset you," I said.

She sank to her knees — actually knelt — her hands sliding down my arms, until the center part in her hair met the cleft of my chin.

"But I *am upset when you say things like that, honey. You know you shouldn't. Sometimes I think you try to upset me, saying things like that,"* a little catch in her throat.

So, she'd heard, all right, she'd heard it all, and her prying complaints were lies, traps. She'd faked it all, was faking this… softening.

"*But I didn't start it. You started it by not saying he cheated us, not saying he stole our berries and then helping him steal some more. Of ours. Like it was all okay for him to cheat!"*

Because it hadn't been at all okay for me that afternoon at Tanner's where big jars of jawbreakers and trays of gumdrops and tiers of candy bars and baskets of suckers and the thick hot juicy smells of cinnamon and licorice and chocolate would get the spit trickling in any kid's mouth. Mother and Miss Jewel were ooo-ing and ahhing over new bolts of fabric in the back, so it was easy to snatch the bubble gum square and peel back the wrapper and the comic strip down inside my pocket where they'd not notice — or even if they did they'd think I was scratching myself, which I'd get scolded for too, only not as much: she hated me doing that, hated more scolding me for it, embarrassed, in public. Anyway, by the time she'd fondled the cloth and put off buying any to another Saturday, and headed for the Plymouth, the gum had gone sticky on my hand, gooey with sweat and lint. And even if I didn't want it then, would've liked to be rid of it, I had to follow through, you know? What I'd done wasn't really done unless I finished it. So when I blew and the limp bubble plooped onto my chin, she understood without asking, and in a minute we were back at the counter, Miss Jewel behind it.

"Spit," Mother said, cupping her hand; and when I did, she flicked it into a grimy old spittoon, sploshing brown sludge out of it.

"Apologize," she said, pinching the back of my neck.

"I'm sorry," I said. "I'm sorry I took your gum."

"Stole," she said.

"All right. I'm sorry I stole your gum."

"Had it in his pocket all the time! Some example you set for other boys, Timothy, and you the preacher's son! How'm I to teach them when there's no getting through to my own boy?" not letting up on the pinch.

"So what about next time?" she asked. "You gonna promise?"

"I promise not to take...not to steal your gum."

"Or anything else?"

"Or anything else."

"I'm so sorry, Jewel; here's a penny for the gum and your trouble. It won't happen again, right, Timothy?"

But Miss Jewel broke in on our march to the door. "They's two for a penny," she said; "you got one comin'. And Tim bein' so nice to 'pologize an' all, seem like he earned a ree-ward. Don' tattle to Mr. T., but here ya go, have three pieces."

"How about a sucker?" I said. "Licorice."

"No rewards for cheats," she said, and dragged me through the door.

"...so just hush up about the strawberries."

She'd hung over me, ranting, and now shook me hard, her eyes like smoky agate. "What's got into you, all this meanness and sass? You think I don't know sin when I see it and hear it? Say! First impertinence and then blasphemy and then lying and now sass! And all over a few berries we don't need anyway. I won't have you sassing me, young man, and neither will your father. Why, what would he say to such talk!"

"Nothing. He never does. And why d'you always have to bring him up anyway?"

"Because he's your father is why. And he's sure 'nough gonna hear about this. You just wait."

"Tell him then! I don't care! Dammit, I don't care. If you're gonna tell him anyhow, why't you shut up on me and go fix your seams. I told you they were crooked!"

Her arm lifted, swept high and back behind her head, showing the caked talcum and black bristles of her armpit, and knifed toward my cheek. I reeled, buckled; but her left arm was there, cradled to my waist. She jerked mine to her body, to the bathroom.

"And swearing! Swearing and disrespect to me and your own father! And to my very face! I don't care you are thirteen, boy, you don't get away with a filthy mouth in my house. Where'd you hear such talk, pick up such rot? Not in my house, you didn't. Nosiree, or use it either. You can't learn to watch your mouth, you'll have it washed. I don't care how old you get, and living in my house!"

She frothed a red washcloth with an Ivory bar and then, one hand tugging my hair, plowed with the other into my mouth, scouring and scraping and screwing her lathered fingers deep into my throat until the gag came, and the grating retch.

"You will be clean," she said.

…Isaiah's lips…the ten lepers…the hemorrhaging woman… the thousand hymns that promise clean: "sinners plunged beneath that flood lose all their guilty stains…."

"You will, if I have to strangle you to do it!"

She turned away. "Wash up now," she said. "I need your help in the kitchen."

All week long, believing berries would come, she'd skimmed and saved the cream topping bottles of milk left mornings at our door. Flakes of it ridged in tiny mounds and valleys around the dark blue bowl.

"Whip it," she said, handing me the wire beater. "Whip it 'till it peaks."

And mad, mortified, but with the badge of her love still burning my cheek, the tangy track of it stinging my throat, I attacked the cream.

Two eerie sounds brought me half-awake, one a low, ragged rasp rising from my throat, the other a high, thin whine from Mark's bed.

"Mom," he cried.

My mouth felt cotton-packed, thick with pillowed mass: smothering breath.

"Mom!" he repeated.

My tongue filled my mouth, blocking passage. Trying to swallow, I gagged.

A shadow appeared in their doorway.

"It's Tim," Mark said. "Why's he making those sounds?"

I pressed on my tongue, sucked breath.

"Timmy?" from the doorway. "It's all right, Mark. Try to go back to sleep. It'll be all right. Timothy?"

I pulled on the covers to hide the arousal below, the other tongue there.

"You'd better come now, Prissy," the shadow said.

I tried to speak, my language like granny's stroke-talk.

In a moment she was there, and sat, tugged my body to hers. I hid myself under clasped thighs, pushed into her breasts, gasping.

"My God," she said, fingers working at my neck. "Dear God, Ernest, I think he's choking to death, choking on his tongue."

"Tim's dying?" Mark said. "I'm gonna throw up."

"Nobody's dying," she said. "Get Mark out of here, Ernest. One mess at a time. Take him off somewhere." But he didn't move from Mark's bedside.

"Get the light," she snapped. "At least you can get the light. I've got to see."

I tried again to speak. Wheezed.

"Don't," she said. She pulled up the sheet to wipe my sweat. I tugged it down for cover.

"His tongue's swollen way back into his throat. Now lie back, honey; lie back and breathe through your nose. It's going to be just fine, I know it is."

In the light I could see she wasn't so sure. Her face shed an oily, yellowish sheen; creases cut around her mouth and puffy eyes; a tiny muscle twitched left of her nose. She bit at the insides of her cheeks, pulling and puckering her lips to one side and the other. Her hands played about my face and neck, probing, caressing.

"I think we'd better pray," he said.

"It must have been the strawberries," she guessed. "Dr. Sawyer said he might be allergic to fruits besides figs. Get the allergy pills, Ernest. And will you please take Mark out of here? Just bring the pills. And," she jerked her head toward my crotch, "do something about that."

I reached to conceal myself but she pinned my wrists. "No," she said, "don't you touch it. You concentrate on breathing. Ernest, call Dr. Sawyer…and take care of that. I want the boy relaxed."

He stared at his hands hanging like dead leaves, brittle and veiny, between his knees.

"Ernest!"

"I'll get the pills," he said. "C'mon, Mark, if you're going to hurl."

But Mark perched on his knees, gawking.

There was no pain, only a long, mellow ache, like an echo, as the strain, above and below, spread and built and arched up and up toward…what?…some crest, some apex, awesome and awful. Breaths came in hoarse, uneven gasps, heaving me against her until she began rocking with me, hugging me as I'd held Peg hurtling, breathing hard herself, lips to my ear murmuring, murmuring something about sorry.

"Here," he said, holding out the bottle, pills rattling. "The doc'll be over soon. How is he?"

"How does he sound?" a sob in her voice. And I felt the tears rise to my own eyes, hot and prickly, in sorrow for her and shame at myself. For I knew, as ever I did, that I'd caused it all, brought all this trouble upon ourselves. All the fantasies, all the squabbling and the urges behind it, all the turmoil of the afternoon at once flooded back, claiming and defining me. And when I tried to speak my shame, I bucked and retched.

"Two," she said. "It's for your own good now, honey. 'Cause we love you. Hurry," reaching for his hand.

The two of them hulked over me, collaborated over me: and the feel and tone and sum of it suddenly crackled with familiarity. For I'd been here before — somewhere, somehow, long ago, before and behind all but the dimmest remembering of it, but here all the same: except turned over, on my belly, the two of them pressing against my rump, shoving a slick wet thing into me…water rushing, spilling over: their satisfied sighing, and my whimper, that it was done, and I clean.

But it was not done.

"Hold his arms, Mark," he said. "You're strong now. Hold him down."

His fingers thrust the capsules down my throat, wedged them through my heaving gags, until she pulled him back.

"We'll have to help him till they take," she said, "get him and the tongue relaxed. Mouth-to-mouth. You first, Ernest. Hold him, Mark."

I shut my eyes against it, felt her fingers close and stroke, smelled the sour as his mouth closed over mine. And accompanied by her chant...

"...in, out, in, out, that's it, together...."

...accompanied by her chant, he pumped himself into me, gave me breath. Then the shudder, spasm, spray, and surcease. I waned, the three of them glued to my flesh.

I awoke to Monte's face leaning over mine, his hand gentling my shoulder.

"Are you okay, Troy?" he said. "It sounded like you're crying."

"I'm not crying, " I said, wiping my eyes. "Really bad dream."

"Sorry," he said. "I pulled up your blanket last night. You were still dressed. That big meal knock you out?"

"I took a pill," I remembered. "They make me drowsy."

He reached out his balm, smeared his lips, slouched onto his bed. "You up for talking?"

"While I pee," I said, crawling out, "how about fetching me a Coke from downstairs? I could use some hydration."

By the time I'd splashed my face and brushed my teeth, he'd returned to his bed, the frosty Coke on the floor beside mine. I flipped him a quarter.

"I wanted to tell you," he said, "we picked out a picture of you for the badge. M&M and I like it a lot."

"Well, let's see it. Where'd you get it?"

"Serendipity. You remember that time you and Scotty got sodas from Lance at the snack bar and went off together? Well, M&M were there too, hanging around the bar, clicking their kodaks, and they caught you in a candid shot. It's a handsome look. You're in your madras, top button open. Fresh haircut. Big smile."

"I'll need to see it. Don't I get some say here?"

"Of course. But Travis has it, to work on the design with. I saw him after you did last night. He thinks it's the right photo, too."

"I'll still need to see it."

"You'll love it, I promise. It's really good. By the way, SS says we can do the badge in color."

I slapped the mattress with open palms. "Why *IS* she being so nice? I don't get it. She's up to something."

"Maybe she's got a little crush on you."

"She's *FIFTY*! Good God!"

"Would it be okay if she's forty-six?"

"Oh stop! No! But why *is* she, being nice, I mean?"

"I told you. She admires your work. And I figure she thinks you may be good for Jubilee. You win, and she'll use you for PR publicity. 'This here'" — he posed his arms in the framing gesture — "'this here is the kind of staff Jubilee hires!' I also figure she's a little embarrassed for reaming us out over the Sparrow Club. She's prob'ly heard how we loved it, and how good for morale it was. Maybe she's kind of making up for that."

"I doubt it. Not the type. But she's paying for the badges?"

"Jubilee authorizes color," he said. "You've become an investment, Troj. Everybody is all in on this thing. And they're all expecting big-time returns. Everybody wants you to win."

"You're not relieving the pressure, Monte."

"Oh, c'mon, man! You know you've got it nailed."

"I don't. And you need to stop saying that. Don't say that around. It's setting me up. You'll jinx the whole thing. So stop saying it, okay? Now: I really do need to see the photo and the designs, before you…what?…go to production."

"All right. Travis thinks he'll have a coupla designs by the weekend. Uh, if you're not gonna drink that Coke…?"

I took a gulp, then another.

"And there's something else," I went on: "I'm not switching crews, and neither are you. I've thought about it, and we're not accepting any 'promotions,' if that's what Steph's offering. And I'm sure as hell not going to be called a 'shit-head.' 'Gopher's' gonna be bad enough. And it's not as though we'd get a raise by switching, just the same percentage of the take as before. Moving us just messes everything up, and to no purpose, unless Steph gets off on ordering us around. And I'm not playing that game just so she can feel important, or you either. Changing will slow everything down till we get used to it, and we've got momentum now, and change'll lose that. And the crew won't accept us bossing them around. They'll resent it, and they'll take it out on us by slowing down. And how could we make them not? Flog them? Fine them? We're not Dallas. We *could unofficially* maybe help everybody pick it up by doing it ourselves and encouraging them to come along. You know, 'Speed it up, Robyn, I'll race you to the finish!' Like that. Maybe get the bakers to promise cookies when we're done? They always have leftovers. But what's Steph's rush, anyway? We're not slugs and sloths. We're not running into the next meal or the crew coming on. What's the hurry? She'll do nothing but screw up the good routine and the good fun and the good morale we've got going, and make everyone cross and crabby. There's no plus in it for anybody I can see. I don't like anything about it, and I want you to tell Steph that. We have to stop this happening."

"That's the longest speech I ever heard you give," Monte said.

"I mean every word of it. I'm not switching."

"Why don't you tell her, then?"

"No, you're her favorite. You can say I refuse to switch."

"She prob'ly won't want to piss you off right now," he said.

"Then tell her she will if she tries to switch us."

"I reckon your arguments will sound better coming from you. Like, stronger. More bite in 'em."

I wondered. "You do?" I asked. "I'm not Bruce."

"But maybe you need to sound like him."

"Well, okay. I'll tell her, to make sure she gets it."

"You want me there? I can come with you."

"No. I'll do it. It's my choice."

"What if she insists?"

"Then I'll quit. I mean it. I'll absolutely quit and head home. Let Wolf have his stupid Goforth title. I don't care for it anyway. If she insists on switching us, I'll pack up and be out of here on the next train, just you watch. There are limits...."

I probably couldn't have told you right then what they were, but I felt that we'd reached them.

"No, no," he said, stepping over to me and sitting. "Hold on there, guy. You can't quit. They won't let you *quit*. And you can't not compete. Switching isn't that big a deal. We'll work out something. But don't start thinkin' about quitting! Not after all this!"

I stood and moved away. "It is a big deal for me, and you need to respect that. I won't have her jerking us around by the necks like so many dumb-ass chickens, for no cause at all, and messing up these last weeks. It's mean and useless and stupid. I'll tell her."

"Don't tell her *that*! She'll fire you."

"Fine. Let her. I don't care. And screw the speech too!"

Somebody knocked.

"Not *now!*" Monte yelled. But Travis poked his head in. "What's going on?" he asked tentatively.

"Well…," Monte began, looking at me.

"I finished my designs," Travis said, holding at the door. "Thought you'd want to see? I can come back."

"No, no," Monte said, his eyes still on me. "It's fine. Come in. Let's have a look. Okay, Troy?"

"Sure. Hey, Trav. Thanks for last night. You bring the photo?"

"Right here," he said, handing it over.

It was a head and shoulders shot, definitely me and complimentary to me, my face tanned, and the blonde, trimmed crewcut bright above it. They must have lightly tinted my eyes a darker blue. The smile was my best one. I handed it to Monte.

"I reckon it will have to do," I grinned. "But what's with the new hair?"

Somebody, presumably Travis, had inked in a few golden wisps of hair at the V of my neck.

"Adding a little sex appeal," Monte said. "But Travis, you left out the cigarette!"

"More cheating," I laughed, uneasily.

"Don't go back there," Monte said. "It's just a little harmless extra illustration."

"See what you think of these," Travis said, laying design sketches on Monte's bed. He selected one, studied it, stepped over to show me.

The octagonal badge cushioned my head against a soft blue background matching my eye color and accenting the straw of the hair. Dixie's white-blonde head, finely combed, rested against my left shoulder, her nose and dark brown eyes ahead, her smile about to open. My teeth gleamed. Forming a ribboned arc around the bottom, in rippling red script, rolled the slogan, "Go-for(th) Troy!"

"It's kind of conspicuously patriotic, doncha think?" I said. "I'm not running for office."

"I like it," Monte said. "Subliminal associations there, maybe. Patriotic can't hurt."

"Dixie's gorgeous," I said. "I mean Bruce."

"He means the dog," Monte said.

But Travis was absorbed in another sketch.

"We could move the dog's head over to the right shoulder. Or set him right in front, like on Troy's lap. Or move Troy's left hand onto the dog's neck, like scratching?"

"Let's see that one," Monte said.

"I kind of like the idea of my touching...um...Bruce," I said. "But you don't have my hand. In a photo."

"I think we do, " Travis said. "In another shot. We could graft it in."

"Troy," Monte said, "do you actually object to the first one?" picking it up again. "We're getting pretty complicated with the graft and such."

"No," I said, "I don't object to any of it except to the whole badge idea. I still think it may be cheating. But I guess we're past that now. I'll go with the first one if you and Trav want to. It's a good photo of us both."

"Then that's settled," Monte declared. "Trav, get with M&M and fine-tune the first one and set it up and let me know. I'll take the mock-up to SS for the final shot."

"Will do," Travis said, gathering the sketches and the picture. "Thanks. Sorry to interrupt." He gave us a curious look, and left.

"You can't quit now," Monte said, reaching for the Coke and taking a swallow. "Maybe you don't need to see SS now?"

"I'll see her," I said, taking back the bottle.

"Give her that same speech," he said.

Steph turned out to be a pussycat.

"Well," she said, leaning back in her squeaking chair, "if you and Monte don't want to captain the ship, I'm not going to force you to. But I think you might learn something about management if you did. And as a start you might tell him to quit the horsing around back there. I know he's not working that hard; and if he would, the others might too, he's such a role model for them. Would you care to recommend somebody else to shift head?"

"No ma'am. You're missing the point. It's not that Monte and I are wrong for the job; it's that the job is wrong for the time and place. The crews are doing their jobs just fine. Ours can speed up if you think we must. But appointing bosses will confuse everything and make us angry and resentful and resistant."

"Yes, you said that. I don't want that; we can't have that. Okay, we'll let it ride for now. But I'll think about how to pick up and streamline and get better work out of yawl. You do too, and get back to me with ideas. And thank you for your opinion."

"Thank you for hearing it."

Corky and the bike appeared to be waiting for me when I left the building.

"I saw you come in," he said. "What's happening in there?"

"A bit of negotiating with Steph," I said. "Calming some troubled waters."

"'Peace, be still'?" he grinned.

"More like Please.... How've you been? Haven't seen you since Christmas!"

"That *was* great fun, wadn't it?" He fingered a trinket hanging from his neck.

"Wait. What is that? Is that the medal...the gift?"

"Sure is," he said, giggling. "I got Travis to engrave my name on the back — see? — and found a chain at the jewelry counter. Like it?"

"Is that the new fashion statement?"

"Maybe," Corky said. "Think it'll go with the badge?"

We laughed. "How about instead of the badge?" I said.

"You want me to get yours engraved? I could ask Travis."

"Ummm. Maybe not just yet. I'm not sure where mine is. I might've lost it. Thanks for the offer, though."

"Just let me know when. See ya!" And he pedaled off.

The next Sunday afternoon Robyn joined Lance and Scotty and Corky and several of us others for a hike up Baldy but suffered a serious asthma attack half way along and had to be helped down to the Nurse's station where she checked his inhaler and recommended bed rest for the remainder of the day. When nobody else did, I volunteered to fill in for him at work; and then Corky also offered, and we stayed there late enough to miss the service.

Heading for the snack bar afterward, we never made it inside the Complex, for milling around outside, milling and roiling, practically mooing like restless cattle considering a stampede, were about two-thirds of the staff, looking stunned and smelling scorched and just about shedding sparks from the sermon laid on them, which must've been even more blistering than usual. The Nulls, of course, always kept their antennae stretched, were forever sniffing the air to measure our moods. And they could tell, as sure as I could, when a crowd was ripe, when primed for a Major Pitch. And before you knew what was happening or how, we'd all been herded and goaded as if by some invisible staff down to the lake's edge, and there we settled. I write "invisible" because it couldn't look planned: no matter how they'd mapped it out, no matter how routine and predictable the pattern every time, it had to look impromptu; it had to feel improvised. But if you'd witnessed as many of these hustles as I had, you'd know they weren't. You'd know to expect no surprises. You'd know how to manage and get through it. So I didn't much mind being caught up in it. And because I figured Monte had to be in there someplace, and Corky too, and been goaded in a different direction and absorbed in the pack.

Besides, the night was sublime, made for pure enjoyment. Post-sunsets, deserts lose their heat in light breezes that tickle the skin, stroke the neck, raise goosebumps and bring shivers. The artificial waterfall on Baldy thrummed faintly, and I imagined the billions of droplets from its crashing spinning wildly away to freeze in glittering crystal against the indigo vastness overhead. Trust me, you haven't seen stars until you've seen them across New Mexico skies — zillions of them, riots of them, spangling the heavens. The lake water gleamed a polished black, like melted slate it whispered along the banks. The soughing pines, punctuated now and again by a lonely owl-note, muffled the cicada's buzz, tempered it into solemnity. Even you too must have known times and places like this, when Nature not only matched your mood but fed it, collaborated with whatever mysterious fevers fired yours to make it richer, rarer, keener. But — wouldn't you know? — just when you're letting yourself sink into it, just when you're relaxing into unreflecting gratitude and appreciation, in the split-second before you give way to the pull of night-music....

A voice piped a few bars of another kind:

Precious Lord, take my hand....

Most of the others joined,

Lead me on, let me stand....

and softly sang other such familiar choruses, until someone, hidden by darkness, felt moved to talk in a stammering, often weepy strain about his changed life, her altered career plans, thanks to the Jubilee experience. The formula then called for a Mr. Null to oil the air with pleas to the rest of us, the few, who either weren't much changed or, if we were, chose to keep quiet about it as nobody else's business. Then we'd bow our heads for silent prayer and eventually an oral benediction informing God of what He'd done and now had better do, and again Sunday would be over, until Monday.

So the departure from that sequence startled me, shot another hole in my Sure Thing syllabus, which had become pretty well ventilated by now. Mr. Null's voice droned on about unclean lips and hot coals scalding them and Isaiah's capitulation — "Here am I; send me" — but then dropped to the pitch Monte said mine should assume in the speech: I mean, Mr. Null began crooning, almost, and told us to stand up and form a circle and take the hand of the person on each side. I couldn't make him out in the dark but I knew it was Monte who came up on my left — you live around somebody and his cologne for a while, you know when he's entered your zone — and took my hand into his cool, hard, dry palm.

"You needn't say a word," the voice went on. "You needn't tell me now. But you should let him know; he's waiting for you to let him know. And you can tell him in your heart. You can make the commitment there."

Monte's hand moved slowly over and around mine, stroked, fondled, gently toyed with it, laced his fingers between and among mine, folded them into his, nestled the grooves, traced the rimples, lightly tickled the palm and heel, ever gentle, never still, as though attempting with a different instrument the same maneuvers he'd used as entertainment on that first afternoon, now to convey or to read some message, some signal.

"You can make your commitment silently," the voice continued. "But if you're afraid to acknowledge and accept his call, he can't, he won't acknowledge you either. If you're ashamed to recognize and yield...."

His hand closed loosely around my fingers, one after another, brushing them, grazing their tips. My breath quickened.

"...he won't acknowledge you. You'll force him to reject you if you reject the invitation he offers, if you delay acceptance too long."

His hand wrapped the back of mine, his thumb kneading, smoothing skin. Nearby, someone snuffled.

"....surrendering your own will to his. He knows it's the hardest decision you'll ever have to make...."

He poked at my high school class ring, pried under it, revolved it slowly.

"That's why we want to help by letting it be as private, as confidential as we can...."

His nails trailed down onto my wrist, feathering it. I shuddered.

"It's just between you and him. He's waiting. He's calling. It's time to let him have his way with you."

His palm moved to match and mirror mine, to companion mine, the fingers threading between mine so to couple the hands, clasp and lock them in possession.

"So let your hand speak. Sign your commitment to the hand holding yours. Just press the hand holding yours, press it to say you accept the call tugging at your heartstrings. He will know, he will bless your commitment, and there will be rejoicing in heaven. Just press the hand in yours. That will be your yes: your sacred affirmation."

I tore apart and flung away — aroused, polluted — into the consoling dark, sobbing my sumptuous shame.

11

Neither of us had mentioned to the other anything about the lakeside event when, three days after it, Steph approached us in the Sweat Shop as we finished cleaning up after lunch.

"Could both of you," she asked, "meet me in my office right away, say, in half an hour? You're not in trouble."

"Sure thing," Monte said, giving me a look. "What's up?"

"Just come. Half an hour."

We headed back to Cactus to change and brush, guessing, but hadn't a clue.

"Sit," she said, pointing at two wooden chairs before her desk. Elbows on the spotless surface, she rested her folded hands against her chin and watched us for a bit, then sighed.

"There've been some developments," she said. "I'm probably not supposed to tell you this, but since you're involved, I've decided to. I've learned some details about the speaking competition."

"The badges are already in production," Monte interrupted. "We can't pull that plug now."

"It's not about the badges. It's about Troy's competition."

"About time," I muttered, but apprehensively.

"Here's what's happened," Steph said, hitching up her chair and sitting back. "I've had a call from the California Convention Headquarters. The Goforth state winner in California has had to withdraw from the national finals here. To get married. It seems she turned up pregnant four months after her church's Valentine's Day Sweetheart Banquet and she'll be on her honeymoon the week of the finals."

Monte snorted and I suppressed a giggle.

"Don't laugh yet," Steph cautioned. "They're sending the second-place state winner to us for the finals." She paused. We waited. "They can do that. It's legit. I called the national Baptist Board in Nashville, and it's okay to do that."

"Who is he?" I asked. "What'd you find out about him?"

"It's a she," Steph said; "the second-place winner is also a girl."

"Didn't you find out anything about her?"

"Yes," Steph said, and took a deep breath. "They thought we should know."

"Know what?" we chorused.

"Well," Steph said: "She's Chinese. And she's a deaf-mute."

I laughed. "Er, Steph, it's a *speaking* contest! You know, with *words*!"

Monte frowned. "What?" he said. "Say that again."

"She's Chinese. And she can't hear or speak."

"You can't be serious," Monte sneered.

"I am serious," Steph said. "I asked Nashville about that too. They already knew. They had to rule on her eligibility for the California competition. So she can participate here."

"The hell you say! No, she can't. It has to be illegal."

"But *how?*" I said.

"She signs her speech. In sign-language. You know. And at the same time her younger brother speaks it. She doesn't hear him but he reads her signing to know where she is, so they can stay and end together. He's memorized her speech too."

"It's already unfair," Monte interrupted her. "That's two of them against one of us. That can't be right."

Ignoring him, Steph continued: "My contact said the California state judges didn't feel quite right giving the win to a mute but were so impressed by her speech and wanted to respect her courage they ranked her second, never thinking…, well, never imagining that she'd get to the national finals here. And now here she is."

"This is insane," Monte said. "We'll have to get her disqualified."

"Give her a pregnancy test," I giggled.

"It's not funny, Troy," Monte said, scowling. "It's a frigging fraud, is what it is. Didn't you even protest, Steph? We can at least stage a protest. We'll have to."

"I don't think protests will change anything. Besides, who would you, who would we, protest *to*? Dr. Mann thinks her participation's a done deal."

"It *is* cheating," I said, uncertainly. "It's *not* fair."

"Damn right it's not," Monte said. "There must be rules. Where do the rules say a deaf-mute can compete in a speech match? It's ridiculous. It's absurd. It can't happen."

"But it is kind of funny," I said.

"Don't you be laughing, Troy," he said. "You really think it'd be funny to go home and have to admit to everybody you lost to a deaf-mute?! I don't think so. There's stuff at stake here. It's no joke."

"No," Steph said; "it's not a joke. Nashville doesn't think so either. And they want us to be extra sensitive, extra careful not to offend...or...shame her. They're worried about that. We have to watch out how we describe her. How we refer to her... well...her difference. Her deficiency? That's what Nashville said. We have to 'respect' her...her...situation. Dr. Mann says we might get sued if we're not fair to her. Treat her just like everybody else."

"Is she American?" Monte said. "I'll bet you have to be an American to compete in this thing."

"She's a citizen. She was born here."

"What's her name?" I asked.

Steph opened a drawer and drew out a pad, rifled some pages. "Here it is, only I can't say it." She spelled it out: "C-h-a-o. Period. X-i-n-g. Last name: W-e-i."

"That means she'll go last," I said. "After everybody else has spoken."

"Not good," Monte said. "Troy needs to be last. Can't we fix it so the order isn't alphabetical by last name?"

"I'm not sure which one the last name is," Steph said, "in Chinese."

"Well find out!" Monte said. "And let's make it official that the order is by drawing straws or something else random. We can control that, can't we? And how would we ever get her to trade places in the lineup if we can't *talk* to her? This is getting stupider by the second."

"Actually, Monte," Steph stepped in, serious: "I don't think there's anything we can do except let it all play out as arranged so far. We try to mess with their plans, somebody's gonna get hurt or pissed, and Jubilee might get a bad rap or sued. Its reputation is sort of on the line here. I'm going to have to ask you both not to change anything, or try to change anything, about the finals. It's probably better if you don't even talk about any of this, lest you slip up and say a wrong thing. I'm not gagging you; I just need you to be really careful what you say. This is a tricky business."

"It's monkey business, is what it is," Monte said. "It's a rotten business. It stinks. And what about *our* plans? What happens to them now? I think we have to challenge this."

"I don't think so," Steph said softly.

"Look," Monte said: "At least we can petition. I can get Lance to draft a petition of protest...to Nashville. At least we can take a stand. Get lots of signatures, that should be easy. Let Nashville know we think this is crap."

"I'm pretty sure Dr. Mann won't allow that," Steph said.

"Then why the hell did you even *tell* us?" Monte said. "If you won't let us try to stop it?"

"I didn't want you to be surprised. Thrown off. By her just showing up that night...and...signing her speech. It would be a shock."

"It's *already* a shock," Monte said. "But listen, Steph: we seriously need to challenge her eligibility. I get the sensitivity angle, but basically she's not qualified to compete. She can't speak. It's that simple. It's cut and dried."

"She speaks, Monte," Steph said. "She speaks the only way she can."

Steph paused for a second or two, tapped the desk with one finger, considered, then said: "I need to see Troy privately. You're excused, Monte."

"What for?" he asked, not politely.

She shook her head, pointing to the door.

"There's something else," she said, when he was gone. "Something you need to know about. I don't know whether you'll decide to do anything about it, but you need to know it's happened."

"What's that?" My heart picked up its pace.

"There's been some confusion around the state that one contestant will represent. Name of Wolf Warren. He's a native Oklahoman but he attends school in Arkansas, and he's decided he wants to represent Oklahoma. Oklahoma didn't have a state speaking competition this year, and the Baptist Convention there would love to have this Warren fellow represent them in our finals. The Arkansas Convention agrees to be represented by the second-place Arkansas State winner, especially as he's already here and they'd save the expense of getting him out here and putting him up. We know him."

I was slow catching up to Steph. "We do?" I asked.

"It's Robyn Byrd. Robyn Byrd was second-place Goforth winner in Arkansas."

"Uh-oh," I said; "that's a complication. I don't see how...?"

"Yes, it could have been a 'complication,' but it isn't. I'm not telling you because there's a problem. There isn't. The competition we're hosting isn't affected by this development. Everything will proceed just as we've planned it. I'm telling you because you need to know — for personal reasons — what's happened."

She paused again, let it sink in. "I don't know what you mean," I said, my heart knocking.

"You need to know that Robyn has decided not to compete in the finals. He says he has 'a conflict of interests.' I don't know what that means, and he didn't explain when I told him about the opening. But he also says his decision is firm. There wasn't a third place winner in Little Rock, so Arkansas will name Robyn the official Goforth state winner. It won't be represented in our finals. Robyn says he regrets that, but 'other concerns,' he said, 'outweigh' his regret."

"Wow," I said quietly. "This is a lot to take in."

"I thought you should know," Steph said, "what Robyn did."

"Yes." I said. "I should."

"It's your decision whether to tell anyone else. I won't. I don't know whether Robyn will."

Monte was waiting for me outside, where he kicked hard at the white gravel, sending a spray of it across the flowerbeds.

"It's a fucking swindle," he said. "It ruins everything. We cannot let this happen. Don't you have any ideas?"

I felt short of breath, slightly dizzy, but saw that I had to pick up where we'd left off with Steph. I'd have to process Robyn later.

"Why're you assuming she'll win? I still might, doncha think?"

"I'm not assuming that. I'm being realistic. Her… 'situation'…is an advantage. It gives her an edge."

"Boy, I never heard *that* before. That handicaps are advantages. That…deficiencies…help!"

"In this context, they do. It means everybody'll feel sorry for her. Surely you can see that."

"The judges can't *feel* anything like that. They have to keep impartial."

"They can't but they will. They won't be able to help it. This is all just so completely fucked up." He kicked again. "Shit, I'm going to talk to Lance about a petition. SS didn't say I couldn't. Or wait. Maybe I'll take it straight to Dr. Mann. Why waste time with SS? Her mind's made up. You want to go with me to see The Man? Two's better'n one."

"You just said back there that two was unfair."

"Don't get smart, Troy. You want to come along, or not?"

I paused, thinking. "No, Monte, I don't think I do. This is all pretty new and raw, and I've not thought it through yet, but I reckon I don't want any part of seeing The Man about it. And I wish you wouldn't see him either. I'm sorry, I hate to disagree, but I think you're all wrong about this." I sounded more plaintive than I felt.

"No, I'm not," he said. "We have to challenge. *It's* what's wrong."

"Let me finish, please," I said, pausing again to think. "We'll both need to consider, but I doubt I'm going to change my mind. Please don't protest. I'm having no part of it, and after all it's my speech. I need some say here, and I'm saying we don't challenge. It's an ugly, nasty thing to do. It's mean-spirited and small-minded. It's petty. It's also futile. California and Nashville have both said she's legit. They're not going to turn around now and say she isn't. And when they reaffirm their first decision, we'll have embarrassed ourselves, humiliated ourselves, and still have to host the contest with her in it. We'll have created a huge uproar for nothing, without gaining a thing. And we'll have shamed and upset Jubilee. Imagine the bad press. But if we play it out and she wins, Jubilee gets points as the site of a breakthrough. Steph will love the publicity. And besides all that, a protest against her participation will look like we're scared of her; we'll look intimidated and gutless, against a handicapped girl. It won't do, Monte. And any protest would be inhospitable at best: they'll say we're beating up on an already disadvantaged person. And what if she turns out to be nice? We'll look rude and crude and discourteous. Challenging Nashville is rebellious; it's insubordinate. It's uppity and out of line. It's only going to bring us and Jubilee a lot of ill will. And we cannot claim it's unfair. Saying it's unfair is an insult to her ingenuity and accommodation and courage. She's actually already earned our respect and admiration by getting this far. We ought to be celebrating her, not chasing her off. We undermine her achievement and disgrace ourselves with petty nitpicking and efforts to disqualify her. We mustn't do it, Monte. So no, I don't want to see The Man with you about protests and petitions. And you should scrap your plan to. And don't go rallying Scotty and Robyn and all them for some big demonstration. We have to drop it and go on with our plan for The Night Of."

He'd played with his balm through my tirade, tickling and twirling and turning it, and now uncapped it as if to oil himself up for a rebuttal.

"Are you *quite* finished?" he scoffed.

"For now," I said.

"You know, Troy, you're a sentimental schmuck. You're a soft-headed patsy. You don't have a clue how she's set us up. She suckered you just like she suckered California and Nashville. It's a canny scam, and you bought it. Of course I'm going to see The Man, especially now you've betrayed our plan by backing her. And of course I'm going to recruit others to help."

"You're one bullheaded asshole, Monte, and you're dead wrong here. She's not a goddamn *threat*!"

"And you know what else? I don't think you *want* to win. I've suspected that for some while, and now I'm sure of it, now you've gone over to the Chinese side. You're *ready* to quit, aren't you? You'd love to chicken out! And now you've found a way, by championing this crooked Chinese foreigner."

"Are you out of your freaking mind?! Of course I want to win. I probably am *going* to win. And I haven't 'gone over' any-where. What is wrong with you? I'm just trying to be fair to this girl...who is doing nothing unfair to us by entering the contest. And I'll tell you something else: what's *really* messed up is us getting so riled over her, so worked up over this stupid contest. I'm pretty sure I've — no, we've — taken it all *WAY* too seriously from the start. It's just a shitty little church thing and we've let it take over our shitty little lives! Why can't we back off and cool down and have a little fun with it? I told you I think this latest wrinkle is hilarious. Why aren't we laughing at it? Instead of quarreling over it? I actually don't like arguing with you, Monte."

"Well," he said, "that's a point. I'm not exactly enjoying it either. But...."

"How about no 'buts' right now? How about we drop it and gear down? Think it over. Come back if we need to. And put protests on the back burner for now. Turned to simmer."

We both grinned, a little shakily.

"Besides," I said, "as long as we're talking, there's this other thing. What was all that business at the lake about?"

"What business? What lake?"

"You know what I mean. With the hands. Sunday night."

"No, I don't know. What're you talking about?"

"After work on Sunday night. I know you remember. I worked for Robyn, with Corky. And then everybody gathered at the lake. Please don't pretend, Monte."

"Oh, right. I didn't go. I went back to Cactus and wrote a letter home and went to bed. Why? What happened?"

"No, you were there. Next to me, lakeside."

"Not so. I wasn't there. Why? What makes you think I was there?"

"You *were* there. I know when you're around. Why're you denying it?"

"Troy! What's this about? Why are you getting upset?"

"I know it was you! Why're you saying it wasn't? I know it was."

"It wasn't. I wasn't there. What did Steph want back there, when she kept you?"

"That's private."

"Ah *HA!*" he said. "She *DOES* have a crush on you!"

"Fuck you, Monte!" I said.

* * *

By lunchtime Thursday badges had begun to blossom around the campus. Corky showed up for work with one pinned at his waistline.

"Whadaya think, guys?" he said; "pretty cool, huh? Dixie looks great, doesn't she?"

"Corky, *no!*" I said; "it's not Dixie. You don't know who she is or whether she's even she! You don't know squat about the dog!"

"Got it," he said, not the least deflated. "But don't you think it's neat? I even like the slogan."

This was my first view of the finished product, and I had to agree that it showed an attractive image, even a striking one positioned there on Corky's hip. He'd hidden another one in his fist and now handed it to me: "I brought you one. You want to autograph mine? I have a pen."

"I don't think there's room," I said; "maybe later," as he did deflate.

"Autographs are Dallas's idea," he said; "he wants you to sell them, with a commission to him, of course" We laughed, Monte too: "Do-Da-Dallas just can't stop, can he?" Monte said.

"Do-what?" Corky said, but focused on pinning my badge. "Here on your left shoulder, I think. Looking good against the white!"

"But maybe I shouldn't wear one?" I said. "Self-promotion and all that. Like I'm my own fan?"

Corky slipped the pin under my T, straightened the badge, patted it into place. "There," he said, "perfect!," and stepped back, nodding his head for me to follow. "Look," he confided, "in case you couldn't find yours, I got another medal from Steph, and Travis engraved the back." He removed a little white sack from his Levi pocket and passed it to me. "You can look at it later, if you'd rather."

"Well, uh, Corky, thanks. You didn't have to...."

"I wanted you to have one."

"Well, thanks."

"C'mon girls," Monte said. "There's work here."

* * *

Thursday: the next batch of guests — members of the W. M. U., aka Women's Missionary Union, had arrived yesterday and settled in with greater dispatch and efficiency, but with more noise and palaver too, than their male counterparts in former weeks. They were the last bunch before the commencement of Youth Week, next Wednesday, on the Saturday night of which the speaking competition finals were scheduled to happen, after Corky and I'd spent the day at Bandelier. Youth Week would end, then, on the following Tuesday, and staff were free to leave for home on Wednesday or Thursday unless detained to help pack up and lock down Jubilee for the season. Monte said that some of us might be. Along with an anticipated excitement over the influx of contemporaries for Youth Week, already a mild melancholy sense of ending, of denouement, seemed detectable in moods and attitudes and preoccupations, in the general spirit and tone of the place — something faintly and sadly apprehensive, doubtfully uneasy.

And then on Friday morning, descending the Marigold staircase, Babs tripped, fell, and broke her right wrist in two places. Monte and I had just finished working breakfast when Corky banged at our door with another message from the Sergeant.

"She wants to see you, Troy, at 11 today in her office. She's on her way back from Santa Fe now with Babs. Babs is okay but her arm's in a cast."

"Uh oh," Monte said.

* * *

"Go on," Steph said to me, "take a chair." She hurried in behind me, bustled about, flipped through phone messages, set them aside. Against her khaki shirt, where medals might have been, the badge flashed when she moved. "I guess you've heard," she said.

"How is she?" I asked.

"She'll be all right, eventually, they think. But she'll be in the cast for maybe three months. It's a compound fracture. We've given her the option of staying through the term or going home now, and she's chosen to leave." She fell silent. I thought of a dozen things to say or ask, but all felt pushy. I waited.

"I've talked briefly with Dr. Mann by phone. I expect you know what we'll need from you now."

"Maybe you'd better say it, though," I said.

"Fair enough. We'll need for you to fill in at the piano."

"Thank you."

"Now there's also Josephine Raddle. You remember her from the auditions? She's okay but you're better. Here's my thinking: you play for the services when you're not working dinner. That's every other night. You'll keep your kitchen crew job, and we'll ask Jo to take the alternate nights. If she can't handle it, there's Mrs. Cobb, who's housemother at Lone Star Hall. She can play passably, we think. Others might turn up."

"Every *other* night for the services."

"Yes, beginning tonight. I'll double your pay."

"How about tripling it?" I asked, in Dallas mode.

"I'd have to see Dr. Mann. But I'll ask him."

"What about the transpositions?"

"Oh, right. I forgot. Babs mentioned them. Here's her idea: any guest musicians want transpositions, Babs says we should ask them to adapt to you, not the other way around. She says they can and will, in the circumstances. It might mean rehearsals."

"What about on the speech contest night," my mind spinning.

"You've already got that one off. Plus the whole day with the car. You wouldn't want to play that night."

"I might. Keep my mind off the speech?"

"I'd have thought.... Let's decide that later."

"But I don't want the job if you're going to keep looking for someone else to take it. What if you find them? How will that look for me?"

"Are you angling for a contract, Troy?" she grinned.

"Are you offering one? It might help."

The grin faded. "Troy," she said, "please don't make this more difficult than it already is. What if I don't look? For another pianist. If any volunteers show up, I'll ask your opinion of their playing, and we'll consider it. That's the best I can do."

"Why would I agree to my own replacement?"

"I'll trust you to be fair about that. You were fair about Babs."

"Will you name me official Jubilee Pianist? After Babs leaves?"

"For your resume? Okay. But you have to put in the dates."

"And I can play for the Jubilates? And sing with them, as usual?"

"Sure, sure. I don't see why not. And that would give us a new way of staging it."

"And the pay?"

"I'll ask. But listen, Troy, and be honest with me: do you really think you can handle both jobs? It might be too much.

And I can always bring in a couple of the grounds crew boys for the kitchen."

"It would be that easy? And I'd play every night then?"

"I don't know how easy but yes, if we replace you on the crew, obviously you'd play every night."

"I kind of like working in the kitchen, though. You know, the camaraderie and all?"

"I do know. Would you like to think about it? Talk to Monte?"

"No, I can think it through for myself. Could I tell you tomorrow?"

"No later, please. I'll hold off on contacting Jo till I hear from you. Also: Dr. Mann wants to hear you play the hymns scheduled for tonight. Three this afternoon? You can practice in the auditorium before. It's not an audition. He just wants to hear you again. Here's the leaflet for tonight's service."

Five hymns I'd known from birth and played a thousand times. With showstopper fireworks.

"And Babs wants a word with you. She's down at Marigold."

"What about?"

"Well, Troy, of course I don't know, but I might guess it *could* just possibly be about the music! Three p.m. today." She waved me off.

I stepped directly over to the snack bar where Lynn was sweeping up.

"Hey, Lynn. Listen, what's Babs's favorite snack? You've heard what happened? I want some of her favorite treats. What would they be?"

"She's devoted to Hershey chocolates. The oversized bars with toasted almonds."

"Give me four of the biggest ones, with almonds. And four cold Dr. Peppers. I know she likes them."

"All the time."

"Could you bag them for me?"

"Tell Babs hey."

Hollis Mosley guarded Marigold from behind the front desk, her badge almost vanquished by the plaid. "Babs is in 206," she said, "and don't forget to yell. What's in the bag?"

"Oh, some treats for Babs." I remembered the Baby Ruth. "You want a Hershey's almond?"

"So long as it's not a bribe," she said. "You don't have to pay your way in."

I'd have three left, and so handed one over. "I won't tell Babs you filched her lunch."

"You want it back? You can have it back."

"No, no, Hollis. It's a joke. Enjoy it!"

At the top of the second floor steps, I did yell, twice, "Male call!" and after the second, a door opened halfway down the hallway, and Scotty stepped out.

"This is her room," she said, "C'mon in."

Babs lay propped against pillows on her bed, the heavy cast across her lap, the badge bright against the tape. A little pale and drawn, she didn't look pained, and almost smiled: "Hey, Troy," she said, "thanks for dropping by."

"Are you getting better?" I stupidly asked, as though she'd been wasting away for weeks with pneumonia. "I brought you these," holding out the sack, then pulling it back, as she had no right hand to reach for it. I wanted to leave and try a second entrance. "Lynn says hey."

"Just set it here next to me," she directed.

Corky hovered nearby, looking as awkward as I felt, while M&M folded clothes for packing into open cases on the second bed. Everybody wore badges.

"Excellent!" Babs exclaimed, smiling broadly. "Exactly what I need," extracting a Hershey bar from the bag. "And Dr. Peppers too, cold, even! This is really, really sweet, Troy, and so thoughtful and kind. *Thank* you. They'll be great on the train tomorrow."

"The badge is very cool," Scotty said. "I adore the dog!" She looked directly at me, her eyes twinkling. "We should feature her in the paper."

"Yeah, he's something, idn' he?"

"She looks like a girl to me," Scotty said. winking.

"Oh," I said, getting it. "Could be, I guess. I mean, we can't really tell, can we? We can't actually see…?" Blushing. Corky covered his mouth and turned away.

"What?" Babs asked.

"It's nothing," I said. "So how're you doing?"

"They fixed me right up. I mean, I'll be out for a while but I'll be fine." Of course I wanted to ask, and in the sudden silence it felt like everybody else did too, but we all held back. So did Babs, looking down at her cast. Then she blinked, shook her head slightly: "So, Troy. I wanted to give you something. Martha, hand me that gray folder there on the dresser; no, wait, don't hand it…I can't… just open it here on my lap, yes, like that, thanks." She turned the large leaves awkwardly with her left hand, pulled out several, tried to even them together, couldn't. "Can you just reach them, Troy? I want you to have them. You see they're my descants for the ensemble, for the Jubilates. I'd like you to take them. Maybe use them? But to have them for yourself. I guess everybody knows them by now for performing, but you might could use them sometime? You *will* be playing for the ensemble, won't you?"

"Actually, I'm not sure, Babs. I don't think that's been decided yet. But yes! Wow! I'd really love to have them. What an amazing gift! Thank you. You did autograph them for me, didn't you? Or you will. No…wait…I'm so sorry. No, of course you…oh, I'm so sorry, Babs. I wasn't thinking."

"No matter. Give them here and find me a pen. I can do my initials left-handedly. And print the date. Won't that do?"

"Absolutely will. That would be terrific! Thanks, Babs. I really appreciate it."

"So if you DO play for the ensemble, and everybody sings, you too, you might get Dallas — M&M, pay attention here — Troy might get Dallas to use your cameras to set up a photo of everybody standing around the piano, dressed up, and Troy at the keyboard, and send it to me, please. I'd like a souvenir of us." She leaned back, spent.

M&M nodded, murmured agreement. Corky teared up.

Babs raised her head: "And Troy," she added: "try singing it while playing it; you just might nail that D-flat!"

"Unless you and Scotty have plans for now," I said to Corky, "how about helping me with something?"

"I'd best help Babs get packed," Scotty said. "Don't mind me."

"You're not wearing your medal," Corky noticed. "Did you lose this one too?"

He had attached it to a thin, tasteful silver chain and asked Travis, presumably, to engrave the back, "for Troy, from Corky, 1959."

"No, it's right here," I patted my pocket. "It's very nice, Corky. I like it. I'm glad to have it. I just think it's a little much to wear with the badge," though he did. "And it bulges under the T and looks odd. I'll wear it later. Thank you."

"You could wear it outside the shirt, like I do," he said quietly.

Good God! Where WAS my stupid mind?! Of course he did, right there in front of me! What is wrong with me?!

"Oh shit, Corky. I'm so sorry," I fumbled. "I take it back. I didn't mean that. I'm just thinking...I'm thinking what I want to talk about. Getting ahead of myself. I'm really sorry. I didn't mean...."

"It doesn't matter," he said. "You're the fashion dude, not me. So what's up?"

"What? No...oh crap. Let it go. Let's walk," I said, leading him out and down to the yard where his bike shimmered in the heat.

"Want to ride?" he asked.

"Not this time," I said. "Can you walk it? I need some advice."

"What's happened?" he said, falling in with my stride, balancing the bike with one hand on the saddle.

"This whole thing happened," I said, a little crossly. "They want me to be pianist. Play for the services. It's very complimentary. I'd kind of like to do it. But I don't know. I'd probably have to quit crew, or play part-time every other night, and I wouldn't feel like the job was really mine. And I *like* working crew with you guys. I don't want to miss that."

"You'd have to be at services every night," he said.

"But I'd have days off. All day. Until after dinner. Except sometimes maybe for rehearsals, like with the Jubilates."

"Who'd take your place on crew?"

"Steph says she'd bring in a couple of boys from the landscape gang."

"Do they even speak English? Would that work? I doubt that would work."

"Do you not want me to do it, Corky? Say so if you don't."

"I can't tell if you really want to."

"I think I might like to. When I applied to work out here, I wanted to be picked as pianist. But then Babs got chosen, and the kitchen turned out the place to be with most of you guys, and Babs was so good not just playing but organizing and everything, and even composing and transposing, I kind of forgot about it until this happened. But if I take the job it's like I'm still competing with Babs, everybody comparing us and all."

"But you *could* do both jobs?"

"Yes, and Steph said she'd pay me double if I did. I think she'd do that for just the one if I agreed to replace Babs. But I'll have to skip crew every other night."

"Awkward for scheduling."

"And that's another thing. They'd have to get another pianist for the speech night."

"Why?"

"Well, Steph thought that might be asking too much, or even giving me too much, like I'd be the whole show that night."

"I don't see that. There's Wolf, for one thing, and all the other contestants. And what's complicated about your leaving the bench for your turn and coming back after? Monte would like the added exposure and the different angle. I think it'd be pretty cool for the pianist to show he's not a one-trick pony. And you might even do a little soft-shoe on your way to the mike!" He did one, and the bike tilted over.

"What if that's an omen?" I said.

"Okay," he said, righting the bike. "But seriously, Troy: what's the downside to taking the job and packing crew for the last week? We've had a good run there, and we can do fun stuff between shifts during the day. I can meet you every night after services with snacks…if you'd like that. What does Monte think?"

"I haven't asked him. We're having a little…disagreement. But it'll pass. I sort of want to decide this thing without letting him make a big deal out of it."

"What do you figure he'd want you to do?"

"Oh, he'd keep me in the kitchen, I'm pretty sure of that."

"Then that should be decisive," Corky said, decisively, but he didn't say which way decisive.

I started. "Really? You think…? But that would be letting Monte decide for me, wouldn't it? That's really what I don't want."

"So what *do* you want then? Look here, Troy: Don't you basically know what you want to do? I think you do. Trust your gut, man! You know you want the new job. You know you'll love the new attention it brings you. It gives you another spotlight; it exercises another of your gifts. You must see it for the opportunity it is, don't you? You've *done* crew, and you might as well get shut of it. There's nothing to finish there. All of this indecisive massaging is just masturbatory. Oh don't look shocked. I mean, it's completely self-indulgent when we both know how this is going to end. So let's cut to the chase. Let's say yes and be done with deciding. All together now, people"— he made the conducting gesture —: "*YES!*" And bounced the bike, emphatically.

"You've got to love the irony," Monte laughed: "she kicks you off one piano and now begs you to command the grand! Brilliant!" He'd rolled the T-shirt sleeve to show the bicep and pinned the badge against it. "You *are* going to take the job, right?"

"Well, Dr. Mann hasn't signed off on the offer yet," I said. "I have to audition for him again this afternoon. And Steph and I are still negotiating salary. But yes, I think I'm going to take it."

"And leave the crew."

"I don't absolutely have to, but I think it's best to. Corky thinks so too."

"Corky? What does Corky know about it?"

"I talked to him."

"I'd rather you didn't," Monte said. He let the ambiguity linger for a second, long enough to be sure I'd caught it. "Leave crew, I mean. I'd rather you stayed on. But I see the opportunity. And I'm pretty sure you want to take it. You never liked Babs's way of playing hymns. So here's your big chance. Grab it! And congratulations!"

"Thanks. But it's not quite mine yet."

"Sure it is. You've got them in a pinch. You can bleed them a little."

I knew he wanted the negotiating details. I also knew what he'd do with them.

"Maybe a little."

He waited but didn't ask.

"So," he said. "We've got a little unfinished business here. Shall we get Cokes and go at it?"

Once more he left for sodas. He was sure to have devised a plan, some scheme formally to register unhappiness, perhaps anger, over admission of the California contestant to the national competition finals without losing me or affecting my uncertain will to continue in them. I couldn't welcome her either, but I understood the foolishness, the impossibility, of mounting any effective offense against her inclusion and the embarrassment to Jubilee certain to result from protests and petitions and public squabbles over it. The risks of exposing all manner of ugly, unreasonable biases even in mild-mannered persons like Corky and myself and possibly Jubilee adult staff were unacceptably high, and I didn't want any of us caught up in scandal, especially right here around the contest finals, for the effect would elevate the competition to a level of importance far exceeding its true consequence. I had to talk Monte down.

Cokes in hand, we sat on the beds. He began:

"I don't like it. You know I don't like it. I think it's illegitimate and impermissible and unfair, and I'm prepared to say that and argue that and defend that. But not now, not yet, partially as a favor to you. Here's what I'll do. We'll let the contest play out. If you win, as we all believe you will, I'll drop and forget any objections or protests. Between now and then, though, we'll research this girl and the California competition and the judges there and the contest history with Nashville all the way back to its beginning for anything we can find or any grounds or any connection to support a protest against allowing a deaf-mute to participate. Or a foreign person to participate. We'll put Robyn on it and maybe Mother Robyn too back home. And if Miss China wins, we'll raise holy hell. I don't think she will, but if she does, we have to be prepared. We'll argue for her disqualification, not that she lost. That's a dead end. But if we get her disqualified, the win goes to second place. That is, you. You can't do worse than second, even with Wolf in the mix. It probably won't get settled till after we're home but we can keep up the pressure from there if we have assignments and keep organized. Can you live with this?"

"I don't think they give second-place."

"They must. They did in California. That's how she got here. I'll put Robyn on it to find out.'"

"Well, Monte," I said, thinking about it, "it's an impressive plan, and I appreciate the support and your effort to help. But I don't want to do it. Or you to do it. I seriously don't want any part of it. We'll just have to make sure I win."

"What's wrong with it? How could it be better?"

Whether this was a request for help or astonishment at the idea of improvement wasn't clear.

"What's wrong with it is its existence. I don't want any protest."

"Well, if you win…."

"That's a big part of what's wrong with it. You think the contest is unfair only if I lose."

"No, I don't. It's unfair anyway. We're talking about protesting if…"

"I can't stop you from planning. But I'm asking you not to, and I won't cooperate with you. Now look: if you do go ahead with all this research and involve Robyn and the others, word will spread about what you're up to and spoil the run-up to the finals and *become* a protest itself even before anybody wins or loses; and if I lose, all the negative flap around it will look like nothing but sour grapes because Jubilee's guy didn't win, and the spat will become Jubilee's protest, Jubilee's very public, whiney fuss. And I will hate that. You should too."

Monte stared. He actually stared. Blinked. Drank. Cleared his throat.

"Damnation," he said quietly. "Damnation, Troj, that's a really good point. Where'd that come from?"

"Protest is a losing proposition from the get-go. Please, Monte: give it up. Let's just focus on winning,"

"Don't beg. I hate begging. It's so...undignified."

"Then don't make me."

He took another long swallow. "Tell you what. I'll think it over for a couple of days. I won't start any research. We don't have a lot time, though, if I have to research. Just give me two days to think, okay?"

"One day. So long as you don't use it to cook up another plan."

"But I already have another one," Monte said, "only not about the contest. Want to hear it?"

"I don't have a lot of time. And I've got to meet The Man at three in the auditorium. You know, for the audition. I'd like to get a little practice in first."

"Okay, I'll walk over with you. I've never heard you play hymns."

"No, wait. Maybe I've got time. What's the other plan?"

"W-e-l-l-l-l," he drew it out in an obvious tease: "do you remember from our first afternoon I promised you something I never delivered?"

I didn't. Plainly, he hoped I did. "How about a hint?" I hinted.

"Water," he said.

"Water? How about another?"

"Indians," he said.

"Sorry," I said, "not getting it."

"Okay. Canoes. Remember I promised to take you canoeing? On the lake. Teach you to paddle?"

"Oh. Sure." Dimly. "What?"

"Next Friday: that's the day before the speech finals on Saturday night, right? And you'll spend Saturday with Corky, somewhere. So I'm thinking you and I should do something special on Friday. Would you like that?"

I understood: Monte wanted to arrange private time to match Corky's with me, maybe to compete with it, best it.

"Well," I said, "what would we do?"

"I might talk SS into letting me skip lunch detail that day so we could *start* relaxing you for the competition. What if I got the cooks to pack us a picnic lunch, and we canoed over to Seraphim? There's a neat little secluded beach on the back far side of it, and we could hang out there for the afternoon, maybe hike around the island, and still get you back in plenty of time to play the service. How's that sound?"

* * *

Dr. Mann had raised the piano lid and sat at the keyboard when I arrived promptly at three. As always immaculately dressed in a suit and tie the heat notwithstanding, the badge on his left lapel, he chorded the familiar measures of "What a Friend We Have in Jesus," softly humming along. I slipped into the second pew and waited.

Finishing the verse, he looked up and smiled. "Hello, Troy," he said quietly. "Just tuning up for you here."

"Hello, sir," I said. "I didn't know you played. Maybe you should replace Babs?"

"No, no," he said; "I'm a complete amateur." But his chords were complex. "I just like to plunk and plonk every now and then."

It was hard to imagine The Man plunking or plonking at anything anytime. "It sounded great to me," I offered.

"Thank you," he said, standing. "Your turn now. I'll take a seat about halfway back. You have the hymn list for tonight? Give me an introduction to the first one — whatever you'd play after the number is announced — and then one verse of accompaniment as you'd play it for congregational singing. And after that, a second verse elaborated, lightly ornamented, if you're comfortable trying that: nothing too heavily embellished, though, or over-loud: we'll still need to hear the melodic line."

The hymns were:

"All Hail the Power of Jesus' Name"

"Blessed Assurance, Jesus Is Mine"

"Love Lifted Me"

"'Tis So Sweet to Trust in Jesus"

"Jesus Is Tenderly Calling Me Home" (committal hymn)

"All Hail" is a robust, almost martial tune, and requires some oomph, some gusto in the accompaniment, but I held back until the second verse and then let fly.

"Very good, Troy!" Dr. Mann called; "maybe a little less volume until the final verse. By the way, we sing all verses of every hymn. You can raise the roof on the last one, except on the committal hymn, which as you know needs a gentler touch. Okay. Just give me one verse on the others for tonight, and at the end of each, if the next is in a different key, try modulating directly into it, or transposing it into your present key, either one."

Uh-oh. The accursed word. But I could do modulation well enough, with three or four transitioning chords, and did.

"Excellent!" Dr. Mann declared when I'd finished. "But a slower tempo on the last one, please. Now let's go back to 'Blessed Assurance.'"

"Was something wrong?"

"Not at all. But on the chorus, at the second 'This is my story,' let's linger on the first, second, and third words for a full whole note, make each one emphatic and determined: prolonged. Then, with the line 'Praising my Savior…,' on '…vior,' just soar, *SOAR* and hold it…hold it….hold it there — you can do some thunder and lightening while they hold — until they're nearly out of breath, and then come back down to normal phrasing and rhythm for 'all the day long.' Do you understand?"

I did. I'd heard it done like that and could play it just as he said to. "Like this?"

"That's it," he said; "exactly like that. Good man. Whoever's drum major that night" — each week's group brought its own song-leader — "I'll talk to him if 'Blessed Assurance' is on the menu, but you should check with him too, so you both can bring the congregation along on the last-verse variation."

This excited him; I could tell. So I wanted to get it right.

"Now, one more thing," he said, stepping down to the piano and standing in the bow. "Some preachers, at the end or near the end of a sermon, and around the committal hymn, like to speak softly extempore over a piano accompaniment — a low backgrounded hymn of a — shall we say? —persuasive disposition: you know, to encourage decisions. Our Youth Week preacher — I bet you've heard of him, Dr. Alexander Abernathy — Dr. Abernathy likes to be impulsive and spontaneous, and sometimes he'll want that, a piano playing softly while he offers the invitation. So let's imagine here the preacher signals you to start playing such a hymn under his appeal, which one would you choose? Think about it and go ahead."

Soft pedal depressed, I began the chorus of "Turn Your Eyes upon Jesus."

Dr. Mann nodded and listened intently for a few measures and then joined me on the bench, placing his hands two octaves above mine and chording the melody with me. We repeated the chorus and were still. He turned his head and looked directly at me. "Perfect," he said, his voice hoarse, his eyes wet.

* * *

The Reverend Doctor Alexander Allan Abernathy was an internationally famous Baptist evangelist. I had heard of him and even heard him: Father had taken me to hear him preach a revival service in the LSU stadium in Baton Rouge, and we'd waited in a long line to shake his hand and his pal Willie's in a press conference room afterward. They'd made guest appearances on popular television shows. They turned up regularly at big Baptist conventions and conferences and rallies as a hugely compelling draw. How Jubilee managed to book them I couldn't conceive. They were phenomena.

For the Reverend Doctor Alexander Allan Abernathy was also from birth a calamitously, piteously disfigured anomaly of human personhood, not wholly disabled but gravely misshapen and impaired. Inarguably grotesque to behold — limbs twisted, joints warped, back humped, trunk contorted, the legs spindly and splayed — he nevertheless walked, with the aid of two canes, and retained full use of his tiny, doll-like hands. At about 5'4", he could not have weighed 100 pounds, his legs and arms showing bone-thin through sleeves and trousers. His head was large, round, and hairless, with neither brows nor beard, and the ears oversized, the neck wattled and scrawny, the skin of the hands blotched and mottled. The eyes and cheeks lay sunken, the nose and mouth pinched and drawn in different directions to the sides, on the eerily white face — a flat white as if bleached, or chalked, of hard alabaster white — ever too animated to seem dead but still disturbingly wan, and utterly free of mark, blemish, or stain, the lips red as blood.

But from them flowed a voice as clean and pure as heaven itself, the Reverend Doctor Alexander Allan Abernathy's vocal apparatus having miraculously escaped damage by defect or disease. A rich, low, mellow tenor, it came to the ear very much as music did, soft as air, and like a touch. His speech was fluent, his articulation flawless, his tones so various and colorful and expressive, ranging up and down the registers, you might almost have thought he sang, his utterance limpid lullabies. Not that he didn't or couldn't preach forcefully, sometimes sternly. But the voice never rasped or grated, never pierced or growled. It purled, like cool, sweet water.

And my oh my, what he did with it! For, you see, the Reverend Doctor Alexander Allan Abernathy was a master ventriloquist. And his virtuosic wizardry in that regard went a long way toward neutralizing whatever check upon normal social relations his physical deformities and handicaps might have wrought. So did his unexpectedly — astonishing! — bright and vivacious personality that electrified his conversations and performances. No maudlin self-pity on display in this fellow! He sparked and sparkled; he quipped and bantered; he teased and laughed and verbally romped: his spirit danced with charismatic vigor and delight. Gregariously affable, he was also exceedingly witty, both in his own winning voice and through his puppet Willie-Nilly, the perfect semblance of the perfect boy, who always opened their show with "Ehhh, what's up, Doc?" in so exact an echo of the Bunny that the house unfailingly roared. And then the Reverend Doctor would introduce the puppet — "This is my dummy, Willie Nilly" — whereupon Willie would open his eyes widely and wriggle his brows and ask with perky sass, "And whose are YOU?" to more laughter. Willie traveled in a black valise the Doctor always carried with two fingers of the left hand that also managed the cane, never permitting anyone else to touch the case. When he stepped onto the stage with it, the crowd applauded and cheered in anticipation of Willie's emergence from it in his signature grey sweat shirt and blue jeans rolled at the cuffs above red and yellow polka-dot socks and black and white Keds. On his head sat a navy baseball cap, its bill crooked to the side so that the Doctor could intermittently straighten it and then flip the hidden switch to crook it again, to the congregation's merriment and Willie's pique expressed in the rolling of his big and vividly blue and always surprised eyes. His right hand clutched a down-sized first-baseman's glove, which Willie frequently used to point or punctuate, or to cover his embarrassment over a particularly bad pun from his handler, or even now and then to tweak the Doctor's nose. He sat on the Doctor's lap, of course, his torso hiding the operating hand, his eyes often closing in on the Doc's lips for signs of movement, after which he'd sigh and wipe his brow in relief and endearingly nuzzle the Doctor's crinkled neck. We spectators couldn't detect lip action either, so skilled was the Doc at "throwing his voice," as it was then called, into the dummy's always working mouth. The Willie-voice had the same rapid-fire rhythm, the same scratchy, nasal grain as the cartoon's rabbit, and even nailed the Bronx accent, all wholly distinct from the mellifluous textures of Dr. Abernathy's natural one; and although we never heard puppet and master sing together, they did counterpoint each other with alternating lines of the same goofy songs and limericks. Their routines included a lot of very clever and harmless gags at the expense of Baptist practices and traditions, and some digs at Jubilee and its customs and even at their own skits but nothing mean or rude or ugly or hurtful. They'd usually carry on for fifteen minuets or so and then wind down, Willie grouching about having to return to his case and then cheerily signing-off with a sweeping wave of the glove, singing out, "That's all, folks!" And the Reverend Doctor Alexander Allan Abernathy would stow the valise under his chair and lurch to the pulpit to preach.

* * *

Following the service that night, Monte and I cruised the snack bar in a futile search for adventure, and then found Corky and Scotty and Hollis back at Cactus looking for us.

"Hollis wants a word with Troy," Corky said; "can we come up?"

Girls weren't allowed into Cactus rooms unless accompanied by adults, but our wannabe guests clearly expected invitations inside; and in these waning days, rules bent and yielded under pressures to test and trespass while time remained. Monte's eyes clicked on mine. I shrugged.

"Of course," he said, holding open the door. "You bring beer?"

Everybody laughed; but Hollis seemed slightly edgy.

"This is all Scotty's idea," she said, " but she wants me to lay it out for you, Troy, since I'm...well...involved."

"How involved?" I asked, now a tad edgy myself.

"It's sort of delicate; we don't want to insult you or anything, or make you feel bad about yourself...but...we've, well, we've noticed something that might be a little handicap for you in the competition. Not really big time, but taking care of it might do you a little favor, Corky and Scotty think. And I'd like to help."

"Do you know what this is about, Monte?" I asked him. "What's happening here? Have you been messing with our speech plans again?"

"I swear I haven't, Troy; but if they've got some ideas for helping out...."

"No, here's the thing, Troy," Hollis interrupted. "Scotty and I have known each other forever, been friends a long time; and growing up, we used to do each other's nails, the way girls do, at slumber parties and such. And then I got interested in it and took some lessons and got pretty good. And sometimes now I do it professionally, you know, for a few clients, and I still do Scotty's once a week when we're home. And she thought maybe you'd let me do yours?"

Monte guffawed. Corky grinned.

"Yours need cleaning up," Scotty said. "Especially now you're Jubilee pianist. Hollis could fix them right up for you."

"What's wrong with them the way they are," I asked, looking at them, feeling mildly vexed by this investigation of my personal hygiene. "Scotty says they're dirty? Is that what you're saying, Scotty? They're not dirty."

"Well," Hollis said, "they're uneven. Irregular. They don't look cared for. They're not shaped. They don't look right for a pianist."

"Is that what you think, Scotty? They don't 'look right'? How're they supposed to look?"

Monte squirmed with giggles. Corky stared at my hands.

"I think they could use some professional care," Scotty said. "Holllis is good." She extended her own right hand, displaying the nails. "She'd do a great job on them."

I studied my nails. In truth, I was only about two years down the road from serious nail-biting, a terrible habit of chewing my nails to the quick; and I had broken it only by the harshest of parental interventions involving quinine and tape; and compared to what my fingernails looked like then — what was left of them — these at the end of my fingers now were absolute gemstones. Only I could see what Hollis and Scotty meant. They were jagged, torn, rough.

"And they need to be smooth and sweet for the speech," Monte said; "you don't want to be up there speaking and gesturing and fondling the mike with dirty fingernails."

"They're not dirty," I snapped, tucking them under my thighs. "I dunno, Hollis; you mean a manicure, don't you? Boys don't get manicures, do they? I never knew one who did."

"Some do," Corky said; "and you do," holding out his own hands, palms down. "Why'd you think they call them '*man*-i-cures'?"

"Wait!" I said, staring at his nails, startled. "They're *shiny!* Have you got polish on them? Good Lord, Corky!"

"No," Hollis said. "No polish. They're just buffed. But they do look nice, don't they? I did them for him this afternoon." She drew from her shirt pocket a small black zippered pouch, and dangled it, with a tease. "How about it, Troy? I could do you and Monte both."

"I pass," Monte said stoutly.

"Just a second here," I said. "Is this some kind of trick? A trap? Is that door going to bust open any second now on M&M snapping pix of Hollis giving me a manicure? Is that the plan?!"

"It's not a bad one," Monte said. "I should have thought of it."

"I don't think so, Hollis. I mean, I'm grateful for the offer and all, but I just don't think boys…most boys…do this sort of thing, sorry Corky, and I'd feel funny about it, you know? Kind of funny."

"You ever look at men's fingernails in movies, Troy?" Corky asked. "In TV ads, up close of hands? They're all beautifully manicured."

"I'm not in movies, or on TV," I said, lamely.

"No," Monte said; "you're just up in front of a thousand people every night showing off your hands all over a white piano keyboard. Don't think people aren't watching your fingers all that time."

"China's nails will be perfect," Scotty said. "Asians are the best at nail care."

"And that spotlight...on you for the speech," Monte added, "showing your hands on that black mike! You don't think your nails will show up? (Hollis: forget that about a spotlight! It's nothing.)"

"Look," Corky said, in his take-charge voice: "It's not at all a sissy thing, Troy, if that's what's scaring you. Lots of men get nail treatments, and not just movie stars. Their *wives* do them if the guys can't. Privately. We don't see it happen but we see the results of it all the time everywhere. You just haven't noticed. You'd have for sure noticed if men *didn't* have manicures. Now you'll notice. Your nails don't look bad, but they could look better. Especially against the keyboard, like Monte said. He and Hollis are right about that. So why not *let* them look better, even perfect? And you'll *feel* better about playing with handsome fingers and elegant nails. It's basic hygiene: your fingers are healthier if they're clean and well-trimmed and polished and beautiful."

"Ya'll keep saying they're dirty. They're not."

"Fingernails," Corky said, "need help to get perfectly clean."

"But what if," I said, grasping, "what if the manicure makes them too sore to play? Couldn't that happen?"

"No, not in my hands," Hollis said, firmly. "I'm not charging you, Troy. I'm free to you this time."

"Does it hurt?" I asked.

"Troy," Corky said, his patience wearing. "It's painless. Actually, it feels good. It's a sort of massage."

"Did Babs get manicures?"

"From me, yes," Hollis said. She reached across and tugged my hand from under the thigh, and took it into her very large one, looking closely at it, stroking it with her thumb. "These are pretty fingers," she said; "but they'd like a little help. I can hear them asking for it! And here help is, right at hand!"

Corky nodded. Monte wagged his head.

"Nobody better tell!" I ordered.

12

Throngs, multitudes, legions of youths with dangerously re-
pressed libidos swarmed over the Jubilee campus on the last
Transitional Wednesday, descending from church and school
and rented buses, vans, trailers, and station wagons now parked
helter-skelter across the grounds; but by Friday, their former
passengers had toured the highlights, learned the routines, and
vanished into the tightly scheduled classes and training sessions
except for meals and services, when they re-gathered, buzzing,
like bees to the hive. So Monte and I expected fairly clear sailing
down to the lake and out to Seraphim for our free time on the
island. Off he went to collect our lunches from the cooks while
I stopped at Central to clear with the Sergeant plans for rehearsing the ensemble at the grand for our first performance since
Babs left. Although official camp pianist now, I wasn't touching any instrument without Steph's "authorization." As I came
downstairs to the Cactus entrance, Corky stepped through it.
We almost collided.

"Oh, hey," he grinned, stepping back. "Sorry. I saw Monte leave and thought I'd run up for a second. I've missed you on crew."

"Well, I've missed you…I've missed you guys, too. Everything okay there?"

"Oh sure, " Corky said; "it's just not the same. Without you there. You like being Babs?"

"You like being popped?" I made a fist but we were both laughing. "I think it's going to be okay. It's just a little lonely."

"I understand lonely," he said.

"But look, Corky," I said gently, "I don't want to seem rude or anything, but I'm in kind of a hurry. I can't visit right now."

"Oh I know, I know. I just wanted to wish you guys a good time today. On your day off."

"Okay." I paused. "But how did you know?"

"Is it a secret?"

"Well, no. I guess not. I just wondered."

"Steph mentioned it to one of the ground crew guys she brought in to replace you…and Monte for today. By the way, they speak English as well as you. He told me. But he didn't think anything of it."

"Why should he think anything of it?"

"I just said he didn't."

"All right. Okay. But I should be getting along…."

"AND," Corky said, "I wanted to tell you: Dr. Mann brought me three books from his home library about Bandelier, with photos and all. I've been reading them, learning about the park. I'll tell you tomorrow."

"That's cool. Very thoughtful of The Man. But I need to get going. Monte's waiting. And I've got to stop at Steph's office."

"I can walk over with you?" Corky asked.

"Prob'ly not a good idea. But I'll meet you there at what, say, 9 in the morning?"

"Great!" he said. "See you then. Yawl jubilate, now, hear?" And he pedaled away, laughing.

By the time I reached the lake, Steph's permission pocketed, Monte was at the boat dock, arranging items in the canoe, among them a large picnic basket.

"What kept you?" he asked.

"I had to see Steph about a rehearsal. Why, are we rushed?"

"For the Jubilates? You'll play? Good. When do we sing again?"

"Not certain. Maybe Sunday."

"The Night After The Night Of!"

"We're not talking about that today," I reminded him.

"We're not. Ready to sail?"

I managed not to tip us as I maneuvered to the prow where Monte directed me to sit, facing ahead.

"Just enjoy the ride," he said; "I'll paddle."

He shoved the canoe off the gravel bank and leapt in, risking capsize, and in a moment we were gliding across the placid blue of the lake reflecting the silver-sapphire of a cloudless sky and, nearer by, the warm yellow skin of the canoe.

"Keep still now," he said, after several hard pulls of the paddle on each side. "I'm going to turn us around for a view back."

So he did, and the expanding vista of the receding campground nearly took my breath away. The sun-scorched adobe of the Complex glared against the sky behind it, and the thickly woven skirt of the flower-gardens draped the slope, falling to the water in a radiant panoply of shimmering color that spread and climbed as we drew away, that soared upward and cascaded down and stretched outward as if unable to restrain its resplendent reach. The gardens piled tiers upon shelves upon layers upon ranks of blazing color, stacked and spilling over into tumbling riots of kaleidoscopic grandeur. He rested the paddle and we floated, taking it in, soaking it up, in the serene quiet. It exacted reverence in a way nothing else on the campus had: it wanted silent respect; it bid awe and compelled worship. One felt its holiness.

"There's another fine view from the island," he said quietly; "but this is about the best one to get...to get...well, to grasp the glory of it."

It was a brutally abused word, but it felt like the right one.

We turned, and slipped silently toward Seraphim.

The mood held while we eased around the island's point and scrunched up onto the pebbled shore of a sweet little cove tucked into the far back side of Seraphim, wholly hidden from Jubilee, where Monte sprang from the boat, the hamper in hand, and flung back the lid.

"*SURPRISE!*" he yelled, unfurling an over-sized beach towel and whirling it around his head while dancing a merry little soft-shoe on the gravel.

"What the hell?!" I said, stumbling onto the bank. "What's this?"

For an answer, he peeled off his polo, kicked away his moccasins, and reached for the top button of his Levis, fingering it, his grin at its broadest and brightest.

I needed no further invitation. Notwithstanding all of my fear and anger at the baptism and my singular deliverance from it, that incident had launched a happy period of immersion, so to speak, in the only sport, other than basketball, at which I appeared to display any aptitude whatsoever, and therefore any sustained interest in, and I pursued it with something approaching zeal, beginning with swimming lessons and continuing through Dry Water camps and bayou skinny-dipping and long, lazy summer afternoons at the Madison pool as soon as the polio vaccine reopened it. Hardly competitive, I nevertheless took to the water and to the erotic stimulation of the element itself, as to the pleasing sights and provocative aromas of the showers and dressing rooms. Monte, of course, swam for Baylor. And although Jubilee provided opportunity and equipment for men's baseball and women's softball games and tournaments, we'd had no appetite for participation, and as a consequence had gone for weeks without significant exercise except for Monte's pushups and the odd short hike. But here, opportunely, arose an occasion for relaxing and relieving and expelling all those muscular tensions and psychological anxieties accumulated over days fraught with nagging perplexities — and on the very eve of the climactic event that, in prospect, had given birth to most of them. I recognized this instantly; and with the shivering transport of liberation, flinging raiment aside, I raced him into the water.

For the balance of the morning, with occasional breaks to rest and sunbathe, we dipped and dived, frisked and frolicked, splashed and splattered, shrieked and shouted, tumbled and tangled with giddy abandon, thrice thrashing to Cherubim and back (he let me win the last race), volleyed and lost and recovered a red rubber ball Steph had included with a handful of balloons she'd passed to Monte with the beach towel — balloons we'd inflated and joyfully bounced and punched and pummeled and burst and even tried to ride, and Marco Polo-ed as well as two players can until we'd worn ourselves down into panting, light-headed fatigue. Monte stumbled up the bank, grabbed the towel to rumple his hair and wipe his chest, and then spread it evenly over a patch of grass for blotting and drying his Jockeys, tugged down his slim hips and shaken out. He signaled me to do likewise.

"They won't take long to dry in this heat," he said, stuffing himself into the Levis.

Yes, I noticed. Guys do, you know. Watch our eyes in the locker room. We look, maybe in sidelong glances, but we look, checking and comparing. And I was sort of on alert *to* notice, and to study what I felt about what I saw. He was a studly dude, this boy-man, obliging admiration. But whether my feelings went farther in any direction requiring intervention by Gaylord Bryce, I wasn't sure. They approved the shapely forms as anatomical facts; other associated emotions pulsed and blurred, surged and faded. But yes, I noticed.

Shirtless, we sprawled on the grass to relax before lunch. Monte dug out his balm and swiped.

"That was terrific," I said. "Thanks for arranging it. You're the champ of arranging, aren't you?"

"I try to be," he said. "Are you all arranged for tomorrow night?"

"We're not talking about it," I said.

"Just for a sec," he insisted. "I need to be sure you're all set to go. Any questions? You remember how it'll all roll out?"

"How could I forget? Yes. I do. Could we move on?"

"I'm meeting the team tomorrow afternoon, while you're off with Corky, to review the plan."

"Just don't overdo it, Monte. Please. Let it be my speech."

"It's all yours, sweetheart," he said, aping Bogart with the endearment, and so neutering it.

"Do we know the order yet?" I asked. "It would help me to know that."

"Oh, SS says she thinks they'll go alphabetically by the state they represent. That'll put China first for California unless Wolf comes from Arkansas instead of Oklahoma, and you somewhere near the middle of the pack unless the contestants we don't know come before L. I'm still trying to find out who they are and where from. And tomorrow afternoon I'll make another bid for random order. Don't you think about any of that, though. Nothing changes our plans. Lights, applause, all that, just like we said."

"Am I playing? The piano, I mean."

"Shit. I forgot to ask. You didn't either? Well, do you want to?"

"I think I should. I'm the official Jubilee pianist. And it's prob'ly too late to get anybody else."

"Okay. I'll fix it with SS. Just show up tomorrow night at the piano."

He turned on his stomach and played with blades of grass.

"I've decided to decide about the protest after tomorrow night," he said. "Since you're going to win, there's no need to decide anything now. Okay?"

"Thank you, But I hope you'll forget it anyway. I mean, either way."

"No slips like that tomorrow night, Troj! You want to practice it now?"

"Stop it. We're done."

Monte lay his cheek against his hands and looked at me.

"What?" I asked.

"You know, Troy," he said, "I've really liked rooming with you this summer. I want you to know and believe that. It's been super fun. You've been a great pal."

"Well, I've liked it too. It's been a blast, um, 'bunking' with you."

"Do you think we'll see each other again? Will you visit me at Baylor?"

"Oh I don't know, Monte. We can talk about it. You might not want me to."

"Or," he went on, "I could come to…what was it… Pineville? Madison?"

"No, you wouldn't want to do that. Neither one is your kind of scene."

"What kind of scene is mine?"

"Louisiana's not Jubilee," I said.

"How about some sandwiches," he said.

Roast beef slices on heavily mayonnaised white bread kept cool with ice packs and complemented by boiled eggs and dill slices and carrots and celery stalks, and chilled bottles of Coke. We didn't even pause for a blessing.

"How come you never dated this summer?" I asked, having wanted to since May but never daring.

"Oh," he said immediately, "I have a girlfriend at home, sort of. Laura McIntyre. Our parents are best friends, and she and I were born about the same time, and we are sort of destined, they say, to be a couple; but she's at Austin and I'm so busy at Baylor, and she travels with her mother to Europe in the summer, so we don't see much of each other."

"Are you engaged?"

"No, no. We date for parties where you have to have one, like frat formals and dinners. But we're both so busy...."

"And you don't write?"

"You'd think we didn't know how."

We were quiet for a moment. Then: "What happened to you and Scotty?" he said. "I thought you liked her."

"So did I. I'm not sure what happened. Maybe something *didn't* happen. I think she's gorgeous but we didn't exactly click that first time, and I never asked her again. I may have hurt her feelings."

"Well," he said, "she's pretty thick with Travis now. Did you know she's wearing his ring?"

"What? Scotty and Travis are going steady? No, I didn't know that."

"Must've been all that time together in the press office! Or the Camels. Scotty's discovered she likes smoking!"

"Wait a second! Scotty's smoking? Naw, not buying that."

"Travis says he's got this private place...."

"Oh, I know about that. I've been there with him."

"...where he and Scotty smoke. He says she's really into it."

Unbelievable! The Queen smokes?! And goes steady with the Oklahoma farmer?!

"When did all this happen? And how did I not know about it?"

"Well, if we'd had a newspaper...."

I looked hard at him, my mind turning. "Wait. What's going on here, Monte?"

"Scotty really wanted your help with it. I think you disappointed her. She may even blame you for the slow start. Anyhow, she's asked me to write a story for it about you and the speech contest — with your help, if you'll give it — how you got into it, how you got this far, you know, background and stuff, leading up to the big finish and the win tomorrow night. How about it?"

"Not a chance. Nope. Not gonna happen. You know how I already feel about all the talk. I hate it. There won't be any story."

"Scotty thinks it's the ONLY story at Jubilee right now. She says *Hughes' News* won't ever get any credibility without running that story. She wants to make the whole issue about it."

"If killing the story will kill the paper, shoot it now."

"You won't tell me? I'm glad to write the article."

"*NO*, Monte! Just stop! This is NOT helping me not think about the contest! And you're about to ruin the day!"

He paused, re-set: "So what about in high school. Did you date there?"

"Oh yeah. Alison and I went steady for two-and-a-half years until I graduated and stupidly decided she was too young for a college man, and called it off. Bad move."

"You still in love with her? "

"I never was 'in love' with her, or she with me, I don't think. We just had one hell of a good time together, you know: kids running around, growing up and stuff."

"We're a couple of cases, aren't we, Troj," he said.

"No," I said. "Why would you say that? Speak for yourself, buddy!" I tossed a rolled-up napkin at him.

He dodged, grinned, and began gathering our litter. "Let's get this cleaned up and go for a hike. I'm pretty sure there's a trail back there." He handed me my shirt, ducked into his, and pinned his badge across the logo.

He found the trail with slightly unsettling ease and led us into the scrubby brush and then among the spruce, fir, and aspen trees, he named them, up a low incline where they closed out part of the sky and cast a cool shadow over the needle-carpeted earth. The air was still; no birds sang. It felt peaceful.

"I wasn't kidding about a visit to Baylor," he said. "It would be great fun, and it might make you think about transferring after sophomore year."

"No," I said firmly. "We can't afford Baylor."

"But look," he said: "Baylor's Baptist, every bit as Baptist as your Louisiana College. Your father'd get the same tuition break you're getting at LC."

"I know Baylor's Baptist. But its tuition is bound to be higher than mine. And room and board, too."

"But there are scholarships. You've got one now, and I'd bet we've got more to offer than LC does. And we'd room together for at least two years, and — who knows? — I might decide to stay a fifth year and get a fourth major, until you graduated too."

"Good grief, Monte! How about slowing down here? You're getting way ahead of everything."

"But think about it: I'd get you into my fraternity, and we'd be, well, brothers. I never had one, you know, and I've always wanted one, and this summer I've even thought you…you're the kind of kid brother I'd like to have…and we could make that work if you transferred, don't you see?"

He had gone a little breathless with this fantasy, and completely floored me with its flattery. I stopped, and touched his arm, holding him back. He turned to me.

"Monte," I said. "Please. That's about the sweetest thing anybody's ever said to me, and I'm hugely complimented. Truly. But we've got so much other stuff on our plates right now...."

"Okay. Just promise me you'll think about it. At least come over for a weekend this fall."

"I'll have to talk to the folks."

"Then do," he said, "as soon as you're home. And call me."

"Should we be heading back?"

"No," he said, "not yet. There's something I want to show you."

The trees thinned toward the crest of the incline and opened on a clearing with an unwalled, spindly A-frame structure, a low platform at the far end of it holding a lectern and facing three backed benches of light wood.

"It's called The Chapel of the Seraphim," Monte said, "and Jubilee guests can reserve it for prayer and meditation and quiet time. But they don't advertise it. You have to know somebody who knows somebody. Let's go in."

My earlier suspicion that this, all of this, had been planned, meticulously plotted, suddenly became a certainty. Gaylord Bryce flitted by.

We sat side by side on the same bench. "Troy," he said quietly, "this may be our last chance before leaving for a confidential talk. Is there anything special on your mind you'd like to tell me or ask me before we have to separate...for a while? Anything pressing on your heart?"

Confident this wasn't where he was headed, I nevertheless said, "Well, now that you mention it, there is something. I'd like to know what was going on with the hands that night by the lake. I know it was you."

He didn't respond right away, just sat, looking down. Then reached for the balm and slowly oiled his lips.

"Could you please not do that?" I said. "And put it away, please?" He did.

"Interesting you should ask. It's not exactly what I thought you might bring out, but it's related. When I said you might transfer to Baylor, I was thinking long term. Like you might come there and we'd share another room and you'd pledge KA and we'd become frat brothers and sort of honorary real brothers and like sworn blood brothers, that close, and then you'd come with me to seminary."

"But Monte," I said at once, "I don't have a calling."

"I think you do," he said.

"But I don't," I said, my voice rising.

"I believe you do," he said, "which is partly why you're so dead set against it. We always *are* dead set against it. It's part of the package."

"I'm not going to argue this, Monte. I know my own mind. I don't have a vocation. And you're going to spoil this very nice day by insisting I do. I don't. And really, you know what? It's none of your damn business anyway. Let it go. Let's us go."

"Don't you want to know about the lake?"

"What d'you know about it? You said you weren't there."

"I was there. It was me. Satisfied?"

"I knew it was. But what were you *doing*?"

"You misinterpreted that." *(The exchange seemed inversely to echo my inquiry with Dale into Monte's whereabouts during the fire. I shuddered at the eeriness of it.)* "You imagined it wrong. You remember what the counsellor said? He said we should squeeze the hand of the person holding ours to signal acceptance of God's calling. I'm sure I squeezed your hand. And I was so sure you felt the same call, and so eager and excited to get your squeeze back, I maybe got a little carried away with encouraging you. I wanted you to be sure enough of me not to hold back yourself. But then you got scared or something and left. I was only trying to help you make the move, commit yourself."

"It didn't feel like help. It felt like…it felt like something else."

"You let your imagination run away with you. You misinterpreted."

"But why did you lie about it? Why say you weren't there when I knew it was you all along?"

"I was afraid you'd be mad, just like you are now. We're sort of re-living the whole thing right here again now, and you're mad, and I was right to fear that."

I took a deep breath. "I wish you hadn't lied. And I'm not mad. I'm upset. We're supposed to be relaxing me for tomorrow night, and you…." I heard how petty I sounded and broke it off. "I'm upset only because you think you know me and my own mind better than I do, and you don't. You need to stop saying you do."

"But what else would you do, for a profession, I mean? You're such a natural for this! Look at the speech and all!"

"That is precisely what I do not want to hear from you or anybody else. I'm sick of hearing it. I don't yet know what I'll be or do, and neither do you. But I won't be that. I won't. Never that."

"But why? I don't get *why*."

"I don't have a calling," I said.

"I think we should pray," he said gently.

"I don't feel like praying right now," I whined.

"A good reason for praying," he said. "I'll lead. I want to pray for your win tomorrow night. And that you'll come to understand and heed your own heart."

"How about praying for a fair outcome tomorrow night?" I asked.

And he did, right there, in those very words. He prayed for those three things, apparently not noting that Number Three Thing voided Number One.

* * *

The next morning Corky and Steph waited for me at 8:55 with the car, the 1955 Ford Fairlane that The Man had promised, a two-door, two-toned gaudy turquoise-and-white number with the chrome V-stripe down the sides and over the fenders, and white-walled tires. Some of Dallas's minions had washed and possibly waxed it, for it glistened in the sunshine and smelled faintly of polish. Corky looked especially chic in a fresh haircut, a pink button-down, and snug, pale blue shorts, the badge bright at his waist and the medal winking against the pink. I'd worn mine too, outside the shirt.

"Like my pastels?" Corky quipped.

Steph also laughed, handing over our lunch sacks. "Chicken salad, meatloaf, an apple, an Almond Joy. A booth at the entrance sells sodas." She removed the shades and pocketed them behind her badge. "Okay, boys, here's what's happening: It's now 8:59. Time yourselves going so you get back here by 4. Troy, you'll meet the other contestants in the auditorium at 5:15 for a drawing to decide the order. You'll also meet the six judges there, three men, three women, none from the states yawl represent. You'll eat with everybody else at 6. The service starts at 7:15, with you, Troy, at the piano by 7. The first pew is reserved for contestants. There's no sermon tonight. Ya'll are the sermon. [I ground my teeth.] The hymns and announcements and offering will run as usual, Troy soloing for the offering. Here's tonight's list of hymns. When they're over, after the offertory, you're done, Troy, except for your speech, of course. You should move to the pew. Because Dr. Mann will introduce the contestants by name and state — stand and turn around when he does — in the order you'll speak. Do remember your number and go directly to the stage as soon as the previous speaker leaves it. He'll also introduce the judges. After the last speech, the judges will retire to confer. While they do, Dr. Abernathy will entertain the crowd with his puppet. He'll keep going till the judges return, but he won't preach. One of the judges will announce the winner and maybe invite him or her back to the stage for applause or something; that part's not scripted yet. And eventually Dr. Mann will pronounce the benediction. And it will be over."

"God speed the hour!" I said.

"Amen," Corky added.

"Any questions?" Steph asked? "All clear?"

"Did you meet her?" I said. "The Chinese person?"

"I did. She's all right."

"What's she like?" I said.

"Inscrutable!" Corky piped. And we cracked up.

We checked our watches and headed out into the brilliant morning, Corky at the wheel. Somebody had put a road map in my seat but Corky said he had directions from Dr. Mann's books.

"It was neat how they applauded you last night," he said.

"You know," I said, "it was," feeling a little warm with embarrassment at the recollection. "Who started that?"

"Not a clue," he said; "I think it was spontaneous."

For the offertory, I'd played a slow, soppy version of "It Is Well with My Soul," maybe hoping it was after Monte mauled it yesterday at the Chapel; the hymn had lots of openings for ripples in the treble and rumbles in the bass, and thick, thunderous chords at the climax of the chorus, and I'd made the most of them.

"I hope so," I said; "I wouldn't want Dallas starting applause one night early."

"No," Corky said; "but shouldn't we keep away from that subject?"

"Yeah, and thanks for the reminder. Closed for the day, against The Night! I was thinking last night, Corky, I know you pretty well from the summer here, but I don't know much, practically nothing at all, *about* you, except for Scotty and the Qwork thing. So could we start with some essentials?"

"Those *are* the essentials," he said; "those, and the bike."

"Yes, but I mean like your folks and high school and Tulane and what you want to be...and even what your real name is and where 'Corky' comes from? Would you care to talk about all that?"

"Sure thing, but you, too."

(What follows here wasn't as one-sided as it looks. Corky asked a lot about me, and I probably told him more than he wanted to hear; but it was all bio you already know or soon will, so to save time I've omitted most of it.)

He is Christopher Caiden Carlisle, "Corky" since seven, because already by then tired of writing it all out on school forms. His father talked about a "Corky" in the "Gasoline Alley" comic strip, and his mother thought it "cute," and he favored the klucks of the k's in it, and took it and adapted himself to it and it stuck.

"If I have to lose it when I grow up," he said, "I'll take 'Caiden' with a K."

The elder Carlisle, Corky said, had plantation in his blood and money on his mind: an Ole Miss alum, he owned and ran the largest of Vicksburg's banks and managed financial operations for First Baptist but leaned left politically and frequently doubted a lot of doctrine he heard preached from denominational pulpits. Mother Ruby, also Ole Miss and frequently queen of balls and parades and festivals at school and home, bore Corky within a year of marriage but suffered damage from a clumsy obstetrician serious enough to prevent more pregnancies.

"When I learned about that," Corky said, "I had to have therapy for a while to get over the guilt. She belongs to a lot of clubs, and volunteers at church, but her main thing now is giving tours of antebellum homes around Vicksburg, and I help her with those. We wrote and directed and acted in a play about Vicksburg history that still gets performed at a plantation on the outskirts. She also wrote a cookbook about Mississippi food. And she spoils me."

We drove west on 285. Close along the road, yucca, cacti, scrub-brush flashed by. To the north, the slopes of the Sangre de Christo foothills clustered with ponderosa pine and pinion and juniper. To the far south, the rugged jaws of the Rio Grande Canyon slashed across the Pajarito Plateau. And straight on, way ahead, rose the hazy peaks of the Jemez range. Corky shared all this information not, it occurred to me, as Monte might have done, boastfully in the knowledge of it, but truly interested, curious, at least mildly awed by what he'd learned from the books now rolled out within view. The immense, flat, stretching emptiness of it all burning under the grander vastness of the blue-silver sky cowed me a little: although we sped, it felt as if we didn't, as if nothing at all moved, as though we and everything else were riveted by the sun in this limitless, tranquil, and pristine desert sea where nothing had stirred for a thousand years, would not change for another millennium, where permanence dwelt, and silence, and peace.

He turned south onto State 4.

"I got my first bike for Christmas at 10 and married it at 11, and as you see I've kept faithful to the domain if not to the species ever since. I figured bike-riding would train me for high school track, and I guess it did, some, because I made the team three years; but I never won a single competitive heat — I prob'ly still hold the record in that department — and dropped out senior year. And organized a badminton team. I just love the way that birdie flies! Sort of erratic and weird and unpredictable: it makes me laugh. So does its actual name: shuttlecock!"

We both giggled.

"One of my mates," he said, "called me 'ShuttleCORK.'"

"Mates?" I asked.

"Teammates. Anyhow, none of the other schools fielded a badminton team, so we folded. I made the Tulane bowling squad last year."

"What about clubs?"

"Scotty got me in Glee Club. Word got around, though, so the other clubs didn't exactly compete to recruit me."

The tuff wall of the Pajarito canyon, Corky called it, jutted sharply from the ground on our left, its face pocked and blotched by shallow grooves, long, jagged fissures, yawning cave-mouths hacked into the volcanic ash and smoke-blackened by centuries of Indian habitation. Like skulls' eye-sockets, those somber chambers stared down at us.

"Did you have favorite courses?"

"Yes, but don't laugh when I tell you. I loved Home Ec. Home Economics."

I choked back a chuckle.

"I had to petition to get in, and write an essay on why I wanted to. They thought it might be for the girls, but I was serious about the subject, and proved it. Of course I took a lot of flack at first, but once past it I actually loved the course."

"Were you — are you — a good student?"

"Your average B goof-off slacker. School was easy, and I didn't work. I didn't get a Tulane scholarship."

"So why Tulane? You know it was my first choice."

"No, really?" He looked at me. "Wow! You never told me that. Just think what...."

We both paused for a beat.

"That settles it," he continued: "You have to visit me this fall. You have to come to New Orleans and see me. It's probably not 150 miles from where you live and go to school. And you can see Tulane. You'll come, right?"

"So why Tulane?" I repeated.

"Simple," he said. "I wanted New Orleans, for the food and the social life. Tulane happened to be there."

The Monument Headquarters and Entrance swung into view just ahead.

"The books said we pay for the horses here," Corky said, "when we get tickets, and they bring them up, all saddled and ready. Let's park and grab sodas and get going."

He rode ahead of me down the narrow trail, suspending conversation except for the occasional remark over his shoulder on this sight and that sound, leaving me alone to contemplate the strange and wonderful prospects. Beyond the Upper and Lower Falls of the Rito de los Frijoles — painted yellow signs on brown wood identified the sites — the path turned south along the steep bank of the Rio Grande. In intermittent flashes through the willows and cottonwoods laced with vines, we saw the river itself far below, boiling and churning around great boulders, flinging spray, still carving its route through the White Rock Canyon. Flycatchers dipped and swooped and sailed through clouds of mist. Nearer by, swallows and swifts scattered at our approach, scolded it. Ground squirrels peeped around tree-trunks and dashed noisily into the shadows; lizards darted across the trail. Corky turned his horse away and pointed back at the rattler end of a snake slithering under brush. The muted voices, identified by Corky as "probably" warblers, tanagers, canyon wrens, and hermit thrushes, flittered through the leaves and branches. Northward through the Capulin Canyon we passed restored game pits, used for trapping by the primitives, some of them fifteen feet deep, Corky said, and wide enough to hold a bear, but with improbably narrow openings. Then it was on to Painted Cave, the expansive rear wall of which displayed mysterious pictographs in dull, faded reds and blacks. And up onto the mesa to the Shrine of the Stone Lions, still a repository for offerings to the gods of the hunt, Corky said, where two crouching beasts sculpted from bedrock scanned the valley below.

Back down into Alamo Canyon, then, and east to Long House, an 800-foot stretch of crumbled talus dwellings on a ledge above the canyon floor, the building's original height marked by rows of caves and roof-beam holes dug into the cliff's face and by a huge, sun-shaped petroglyph scratched into the rock over the central door. We tethered the horses and crawled through a number of these gloomy caverns, deemed them fearful and cozy, and headed out for the Tyuonyi ruin, the largest in the park. The trail widened now, so we could ride abreast. We saw Tyuonyi first from a slope to its south, a pattern of mouldering cubicles laid out in concentric circles around a huge central plaza. Originally, Corky told me, it had contained at least four-hundred rooms in three stories of pueblo architecture, but only the first floor remained, eight apartments deep at its widest point, its walls about five feet high. A short distance to the east, centered on the Frijoles canyon floor, lay the Big Kiva, a subterranean ceremonial chamber, circular, walled with stone, eight feet deep and almost fifty across. Of the ceiling, only the butts of six beams survived, but formerly, the single access to, the sole visible sign of, the kiva was a ladder projecting from a tiny hole in its roof.

"The boys and the men," Corky explained, "they'd hole up down there and chant and pray for days and days and do stuff with each other, the books didn't say what. But like initiation rites, I figure, weird rituals to make the boys into men, and brave, grown-up members of the tribe. Prob'ly not your average Boy Scout over-nighter."

We explored other, smaller kivas hollowed into the surrounding cliffs, some with crude murals or incised designs on their sooty walls, all still vibrant with esoteric custom. Our last stop was Ceremonial Cave, a shallow rock overhang 150 feet, Corky said, above the canyon floor, housing remains of a few masonry dwellings and another small, excavated and re-roofed kiva. Corky scaled the series of ladders ahead of me and, scrambling onto the ledge, reached down.

"C'mon," he said, "give me your hand." I did, and he hoisted me up. It was the first time we touched, skin to skin.

The view, a grand spectacle of where we'd been, was a thrill to behold. We breathed and took it in for a few moments.

"Magnificent!" Corky said. "This is perfect for lunch."

We climbed back down to the horses, grabbed the sacks, reascended the ladders, and, panting, laid out the fare. Cross-legged on the rock, still awed by the spacious stretch, we munched and sipped silently for a while.

"You were saying," I began, "that you wanted New Orleans."

"For the food and the social life, yes. You know, you asked me before what I wanted to be. This might be part of the same story. I like food. I like thinking and talking and reading about food. I could probably write you the recipe for this meat loaf right now. I know for sure it has way too many bread crumbs. Ugh. I helped mother with the cookbook. I got an A in Home Ec. I've read about New Orleans restaurants and chefs and Creole and Cajun cuisine. I might, I *might,* after Tulane, I might want to apply for culinary training, maybe in New York or Boston, or, hey! why not France?"

"Really, Corky?" I said. "That's very cool! You'd do that? Could you maybe apprentice in New Orleans now?"

"I might try. Now after freshman year, I might have time."

"And what about New Orleans social life? I mean, what about New Orleans social life interests you?"

"*Everything!*" he said brightly, lifting the Coke bottle as if toasting. "But, Troy: are you sure you're ready to talk about this? Now? Right before tonight, I mean?"

"I'm sure as hell not ready to talk about *that.* So just get on with it."

"You sound mad. Are you mad?"

"I'm not mad. I'm impatient!"

"All right. But stop me if this isn't something you're ready...."

"Corky. I'm ready. I think I'm ready. Fire away."

"I'm not a weapon, Troy."

He stretched out along the ledge, leaned back on his elbows, his lean muscled legs as brown as earth.

"Okay. You know about The French Quarter?"

"I know it's probably the biggest reason my folks wouldn't let me apply to Tulane, that and the high tuition. But no, I don't actually know anything about it."

"Well, New Orleans is a pretty liberated city. Most folks are open and tolerant and accepting. It's what they call a permissive environment. And the Quarter is especially welcoming to, well, you know, difference. To strange types and behaviors."

"You mean Qworks."

"All sorts of odd types. And besides lots of fantastic cafes and amazing shops, the Quarter has bars and clubs that cater to guys who like to hang around with other guys and maybe make plans with them to have dinner with them and see a movie or visit their homes. Some of the bars have live music, and they all have juke boxes and sometimes guys dance with each other. All serve beer and some have hard stuff and wine, and a couple serve food. They stay open real late."

"You've been to them?"

"Illegally. I have a fake I.D. They're easy to get, and the bars aren't very strict. I've only been carded once."

"How many times have you gone to them?"

"I don't know. Several."

"By yourself?"

"Yes. I was scared the first couple of times but I got over that, except at one where everybody was way older."

"Did you ever dance with another guy?"

"Coupla times. I'm not very good. Scotty taught me a few steps."

"Fast or slow?"

"Both."

"Did you like it?"

"Yes. This feels like the third degree."

"How do you know where to go?"

"You ask. Taxi drivers. Bartenders. You check out neighborhoods. You scope bars. It only takes a minute inside to tell."

"And this is what you went to New Orleans for?"

"Partly, yes."

"I don't understand why."

"You're not trying. Look, Troy: I like guys. I like to be with boys. Like me. I like to get comfortable with guys. New Orleans allows that."

"Do you have a special boyfriend?"

"Not yet, no. I know I'd like to."

"And do boys date? I mean, do you want to…like…go out on dates?"

"Yes. I do. I think I'd like that very much."

This was all interesting and illuminating to me but it wasn't getting where I wanted to go, not that I was quite sure where that was. I tried again.

"But how do you *know* that's what you want?"

"I've known since I was twelve. I get along with girls just fine — take Scotty — but I *feel* different about guys. I'm friends with girls, but friendships with guys are, I don't know, *stronger*. Deeper. Sort of warmer. More, well, intense. I just feel *closer* to guys."

"And how…how do guys, you know, how do guys *express* those feelings?" I heard the tremor in my voice. Corky looked hard at me.

"Well," he said after a pause, "I can't exactly tell you. Not from experience. I don't know exactly how the feelings get 'expressed.' I'm still a virgin, Troy. I mean, I've heard things; I've read stuff. You must've heard stuff. But I don't know…like…for sure. I think, though, when the time comes, it won't be all that hard to figure out what to do. I think it will be, well, mighty great fun to figure it out, you know, together, don't you?"

"But for now, how can you be sure you're on the right track? How are you sure? What if you're wrong?"

"All right. Okay. I'll tell you. There's a way. There is one absolutely foolproof, fail-safe way of knowing for sure whether one is or is likely to be a Qwork…to be the sort of person we're talking about here. That is, to be like me. Do you want to know what it is?"

Did I? I suddenly wasn't at all sure I did. But what if I said I didn't want to know? What would that mean? Was this a trap? Gaylord Bryce darted past.

"Tell me," I said, hoarsely.

"Answer this question honestly and you'll know for sure and forever: Who do you think about when you masturbate?"

"Wait…what makes you think I…?"

He bleated laughter. He actually laughed. "Oh, please," he said, recovering. "Don't be stupid. Of course you masturbate. Everybody masturbates. It's what we do. That's not the point. It's who you think about *when* you masturbate."

"It's as easy as that? Knowing, I mean. It's that simple?"

"I don't reckon it's scientifically definitive proof, but I think it's a damn near infallible indication."

"You believe it then," I said.

If I granted it the privilege, if I allowed it, this would be revelational. To write that I was stunned doesn't even begin to capture my emotional response. Shock gets closer. And yet. And yet. Was that relief edging the slippery recessive niches of my mind? Was that abatement, even balm, stirring my baffled heart? Something had cleared. Something ceased, let go.

"Maybe we'd better head back," I said.

* * *

Back in our Cactus room I found a telegram from the folks wishing me "Godspeed" with the speech, and a colorfully wrapped and ribboned package with an attached card signed by all our group and a few others under an inscription: "We're praying for you tonight!" Inside lay a sedate, diagonally-striped, navy-gray-blue bow tie perfectly matched to my business-gray suit. Shampooed, showered, and shaved, I dressed with unusually studied care, and pocketed the card.

They had gathered, the five of them, down front in the auditorium, with the Sergeant, sans shades. Two were easily identifiable. First, Wolf Warren: tall and tawny, broad and brawny, his face a square box of sharply cut angles, his shiny black hair pulled back into a tight braid down his neck, his brows heavy over gleaming black eyes. Then Chao-xing Wei, nearly as tall, slender, stately, pale under glossy black hair in bangs and cupped against her ears, wearing a red silk, skin-tight, short sleeved, ankle-length dress with yellow floral patterning above lightning-white heels. She was luminously beautiful, and her brother hardly less so in a tailored dark suit, white shirt, and yellow knit tie, his own glistening hair parted on the right and combed into a discreet pompadour, links of gold flashing from his cuffs. They would sparkle in his signing. Probably about my age, he too seemed slightly pale, and stiff with dignity and propriety, but he smiled warmly when we shook hands, and spoke crisply without a trace of an accent. The others — Ginger Davis (Colorado), Stephen Clark (Oregon), and Reggie Brightwell (Kansas) were also cordial with smiles and murmured greetings but showed the nervousness I felt creeping into my own gut. It didn't dissolve when Wolf entered my little orbit, his size swelling the intimidation of his eyes. His grip hurt.

Steph explained Chao-xing's presence and her brother's role, and then repeated everything she'd told Corky and me that morning. "Take one," she said, handing round a basket with folded strips of paper, "and hold it unopened till everybody has one." The brother drew first, and by the time the basket reached me, only one slip remained. "Okay," Steph said, "open, and whoever has #1, hold up your hand." Wolf would lead off. China and bro were fourth. I was sixth and last, just as Monte had wanted. I don't see how he could have rigged it, but I worried that he had.

He whooped with elation when I told him. He'd left the Sweat Shop to find me among the diners to learn the order and to wish me well. "This is great," he said, "just perfect! We're all set. Everybody's primed. How about you? The tie is super! You ready?"

Corky, still in his apron too, caught up with me in the crowd heading for the auditorium. He placed a note on my palm and fled back to work. Once in the light, I read: "Dixie says 'SPEAK!' Love, C."

Exeunt

The early portion of the service proceeded routinely enough, although the anticipation of competition palpably stirred the air and raised the volume of youthful voices singing hymns so familiar to me too that I needed no score for accompaniment; and it probably quickened my fingers into extravagant embellishments that would have outraged poor Babs and should have embarrassed me. But if I could work off some tension at the keyboard, I might deliver a smoother speech. A crowd had turned out and continued to grow as staff finished work and trickled in, badges prominently displayed. The other contestants and the brother were seated on the front pew, where I joined them when finished at the piano.

Black Wolf rose and climbed the five steps onto the dais. He truly was an impressive specimen, and stood, poised, statuesque, without lectern or mike, in the middle of the stage, nearly immobile, for the duration of his speech, which stressed physical fitness as essential for effective Christian witness. He pointed to the strength and endurance of the Israelites who built pyramids, to Moses who walked them out of Egypt and across deserts, to boy David's triumph over Goliath, to Samson, to the sturdy fishermen among Jesus's disciples all of whom walked and walked the roads of Galilee, to Philip racing after the Ethiopian's chariot, and then to his own volunteerism at kids' summer camps as director of athletics and exercise trainer. It was straightforward and clear and I thought a little hokey, and I figured Robyn admired Wolf more than he admired Wolf's speech, but for the whole I gave him a B.

Reggie Brightwell and Ginger Davis each followed the standard Baptist formula of "three points and a poem" about a chosen Bible passage, he the feeding of the five-thousand with the kid's fried fish and cornbread, she the calling of boy Samuel and his misunderstanding of it, which fell squarely in line with Youth Week's emphasis and Monte's line yesterday. Hers was a savvy choice of subject certain to please the judges, and I gave her a B+ for it; but her effort to apply it to herself was unsuccessfully sentimental, and the poem, which she'd composed, utter swill, and dropped her to a D+ in my book. Reggie's reading of the loaves and fishes parable was no better than the other hundred I'd heard on this story, and sounded a lot like them, and earned him a flat C. I'd always wanted some preacher to focus on the boy, on what the *boy* thought about, what he felt, after having his lunch taken away and the hocus-pocus put on it.

China and her brother floated onto the platform and stood about a foot apart at its center; and when she began to sign, the congregation fell into total silence and stillness, whether in surprise or approbation I couldn't say. The pale arms and hands moved with fluid grace, the fingers slow-danced, gliding from shape to shape like tiny birds, like melodies if you could see them, without jerks or bumps or abrupt shifts, nothing but gentle smoothness and slow, supple sculpting of the air. Brother's voice was similarly slow and soft and silken, like lightly strummed harp strings. Together they told a story some of us well knew part of, and it too showed genius in the selection: China's grandmother, we learned, back in the home country, was a convert to the Baptist faith under the ministry of Wilomena Goforth Peter for whom this contest was named; and China simply recounted the narrative of that religious experience as her grandmother had reported it, and then the terrible, tragic accident of the stampeding water-buffalo herd that had killed Wilomena and her husband, the Revered Silas Blueford Peter, and how, in the shocked aftermath among Baptists worldwide, believers had established this memorial competition that encouraged so many young people to dedicate themselves to continuing proclamation of the Gospel of Jesus Christ, among whom China herself was one, to a special community of disadvantaged persons like herself; and she'd soon begin work at a seminary devoted to the training of disabled persons for the Christian ministry. They both bowed deeply, in perfect synchrony, and returned to the pew, with straight A's from me.

I would not have wanted to be fifth, Stephen Clark of Oregon, to follow that. But he did follow, I thought a little shaken, and got through another three points and a poem speech, this one based on the Book of Jonah, a perennial favorite of Baptists everywhere but a risky choice, I believed, because so familiar and so likely to divert itself and congregational attention onto doubtful details and fantasies of life in the belly of a whale for three whole days. Stephen found nothing new to reveal in these connections and, worse, ignored the ending of the Book, as is so often done in my hearing, and so rated a flat C.

I am on. I strode to the pulpit, removed the mike, and returned to center stage. The houselights blinked off. The spot beamed on and found me. I spoke. I crooned. I stroked. I whispered. I practically French-kissed the mike. I enshrined Bruce. Applause thundered.

From the first pew, we watched the six judges, notepads in hand, file backstage to confer, the Sergeant leading them. Like the jury they were, they didn't look at us. Shyly, we exchanged congratulatory sounds with each other, eased into cordial chatter, cracked a few lame jokes as the congregational buzz grew louder in the absence of stage action. Then Dr. Mann appeared from the wings accompanying The Reverend Doctor Alexander Allan Abernathy on his canes, the black valise gripped in the fingers of his left hand. Our entertainment for the interim. As always, Willie Nilly proved a huge hit, and pretty much silenced chatter about the contest and turned minds to himself and his master for an extended and very funny riff on Baptist "revival meetings," gently ridiculing everything from the fat evangelist's ruddy face and sweaty hanky to the repeated passing of collection plates to get up his fee and his stubborn refusal to stop the "invitation hymn" after ten verses. But after about twenty minutes the Reverend Doctor either ran out of material or sensed the restive impatience in his audience and began to pack up Willie for his "That's all, folks!" exit line. Dr. Mann quickly reappeared and signaled to me. My heart jumped, but he pointed to the piano and addressed the crowd:

"Our judges have been briefly delayed. While we wait, let's give Dr. Abernathy and Willie a big hand…," which we obligingly did, "and enjoy some choruses."

"Choruses," he mouthed to me.

But as I sat at the keyboard, dredging up some titles, Steph appeared through the rear stage curtains, leading the judges. They lined up center stage, and one man stepped forward. The congregation hushed.

"Before announcing the results," he said, and the rustling started up again; "we'd like to take this opportunity…" blah blah blah with thank-you's and such, and we all tuned out. We may have envied China.

"So," he said at last, "the results." He studied his pad and cleared his throat. "Unfortunately," he continued, "unfortunately — and the judges are unanimous in these decisions — unfortunately one candidate has been disqualified for unauthorized special effects. So our winner of this year's Silas and Wilomena Goforth Peter Young People's Speaking Competition is California's Chao-xing Wei." He smiled down and waved her up to the stage. The applause was light and scattered.

Corky and Scotty and Monte and Dale were immediately at my side, and I could see Travis and Robyn and Hollis pushing toward us through the erupting melee.

"The party's off," Monte said, swiping his lips. "Obviously. Pass the word. But tell everybody to stop by the snack bar anyway and pick up the treats we bought for it. Everything's paid for. Then get everybody to Cactus Lounge. Right now. We need a meeting."

Nearly apoplectic, he was breathing hard, his face red and sweaty. Tears showed in Scotty's and Corky's eyes.

"No," I said. "Don't. Please don't cry. It's not sad."

Was it? I didn't feel sad. Not sad at all.

"This is absolutely *insane!*" Monte said, almost shouting. "What in hell are 'unauthorized special effects?' And who's guilty of them except Miss frigging China?! How can she win when she's the frigging queen of special effects?"

"Monte," Corky said, "let's cool it, can't we? You're gonna give yourself a heart attack. Let's just get out of here."

But Monte wasn't cooling. "I have to find Steph. I've got to find out what happened. Who they disqualified."

"Don't, Monte," I said. "We know who. It's over. Let's just go."

"Oh no," he said; "it's not ending like this. I'm not having it end like this. This is another fucking swindle, I swear it is!"

But Dr. Mann was there. "Leave the building, Monte," he said firmly but quietly. "Or get sent home. And see me in my office tomorrow, when you've collected yourself."

"We have a meeting, sir," Monte said. "I'll see you tomorrow."

We bunched around him and walked him out and toward the Complex, alerting others along the way to the change of plans and to free goodies at the bar.

"They *cannot* do this!" Monte declared. "They can't."

"They just did," Corky sensibly said. "And we cannot undo it."

"I think we can," from Monte; "and we will, too."

We milled for a few minutes, picking up whatever treats we wanted from the baskets piled with them, and bottles of sodas from iced buckets. Everybody seemed to be there. I made my way to Wolf, standing alone.

I put out my hand. "Again, I'm Troy. You were terrific."

"Horseshit," he said. "Trojan horseshit!" We both cracked up. And shook hands, his grip tight and gratifying.

"Why'd he leave?" Robyn said, coming up. "I wanted to say hey. I know him, you know."

"Pissed he didn't win, I guess," I said.

""Well," Robyn said, "Now he knows what it feels like." He reached for his hanky, removed his glasses. "I guess I don't need to see him again. He probably knows he was better in Arkansas."

"Arkansas didn't have China," I said.

He turned toward the baskets. "Hold on," I said. "There's something...."

Time froze the two of us facing each other in a temporary tableau. Of course I'd reflected on why he'd declined to participate in the Gorforth finals here, but I'd reached no satisfactory conclusions in that regard. Was he scared of losing to Wolf again? I could understand that. It would be a re-match: why expect it to go better or differently than it had before. Had he removed himself for my sake? That I didn't understand. Robyn wasn't confident enough to suppose he could beat me. But losing to me might embarrass him in our group. And how did Robyn feel now, after my loss? I didn't know, and I didn't want to guess wrong when approaching him. But I owed him a reaction. I owed him a response to his decision. Of that I was certain. I owed Steph one, too, for telling me. And this looked and felt like the moment for a response to him — an intersection for resolution, my unpreparedness notwithstanding. I offered my hand.

"Mr. Robyn Byrd, sir," I said, "you are a true gentleman and an honorable man, and I'd be proud if you accepted this expression of my heartfelt gratitude."

"I try to be," he said, taking my hand, "but you sound like Lance." I'd heard the hint of unintended parody in my words, and regretted it, too late. His eyes brightened. His smile broadened. His hand was dry and his grip secure. With his other one he covered ours, lifted them once, lowered them in a single, decisive shake, and stepped back into the milling crowd, favoring me with an emphatic thumbs-up.

"Let's go," Monte said. "We need to get started."

"Wait a sec. I should congratulate China. Where is she?"

"She wouldn't hear you if you did," Monte said. "Why bother?"

"We should've invited them," Dale said.

"The party's off. I told you," Monte said.

"Whose idea was this party anyway?" I asked.

"It's what I was 'arranging,' while you and Corky had yours."

Everyone had packed into Cactus Lounge when we got there. Monte shoved and pushed our way to the piano. "Bang on it to get their attention," he ordered.

"All right," he shouted, "settle down and listen up! I don't know what happened back there but I do know it's wrong, and it's going to get fixed. I'm seeing Dr. Mann in his office tomorrow to start the fixing. We're not going to let this stand. We did not lose this competition. If anybody used 'unauthorized....'"

But I cut him off. "Don't even say it!" I shouted over his voice, and everybody got even quieter. "For God's sake, Monte, just don't say anything else. For once, please sit down and shut up. I want to say something. I need to say something. This: Nobody's fixing anything that happened tonight. I lost. China won. We know who used 'unauthorized special effects,' and who got disqualified, fairly disqualified, for doing it. I was. What the

judges said without saying it is that I cheated. And that's true.
I don't want a title I cheated to get. And to tell you the truth, I
hate that title anyway. NO, Monte, shut up! It was completely
my fault. I let it happen, helped it happen. Blame me. I know
Monte's going to want to stage some sort of protest, send petitions around for signatures to overturn the decision, and I'm
begging him not to. Please don't let Monte take *this* away from
me too! I'm accepting the decision as final. This thing is over.
And — here's the important thing, so pay attention: I'm glad
I lost. That's right. No kidding. I'm actually happy I lost this
damn thing. And you know what else? I think it's hilarious that
I lost to a deaf-mute! Have you even thought about how funny
that is? How completely hysterical that is? How does anybody
ever manage to lose a speaking contest to a mute person? So
laugh already! Giggle or something, you morons! And celebrate
the end of this damnable thing! Make that what this party's
about! That it's *OVER* ! *And* it finished the right way. So eat
some cookies. And trash your badges on the way out!"

"Was that a 'come to Jesus' moment?" Corky asked me,
laughing.

* * *

"What happened to Double-Ass Dallas?" Monte asked, back in
our room. "I didn't see him. He was about the only one who
didn't show at the not-party."

"I dunno. Maybe hustling tips somewhere?"

"China's folks looked rich, didn't you think? Maybe
Dallas'll marry her!"

"Well, at least he stuck around to start the applause."

"No, actually, he didn't," Monte said. "It was late to start. I had to start it. At about five long seconds after you finished and the spot went off."

"Really? You think he lost count?"

"Possibly. Or maybe deliberately? Would he do that? Why would he want to screw up the plan?"

It was a throwaway line but it caught my interest. "But he might've," I said. "Think about it. You pissed him off. You took the Sparrow Club away from him. You never let him act on any of his ideas, loony as they were. You wouldn't let him into the ensemble. The same reason he finally left us, more or less, for his bellhop business. You stifled him. You shut him out. And we didn't respect the Lees. It sort of piled up, when you think about it. Maybe he'd had enough and wanted payback?"

"But to screw up our plans like that? What if I'd waited? To start the applause?"

"Monte, it wouldn't have made a bit of difference. The decision was in. Forget Dallas. He probably just slipped up. It doesn't matter now."

"Well, I can see he doesn't come back next year."

"Don't do that. And don't blackball him back at Baylor either. He'll grow out of it."

He leaned back against the dresser, hooked his thumbs, looked hard at me.

"Doncha think," he asked, "don't you think your mea culpa down there was even a little bit over the top just now?"

"The offense earned it," I said.

"Offense! What offense? We didn't offend anybody."

"I'm offended. You should be. The whole thing stinks."

"And just when did you decide *that*?!"

"Look, I took the blame. All of it. I accepted responsibility."

"And you were pretty hard on me. Kind of nasty. You might have cost me some votes for Mr. Staffer."

He referred to the popularity contest that would culminate at the big ice-cream-and-cake farewell party on Tuesday afternoon, when eight "Jubilee Staff Favorites" would be announced, and the boy and girl winners of the most votes named "Mr. and Miss Staffer 1959," and the remaining six, three of each gender, the other favorites. Voting began today. Nobody campaigned for these honors, but factions and cliques whispered and conspired to promote choices, and interest ran fairly high especially among the women. I considered it all pretty juvenile and wasn't involved. That Monte cared enough to count votes surprised me.

"Didn't know you were running," I said.

"And you needn't have told them to trash their badges. They'd make nice souvenirs of the summer."

"They're lies, Monte. The badges lie. They don't deserve to live."

"And neither do those judges. They lied, too. Jeeze, Troy, I don't understand how you can accept what they said. They're so wrong. And so unfair. We didn't lose."

"I lost. We beat ourselves, going away. So stop. Now. Moving on: don't forget ensemble rehearsal at 3 tomorrow afternoon for Tuesday night, Commitment Night. Also: I'm rejoining crew tomorrow morning. Wake me up for staff breakfast."

But just then someone rapped on our door. It was late, already past lights out. We were both in our underwear, ready for bed. We looked at each other, clueless.

"Just a sec," Monte called. "Coming." He grabbed his robe from the closet, slung me mine, opened the door a crack.

"It's us," Travis said, "Scotty and me. Can we come in for a minute? It's kind of important."

They slipped in, stood with their backs against the door. Travis held a large manilla envelope with both hands, in front of his crotch, as though hiding it. For the last couple of weeks Travis had traded his overalls for Levis and a navy sports coat over a collared white dress shirt, which he shed for the T underneath it for crew, and brown moccasins. Scotty filled out a white, short-sleeved sweater and a snug blue skirt. Travis's ring hung on a thin gold chain from her neck. She sparkled. She glittered. Something was up.

"Sorry to come so late," Travis said. "Glad you're still up. We wanted to show you something. Give you something." He brought the envelope up to waist level, but held onto it.

"Give it here," Scotty said, "I'll do it."

She squeezed the little metal brackets pinning the flap on the back — cautiously, for her hands trembled — and drew out a sheet of newsprint the size of the envelope. The exposed side was solid with print, unreadable from where we stood. She held the other side against her chest.

"The first edition of *Hughes' News*," she said. "And the last. A souvenir for Troy."

They both giggled as she slowly turned the page around. The huge black headline blasted: TROY DEFEATS CHINA, and under it spread an oversized photograph of the image on the badge, Dixie and me in garish living color! The byline for the article read "Staff." She handed the sheet carefully to me.

I looked at it, passed it to Monte, who looked, laughed, and passed it back to me. We were all laughing now, laughing hard, the giggles spilling unstoppably out as we gasped and chortled and cackled and whooped at the transcendent absurdity of the thing as I held it high and danced around the room!

"Has Corky seen it?" I asked.

"He has a copy," Scotty said. "And I do, and Trav. There's another here in the envelope for Monte, if he wants it. They're the only copies. We're not printing others."

"Monte," I said. "Empty the trash can into the hallway."

He looked at me, uncertain, but did it.

"Travis," I said, setting the trash can in the middle of the room. "Now the matches, please." Scotty handed over her lighter.

* * *

The Sergeant whistled us to attention the next morning over breakfast. "Important Announcements Coming Up," she said, "so listen here. First: the farewell party starts at 3 tomorrow afternoon at the Complex. Casual dress. Be there! It's always fun. Second: Attendance is mandatory tomorrow night at the Commitment Service. It's major, so dress up and be on time. Third: Campus Clean-Up Crew works breakfast Wednesday morning and starts the break-down right after, so you're all done working after dinner tomorrow night. No work for ya'll on Wednesday!" Applause! "If you're going home by bus or train — now LISTEN! — coaches and buses will depart from Central every hour on the hour for the Sante Fe bus and train stations starting at 6 a.m., the last one leaving at 4 p.m. Allow 90 minutes for the drive to Sante Fe. Don't count on the local to stop at Jubilee. Take the coach to Santa Fe. You don't need to check out but clear your dorm rooms completely by 2 p.m. Please don't leave belongings behind; we can't ship what you forget, so don't ask. Be careful moving around on Wednesday: there'll be heavy traffic on the grounds all day. Any questions, see me later. Bless this food, O Lord, and us in Thy service! Amen. Safe travels, everyone! It's been a ball!"

"Will you have me back?" I asked as she thumped by our table, "for breakfast and lunch today and tomorrow and Wednesday. Oh, no, not Wednesday. No extra charge! I'll still play for services tomorrow night."

"That might actually be helpful," she said. "Staff are starting to leave, without leave, and I may run short. For today and tomorrow, just help out back there whoever needs some. Thanks, Troy."

*　*　*

They'd shown up, on time, I figured to check me out as Babs's successor not so much at the piano as ensemble director, for this was my first and final shot at attempting it. With her in mind, of course, I worried about comparisons, and feared embarrassing myself and spoiling their performance by screwing up, and disappointing Dr. Mann's and the Sergeant's trust in me with the appointment. Further, we'd been displaced from the dais to the main floor of the auditorium, and so required rearrangement around the piano and new audial balancing and blending tested and adjusted. And I'd never before played for and with these people except informally in casual singalongs. There's an art to accompanying, maybe not so much for congregational singing — but try telling that to Babs — as for formal solos and groups, a fine-tuning by ear to nuances of voice that make or break a musical match, and I wasn't at all sure I had the gifts or the skill to bring it off. And then there was the other really big thing.

"Okay, guys and dolls," I said from the bench, "gather round, and bear with me for a minute. I want to try something. I've picked 'Wherever He Leads' as our number for tomorrow night — no, don't roll your eyes, Robyn, give me a little break here. It's the right hymn for the Commitment Service, the best one, and we can warm them up with it, just the way Babs taught us to. And she also gave me a tip about…well…about my cursed note, and how I might find it. Here are her descant sheets if you need them. M&M will do the descant. But first let's run through verse 1 and the chorus."

I felt jittery about trying this hymn again after having such trouble with it before, but I'd nailed my note that time in the Cactus Lounge, and I decided that Babs's tip, though offered as a joke long afterward, was worth a shot. If it — or I — failed, I had backup selections in mind. So I introduced the song with more robust and dynamic chords in the opening measures to raise expectations of stronger backing than Babs used, and thus might require greater volume from my ensemble. Knowing that the problematic passage approached near the end of verse 1, Corky edged nearer and then actually sat down next to me, and leaned his face in toward mine. It might have looked daring to already suspicious eyes, and Scotty's might have shown awareness but not mistrust. We were, after all, merely trying to harmonize a challenging mix of unlikely notes. The D-flat lay straight ahead.

"Was that it?" I asked, once past it. "Did I get it, Robyn?"

"It sounded right to me," he said, kindly.

"You nailed it," Corky said.

"Again," I said, "from 'I gave….'" We repeated the strain.

"That's it," Robyn said. "Great chord!"

"How d'you get it now?" Monte asked. "When you never could before?"

"He's playing it now, right, Troy?" Scotty said.

"How can that matter?" Monte said.

"I don't know," I admitted, though with a smile. "It's Babs's idea. She thought playing that D-flat might somehow clue my voice and ear, and I could hit it. And yawl say I did? Really?"

Agreement all round, to my intense relief.

"But let's run through it a coupla more times, to be sure. From 'I gave….'"

Corky stood and moved back. But would he need to be there, next to me, so I could hear his own D-flat? Superstition!

"Again," I said.

"We've got it," Robyn said.

But something else wasn't quite right; balance was off. I shuffled them around so they formed a crescent behind me, with M&M in the bow, facing the others. I stationed Corky at the end of the keyboard to my left.

"I'm going to make another change," I said. "Dale, you take the lead on verse two, with M&M on the alto line, and then Dale will solo the descant on the final chorus with us humming four-part harmony behind him, and repeat that, very softly, to end. Let's go all the way through it now, with those changes."

Finished, we stood immobile in stunned silence. Somebody sniffled; somebody cleared her throat. "*That*," Robyn finally said, "was sacred music!"

"Beautiful," I added, moved myself. "Great work, guys. Do it just like that tomorrow night, in those positions, with those changes. Jackets and ties and heels, please. M&M will get photos for the yearbook, and to send Babs. Don't overdo the cake and ice cream. Thanks for being so...*perfect!* And thank *you*, Babs!"

* * *

Monday night services had been canceled so that a drama troupe drawn from several Sante Fe Baptist churches could stage a play for us they'd performed around the state to some acclaim. Promos and posters told us it depicted a domestic situation disrupted by the devastating effects of alcohol consumption. Jubilee had reviewed it and found it a worthy parable of valuable instruction sufficiently entertaining to merit presentation before the susceptible, vulnerable flock assembled for Youth Week. Notwithstanding the welcome variation in routine this opportunity afforded us, the teaching it freighted was as familiar as dirt, and as boring: it repeated an unremitting drumbeat of Baptist tradition: sermons, devotionals, lessons, workshops, films, books, and study groups hammered the point with relentless insistence. At least once a year from tyke-hood we were urged to sign pledges vowing lifelong sobriety. The indoctrination didn't preach temperance; it didn't plead moderation. It demanded abstinence. By now the drill had become so tedious, so stale and tiresome, that the temptation to trespass proved too much for Travis, who invited Corky and Monte and Dale and Lance and me to his and Robyn's room for a "stag party" during the play.

We waited on other staffers headed for the play to clear
Cactus before trooping down to Travis's room where the two
Mexican boys — Carlos and Luis — recruited to be me in the
Sweat Shop had brought in Camels and six-packs of Pabst Blue
Ribbon, they having access to contraband that we didn't, although Travis made it plain he'd paid. Luis dug out a bar blade
and laid it by. Carlos, bearing a second large paper sack, a long
stick, and an instrument case, piled them under the windows
and perched on my bed, near the pile. Robyn bent over it to
open the windows, and handed round empty Coke bottles
for ash trays. The rest of us distributed ourselves around the
cramped space while Travis made a bit of a show by slowly unwrapping the Camels, peeling back the foil, and tapping out
five in the perfect staggered-towers shape. We each took one —
Robyn tucking his behind an ear — lit up, and passed around
the bar blade. It came out right away that all of us white boys
had taken that famous abstinence pledge once or more over the
years, and all but Robyn and I had broken it, also more than
once. So Corky ceremoniously poured suds over our two heads,
officially anointing us members of The Bibling Brotherhood to
laughter that cracked the ice, and we relaxed. I didn't much
fancy my first sip of the beer, or the second either — Monte said
nobody did — and the ripple of frisson in my gut almost certainly registered my satisfying sense of violation rather than any
pleasure of the palate; but the smoke agreeably complemented
the suds, and with my third sip I began to get the appeal. And
if I ended down in hell for it, Corky would welcome me and
Monte would show me around.

We drank and smoked and yakked and giggled: sports
(folks still gabbed about LSU's Sugar Bowl win last year over

Clemson; Harvey Haddix's perfect game for the Pirates back in May); girls (we trashed some tacky staff types); what kind of private life Steph might have and whether there was a Mrs. Dr. Mann; remembered good times and bad in the Sweat Shop and imagined getting home, and learned a little about Luis's and Carlos's lives; and were feeling pretty mellow when Monte brought up the competition.

"Don't," I said.

"I just want to know what everybody thought of how it ended. What's wrong with that?"

"Furthermore, it was wrong for Troy," Lance said.

"It was shit for Troy," Travis corrected.

"I thought Troy won," Robyn said; "I think he whipped Wolf."

"He was a lot better than last year's winner," Dale said (having "remembered" more).

After a beat or two Corky said: "I've been thinking about it, and I have a little theory to float." How he spoke — a little loud, a little sternly, without a grin — silenced the rest of us. We stared at him and waited. "I've been thinking," he went on, "specifically of what that judge said, how he told us what they decided. Does everybody remember?"

"I do," Monte said. "He said...."

"You're not the best witness," Corky interrupted him.

"He said China won," I said, dismissively.

"Not exactly," Corky said. "Here's what he said: 'Unfortunately' — he said 'unfortunately' three times — he said, 'Unfortunately, one candidate has been disqualified....'"

"Do we really have to hear this again?" Monte asked.

"Do shut up, Monte," I said, "and let Corky finish."

"The judge said, 'One candidate has been disqualified...so our winner is....' Now listen to that 'so.' What he *said* is: *because* one candidate has been disqualified.... That is, as a *consequence* of one candidate's disqualification, another one won! China won as a *result* of Troy's disqualification. Which means, don't you see, that Troy actually *won*, and then lost because disqualified. So Troy beat everybody else by giving the best speech, and then lost on a technicality."

Nobody spoke. My pulse raced.

"Damnation," Monte finally exclaimed. "Damnation, Corky, that's fucking *right*! That's brilliant! Troy won! I said so all the time. I knew it all the time. Holy shit, this is *great* news!"

"No, Monte," Corky said evenly. "Troy lost the competition; on a technicality, yes, but he lost. We know, though, that he gave the best speech, and the judge said so, the judge said he did in his verdict whether he intended to or not. Are you okay with this, Troy?"

"I'm fine," I gulped; otherwise speechless.

"Now understand that the price for your knowing this," Corky went on, "is silence. I mean it. Total silence forever. The contest is over, the decision is final. It won't be disputed or protested or argued. We have the satisfaction of knowing Troy gave the winning talk...about his late lamented dog Bruce. But we never ever breathe a word about it. Not even to parents, Troy. It does nobody else any good to know what we know, and spreading it around will hurt and upset a lot of people to no purpose. So I'm swearing you — you too, Carlos and Luis — on your sacred word as Bibling Brothers, never to speak what I just did! Say it!"

And we murmured assent. Even Monte. Even I. And I've kept my word, till now.

"How about a little late Cinco de Mayo?" Carlos asked, reaching for the instrument case. "We're about three months along from the day itself but I might remember enough to liven up this party with a mariachi tune or two if you'll give me a little rhythm." I don't think he meant applause but we gave him some and rearranged ourselves into attentive mode as he unpacked the guitar and tuned up. "If anybody knows Spanish and the song, join in!" Nobody did, but we all found the duet a charming gift from across the border, so to speak, and rewarded it with such generous applause we got a third, spirited song that, had we space, might have inspired dancing, for Luis moved his feet rhythmically and raised the bedcovers to reach for the metal bed-frame and tapped out a syncopated beat grounding Carlos's strings. I figured we could have used Luis's rich tenor in the ensemble. They finished with a flourish of strums to more claps and laughter, and Carlos reached for the second sack.

"No Cinco is complete," he said, smiling broadly, "without a piñata!" And out of the bag he carefully drew quite a large papier-mâché horse in vivid primary colors plus green and orange and purple and black, trailing vari-colored ribbons and tinsel and streamers, and several bright feathers incongruously pricking its back and flanks.

"Oh, wow," Robyn gushed: "It's really beautiful!"

So it was. And we clapped again.

"My grandmother makes them," Carlos said, "and sells them; and we" — waving Luis in — "thought ya'll might like to play with one. You know how it works?"

We sort of did, or said we did, but Carlos caught some un-
certainty and explained, holding out a string attached to the
horse's red head and scoping out the overhead light fixture.
"We'll hang him from up there," he said, "and one of ya'll will
volunteer. We'll blindfold you and turn you around and around
five times and give you the stick" —Luis held it up —"to slam
the horse. The idea is to slam it hard enough to explode it!"

"'Explode'?!" Robyn said, alarmed.

"Break it apart," Carlos said; "smash it to bits."

"It's pretty tight in here to swing that stick," Robyn said.

"Yeah, it is," Carlos agreed, looking around. "Everybody
will need to stand on the beds up against the walls."

"Why not just shorten the stick?" I asked. "Couldn't we
break it in two? It's just a stick, idn' it?"

"And," Corky added, "have the guy use it up and down, not
swinging in half-circles like a bat. Wouldn't that work?"

"I could run get my bat," Dale offered.

"That would give you an unfair advantage," Monte said.

"All things considered," Lance said, "that's a crock."

"It would work," Carlos said to Corky, setting his knee
against the stick and cracking it. "Swing it either way now, or
poke it like a sword."

"A little risk is half the fun of it," Luis said, swishing and
slicing the stick.

Carlos cupped his hands and lifted Luis to tie the string to
the overhead lamp, tugged the horse to test its security.

"So, who's first?" Carlos asked. Nobody moved. "Okay," he
said; "I'll go, just to show how. But I won't swing to break it."

He took out a bandana and held it up to the light. "See? No
holes for peeking." He folded it over into a mask and knotted

it firmly against his face. "Now somebody turn me around five times and walk me back and forth so I don't know where I am."

Monte put the stick into Carlos's hands and turned him, walked him, waved a hand before the mask. "See anything?"

"Nope. Just black. Flatten against the walls, guys. Watch out for the pictures. Okay, somebody set the horse swinging."

He walked straight into the closet, the stick rattling the hangers, backed out, walked into the opposite bed, nearly tripped into it, stepped back, poking the stick, and walked smack into the dangling horse. Laughter all round. "That's how not to do it," Carlos said, tugging off the mask. "Next?"

"Let me try," Monte said, taking the stick. He stood where Carlos left him and swung wildly, first around, then up and down, took two steps forward, and bumped noses with the horse, which Carlos then pushed again. Monte tossed the stick into the air; it glanced off the horse coming down.

Then Travis; then Dale; then me; then Lance. Much hilarity all round with every miss.

Robyn stepped up, oriented himself as Carlos prepared the mask, balanced himself, spreading his feet, and turned slowly under Carlos's hands. "Now," Carlos said, stepping away. Robyn did a 180 and moved the stick slowly through the air, first up and down, then side to side at several levels; then, a 360, repeating the maneuvers with the stick...and touched the horse. Holding the stick level, he felt the air slowly, touched the horse again and steadied it, steadied it, and then swiftly pulled the stick back over his right shoulder and with both hands swung hard to the left, striking the horse broadside, splitting its belly — to shouts from us all! — from which spilled tangerines, plums, guavas, confetti, cigarette packs, suckers, balloons, candy bars, jawbreakers, Lifesavers, bubble gum, and…and…condoms! Condoms! Each flashy packet flouting my name!

"HOLY CRAP!" Corky cried. "AUTOGRAPHED CONDOMS!" he said, pocketing two.

Everybody scrambled and grabbed, nearly hysterical with glee.

"Hey!" Corky added: "Was that the TROJAN horse?!"

Later, he and I collected the empties and hauled them to the ash cans out back.

"The sanitation guys will notice," he said.

"We'll bribe them," I said. "With autographed condoms. Beats badges as souvenirs."

* * *

The spread across the sand behind Central looked pretty and inviting: tables clothed in white piled with pyramids of vanilla ice-cream cups and mounds of chocolate brownies with walnuts fresh from our bakery; glistening coffee urns and white porcelain cups and saucers set out at the ends of each; multicolored bouquets bloomed from dark blue vases.

"They shouldn't have called it a 'farewell party,'" I said to Corky. "Nobody likes saying goodbye."

"Oh, they seem to be enjoying themselves," he said. It looked to be mostly true. Merriment appeared manifest as the brightly dressed girls flitted and skittered about with autograph albums for scribbling contact information and sugary endearments; boys swaggered and shoved and slapped and elbowed in rough, affectionate scuffling; couples touched and shied and flirted and giggled. People ate, briskly, stirring and guzzling.

"Just watch," I said; "and listen."

I wanted him to notice how everything moved in undirected hurry and hustle and scuttle.

"Nobody's sitting," I said.

"There aren't many chairs," Corky said.

We laughed. "All of them empty," I said. Folks stood, restlessly, in twos and threes, switching from foot to foot, inattentive, scoping out other sets nearby and moving to them and then away again. They shifted about aimlessly, itchy and fidgeting, gestured in chops and jabs and spasms. Encounters were brief and abruptly broken. Voices sounded shrill and strained. The groups looked edgy, scattered and incoherent. Tensions rattled the air.

"Do you see it?" I asked Corky.

"I dunno," he said; "I *feel* something. What's going on?"

"I'm not sure, but something is. Don't they all seem...well... nervous? Sort of antsy?"

"Yes," he said, "and watching them makes me, too. Like it's infectious or something."

"You think it might be nerves about the 'Favorites' election results?" I asked. "That announcement should happen soon."

"Is anyone thinking about that? I'd forgotten. Maybe they're worried about leaving. Or excited to be leaving?"

"That's my thinking, too," I said, delighted that he'd also stumbled onto it. "I think that's exactly what's on their minds, making them so jittery. Maybe us too. We're all about to disconnect. Weigh anchor. Uproot. It's literally unsettling. And it's scaring all of us."

Corky looked at me. "That's actually pretty interesting, Troy. I'm sort of anxious myself about leaving."

"'Anxious' is the word," I said. "Do you know what 'separation anxiety' is?"

"Oh sure," he said, "we read about it in Psych 101."

"We're looking at it," I said. "Out there."

"You think everyone's tense about going home?"

"Not exactly and entirely. I think we're all *apprehensive* about going away, splitting up, maybe never seeing each other again. My psych prof said that every separation 'rehearses' the last one, the final one, and reminds us of it, unconsciously at least. So no wonder we don't like them. No wonder we get antsy around them."

"I don't remember that part...," Corky said.

"Maybe you deliberately forgot it?"

"...but it's kind of interesting if a little morbid. But what does it have to do with anything? Why are we talking about it?"

"There may be a connection. You want some dessert first?"

We did, and ambled out to the tables, trying not to look uptight and "anxious." We nodded and greeted and waved but — we both noticed — didn't stop to chat. We stood, and gobbled and gulped.

"So," I said, leading Corky to the edge of the set-up and easing down to sit cross-legged on the warm sand. "I've been trying to work out something. It's kind of crazy, I guess, but can I try it out on you? It won't take long."

He sat too. "Crazy can be good," he said. "Go."

"Okay. What if all this restiveness is related to tonight, to the 'Commitment' service tonight? What if, way back, some super-savvy Jubilee shrink who understood the Jubilee agenda and its objectives...what if he imagined an occasion that created a condition that could be cured or relieved in one fell swoop by a simple opportunity? Keep that in mind. Now think of another word to describe what we've just seen out there, for all that nervousness and fret."

"What's wrong with 'anxiety,' like we just said?"

"How about another psych word?"

"'Dis-ease'?"

"'Instability.' Now what's the opposite of 'instability'?"

"Well 'stability.'"

"And what's the cure for instability? What relieves it?"

"I don't know where you're going with all this, Troy. What you want me to say."

"Sorry. I'm not doing it very well. Let me try again. Directly. I'm guessing, I'm proposing, that commitment is an antidote for anxiety. Commitment cures agitation. It calms upset. What relieves doubt faster than commitment? It steadies instability. Are you following?"

"Yes," he said, a touch unsteadily. "So...?"

"So, I know it's a stretch, but what if, noticing that staffers 'agitated' over the prospect of leaving, what if Jubilee figured out that offering opportunities for 'commitment' might ease and relieve the tensions and anxieties accumulated around separation at the end of the session? Of course there are all kinds of commitments, but a religious one — a comforting, healing, restoring, church-approved one — what better conclusion to Youth Week? Eureka! 'Commitment Night'!"

"Are you joking?" Corky asked.

"Not entirely," I said, respectful of his skepticism and honoring my own. "I'm not suggesting a conscious, deliberate Jubilee plot or strategy. I doubt, but I don't absolutely reject, the idea that Jubilee might take advantage of a psychological condition to capitalize upon it. We know from this summer that it practices manipulation, and very skillfully too. I'm only pointing out a possible connection between this social event and the agitation it obviously arouses, and tomorrow night's design and purpose."

I could tell he was debating it, puzzling it out, probing for weak spots, and — oddly — almost wanted him to find some. "It's intriguing," he said; "I'll give you that: it sounds plausible, the way you put it. But it's all kind of...well...complicated. And, I don't know, sort of scary itself. How'd you come up with it?"

"It just popped into my head when Steph mentioned the two events in some announcement, and they got stuck together: I couldn't, um, separate them, and just kept working it out. And it seemed to fit with the whole Jubilee manipulation drama. If it's scary, don't think about it. We can talk about something else."

"No," he said, "it's fine. I'll think about it at the service tomorrow night. See if it makes sense there. Want some coffee?" he asked, standing up.

"Speaking of leaving," I said, "how are you getting home?"

"Oh, train. Same way I came. You?"

"Also train. Wait, what's your routing?"

"Steph says we can't use the Jubilee stop, so I'll grab one of the buses to Santa Fe and board there."

"Yes, but what then? How do you get to Vicksburg?"

"Southern route. I change trains in New Orleans."

"So do I," I said, grinning.

* * *

Steph's whistle shrilled.

"Attention, people!" she ordered. "Remember: service attendance tonight is mandatory. Dress-up clothes. Tonight's Love Offering, too, so look your best. I'll mail final paychecks to your home addresses. Remember to allow 90 minutes for the bus drive to Sante Fe. No meals after breakfast here tomorrow, so if your folks are picking you up, plan on road food. Your yearbooks should arrive by mail in two months or so. Don't write us about them. Rest well and safe travels! Now how about a big hand for our bakers!" And when it subsided, Monte called out, "And one for Steph the Sergeant!!" Louder applause; shouts and whoops and whistles. She waved with both hands, removed the shades, smiled broadly. And then performed a very lady-like little curtsy. We roared.

"Final item," she said. "Here are the results of the Jubilee Favorites balloting: our six favorites are, in no particular order: Monte Trevalyn, Scotty Hughes, Corky Carlisle, Jordan Jamison (registration desk), Troy Tyler, and Mary and Martha Moon, which makes seven, but as we all know the last two are inseparable! The boy and girl getting the most votes, and so the 1959 Jubilee Miss and Mister Staffer are: Scotty Hughes and Corky Carlisle! Warm congratulations to all!" Hearty huzzahs and cheers!

I clapped Corky on the back and shook his hand for a while. He let me.

"Mister Staffer!" I said to him. "Wow! This is great! Congrats, good buddy!"

And to myself I said: "My All-American boy, Mr. Staffer, and him a Qwork! How cool is that!"

* * *

"They must've voted for the couple, before Scotty found Travis," Monte said, a little sourly, knotting his dark tie under the stiff white collar points. "Two against one isn't fair."

"Or maybe they voted for the bike?" I quipped; but he was having none of it.

"Yeah," he said; "it for sure got him lots of exposure. How is a bike even legal out here? That wasn't fair either."

To make him feel better about losing to Corky, I'd asked Monte to sing with Scotty and Dale the offertory at tonight's service. Normally, I'd play variations on hymns while they passed the plates, but for a change — another one — and because I could, and because it was Love Offering night, I figured a sweet little quartet surprise to my accompaniment might shake loose some extra change. "'Softly and Tenderly,'" I explained to him and Scotty and Dale, "verses 1 to 3 in two part; I'll come in on the chorus with the repeated 'Come home' in the lower register; keep that for verse 4, when Dale will sing the descant, and we'll repeat the chorus, and repeat it again a cappella, with Dale's descant. No need to rehearse. Just remember these changes. And harmonize your hearts out!"

"I'll do it," Monte said later in the room; "but I'm not forgiving you for replacing me with Dale. That was pretty mean. And you could have told me before. Springing it on me in front of the group like that, so I couldn't respond: that was shitty."

"I'll take blame but it wasn't my idea. Remember those sheets Babs gave me right before she left? She'd written a couple of new descants, with a scribbled note assigning the tenor part to Dale. I'm honoring that. And I also like it. A lot."

* * *

Still packing in when we arrived, the auditorium crowd continued visibly and audibly "agitated," possibly from the sugar and caffeine high of the afternoon, possibly from energy around leaving, but loud, boisterous, unsettled, bordering on rowdy. The ensemble, on the other hand, looked serene, composed along the front pew, on the piano side, splendidly and tastefully decked out, the girls in frilly light blouses and slim skirts, the boys in jackets and ties, mine the gift bow for my speech. The familiar hymns were spirited, brisk, imperative ("Stand Up, Stand Up for Jesus," "All Hail the Power of Jesus's Name," "Crown Him with Many Crowns," "Praise, My Soul, the King of Heaven"), perhaps to help absorb the energy overload of the gathered throng. By the time we reached "To God Be the Glory," vigor and volume had marginally waned, and even I felt ready for a break, which we sort of got with the offertory. It turned out that Scotty-Monte-Dale-Troy voices tonally matched for the seductive "Softly and Tenderly," which also agreeably combined with the commitment theme of the evening. Following, our ensemble took their assigned positions around the piano for "Wherever He Leads," and the congregation quieted. M&M absolutely soared on the descant, Dale gilded the tenor line, I nailed my note, and as we repeated the chorus a cappella one final time, the Reverend Doctor Alexander Allan Abernathy tottered on his canes to the dais chair, his black valise in hand. The crowd erupted with applause, whether for us or in expectation of Willie Nilly, I needn't say.

He sat, unpacked Willie, and arranged the puppet on his lap. But Willie skipped his routine opening question and, his brows lowering, his wide eyes batting at his handler, he gestured toward our ensemble and asked, indignantly, "Why can't you make *ME* sound like that?!" Plainly an accusation, it brought down the house, and, as I chose to believe, complimented us, if off a dummy tongue. The Doctor restarted with the Bugs query, and the two of them bantered and bandied for an amusing while about Jubilee features and customs, and even got off a few gentle jokes at the expense of Dr. Mann and Steph.

And then Willie said, his Bugsy voice rasping, "I heard tell o' this fella workin' here, name of Troy, near 'bout won a preaching contest the other night — *SHOULDA* won it, too, lotsa folks thought."

"That so?" the Doctor asked. "Why, I'd sure like to shake that fella's hand, wouldn't you?"

"Yessir, I would," Willie said. "How 'bout we call 'im up, let 'im preach a little piece of his shoulda-won sermon to the folks here, whadaya think of that, Doc? Wouldn't that be a fine thing?"

"For sure it would," the Doctor said. "Let's do that!" And they both — Willie's eyes popping, his head swinging from side to side — they both began to scan the crowd, Willie shading his eyes with the baseball mitt, both alternately calling out, "Troy? Troy?"

Instantly on his feet in the aisle to my left, Monte waved his arms at the dais, pointed at me with short, blunt stabs. I leaned over to catch Corky's eye down the pew, locked onto it for a second. The throng picked up the cry. "Troy! Troy! Troy!" they chanted, and began to clap in rhythm with the name. Willie pumped his fist. Dr. Abernathy beamed. "Troy! Troy! Troy!" the syllable a strident pulse. I stood, slightly giddy, and strode down along the pew toward Corky, the peal of "Troy! Troy! Troy!" blasting like blows. Standing close before him, I extended my trembling hand. He gave his into mine. "We're leaving," I said. He nodded, stood. The chants quickened, amplified.

We moved down the row toward the center aisle, dodging the appalled, gawping, speechless Monte, and stepped into it, our hands clasped, and ran, ran, suddenly burbling tears and laughter, we bolted pell-mell hell for leather, hurtled past the astounded faces toward the rear doors and burst through them into air, sucking at it. Corky lay hold of the bike, mounted it, side-saddled me onto the crossbar where his biceps caught and cradled me. He stood on the pedals to push off, leaned into me, and kissed the back of my neck. I let him.

Alternating in the saddle, we rode and rode along the still deserted paved paths, rode the highway shoulder, our faint lamp alerting the few cars out. We rode: decompressing, chilling, pondering.

"How about the lake?" Corky asked.

"Yes," I said, " all right."

We lay side by side on the bank. I tugged off my bow, folded it away, and opened two shirt buttons. So did Corky. Both medals showed.

"Would you please hold my hand again?" I asked.

"If you'll hold mine," he said, and we giggled at the childishness of it.

After another quiet while, I said: "What have I done, Corky? What *have* I done?"

"You did what they forced you to."

"Did I? It sure felt like I had no choice."

"You didn't. You couldn't have done what he said. What they wanted."

"But I've disgraced myself. Ourselves. I've embarrassed everybody who knows me. I ruined the service. How can I ever...?"

"Stop. Don't make it worse by feeling sorry for yourself. There's no reason to. They disrespected you. They insulted you. You defended yourself. And you defeated them."

"No, I ran away. I really hope I didn't run away. I don't think I could stand that, if they say that."

"You didn't. You escaped. They tried to lock you up, and you dodged the trap. You ran for your *life*! You claimed yourself. You affirmed yourself. It was brave and honorable. You should be proud of that."

"I don't feel proud. I feel ashamed."

"Then I'll have to feel proud for both of us."

"I 'claimed' myself?" I liked the sound of it. "Is that what you said?"

"I did. You did. You found and claimed your real self, not the one they cooked up for you. You basically said, 'Just shove it,' which I think you've wanted to say, wanted to yell, for a long, long time. You said it. Leaving was the only honest thing to do. You were honest and brave. And I am honored to have been a part of it. What's not to be proud of in that?"

It shut me up for a moment, and the "honored" part nearly brought tears. "You really believe that, Corky?"

"I do. And you must too. It's completely true. Can't you feel the truth of it? Are you going to be all right now, Troy?"

And I did tear up again at the tenderness of the question. He gently squeezed my hand.

After a few more breaths, some deep and shaky, I said: "I don't want to go back to Cactus tonight. I can't deal with Monte tonight. Maybe not ever."

"Don't be rash. He's your best friend."

"Not tonight he wasn't. Maybe not...."

"Don't say it. Things might change. Feelings might."

I released his hand and rolled over onto my stomach, and a quick stab of pain pierced the top of my thigh. "Ahhhh!" I cried, grabbing at the spot. I'd turned onto a rock that pressed a pocketed object hard into my flesh. "Damnation," I growled, tugging out a tube of Monte's balm, the one he'd planted on my palm our first day. Although I'd never used the thing, I'd developed the thoughtless habit of including it among change and keys, and carrying it around.

"Is that what I think it is?" Corky said. "Montesque revenge already!"

Laughter vanquished the somber mood. I hurled the tube with all my pent-up might into the far and reaching middle of the deep, dark lake, the faint plinking of its plash a feeble, final comment on its fate.

I sat back down, facing what I could see of him.

"Listen, Corky. I've been thinking."

"Uh-oh," he said.

"Are we actually going to travel home together tomorrow? On the same train? All the way to New Orleans?"

"Don't you want to?"

"Of course I do! Don't you? How did we not know until today we could?"

"Never came up. You just said people don't like to think about leaving. We didn't."

"But it's such a cool thing! We should plan to, okay? I've been thinking."

"Ditto the 'uh-oh.'"

"You know all those buses and coaches we passed tonight parked everywhere? Every one of them will head for Sante Fe tomorrow, and will unload at the train depot there. We'll be on one. What if we board it tonight?"

I could tell he was looking hard at me.

"Go on," he said.

"Let's find an unlocked one, or doors we can pry open, and spend the night there. The overhead bins will have blankets and pillows. Tomorrow morning we can either get off and board another one at Central, or talk the driver into letting us hitch since we're going anyway. How's that sound?"

"But what about our stuff?"

"We leave it. It's nothing but T-shirts and jeans anyway, and my madras, which are already bleeding in the wash. And we're wearing our best. Your bike can go in the big luggage hold underneath, and in the baggage car on the train. Are you with me?"

"I dunno, Troy. I don't want to get us in trouble."

"We're IN trouble, Corky, or we could be. I'm getting us out of it. Do you have your ticket home?"

"It's in my room. I'll have to get it."

"No, we're not going back to Cactus. Do you have cash?"

"Not enough. But my Dad gave me an American Express card last year. I've never used it but I've got it."

"My return ticket's in Cactus too. Could you stand me the fare till we're home?"

"I'd love to do that, Troy."

"Are we serious here, Corky?" I said. "Are we actually doing this? I believe I am."

"I believe we are," Corky said, taking my hand, pressing it.

* * *

We'd nabbed bus seats across the aisle from each other, and stretched out against the windows.

"I feel better," Corky said, "a lot better. No more...what was it?...'agitation.'"

"Yes, me too," I said.

"So what happened?" Corky asked. "Why do I feel better? Why do we?"

"Did commitment happen," I asked. "I think commitment happened."

"And 'recognition'?" he breathed.

We were quiet, with wonder.

"Good night, Qwork," he said.

"Good night, Queer," I said, snuggling into the blanket, lightly stroking the medal at my throat.

Epilogue

Dear Troy,

Please find enclosed your final paycheck. We've added in extra for your time in two jobs.

We're glad you and Corky got home safe.

Monty said you'd visit him at Baylor, so we let him take your things, and the music.

Dr. Abernathy blamed everything on Willie, said he was just a dummy. But we know who the dummy was.

What you did took guts. That was some tough shit.

Good luck to you and Corky.

Your friend,
Steph

P.S. Dr. Mann says hey, and to turn your eyes upon Jesus.

Amen.

ACKNOWLEDGMENTS

*Of Jack, with loving gratitude for patient,
steadfast encouragement.*

Of Kenny, in thankful recognition of wise and artful guidance.

*And of the boys to whom this story is dedicated,
whose enduring presence steeps my every line.*

~Paul Elledge
Nashville 2021

CPSIA information can be obtained
at www.ICGtesting.com
Printed in the USA
LVHW081325070322
712825LV00015B/124

9 781638 374893